# WARRIORS

## JACK LUDLOW

Allison & Busby Limited
13 Charlotte Mews
London W1T 4EJ
*www.allisonandbusby.com*

Hardcover published in Great Britain in 2009.
This paperback edition published in 2010.

A CIP catalogue record for this book is available from
the British Library.

10 9 8 7 6 5 4 3 2 1

ISBN 978-0-7490-0704-1

Typeset in 11/16.5 pt Century Schoolbook by
Allison & Busby Ltd.

The paper used for this Allison & Busby publication
has been produced from trees that have been legally sourced
from well-managed and credibly certified forests.

Printed and bound in the UK by
CPI Bookmarque, Croydon, CR0 4TD

JACK LUDLOW is the pen-name of writer David Donachie, who was born in Edinburgh in 1944. He has always had an abiding interest in the Roman Republic as well as the naval history of the eighteenth and nineteenth centuries, which he drew on for the many historical adventure novels he has set in that period. David lives in Deal with his partner, the novelist Sarah Grazebrook.

*To the memory of*
*Edward Dyson.*
*A school friend of my son*
*who for many years was part*
*of that golden group of boys who*
*helped, through sport and just contact,*
*to keep me feeling young.*

# ITALY IN THE 11TH CENTURY

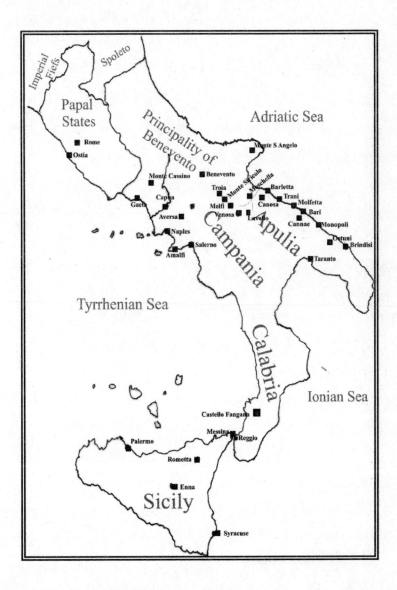

Imperial Fiefs

Spoleto

Papal States

Principality of Benevento

Adriatic Sea

Rome

Ostia

Monte S Angelo

Monte Cassino

Benevento

Capua

Troia

Monte Siricolo

Meschella

Barletta

Trani

Gaeta

Melfi

Canosa

Molfetta

Aversa

Venosa

Lavello

Bari

Naples

Cannae

Monopoli

Campania

Apulia

Ostuni

Salerno

Brindisi

Amalfi

Taranto

Tyrrhenian Sea

Calabria

Ionian Sea

Castello Fangam

Messina

Reggio

Palermo

Rometta

Enna

Sicily

Syracuse

# PROLOGUE

✠

Apulia was in turmoil and the Eastern Empire had only itself to blame: all the way up the Adriatic coast, with a few exceptions, the Byzantine possessions in Southern Italy were in open rebellion, the strife extending from the great trading ports to the rich agricultural lands that ran west to the high mountain barrier of the Apennines. Seeking to take advantage of a division between the Saracen emirs of the island of Sicily, Constantinople had decided to invade and reconquer that valuable possession, but in doing so, in order to find the soldiers necessary for the task, harsh methods of recruitment had been employed in their nearby Italian fiefs and the results of that had come home to roost.

Like the Roman Empire of antiquity, the Byzantine

Empire was rarely free from trouble in its distant possessions; it could be no other way with borders that ran for a thousand leagues from the toe of Italy, through the mountainous Balkans, over the narrow neck of the Bosphorus and on into the wilds of Anatolia where it faced the newly emergent Turks. Apulia, as a province, was more febrile than most, containing within it a sizeable population of Greek rulers at permanent loggerheads with the indigenous Italians.

But there was a third, numerous and more seditious group to contend with: the Lombards, heirs of a northern tribe who had invaded five hundred years previously to conquer the whole of Italy. Rapacious as rulers, fractious by nature and unwilling to assimilate, they had never been popular and had, in their turn, succumbed to the combined might of the Emperor Charlemagne and overwhelming Byzantine force, hanging on as subject overlords only to the dukedoms and principalities of Campania and Benevento.

As a race they had never forgotten they once also ruled in fertile Apulia and were thus ever ready to fan the flames of an insurgency. Added to that they had, on both the western and northern borders, powerful Lombard magnates to whom they could appeal for aid, given they all shared a dream of one day creating an independent kingdom which would embrace all of Italy south of the Papal States.

The Eastern Empire had several assets to counterbalance that dream: a kingdom required a sovereign lord and no Lombard ever fully trusted or was willing to serve under another. In the past they had quarrelled amongst themselves and engaged in betrayal with more purpose than they ever brought to a common enemy, and Constantinople had long been expert, using streams of gold as well as brute force, at the tactic of divide and rule, both within and without its external borders.

Constantinople also enjoyed a steady supply of enterprising generals – men who knew how to pacify revolt – and young Michael Doukeianos, newly appointed as the Catapan of Apulia, was no exception. The one port still utterly unaffected – being the largest, and ruthlessly governed by Greeks – was Bari, and from there, with few trained men and even less in the way of resources, Doukeianos set out to pacify the region known to his imperial masters as the Catapanate.

Speed of movement, paid-for betrayal, allied to that lack of cohesion amongst those he sought to overcome, were his most potent assets, giving him the ability to arrive outside a rebellious town or city before those inside were aware he was even approaching. Ill prepared to withstand his sudden assaults, with defences more often than not in an unready state, poorly led and bereft of external support, they fell one by one and the rebellion began to falter and die out.

Retaking imperial possessions was one thing; continuing to hold them with limited forces another. Every town and city in the Catapanate was partly or wholly fortified, most badly, a few formidably so: ports like Bari and Brindisi had stout walls and fortified harbours so strong that in the past they had withstood attempts to capture them lasting over a year. If inland towns had walls in different states of repair, they also had populations in a state of discontent, while to the north and west protection was needed from the Principality of Benevento and, on the eastern side of the Apennines, from the powerful Lombard fiefs of Campania: Salerno, Capua and Naples.

High in the mountains to guard against this lay a pair of immense forts, Troia and Melfi, strong enough to repel even the mighty forces of the heirs of Charlemagne. The danger for Doukeianos was simple: help from beyond those borders might still come and that would encourage those who had just rebelled in his bailiwick to rise up again. He did not have the troops to hold the vital Adriatic coastline, pacify the inland littoral and simultaneously man the mountain passes through which danger would come.

Norman mercenaries held the northern fortress of Troia, facing a papal fief, the Principality of Benevento, men who had been in the pay of Constantinople for nearly two decades. But further south stood the now ungarrisoned bastion of Melfi, which controlled the route into Campania. Here an ally had to be found or bribed and he could only come from the indigenous population, including Lombards, not all of whom were adverse to Byzantine hegemony; that race contained amongst its number men who had often served the empire faithfully as paid retainers.

Arduin of Fassano was one such, and his record in that regard was exemplary. He had just returned from the faltering reconquest of Sicily, where he had led a contingent of Apulian pikemen in the Byzantine service, until he fell out with the irascible general in command, an arrogant giant called George Maniakes. Called upon by his fellow Lombards, on his return, to join in the revolt, he had declined to take part and cast his lot with the catapan. As an envoy he had gone some way to brokering reconciliation with many rebel strongholds on behalf of Doukeianos, thus avoiding bloodshed.

If he was seen as helpful to Byzantium he possessed one other quality, equally important: the assurance he could engage reliable men to man the border, suggesting the Normans of Campania, warriors he had fought alongside in the Sicilian campaign. The fiercest, most disciplined fighting troops in Christendom, and mercenaries, Normans could be relied on to oppose the enemies of whoever paid them. Scattered throughout the southern fiefs of Italy, these men from the Atlantic seaboard had, in the last twenty years,

become numerous, so much so that in many places
they provided an essential tool for anyone wishing to
gain or hold on to power.

Arduin's argument for employing them was also
telling: having returned from Sicily – they too had
fallen foul of the same arrogant Byzantine general –
they were at present unemployed; if Doukeianos did
not pay them someone else might, possibly causing
him more trouble than the revolt he had just crushed.

'The Normans are bred for war, Catapan, and they
live off it. They will not sit idle and just polish their
weapons. Better they are in your service than they be
employed by another, or left free to raid and plunder.'

'The men you encountered in Sicily are loyal to
Guaimar of Salerno.'

'They are loyal to his purse, Catapan, and I think,
now they have returned, the Prince of Salerno, who
has been troubled by their presence before, would
welcome the notion they be engaged elsewhere.'

The Lombard held his breath: how much did
this young and inexperienced catapan know of the
Normans of Campania and the bubbling stew of
Lombard politics? He would know the Norman leader
was Rainulf Drengot, of advancing years now, but
a man who had, as a young knight, taken part in a
previous Lombard revolt in Apulia, one eventually
crushed by another great Byzantine soldier called
Basil Boioannes.

Beaten to the east of the Apennines, Rainulf and the men he led had prospered in the west through a combination of brute force, outright banditry and utter unreliability. Drengot had made himself militarily indispensable to one warring Lombard magnate in Campania, the late Duke of Salerno, only to later betray him by giving his support to his rival, the Prince of Capua. But Rainulf had gone one step further: thanks to another switch of allegiance, and by deserting Capua, he had been elevated to the title of the Imperial Count of Aversa, granted his gonfalon by no less a suzerain than the Emperor Conrad Augustus, heir to mighty Charlemagne.

'Would they serve?'

'They will if Constantinople will pay them.'

'It is I who will pay you, Arduin. I have no wish to deal with them directly.'

At least the catapan knew that much: the Normans were difficult people with whom to do business – demanding, quick to see weakness, sharp when it came to their own advantage and careful of what they perceived to be their honour.

'As long as I have the means I am sure they will serve me, but you must tell me what it is you require.'

'The key to protecting the border with Campania is the fortress at Melfi. As long as that is in my hands no force of invaders from there can hope to sustain itself in Apulia.' Arduin knew the truth of what was being said, but he was also holding his breath for what he hoped was coming next. 'And I am offering to you the post of *topoterites* of Melfi, if you can secure the services of enough Normans to hold it secure. I do not have the forces, myself, to garrison it properly and control the rest of the Catapanate.'

'Will the emperor not send you more men?'

'The Emperor Michael has no more men to send. He has serious trouble in Anatolia with the Turks and his armies are committed there. Do you accept my offer of Melfi?'

'A great responsibility, Catapan,' Arduin replied. 'You do me great honour.'

'I am sure you are worthy of it.'

Michael Doukeianos looked into a smiling, eager face. Had he been able to see behind that smile, as well as the dark brown eyes and the round, pallid face of the man before him, he would have been unsettled. Arduin of Fassano was a good soldier and had proved his worth to Byzantium both in Sicily and in the recent rebellion. To give a man of his experience the captaincy of such an important fortress was, on the face of it, sound policy, but Doukeianos should have remembered he was dealing with a Lombard, and they were a race much given to duplicity.

Arduin had not joined the revolt just crushed for one very good reason: with an experienced military eye he had seen it was doomed to failure, but that did nothing to dent his feelings for Lombard aspirations. Yes, he had served Byzantium; he was a soldier and had gone to where there was a war to fight with pay and plunder to be gained, and once there had done his very best and earned the plaudits of his peers and superiors by turning unwilling Apulian conscripts into effective soldiers, but in his breast the flame of independence had never dimmed.

His father had been a soldier in the great uprising of twenty years past, led by the late and revered Lombard hero, Melus of Bari. This was the very same revolt which had seen engaged the likes of Rainulf Drengot – and Arduin's father had died fighting Basil Boioannes. As a lad he had been fired by parental ideas, and those he had never lost. It had been drummed into him that the time must come when Byzantium would be weak, when they could not find the forces to hold on to Apulia, told that would be the moment for the Lombards, under a competent leader, to strike and take back the power they had once held. Never mind that Melus of Bari had failed; was now the time and was he the man?

As he replied, he was aware of his rapidly beating heart, just as he was aware of the need to keep his voice, as well as his excitement, under control. 'Before I accept, Catapan, I must be sure that I can do as you ask. I must go to Aversa, and parley with the Normans.'

'Go to Melfi first, and see what needs to be done. Make sure the locals are loyal, and if they are not, do what is required to get them on your side. Hang or bribe the leading citizens, that I leave to you, then you can go to your Normans.'

'If I am to bribe and recruit, both require funds and any Norman worth his salt will want to see coin before they commit themselves.'

'Never fear, Arduin,' said Michael Doukeianos, grinning. 'If Byzantium is short of fighting men, it is never, ever, short of the means to pay for support.'

# CHAPTER ONE

><><

Any gathering of the sons of Tancred de Hauteville was
bound to end up in reminiscence and this, taking place
in the vestry of an Italian cathedral, given there were
five of his offspring present, was no exception: they
recollected the memories of growing up in the unruly
Normandy region of the Contentin, of escapades, past
quarrels, fights they had engaged in with each other,
but more importantly with their neighbours, as well
as raiders from the islands that lay off the Norman
coast. And they talked of their father, sometimes in
awe, sometimes with gales of laughter, but mostly
with wry affection.

Tancred de Hauteville had been a noted warrior,
as well as a man who bred sturdy and numerous sons
– there were another seven brothers still at home,

the product of two wives – and he had raised them
to be puissant warriors like himself; their rank as
the offspring of a petty Norman baron required no
less. From their very first-taken steps they had been
tutored in the use of weapons, toy wooden swords and
shields, replaced by metal as soon as they could handle
the weight, growing strong by constant practice, gifted
on land and in water, swimming in the river that ran
through the family fields and then in the crashing
waves of the nearby great ocean.

The time came when they could mount first a pony
and then a horse; they had been taught to ride and
use a lance so that one day they could, if fortune
favoured them as it had their father, serve in battle
under their liege lord, the Duke of Normandy, as part
of a mounted fighting force greatly feared throughout
Europe. Well fed on the produce of Tancred's fertile
demesne, the sons came eventually to match and even
tower over a parent whose own great height was often
remarked upon.

Tancred never let them forget their Viking heritage,
or that the five elder boys, through their mother, were
half-blood relations to the ducal house. They came
from a race and a lineage bred for combat: it was not
for them but for others to cut timber, grow food, to
sow and reap crops, to work the family salt pans and
exploit the fishing rights which provided the means by
which they could be armed.

Each had been provided with the weapons and equipment necessary for the tasks that lay ahead: the horses needed to carry them and their equipment to war, as well as a destrier to ride in battle, a sharp-tipped lance, a heavy, double-edged sword, a shield framed in metal, covered with hard wood and leather and painted in the de Hauteville colours of blue and white. Most expensive of all, but vital, each had been gifted a set of protective armour: a chain mail hauberk, gloves and a helmet.

The duty of vassalage obliged Tancred to provide to his duke ten lances, and that he had done – a task made so much easier as his elder sons, one by one and a year apart, grew to match then surpass his fighting ability. They also aided him mightily in his endemic disputes with neighbours, usually over land, water, or rights to the produce of the Atlantic shoreline, and given their talent for combat the name de Hauteville had soon become one to be respected in the Contentin.

Yet that very number of sons brought with it a greater problem: the petty barony of Hauteville-la-Guichard could feed them as they grew to manhood, could arm and mount them to be warriors, but it was too small a demesne to satisfy their needs as adults. They required land of their own on which to raise families and to provide for them the revenues which supported a fighting knight.

Tancred had sought to get them placed as personal

knights, part of the *familia* of his liege lord, the son
of the man he himself had served so faithfully. That
suzerain, Duke Robert of Normandy, had ignored
written requests more than once, and had then
rebuffed the same appeal in a face-to-face meeting.
For men bred to war, with no hope of advancement
in their homeland, the brothers de Hauteville, first
William and Drogo, and now joined by Humphrey,
Geoffrey and half-brother Mauger, had taken the well-
worn route to Italy and mercenary service, where the
martial prowess of the Normans was highly prized
and well rewarded.

'Enough,' William insisted, as Drogo continued to
relate those amatory adventures he had indulged in
at home, quite forgetting the trouble his activities had
caused: he was the father of more bastards than could
be counted on the fingers of his hands. 'Home is far off
in time and distance. We must turn our thoughts to
that which concerns us here.'

Drogo frowned more from habit than irritation;
William might be the oldest and Tancred's heir, but
too often in their growing years he had assumed near-
parental powers.

Yet he deferred to him, not just as an older sibling
but also as a chief; Rainulf Drengot commanded the
Normans of Campania, but William was his senior
captain and had led the mercenary contingent in the

recent invasion of Sicily. A measure of his stature, gained in that conflict, was his soubriquet: he was now more commonly referred to by those he led as *Bras de Fer,* a title bestowed on him by his confrères after a single-combat encounter outside the walls of Syracuse. William Iron Arm had fought and defeated the ruling Saracen emir, a giant of a man who claimed to have on his belt the notches of a hundred skulls.

Humphrey, his beetle brow furrowed, stood suddenly, and went to the door that led from the vestry to the chancel of the cathedral, opening it to ensure no one was listening.

'Suspicious as ever,' said Mauger.

'The only people I trust are in this room,' Humphrey insisted, before sweeping the assembly with a glare on a face that, with its large overbite and close-set eyes, lacked beauty, 'and that is not wholehearted.'

'You sleep with your purse between your legs,' scoffed Drogo, Humphrey's parsimony and mistrustful nature being a family joke.

'He would when you are around, brother,' crowed Geoffrey.

Drogo laughed. 'He has not got between his legs anything else to tempt me.'

'I cannot think why you bother, Humphrey,' William said with a weary air, looking at the now closed door. 'Who would want to overhear this foolishness?'

'You should slacken sometimes, Gill,' Drogo insisted.

'A little foolishness would do your soul good.'

For 'foolishness', Drogo meant gaiety and that covered much of the ground that lay as a difference between the two eldest brothers. Drogo was mercurial by nature, laughing one second but equally likely to resort to a fist fight the next if he felt impugned. He was also a womaniser, never without a concubine to bed when he was at what passed for home, and ever on the lookout for companionship on campaign or when travelling. William was steady and serious, and while not, as Drogo called him, a eunuch, he was restrained in his carnality, engaging in the odd liaison, without ever forming permanent attachments.

'I'll leave the priests to worry for my soul, brother, because I have four of you to use up all my concern.'

'We can look after ourselves,' Mauger responded, with all the confidence of the youngest present.

'Can you?' William replied, looking past Mauger at the crucifix on the bare stone wall, the son of the God he had been raised to believe would see everything, and who would one day judge him for the sins he had committed in life. Then he looked at his brothers, all big men and broad of shoulder, all with golden hair and faces made red by the Italian sun. 'I thought that too. I thought I had become heir to a brilliant future, only to have Rainulf snatch it away.'

'His child may die.'

William responded to Geoffrey with a withering

look. 'And with a willing bedmate he may breed many more.'

That induced a long silence, as each of the recently arrived trio contemplated what had happened since William and Drogo had come to Italy. Both had taken service with Rainulf Drengot and both, through sheer ability, had risen to lead companies of men, William even more. He had become Rainulf's right hand, to be consulted frequently at a time when Campania was in turmoil and the mercenary leader had himself felt under threat.

Drengot had betrayed the Duke of Salerno, a trusting soul who had granted him not only the hand of his daughter but also the dowry gift of the Lordship of Aversa, raising him from mere paid retainer to the status of influential landowner in his own right. Rainulf had shown little in the way of gratitude: when his wife died he had switched his allegiance, and thus the overpowering force he could put in the field, to a fellow of staggering mendacity called Pandulf, Prince of Capua, marrying his sister to seal the bargain. A termagant and an unwilling spouse, that was a union Rainulf had come to much regret.

Even for a Lombard, Pandulf of Capua, known to all as the Wolf of the Abruzzi, had shown a greed and lack of integrity that was remarkable. Having deposed the Duke of Salerno and dispossessed his remaining children, he had grown even more grasping, bearing down on subjects in both fiefs, people who hated him, and stripping from them, with Rainulf's help, ever-increasing wealth. No one, petty baron, trader, farmer, priest, bishop or monk was safe from his depredations.

Pandulf loved gold, not God, and like all avaricious men, he had, in time, overreached himself, attacking and ravaging the lands of the wealthy Monastery of Montecassino. Not content to merely seize its treasury, he threw the elderly Abbot Theodore into his dungeons and parcelled out the monastery's extensive lands to Normans, men he had suborned from Rainulf's service. Indeed, from being the greatest source of Rainulf's wealth Pandulf had become too powerful, a threat to the now ageing mercenary leader – childless, and, thanks to his tempestuous marriage, much given to taking refuge in drink.

The Wolf's depredations had, through the intercession of Guaimar, the Duke of Salerno's son, reached the ear of the Western Emperor, Conrad Augustus, but it was what he had done to the holy men of Montecassino that proved his downfall. The irate emperor had come south from Germany with a great army to restore Montecassino and put the villain in his own dungeons. William de Hauteville, advising Rainulf to leave his untrustworthy ally to his fate, had engineered a truce with Conrad – a combination of force that obliged Pandulf to flee.

The reward for Rainulf had been imperial confirmation of his title under Guaimar, the newly elevated Prince of both Salerno and Capua. This, for a Norman who had come to Italy with nothing but his horses and his weapons, was elevation indeed, a title and fiefdom from which only the emperor could remove him. At the ceremony of investiture outside the walls of Capua, Rainulf had brought forward William and embraced him, bidding him kiss the gonfalon that denoted his title, an indication from a man without offspring that his senior captain should be his heir.

William had gone off to Sicily leading all but a hundred of Rainulf's men, sustained by that promise of a brilliant future; he had returned to find Rainulf's termagant wife shut up in a nunnery, a new young and lusty concubine in his bed, the Imperial Count of Aversa sober and cradling in his arms a mewling male infant he called Hermann, who would one day, he made plain, succeed to his lands and title; William de Hauteville would get nothing!

'Put the matter to the vote,' Drogo suggested, not for the first time. 'Let the men decide who to follow, you or Rainulf.'

William looked at Drogo long and hard. They had been through much together, growing up, in coming to this place and what had occurred since. Drogo had been his lieutenant in Sicily and had not in any way let him down; he was a fighter any man would be happy to have at his side. His flaw, if you excluded his inability to pass a woman without trying to bed her, was his lack of judgement. Yet looking around the faces of his brothers he saw they too shared Drogo's view.

Perhaps because William was the eldest of a large and unruly clan he had a better grasp of reality, the very quality which had led Rainulf to previously rely on him for advice. All his life, when Tancred and his parental wrath needed to be kept in the dark about some family problem, he had been required to intercede with one brother against another and, in Drogo's case, with more than one irate father. For every time his judgement had been accepted, there had been many more where he had been obliged to ensure acceptance of the right course with a thump around the ear. That would not serve now they were all grown men. Yet he needed them on his side.

'Right now it would break the band apart, Drogo. Not all the men would follow me and Rainulf would not let such an insult pass. A split like that would lead to bloodshed, which, I suspect, might please many people, but in the end it would resolve nothing. Rainulf would still not reinstate me as the heir to his title and I am not prepared to fight and kill my fellow Normans for something I cannot have.'

'Go back to Prince Guaimar,' suggested Humphrey. 'He has the power to force Rainulf to keep his word.'

Having tried that once, and been rebuffed, William had no desire to do so again. 'That would be to beg and, besides, you are wrong. To make Rainulf bend the knee in such an important matter would cause Prince Guaimar more trouble than he desires to have, and do not doubt for a moment he takes pleasure in our mutual dissension.'

'So you just accept being cheated?'

'It's Duke Robert all over again,' said Mauger.

That took William back to Normandy, just days before the first major battle of his life, to the great ducal pavilion hard by the hamlet of Giverny, in which he had first laid eyes on his then liege lord. Duke Robert had not been happy at the way Tancred de Hauteville, leading his sons, had forced his way into his presence, even less joyful when he had been reminded that five of those boys shared with him a bloodline through their late mother, albeit one carrying the taint of illegitimacy.

It had been a less than joyful interview for a man who liked to be styled Robert the Magnificent: Tancred was not one to show excessive respect, of the kind Robert had come to expect from fawning courtiers. Like an uncle to the family of the duke, this was a man he had known since childhood, who he had, along with his elder brother, tossed high in the air. Rumours abounded that Duke Robert had poisoned that elder brother to gain his title; those who believed such an accusation to be a literal truth called him Robert the Devil.

Tancred had raised his sons with one aim in mind: the prospect of joining the *familia* knights of the ducal household, the men who served their liege lord close and would die in battle to keep him safe, the reward for good service being the captaincy of a castle, maybe even lands and possibly a title of their own. Duke Robert had disabused him: he had no trust in the connection of bastard blood, even less in Tancred or his sons.

He would not allow any de Hauteville to serve him close, for fear of what they might do to his own born-out-of-wedlock son, who was now, following Robert's death, the reigning Duke of Normandy. Rabidly ambitious himself, Robert could not be brought to even consider that these tall and sturdy boys were free of that trait, nor that the solemn vow Tancred had made to his own father would bind them to his service, a refusal which had brought them to this place and this conundrum.

'We have no choice but to do now what we did then,' William insisted. 'We must look for good fortune elsewhere. I want to be sure that whatever I do I can count on your support.'

'To whom else would we give it?' asked Mauger, who could not hide the look in his eye, one that told all present how much he worshipped a brother many years his senior.

That brought forth a smile. 'No one, Mauger, but I wish to remind you all we are bound together, that we are de Hautevilles, in the same way our father was wont to remind us—'

'Endlessly,' Humphrey interjected, champing those very prominent top teeth, he being one son who was sure he had never truly enjoyed his father's love.

Geoffrey spoke next. 'You are our leader by right as well as birth, William.'

'Is it sacrilegious to puke in church?' asked Drogo, though he grinned to make sure all understood he was joking.

'From now on there are two worlds, that outside and ours. I will seek your support when there is no time to explain why, but know this: I will always act in all our interests, not just my own. I ask you, as our father did, to swear on the Holy Cross that you will follow me wherever that may lead us, and I ask you to renew the vow he made us all swear before we left Normandy, never to raise a weapon against each other.'

William hauled out his sword and knelt, the others following, each using hilt and pommel as a personal cross, to take the oath William had asked of them, their eyes fixed on the crucified Christ as they pledged their word.

'You said elsewhere,' Drogo said as they stood again. 'Where would that be?'

'Apulia.'

'Why Apulia?'

That question was posed with a look of deep suspicion. William, he well knew, was capable of laying deep and long-sighted plans. He was also inclined to keep such things to himself and this time was no exception.

'Wait and see. Now stir yourselves, it is time we ended our devotions and returned to camp.'

'What devotions?' Geoffrey demanded, a reasonable question since no prayers, barring the oath just taken, had been said.

William smiled. 'The ones I told Rainulf were due today, a Mass for the soul of our late mother.'

'But...' Geoffrey paused before stating the obvious: this was not the day on which the mother he shared with everyone except young Mauger had passed away.

# CHAPTER TWO

✠

A mock tourney it might be, more a way of exercising fighting men to avoid them becoming rusty, rather than proper warfare, but today would, nevertheless, be brutal. No one should die, but none would emerge lacking a bruise and quite a few would need days in their cot to recover, added to the ministrations of their womenfolk and, perhaps, a mendicant monk from nearby Aversa. William de Hauteville, still the senior captain, had arranged the fighting contingents, several of them led by his own brothers – but if they were united by blood, they were also animated by the desire to prove their fighting worth; no sibling could expect gentility from another.

On the open agricultural plains of Campania, finding room to deploy four hundred mounted warriors presented little difficulty, and if some crops got trampled in the process, well, these were Rainulf's own lands, the peasants his to command, the rich soil his to exploit, so they would be obliged to watch the destruction of their careful husbandry and ploughed fields in silence.

William, aware of this, and as a sop to their depleted larders, had arranged they should participate in the feast which would follow the tournament – several oxen were already roasting on spits – an act which had earned him a snort of disapproval from his chief.

'They will not love you for it,' Rainulf insisted, looking up at a man who towered over him by several hands, his purple-veined face censorious. 'The Italian peasant understands only hard treatment, and if you are soft on them, your reward, one dark night, will most likely be a knife in the back.'

'Part of the crops we destroy are theirs to live off. If we are taking the food from their mouths, it does no harm to put some back.'

'My crops, my food! I could overrule you.'

'You could,' William replied, his tone as cold as his stare.

The locked eyes and stony expressions, which followed that exchange, underlined how things had altered between these men in the last two and a half years. At one time Rainulf would have welcomed the suggestion from a man he trusted absolutely; now there was some doubt if he could tolerate the speaker's presence.

'It is time and Prince Guaimar is waiting,' William said, indicating with a finger that the powerful Italian sun was well past its zenith, that the day was cooling and so it was time to commence the tourney.

Mention of his titular overlord had Rainulf looking to the elevated, shaded pavilion he had erected so the party from Salerno could watch the tourney in comfort. Prince Guaimar, at a mere twenty years still looking too young for his title, was seated next to his wife and young son, she holding a newly born daughter still at the suckling stage, while his sister, Berengara, her radiant beauty evident even at a distance, sat on their left. On the right of the prince sat another Lombard called Arduin of Fassano, a fellow known to William but not to Rainulf. Behind the prince, alongside the various officials from Guaimar's court, sat Rainulf's slender young concubine, his new bedmate, holding his restless child, Hermann.

'Odd,' Rainulf observed, with no attempt to disguise a degree of contempt. 'Guaimar is a prince who has never led men, never seen a real battle, yet I, who have seen and spilt much blood, must bow to his title.'

William was about to reply that the prince had in his veins the blood of his forbears, but he checked himself: to mention such a lineage was to raise the spectre of Rainulf's bastard son, a subject best avoided.

'He has the good sense to let we Normans do his fighting.'

'The other fellow, Arduin, you know him from Sicily?'

'I do.'

'And?' Rainulf said querulously, not happy at having to drag out information.

'A good soldier, he commanded the contingent of pikemen from Apulia, and given they were reluctant to serve, he trained and led them well.'

'Trustworthy?'

'He's a Lombard, Rainulf.'

The squat older Norman nodded, which made the spare flesh under his chin more pronounced; that remark required no further clarification for a man who knew the Lombards better than most and shared with them a history of conspiracy.

'Any notion of why he is here?'

William knew very well why he was here: realising that Rainulf was intent on breaking his word regarding the succession, he had gone to see Prince Guaimar in Salerno, and, in a disappointing interview, in which he had tried and failed to get him to remind his vassal of his promise, the prince had told him about Arduin and his appointment as the *topoterites* of Melfi. He had also told him of the plan to betray his new master, Michael Doukeianos. It was telling that Guaimar had yet to inform Rainulf.

'My guess is he will be looking for lances.'

'To fight where?'

William just shrugged.

'Then it is time we showed him of what we are made.'

Rainulf was now too long in the tooth to spend much time in the saddle; he would watch with Guaimar, and no doubt use his proximity to press the prince once more for help. He had asked the Papacy to grant him an annulment of his marriage to his second wife, without which he could not legitimise his child, Rome being a place where a Lombard prince could apply more weight than any Norman. William knew he was wasting his time, and not just because of the tangle of Roman politics: Guaimar had only borne his title for less than three full years but had learnt very quickly that the best way to sustain his power was to keep alive dissension amongst those who might oppose him.

He would no more act as Rainulf requested than respond to William's appeal, and for the same reason. All the advantage for him lay in the strained relations between the two Norman leaders. In fact, there were very good grounds to suppose that Prince Guaimar was doing the very reverse of what Drengot required – this made easy by the endless jockeying of several claimants to the papal title – using whatever influence he had in Rome to block that which Rainulf sought, and thus keep him dependent.

Guaimar had grown in acumen as he had become accustomed to power and, no doubt, fatherhood had sharpened his resolve. He was no longer the young innocent William had first encountered – the dispossessed son of the previous ruler, easily outwitted in negotiation. Now he had a mind that could calculate where his advantage lay and he applied it well. He might smile at Rainulf, but he would never fully trust him, never forget this was the same man who had betrayed his father.

Should he falter in that resolve his younger sister was ever present to remind him. Berengara had her beauty, but that was leavened by a degree of spite aimed at the Normans, any Norman, which made speaking with her an exercise in bile. She hated the men who had betrayed her family with unabated passion, and rumour had it she had traded her virtue to put pressure on Conrad Augustus to come south and restore her brother to his fief. The Normans, when the news came that the Holy Roman Emperor had expired, were inclined to put his demise down to her poisonous embrace.

William's relations with her were no better than those of his confrères, but he was prone to guying her when chance presented itself, given that she never failed to react. Much as he despised Frankish customs – no true Norman had any respect for their French or Angevin neighbours – he had heard that the knights of Paris and Tours were wont to request from a lady, prior to an event such as this, some favour to decorate their weapons. Thus, before he rode out to commence matters, he stopped before the pavilion and lowered the padded point of his lance till it was before her face.

'My lady, I am told it is the custom of the northern courts to beg support from a fair maiden prior to combat.'

Berengara knew she was being played upon, and if she had had any doubts, the smile – or was it a smirk? – on William's face, would have told her so.

Her brother sought to head off her angry response, by speaking first. 'It is not yet the custom in Italy.'

'You may have my favour,' said Berengara, swiftly, removing a thin shawl, which had covered her bosom, pleased by the way William's eye was drawn to that which was revealed. She was still smiling when she spat on it, followed by a swift twist round his lance. 'And also you now have my sentiments as well.'

William laughed out loud, which wiped the acid smile off her face, before he hauled round his mount and headed out into the open, past the curious peasantry, to where the entire force of Rainulf's mercenaries was lined up.

'He has pride, that one,' whispered Arduin to Guaimar, 'and has the gift of command as well. I saw him fight outside Syracuse, and he is formidable both in single combat and in battle.'

'They all are that, Arduin,' Guaimar replied in the same soft tone. 'So much so, that they are also a menace. You will do me a service if you take most of them out of my lands.'

The sound of a battle horn, a single long note, floated across the open fields, the signal for the tournament to commence.

'It is the catapan's gold that will take them there, Prince Guaimar, and I will give them Melfi, but they need two other things if we are to foment a real revolt that will not only break Byzantium, but elevate the Lombard cause: a leader and a purpose.'

'Will you not lead them?'

'I am but a soldier, with no land and only the title gifted to me by the catapan. Militarily I can command, but to head the enterprise I have outlined requires a nobleman of stature, someone under whose banner the Italians and Lombards can unite against the Greeks. It is not modesty, but truth, to say they will not follow me.'

The invitation was obvious in the words and look, a request that Guaimar should raise the banner of Lombard revolt in Apulia, an offer he would decline. Arduin might say, and indeed might believe, Byzantium was uniquely weak and vulnerable at this time, but if revolts had failed in the past they could do so again and, previously, retribution had been bloody and swift. Whoever raised the standard would, if things went against him, pay a heavy price.

If an army could invade Apulia, a rampaging Byzantine host could do the same to Campania, quite apart from the prospect of a powerful fleet sailing from the Bosphorus, then appearing in the Bay of Salerno, which had also happened before. Guaimar had held his title for too little a time to place it in jeopardy; let another take the risk, as long as he was around for a share of any reward should they enjoy success.

'I think when you leave here you should pay a call upon the Prince of Benevento.'

'You think Prince Landulf will take the lead?'

'I was thinking more that Argyrus, the son of the great Melus, now resides in Benevento.'

Melus was a potent name, as the man who had so nearly succeeded in the task Arduin was now setting out to repeat. Argyrus, his son, had only recently been released from imprisonment in Constantinople, as a sop to Lombard sensibilities. He was, as of this moment, an unknown quantity, but his name was worth half an army.

'His presence is known to Byzantium. To lead another revolt he must have permission from the Prince of Benevento. Would Landulf agree to let him participate?'

'I think he might. Benevento has much to gain if there is any success.'

*So do you*, Arduin thought, but he kept that to himself.

\* \* \*

There was no metal in use this day, for the very simple reason that every one of the men assembled was either young or too seasoned a fighter. The former were, by nature, hot-headed in battle, the rest too proud to take lightly being bested by another. No trust could be placed in their restraint, and the use of swords and metal-tipped lances would lead to multiple deaths. What William wanted was to exercise the horses and men, not in the tens of the standard Norman conroy, but in the mass, to underscore the lessons learnt in Sicily. He wanted them to behave as the mounted component of an army.

The purpose of doing so he had kept from Rainulf: in his meeting with Prince Guaimar he had as good as acceded to the notion of taking service with Arduin. He would follow the Lombard to Melfi and take possession of the fortress, and, under his command, invade Apulia. But on this expedition he was determined to act on behalf of himself and his family. If Rainulf Drengot could gain land and title in Campania, then William de Hauteville was determined he would do the same in those fresh pastures.

There would be many obstacles along the way, not least the Byzantines, who were formidable in adversity. He would also have to outwit the Lombards, Prince Guaimar, and Rainulf, all of whom would see him only as a mercenary, or in the Norman leader's case, a captain, acting on his behalf. His brothers, in that vestry, had more or less accused him of allowing himself to be cheated; they too would learn that their elder brother had the wit and guile to outmanoeuvre those he felt had duped him.

The mercenaries had been broken up into bands of one hundred lances, and their first task was to attack a long false wooden shield wall William had had erected fifty paces from the front of the elevated pavilion and the assembled guests; let them feel some sense of what it was like to face a Norman host. Taking station to the right of the first line, commanded by Drogo, William ordered them forward, noting that no command was required for another captain, called Turmod, to advance his own century after a slight gap.

Humphrey, with Rainulf's blessing, had been elevated to command for the day, and so had brother Geoffrey, which left Mauger fuming as the only de Hauteville not leading one of the four assault lines. He was obliged to act as William's aide, which, hero worship notwithstanding, was not enough to mollify him, and as he sat alongside his elder brother his frustration was not something that could be hidden by either helmet or nose guard.

The strength of Norman cavalry lay in their use of weight as opposed to tempo. Horsemen of other armies charged, hoping by sheer brio to break an enemy line, which inevitably led to some moving at more speed than the rest so they arrived at the point of battle as a disorganised melee. The Norman line was solid, the destriers they rode chosen not for fleetness but for their sturdy nature. Both horse and rider were trained to hold their line and hit an enemy position as a formidable mass.

This required well-practised horsemanship and constant attention; no steed next to another could entirely be weaned off the desire to race: a horse did not require to be told *how* to run, but when. To hold them in exact relation to their neighbouring mounts took endless training as well as strong hands and thighs, the latter becoming immeasurably more important as the point of actual combat approached: the rider would be looking to use his hands for his lance and his shield, albeit he would still hold a rein. Once battle was joined, the main pressure a warrior would have to control his mount was those thighs.

No mock tourney could ever be like the real thing, but for the likes of Guaimar, who was no soldier, the sight of a hundred lances attacking in his direction made him tense, even if he knew they were blunted and it represented no threat, so much so that he put a protective arm around Gisulf, his young son. Looking past his wife at his sister, he was surprised to see how excited she was, her body tensed and leaning slightly forward, her mouth open and the one eye he could see alight with anticipation, nothing like the frisson of fear in his own.

The Normans were now standing in their stirrups, the hooves of their horses kicking up a huge cloud of dust, their lances couched under their arms and their teardrop-shaped shields, coloured in the red and black of Rainulf Drengot, set forward to protect both themselves and the flank of their horse; two hundred eyes and those padded lance points, in Guaimar's over-vivid imagination, fixed on the point of his chest.

Berengara's body jerked as the points hit the wood, a hundred thuds like a tattoo of many drums melding so close as to be as one, mixed with the battle-cry shouts of the attackers. It was what happened next that was most impressive. At the sound of a battle horn all hundred riders spun their horses to run parallel with the wall and, jabbing their tipless lances at imaginary foes over the top of the shields, they moved as one at a steady canter, and there, behind them as soon as they were clear, were another hundred lances a few grains of sand away from contact.

That century turned right to get clear, and the sight of another attack was repeated twice more, in a series of sounds and cries, each one of which seemed to pass like a lightning strike through Berengara's tensed frame. But her excitement did not end there, for Drogo's century was approaching again, this time with lances held high, to be thrown on command at the straw bales which lay in front of her. Those dispatched, swords were unsheathed and the wood hacked at with great force, sending splinters flying from the edge as they again made their steady way to the left to be replaced by another century executing the same manoeuvre.

'Few would stand against this, Prince Guaimar,' shouted Rainulf, also in a state of high excitement. 'Most would have broken by now.'

Locking eyes with the Norman leader, the young Lombard wondered if there was an implied threat in the observation. Was Rainulf telling him that no army of conscript Italians and Lombards could sustain him if he chose to challenge such a host?

'The Varangians would stand,' called Arduin.

That reference to the axemen of Kiev Rus brought to Rainulf's face a deep frown. He had fought them in the Lombard revolt led by Melus, and he had lost his elder brother in the final battle. A force of Norse lineage provided to Constantinople by the Prince of Kiev, the Varangians were indeed formidable and their chosen weapon, axes swung and thrown, were deadly against both horse and rider.

'I saw them in Sicily, Count Rainulf, and I came to admire them greatly.'

Rainulf just jerked his head to look to the front; he did not want to talk of Varangians or of campaigns led by William de Hauteville. His eyes were now on the two lines of Normans who had taken station facing each other, and at a command they closed, first seeking to unhorse the men they fought, then, once the lance had been used or abandoned, fighting each other on horseback with hardwood swords. No mercy was shown to anyone who left an opening: several jabbing and slashing men were dismounted to fall at the feet of, and scrabble away from, the heaving mass of hooves, more dangerous by far than that which they had faced in the saddle.

At the sound of the horn they disengaged and were replaced by the other two centuries, the whole confrontation repeated with the same level of effort. To the rear, men could be seen limping away both from the previous battle and this, while the odd mercenary lay comatose where they had fallen, as their confrères tried to continue to jab, slash and parry without simultaneously trampling them.

'Look,' cried Berengara, as the two lines disengaged and withdrew.

She was pointing to a line of marching Normans, making their way through the clouds of dust left by their previous mounted engagement. Only on foot could you truly appreciate that these warriors were likely to tower over any enemy they faced. Every one was well above whatever height could be named as average, and in the middle of the line it was impossible to miss William de Hauteville, taller still, with his brother, Mauger, a hand smaller, at his side.

He led his men to the shield wall where they began hacking away, reducing what was left of the wood of the defence to shards, which set young Gisulf to crying, a sound which had no effect on the swordsmen but one which had his mother take him away from the noise. Destruction complete, the Normans retired, exchanging their weapons for wooden replacements, as two centuries faced each other in foot combat, coming together with a series of loud cracks and screaming imprecations as they fought each other in mock battle.

William had by this time remounted, and it came to the point which interested him greatly. There was a tactic he knew his men could use mounted – the false retreat. Could they do it on foot? He had deliberately left till last a fight between men who had served him in Sicily, under Drogo's direct command, and those of Turmod's troop, who had stayed behind in Aversa to protect both Rainulf and Prince Guaimar, knowing there was a deep degree of rivalry between them.

Only Drogo knew he was going to give the horn signal for a false retreat; would his men realise that it applied to them unmounted? Drogo was key, as was any commander in a conflict, but in this the Normans had their other great asset: close battlefield control. They knew the commands just as they knew they must be obeyed; it was not their job to think but to obey. The horn blew its triple notes and William saw his brother's sword in the air, waving as he fell back, pleased to see that his shouts and gestures were bearing fruit – his men had disengaged.

Turmod's men should have known better: they were Normans too, but they could not resist moving forward to pursue, a fatal tactic, because they did not all do so at the same pace, creating dog-leg gaps. William signalled for the horn to blow again, and watched with pride as Drogo turned his men round in a tight line and rushed them forward, completely overwhelming their opponents and driving them back, inflicting more bruises on that century than had been suffered by any other in the day.

If he had been looking at the pavilion, he would have seen an irate Rainulf ranting about the deviousness of his senior captain, for he was soldier enough to know it had been he who had initiated the manoeuvre. William would not have cared: as a leader he had just added another string to his tactical ability; everyone in Rainulf's band had seen it, now all four hundred lances would know what to do in the future.

The sun was sinking, the light going, the wounded were being helped away, and in the gathering gloom the fires of those roasting oxen glowed, while torches by the hundred were being lit around twin rows of great tables. It was time to eat and drink.

# CHAPTER THREE

'I can give you another captain, just as skilful and as brave as William de Hauteville,' insisted Rainulf.

'You forget,' Arduin responded, clearly unconvinced, 'that I have seen the Iron Arm fight, and I have seen him lead men – your men.'

'Iron Arm!' spat Rainulf, his high-coloured face picking up the light from the numerous torches. 'Such posturing means nothing, it is but a name. Old as I am I would not fear to take up arms against him.'

Prince Guaimar and Arduin nodded insincerely in response to the glare with which he fixed them, taking the statement for what it was, an idle boast from a man who could not admit to being the ageing fellow he saw in his piece of polished silver each morning. Berengara, who should not have been part of the discussion at all, was not one to let such an opportunity pass.

'I think you should challenge him, Rainulf, and I will persuade my brother to provide a healthy purse for the victor.'

The look that got her was one full of detestation, an emotion she returned in good measure. If she hated Normans, then Berengara hated Rainulf Drengot most of all! The day she and her brother had been dragged out of the Castello de Arechi in Salerno was seared in her mind. Rainulf had been there, sneering at his one-time father-in-law for his protestations of betrayal. The events of the day had broken him: the old duke had retired to a monastery, and with his heart and hopes destroyed, it had soon brought about his demise.

'The loser,' she added maliciously, 'should have nought but a pauper's grave, a place for dogs to piss and defecate.'

'I am curious, Rainulf,' said Guaimar, heading off his angry response, 'why not William?'

If it was possible for a man with so purple a countenance to flush, Rainulf did so then, aware, as he was, that the prince was pricking him just like his sister; not in the same outright manner, but discomfiting nonetheless. Guaimar knew very well Rainulf's objections were brought about by fear of a man who might have too much support amongst the men he led, a man too powerful to openly challenge. Yet he had his justification well prepared.

'He has had opportunity already, in Sicily. It is time to give such a gift to another.'

'No!' snapped Arduin.

'Turmod has been in my service longer than any of the de Hautevilles, and that is another factor. If William goes he will take his brothers.'

'I would expect nothing else,' Guaimar replied.

Arduin spoke again, his look deadly serious. 'This is not skirmishing in Campania, which is all this Turmod of yours has ever done. We are talking about fighting the might of the Eastern Empire—'

Rainulf's interruption was bellicose. 'I know that!'

'Just as you know from fighting them yourself they are difficult to overcome.'

The pair glared at each other. The subject raised was the defeat at Cannae, the very same field upon which Hannibal had massacred the Romans in 216BC. The Lombards and Normans, led by Melus, had not suffered so final a fate in the rout, but the battle had been bloody, the mercenary cavalry left with barely enough horses to flee the field, leaving behind the Apulian *milities* as they did so to die under a Byzantine sword or a Varangian axe. After every battle lost, there were recriminations: the Normans maintained it was the Lombards who had broken; they, the too confident Normans who had failed.

'If we are not to repeat what happened previously,' Arduin insisted, driving home his point with a jabbing finger, 'then I want a cavalry leader who has experience of real battle, not something barely a step up from that which we witnessed today.'

'He has the gift of previous success,' Guaimar added, driving home Arduin's point; not even Rainulf could match William de Hauteville in that regard. There was also the delicious pleasure of reminding the Count of Aversa that in a proper battle, as opposed to skirmish, he had known only loss. 'I fear, as your suzerain, Rainulf, I would be bound to insist you grant Arduin that which he wishes.'

There was a moment then, pregnant with threat. Rainulf was an imperial count mainly through Guaimar's good offices: it was the disenfranchised young heir to Salerno who had first suggested to Conrad Augustus that, instead of seeking revenge against the man who had betrayed his father, only such an elevation would detach him from support for the rapacious Pandulf. Rainulf had turned to Guaimar, who had stood by as he accepted his gonfalon from the imperial hand, to then acknowledge the new young prince as his immediate overlord.

Yet there had not been, since that time, a point on which they could disagree on any vital matter and there was no certainty this Norman, who had made so much trouble in the past, would acknowledge.

Guaimar's right to make such a decision. The test had to come at some time: who was the lord and who was the vassal? Odd that it should be over William de Hauteville, the very person who ensured the Count of Aversa felt insecure, and also the very person who had brokered the actual pact with the Holy Roman Emperor to get rid of Pandulf.

'Perhaps I should lead my men myself.'

'I need you to stay close with a number of your lances to protect my fiefs and impose my will.'

The pause was long, the looks unblinking, until Rainulf, who had drunk sparingly throughout the feast, picked up a full goblet of wine and drained it in one, pushing it out towards a flagon-bearing child to demand a refill. He did not speak, but then he did not have to.

William was eating at the same high table, close enough to Rainulf and his main guests to observe the depth of their conversation, but he was not near enough to actually hear what was being said, that made doubly impossible by the hubbub of talking and shouting which surrounded him – there was dancing too around a great bonfire – though he had no doubt it involved the proposed invasion of Apulia. It was galling that these matters were being discussed without him; he was in no doubt that he was the one who would have to carry out the task.

So in his mind he ranged over the problems he would face, firstly those of a military nature. Arduin clearly desired to have overall military control, and that was as it should be; if the assault on Apulia was to be based on the notion of Lombard independence, then it required one of that race to be in command. If Michael Doukeianos had trouble holding the many fortified towns, any Norman-led force would have just as much trouble subduing them, and besides, that was not the object: they needed to be won over to the cause, not besieged and forced into surrender.

He would have at his disposal a formidable body of Norman cavalry, but that would not be sufficient: he would need more to face the power of Constantinople, an empire with millions of subjects and, William knew from Sicily, a bottomless treasury. So word must go out from him to other Norman bands in South Italy, enticing them with the possibility of rich rewards. Then there was the man he would face!

Byzantium had different types of commanders, and they ranged from the very good to the utterly useless, the quality and the person depending entirely on intrigue at court. The armies they fielded away from their constantly threatened eastern possessions tended to be bought-and-paid-for fighters, or unwilling *milities* raised locally. The latter could be a weakness, sometimes more trouble than they were worth, but no army could fight without foot soldiers of some

kind, and Arduin would have to raise those. It was
necessary they should come to the banner willingly,
for the catapan would be obliged to conscript his.

Would Arduin have a force of crossbowmen? If not,
they must be recruited, for they were an essential tool
against any army in a strong defensive position, and
William reckoned, if Byzantium was presently weak in
the Catapanate, then a wise general would force the
people he saw as rebels to attack him rather than seek
open battle with an enemy strong in cavalry. Finally,
nothing could be complete without the reduction of
the Adriatic ports, that is, if they failed to support the
revolt or were held by the catapan; that might mean
siege equipment and artisans to construct them on
site, weapons of which the Normans knew nothing. He
was still ruminating on such problems when he looked
up to see Arduin standing behind his shoulder.

'Rainulf has agreed that you should lead his men
into Apulia.'

'Was it ever in any doubt?' William enquired,
looking towards Rainulf, who avoided his eye. Turning
back to Arduin, he could see, as much as the Lombard
tried to hide it, that had indeed been the case.

'I hope you are willing to serve under me?'

'I am,' William replied, seeking to control the anger
in his voice, lest Arduin think it directed at him. 'As
are my brothers.'

'All of them?' When William nodded, Arduin laid

a hand on his shoulder and said, 'Good! I have asked
Prince Guaimar to meet with us tomorrow, to discuss
the campaign.'

'I look forward to it.'

That was when the fighting started, round that
bonfire; the combination of food, drink and women had
worked its usual magic on the many present rivalries
to produce a brawl. Normans who had been to Sicily
would take a swing at those who had not, added to
Italian peasants who resented the mercenaries long
before they sought to interfere with their womenfolk.
Drogo would be in there somewhere; he always was
when there was trouble. There was a time when
William would have gone in to seek to cool things
down and to ensure Drogo, and for that matter his
other siblings, did not suffer from trying to take on too
many opponents.

He was not inclined to on this night, which made
him wonder if perhaps he was getting old. Turning
away from that to glare at Rainulf he saw Berengara
leaning forward, watching the fracas with deep
concentration. She looked stunning, but it was her
evident pleasure, and the flush of blood in her cheeks,
picked up by the torches, that was most evident. Was
it caused merely by the fighting, or the thought that
some Normans might be getting what, in her mind,
they deserved?

* * *

There was a certain amount of amusement to be gained from observing the way Prince Guaimar sought to exercise control over the direction of what was proposed while at the same time he made it perfectly plain that Salerno and Capua were detached in terms of interest in the outcome, clearly trying to have the best of both worlds. Watching the other faces was also instructive: Arduin disappointed but resigned that he would not have Guaimar's complete support – Salerno would provide no foot soldiers, in fact nothing but sustenance on the route, and that would be paid for; Rainulf, obviously suffering from a night of excessive imbibing, looked morose, when not openly furious.

The conference was taking place in Rainulf's stone donjon, a square defensive edifice that had stood in this place for centuries, possibly since Roman times. The tower lay at the heart of his impressive operations – no less than what amounted to a standing army – and was surrounded by the huts which accommodated his men, as well as their concubines and bastards, a huge barn in which feasts could be held, a manège for training in the use of all kinds of arms, and a square league of paddocks which contained the horses without which his lances were useless. Added to that was a stud which bred even more mounts of the various types Norman cavalry required for movement and combat.

Faintly, through the doorway that led to a long

sloping ramp – one that would be pulled up and in when danger threatened – came the sounds of the morning's exercise. The men might have been drinking heavily the night before, not to mention fighting each other with their fists, but that did not obviate the need for daily practice. It was this constant training, as much as the quality of the men he commanded, which had made Rainulf Drengot so formidable a presence in Campania.

The day William and Drogo arrived – and the same had happened to their brothers – they had been obliged to enter that training manège and prove their ability with sword, lance and fighting mount. Rainulf had a very simple attitude: they were in a foreign land and paid to fight and he wanted no one in his band who was not accomplished at that.

When there was no actual combat they trained hard for their task, so that when they did ride out for whatever purpose they were warriors at their peak, men whom no one locally could hope to stand against. Thus their reputation, which included their inclination to cruelty, went before them, often defeating opposition without the need for them to draw their swords.

Arduin had the floor; he had been given enough gold by Michael Doukeianos to pay for fifty knights to garrison Melfi for a twelvemonth, and that was enough to purchase supplies for three hundred lances to get to the fortress and take it over. If he had hoped that

Guaimar would dip into his princely revenues to fund anything, that too was a disappointment, but he was no doubt sustained by the rewards he would acquire for success. What those would be were a matter of some interest to William, but that was what they would have to remain: there was no way he could ask, and even if he got an answer, no way of knowing if he was being told the truth.

'Initially,' Arduin insisted, 'we can live off the land, for it is fertile. For the future, the revenues that Byzantium now enjoys will come to us, and that can be used to reward success.'

'Is there any possibility the inhabitants of Melfi will close the gates against us?' asked William. 'They have no reason to love Normans.'

'They do not hold the castle.'

'Right at this moment no one holds the castle. You have no garrison, which means the townsfolk have nothing to stop them taking it over.'

'I am the *topoterites* appointed by the catapan. They will not, and cannot, deny entry to me, and if I choose to lead you in...'

The fact that Arduin did not finish that sentence was proof enough to William that he had raised a real possibility, and one that would fatally compromise the whole endeavour. Melfi had to be their base as well as their refuge, and having avoided it more than once as he and Rainulf's men raided into Apulia he knew how strong it was. Even with untrained townsfolk it could be held for an age if they had enough food, certainly long enough to alert Byzantium to what was happening.

'Might I suggest that you only approach the town with the fifty lances; in short, the garrison the people can be persuaded to accept. Once they are inside the fortress, the Melfians can object as much as they like to another two hundred and fifty more joining them, it will be of little use.'

'That smacks of you being fearful,' Rainulf growled.

'I am that,' William replied. 'I have found it helps to be so in a campaign. Michael Doukeianos will hear soon enough of our arrival and the purpose for which we are there. He will have no choice but to bring everything he can muster to evict us. Arduin needs time to gather local levies so that we can meet him with an army, and we have to find crossbowmen from somewhere since we will not have time to train them.'

'Let him besiege you,' Rainulf suggested. 'Let him waste his strength before your walls.'

William looked at Arduin, who nodded, bidding him continue. 'What message will that send out to Apulia, Rainulf? That we are afraid to meet him in the field? The best way to rally support across the province and beyond is to give Doukeianos battle, at a time and place of our choosing, and beat him.'

'We must,' Arduin added, 'attack and take some

of the nearby towns to encourage him. The quicker he seeks to defeat us the better because of his lack of strength.'

Rainulf was shaking his head, possibly from the memory of the previous defeat, but more likely because he was inclined to disagree with whatever was proposed on principle. There was no doubt he saw what was happening as a diminution of his standing: orders and actions were being proposed for his men and he was not the one deciding on the tactics to be employed. William could see that Guaimar was paying him close attention, watching his every reaction, knowing that each rebuff was a test of his authority.

'The time will come, Rainulf,' he said, in an encouraging tone, 'when Arduin and William have laid the ground for our open support. Every one of us will gain eventually.'

That was so blatant a piece of hypocrisy that William had to fight not to react, and he was not helped by the look on Arduin's face, which could only be described as contemptuous, hardly surprising given the cynicism of what Guaimar had just said. Clearly the prince realised he had made an error, had spoken too truthfully about what he hoped for the future, for he added quickly and earnestly.

'Byzantium evicted from our borders can only do us good.'

'So you still wish me to approach the Prince of

Benevento about Argyrus becoming titular leader of the revolt?'

The positive reply was a stammer: Arduin had brought out into the open something meant to be kept close. It was pleasing to see Guaimar discomfited; since his return from Sicily William had not, until this day, seen the younger man put a foot wrong in the way he had played him and Rainulf off against each other, and he was obviously, given the mention of Benevento, planning to play the same game with his Lombard neighbour.

Benevento was a papal fief, answerable to Rome, not an imperial one whose suzerain was the Western Emperor in Germany, thus Guaimar could justifiably insist to Constantinople that they were acting alone: he had no involvement in any Apulian uprising and the ultimate responsibility lay with the Holy See.

If Byzantium managed that which it had done in the past, and massively reinforced the Catapanate, and either defeated Arduin or forced him to withdraw, then no blame – even if there were good grounds to suspect it – could be attached to the Prince of Salerno, and while whoever was sent from the east to chastise Apulia took out their ire on Benevento, he would have ample time to negotiate for a settlement of any perceived grievances with the victorious catapan. The Normans could be explained away as they always were, as greedy mercenaries not under his direct control.

Should the revolt succeed, Guaimar would, no doubt, claim to have been the magnate to instigate it, and he would thus be able to put himself forward as a future ruler of that dreamt-for Lombard Kingdom. Any other nobleman prepared to contest that claim would know that, through Rainulf, he controlled the Norman host, a force impossible to stand against, and that would apply to the Adriatic trading ports as well. The Prince of Salerno might get himself raised to the purple, and Rainulf Drengot would be rewarded with more land and titles to ensure his support.

As a piece of chicanery it was a perfect example of the politics William had come to expect in Southern Italy, one of the reasons no Lombard overlord had ever succeeded in leading a successful rebellion; they were too busy manoeuvring to see the wood for the trees. The second reason was one they were even less able to discern: the way they bore down on their subjects, with arbitrary methods of rule, especially in the area of taxation and law.

No Italian ever won a legal case against a Lombard in courts where those sitting in judgement were either of that race or Lombard appointees; no citizen of any of their lands could be sure that, having paid what taxes their overlord demanded, there would not be a sudden claim for more, with outright seizure a permanent possibility. Even Guaimar would be tainted with that tribal habit, not yet perhaps, but sometime in the future when he felt his coffers to be too low.

So, when they conscripted Italians to fight in their campaigns, often Lombard versus Lombard, they had under their command reluctant men forced to war for something which would provide them little gain, if any at all, excepting death. No wonder they had never managed to form that kingdom these lords of fertile lands all dreamt of; no wonder they needed Normans to fight their wars.

Rainulf was quick to see the ramifications of what had just been said: Guaimar would involve him when he took a hand himself. There would be ample rewards with no prospect of loss and he would, by right, reassume command of his own men and put William de Hauteville back in his place. For the first time that morning he smiled.

To move a force of three hundred cavalry, more than forty leagues, over different types of terrain, was a huge undertaking. Each lance required three horses: a destrier and a packhorse carrying his personal possessions, both led, plus the mount he rode, and that took no account of the spare animals needed for a force expecting to fight, which, given the delicate nature of the beasts, always led to more equine casualties than human. Naturally there were also losses through normal activity: age, sickness and laming.

To a Norman knight these mounts were paramount possessions, the means by which he got to the point of combat; usually – though they often fought on foot – the instrument, along with raw courage, his sword and lance, of victory, as well as, should things go badly, his means of flight. Every one of the men under William's command had been raised, as had the de Hauteville brothers, in close proximity to horses; they knew their sires and mares, had often attended the foaling of the mounts they rode, had trained them from yearlings, treating them with a combination of strict discipline, affection and careful attention to their well-being.

But they were not sentimental regardless of the attention they lavished; each horse had a purpose. The lesser breeds as beasts of burden, the travelling mount required to be fleet as well as full of stamina, the destrier to be unflinching in the face of the enemies the rider would fight – men with pikes, axes, lances and swords, who, yelling in their thousands, could create enough of a din to act upon the nerves of a prey animal, for in the wild state that was what a horse was, thus being highly strung and so nervous they reacted to any unusual sound or sight. That they could be made fearless was remarkable.

Even in Italy, where Roman roads still existed, there were many areas – and the approach to Melfi from both east and west was one – where the only reliable transport for an army on the march had to be hoofed: not carts but packhorses, mules and donkeys. When they got to the town and castle that lay beneath the towering height of Monte Vulture, and to the fighting which lay beyond, William and the men he led, as well as their animals, would be required to live off the surrounding land.

For now, fodder could be gathered from the various fortresses and petty barons on the way, each one required to be a storehouse for Guaimar, their liege lord, but the main requirement was water, which meant that the route was dictated by the river system, at least until they got into the mountains where there were deep and abundant lakes. Men had to be fed and cared for as well, and the Norman host had with them enough camp followers to cook and see to their needs, as well as an armourer, a farrier, a saddle and harness maker, and a priest to say mass every day.

They travelled early morning and late afternoon, when the sun had lost some of its fire, resting up in the midday heat in places located by the advance party, sent ahead under Mauger. He was tasked to find not only ample water but shade and pasture, and the journey was not rushed – at five leagues a day – to keep fresh the horses. It took eight days, time for Arduin to both travel to Benevento to talk to the reigning prince and to make it back to rendezvous with William, with a view of Monte Vulture, but out of sight of the town and castle of Melfi.

The news Arduin brought to that encampment was by its nature mixed. The Prince of Benevento had refused to agree that the son of Melus, even given the power of his father's name, should act as the standard-bearer for the revolt. Instead, no doubt fired by greed, he had put forward his own younger brother, Count Atenulf, with the proviso that, should matters go against the insurgency, he might be obliged to disown him in order to appease Byzantine wrath. William's comment, made not to Arduin but to his brothers, was, 'Typically Lombard!'

The next morning Arduin and William rode ahead with fifty knights, knowing their approach would set off the alarm – in this part of the world every commune looked out for signs of approaching danger, which fifty mounted men wearing Norman mail and helmets certainly represented – and it came as no surprise to find the mass of the townsfolk had decamped from their dwellings to the castle and slammed shut the gates.

# CHAPTER FOUR

>◊<

Neither was it a surprise to see Kasa Ephraim in the Castello di Arechi; as the Collector of the Port, the Jew was a powerful official in the government of Salerno, holding an office of high and consistent profit to both Prince Guaimar and himself. A look over the Castello battlements would show why: the bay was full of vessels arriving and departing, the harbour berths packed with trading ships from both the Levant and the territories to the north, eager to take back to their home ports the produce of fertile Campania, every one obliged to pay customs dues for the goods fetched in and transported out.

Ephraim was the man who had helped the young heir and his sister to escape the clutches of Pandulf, murderous enough to have them both killed, by smuggling them away to sea, then ultimately to Rome and the Imperial Court at Bamberg. He had also used his contacts in Rome to provide funds with which to appear at the court of the Holy Roman Empire in some style. The Jew had claimed that valuable office as his reward for the service, and any fears Guaimar might have had about the way he would conduct himself had long been laid to rest.

An examination of the tally books proved that in the time of his tenure in the collector's office Ephraim had increased the revenues of the port substantially, monies which allowed his young master to be a liberal benefactor to his lesser nobles, the church and the poor; for the rest of the population, he satisfied their needs with pomp and display at the numerous religious festivals, both in the Latin rite as well as the Orthodox, which punctuated the Salerno year.

'I give you good day, honourable one.'

This Ephraim said as he entered Guaimar's private apartments. Under his arm he had his tally books so that the prince could see the extent of the month's revenues which, in gold and silver coin, were at that very moment being handed over by Ephraim's servants to the prince's official treasurer, whose domain lay deep in the vaults of the Castello. These would be placed in the brass-bound state coffers, which lay behind two very heavily barred and constantly guarded doors.

Guaimar having dismissed his servants, no one saw, apart from the two principals, the single bulging leather purse the Jew gave to his master for his private use, the monies he extracted as bribes from those who smuggled goods in and out of that same port. Kasa Ephraim had explained, long before the young man came into his inheritance, that smuggling could not be stopped in a port like Salerno, with its long, deep bay and shallow sandy beaches; therefore it must be controlled.

So the collector oversaw it, kept it from growing into a burgeoning problem, provided an occasional malefactor to be stoned by the mob, usually someone who had gone too far or tried to avoid paying a bribe, to prove to all he was carrying out his official duties, thus raising monies from the contraband trade that would otherwise have gone missing.

It was a duty the Jew had carried out for the young man's father, providing him, too, with sums of money that were never seen by the treasurer who recorded the income of the duchy, or the chamberlain who helped his lord and master to spend it. It was a fact that even the richest magnate required funds which he could disburse in secret to increase or merely just to maintain his power. The one question never posed was how much the Jew took as commission for his services: nothing was ever committed to paper.

'I received word, this very morning, that our Normans are close by Melfi.'

Kasa Ephraim nodded. He was a tall, good-looking man with, apart from a somewhat sallow Levantine complexion, none of the features so associated with his race. As well as his duties in the port he had become an unofficial advisor to the young prince: not part of his court, yet close to it, a man in whom Guaimar could confide without a record being kept of what was discussed, and one whose wisdom and discretion he respected.

'But they do not yet have possession of the castle?'

Guaimar dropped his eyes then, so that Ephraim could not see the train of his thoughts: the Jew had sources of information every bit as good as those of his prince, perhaps, in some regard, even better. Had he made that assertion regarding the Normans from knowledge or deduction?

'I await news. I hope also that the Prince of Benevento will accede to a request from Arduin, and give permission to Argyrus, the son of Melus, to raise his standard as leader of the revolt.'

The Jew was clever, Guaimar knew that, and, lifting his head again, he gave him a look from under half-hooded eyes, accompanied by an enigmatic smile, which implied much but conveyed little.

'And if this is the case, what will it portend?'

'Should it tell me more than the fact that the revolt in Apulia can proceed?'

'I sense, honourable one, that it will give you cause to examine your policy.'

'How so?'

Kasa Ephraim had become accustomed to this game, one the prince played with increasing frequency. It was natural as a head of state that he thought of nothing but the good of his patrimony, which in essence meant he indulged in a high degree of self-interest, since the fate of Salerno and the fate of its ruler were inextricably intertwined. It was also the case that the public face he presented was often at odds with his private thoughts: there were things a wise ruler needed to keep even from his everyday advisors.

'The forces that shape our destiny are many and varied, Prince Guaimar.'

'And must be treated on their merits.'

'Or faults, honourable one.'

'Even if they take possession of Melfi, it will be some time before Arduin can launch any kind of deep incursion into Byzantine territory.'

'And you are curious, I sense, as to how the catapan will react?'

'It is my duty to be.'

'I sense you would not now wish that which is about to fall upon him to come as a surprise?'

Guaimar smiled, an expression both full and satisfied. 'You have, as usual, my clever friend, nailed the predicament. If I wish, and I do wish, the catapan to believe that Salerno has had no hand in this revolt, how can I reassure him?'

'Only by forewarning him.'

'Is that a wise thing to do?'

The strands of what the prince was saying were very obvious to a man who would have openly and proudly admitted to being in possession of a very devious mind. He also had much experience in the byways of other men's thinking – the processes by which they justified to themselves acts of questionable virtue – a very necessary ability for one of his race in a Christian world that was not always overly fond of the Sons of Abraham.

Guaimar wanted to protect Salerno from any chance of Byzantine reprisals, which would surely follow if Arduin and his Normans failed in Apulia. It would be pointless to protest to a lack of knowledge after matters were settled in favour of Constantinople: he would not be believed. Were the Normans not from his fiefs, were they not men who had been in his service? The leaders, Arduin and this Argyrus, were Lombards, as was he, for Michael Doukeianos would soon discern that the latter was no more than a figurehead, and this might expose the tentacles that led back to Campania.

Yet Guaimar had a need to be careful: what if Rainulf Drengot found out that his liege lord had sent information to Bari, which he would certainly do if this matter was discussed openly in the prince's council? Never mind his reservations about William de Hauteville, Drengot's men were about to take over Melfi, and surprise was an advantage that would stand them in good stead when it came to the first encounters with the enemy, something that definite information given to the catapan would possibly destroy. An angry Rainulf might bring them back to fall on the man he felt had betrayed them.

'If he is a wise catapan, honourable one, he might already know.'

'You are saying he has spies in Salerno?'

There was no irritation in the question; both men knew the strands of Byzantine influence were long and deep, given they had once ruled in this part of Italy, just as they knew their own city. Constantinople had eyes and ears in every court that might pose a threat: Rome and Bamberg, home to the Western Emperor, especially. Salerno, Naples, Amalfi and Gaeta, all trading rivals on the Western Italian coast, each contained within them Greek traders, while substantial parts of their Italian populations still worshipped in the Orthodox rite and looked to the Greek not the Roman church for guidance. Loyalty was a movable feast even if you excluded payments for information.

'We are a busy trading port, honourable one. Ships go in and out of Salerno by the fistful every day, and many go east to the Levant and the Bosphorus. It would be foolish to think some hint of Arduin's intent has not left with them. The port, indeed any port, must be a hotbed of rumour and gossip.'

'So no warning from me would serve?'

'On the contrary,' Ephraim insisted. 'If what I suspect is true, and the catapan will be forewarned anyway, it would be sound policy that something of the same should come from you.'

There was a moment when both men ruminated on what the Jew had said: there was a great difference between gossip and hard, irrefutable fact. Michael Doukeianos would wonder if there was truth in the former; word from a Prince of Salerno would be taken as truth.

'And Benevento?' Guaimar asked.

Kasa Ephraim was at pains not to smile, for what Prince Guaimar had been saying so far was in the nature of being obvious. Now he had come to the salient point: here was the true nub of that at which he was driving. To inform the catapan of the involvement of Benevento could have unseen benefits, first by definitely diverting suspicion from Salerno, and secondly – and again this was based on the possibility of the failure of the Apulian revolt – with that information given early, any reprisals would be directed against his fellow Lombard prince and that could present opportunities in the aftermath, which might see the expansion of Guaimar's territory at the expense of his neighbour. It never did any man harm to be on the side of the victor.

He did not smile, because he was too wise to let even his lord know of his thoughts, instead he looked grave. 'We know from the past that the Eastern Empire does not forgive those who see it as its enemies.'

'Are there ships at present in the harbour who might have reason to call at Bari?'

'It can be arranged, honourable one.'

If Guaimar detected any irony in the way Kasa Ephraim addressed him, it did not show.

'A secret letter then, with my seal?'

Ephraim shook his head. 'No seal, my Lord, not even your name on the message. It would not be wise to gift Constantinople something with which they could later undermine you.'

'That is wise. I must go now to my council, where we are to discuss the matter of Amalfi.'

'A troublesome thorn, honourable one.'

In saying that, Kasa Ephraim was identifying a truth to both him and his prince. Not only was Amalfi Salerno's closest trade rival, but, positioned as they were, on the direct route west to the Tyrennian Sea, they could board and seize goods at will, interfering with shipping going to and from this port from half the Mediterranean. These interceptions were based on the flimsiest of excuses, but they diminished the revenues of the much larger principality. It had long been Guaimar's intention to put Amalfi in its place.

'They think by denying piracy, by claiming imperial edict, that I will believe them.'

'No thief lacks justification for his crimes, honourable one.'

'You see I have just cause, do you not, to subdue them by force?' Ephraim merely nodded: it was, in truth, not a dispute in which he wanted to become involved, having as he did his own interests in the port of Amalfi. 'And besides, we must keep Rainulf Drengot occupied, for if he is not he is inclined to mischief.'

*So, the territory of Amalfi will be invaded,* Ephraim thought, and the concomitant of that was what he would need to do about his own investments.

'Might I also suggest, honourable one, that you lay upon them, at some time in the future, the accusation of alerting the catapan to what is about to fall on Melfi?'

The deviousness of that suggestion pleased Guaimar enormously, for he was grinning widely as he spoke. 'How I wish I could have you as one of my council, but, of course, it would never do.'

Arduin stopped William and his knights far enough off to tempt out, through the gates of Melfi, the leading citizens of the town, those who had left their homes to whatever they feared these Normans might do. He was alone as he addressed them, a man they already knew, who had feasted and flattered them on taking up his appointment, yet it was with obvious suspicion that they listened to the blandishments of this *topoterites*, as he sought to persuade them that they had nothing to fear.

'These are the men I have engaged at the express request of the catapan. If you deny them entry to the castle they are supposed to garrison in your defence you will defy him and the emperor, not just me.'

'They are Normans,' one elderly worthy growled.

It was a telling interjection, which brought forth a swelling murmur of agreement from the assembled crowd; the people in these parts had encountered Normans before in the last two decades, and suffered much from their unbridled banditry. The castle they left alone – it was too strong for the roving bands – but the mailed knights took what they wanted in food and comfort from the surrounding countryside, burning and destroying what they could not carry if faced with resistance.

'This is different. Who do you think holds the fortress of Troia?'

He waited for a response but none came; he found himself looking at bowed heads, doubting if indeed they knew the answer. These were people who lived in ignorance of what occurred in the neighbouring valley, never mind a fortress ten leagues distant.

'They are Normans, the very same kind of men you are damning now, and they protect the people thereabouts.'

'The Normans are brigands.'

'Not those I command,' Arduin replied softly. 'They are soldiers in the pay of the catapan, as am I, as are the Normans of Troia.'

Quite a few of the faces were diverted then: Italians did not like Lombards any more than Normans. Arduin did not miss it, he merely ignored the reaction: he was not without the arrogance typical of his race and he had lived among these people too long to be bothered. Besides, they rarely had much affection for each other, never mind those they saw as interlopers.

'Observe what they do now,' he said.

Arduin pointed to William's band, dismounted by the gurgling stream that ran off the high peak of Monte Vulture and through the huddle of buildings that made up the town. They had unsaddled their mounts and were busy grooming them with combs and brushes, this while the horses munched at piles of hay.

'Do they torch your homes, do they break your watermill? No. They have not even touched your wine.' That led to some shuffling of feet, which made Arduin feel he was getting somewhere.

'For I must tell you, if you do not admit them they will not leave, and I will have to send to the catapan to tell him of your intransigence, which is nothing short of a revolt against his authority.'

Such an accusation set up a howl of protest: if these people were wary of Normans, they knew enough to fear an angry Byzantium even more.

'And can I tell you what he will do? He will come and he will fire your houses and smash that watermill. He will also burn every man amongst you to a cinder, those he does not hang from the castle walls, once you have been disembowelled and seen your own entrails slither from your belly.'

That made them pale, but Arduin was not finished.

'Then he will let those Normans, and his Greeks, loose on your women and you will hear their screams as you die. Your children will be sent east to slavery, perhaps to the brothels of Constantinople, which cater for every vice. And then he will send word around the country to say that valuable land, well irrigated and fertile, is empty and there for the taking, so other hands will work this soil and prosper, using your women as slaves and your crushed bones to help nourish their crops.'

'We hold the castle.'

'Can you hold it against an army? Are you fighting men?' He waved to the Normans once more. 'Look, they are fighting men. Can you face them even with walls to protect you?'

If they were wavering they were yet to be convinced, so Arduin changed tack.

'Let me send to the catapan and say that the good folk of Melfi are loyal, that they are people who deserve relief from too heavy a taxation, if not monies provided to help develop what they already have. What one of you could not use some Byzantine largesse to increase your yields, to stock your pigsties and sheep pens, to increase your oxen? Would it not be wondrous to say in years to come that this was made a golden part of Apulia where men work for reward, a place where women sow and reap in plenty, that children grow up strong and to a good age so that those who bore them have ease in their later years?'

Arduin had a silver tongue, one which had served him well with his reluctant soldiers in Sicily and it was having the same effect here, for what he was holding out was a tempting prospect to people who toiled as long as it was light to get from the soil that which was needed to both maintain themselves and satisfy the demands of their overlords, nothing less than the sum of their dreams – a life free from the threat of famine.

These were not the fertile plains of two harvests a year, which lay to either side of their lands, but the mountains where the soil was shallow and supported by hard rock, the weather more fickle. There was never truly enough, for if times were good the population grew to consume whatever the land produced. But there were also those bad years, of blighted crops and endless foul weather, times when cattle and flocks were ravaged by maladies for which they had no cure, so that people came close to, and sometimes even succumbed, to starvation.

'And, my friends, with this garrison in place, I can ask – no, demand – the castle be well supplied, food that would be there for you, should nature fail you.'

'We must talk, *topoterites*.'

Arduin nodded: the use of that title indicated he would get what he wanted.

William waited until the castle had been vacated, watching as the locals made their way back to their homes, few willing to exchange a glance with these mailed giants who would now live amongst them. They were stocky folk in the main, of truncated height to a Norman, but it was easy to see they had a strength brought about by endless toil; that is, those who were not too bent by the same condition of life to stand upright.

Despite sharp commands from angry parents the children could not contain their curiosity, and were much taken by the horses, for in this part of the world, where oxen did the burdensome work, the possession of such a beast was only for lords and masters. Nor could the younger females stop themselves from throwing what they thought were discreet glances at such tall and striking men. For that they got parental blows, not hard words.

Watching them, and the contrast with their nervous elders, William thought back to his father's demesne in the Contentin, to the serfs and tenanted villeins who supported the de Hauteville family, people whom his father saw as his responsibility. The indigenes who had occupied the land before the Norsemen came were not dissimilar, hardy folk inured to endless toil and the need to eke a living from the soil. Yet his forbears had intermingled with them, married their womenfolk and bred children by them, and they had also protected them in an uncertain world. Could he, and the men he led, not do the same here?

'Mount up,' he called when the last of the townsfolk had passed.

Riding up the wide, winding causeway that led up to the great gates of the Castle of Melfi, itself with a defensible wall, William found himself increasingly impressed by an edifice he had only previously observed from afar. Imposing from a distance, with its great square keep and hexagonal corner towers, it became more formidable still at close quarters, where he could see how soundly it was constructed, from the stone bridge that spanned the moat to the twin curtain walls that contained a killing zone between them.

An attacker must cross that narrow, high-arched

causeway to even attempt to take the outer wall, then get through a gate to be faced by yet another ditch with a raised drawbridge. Caught between the two they would be at the mercy of anyone on the inner wall and they would need a great effusion of blood to overcome the defence. Those walls and towers were made from the hard stone of the mountains in which the castle was sat – rock so hard the walls could not be undermined – and they were well buttressed to withstand assault by ballista, while being tall enough to make firing anything over the top near impossible, the whole edifice high on a hill that dominated the town below, as well as the valleys that led to the east and west.

Overlooked by the even higher peak of Monte Vulture, that too was part of its defence: no substantial force could hope to approach from any direction without being seen a whole day's march distant. Inside, the fortress was spacious, with well-constructed buildings that could house hundreds of knights, sufficient stabling for their mounts, and vaults below and lofts above that could store enough supplies to sustain them for an eternity, while the keep was large enough in which to train to fight so that no warrior could become rusty by confinement.

Built by the Byzantines on the site of an old Roman watchtower, it had a water supply that could not be stopped, several deep wells that sat inside the very rock on which the castle stood, and on three sides lay steep escarpments which reduced the options for any attacker to a frontal assault up the causeway to the crossing, at the end of which stood huge oak gates, studded with metal. On either side of the outer castle entrance stood a pair of towers, barbicans that made the area before the drawbridge a deadly place for any man at the mercy of besieged crossbowmen.

Arduin was already inside, back in the place he had come to occupy when first appointed, and he was on the steps that led to the great hall when his first Normans entered through the castle gate. In his mind he could see what was to come, himself at the head of a formidable army, taking from Byzantium towns, cities and especially the great ports which sustained them with their fabulous revenues.

There was another vision: he might need a figurehead to give him the legitimacy needed to persuade others to revolt, but he would be no more than that. Men had risen before from seemingly humble origins to a noble estate, why not he? His arrangement with Prince Guaimar was for an equal division of the spoils, but that might be something he could circumvent with success. In part, the happy face with which he grasped the arm of William de Hauteville and the first contingent of knights was fed by such thoughts.

'A messenger, William, to bring in the rest.'

'Already sent, Arduin,' the Norman leader replied. 'I would also ask a message be sent north to the Normans of Troia, suggesting they desert Byzantium and join us.'

'Do you think they will be tempted?'

'No, they have prospered too much from serving the Eastern Empire, but not to ask might make them more of an enemy than we now need and I would want them neutral. It never does to wound Norman pride.'

Arduin flashed a look at William de Hauteville then, wondering at the level of his pride, indeed the pride of the whole clan; all twelve of them.

# CHAPTER FIVE

✂◇✂

The great castle of Moulineaux stood stark and pale
grey, high on the hillside, set against the deep-green
and corn-gold fields of the Normandy landscape,
dappled by sunlight and high white clouds, with a
rolling slope, part cultivated fields, part woodland,
reaching down to the silver ribbon of the winding River
Seine, the whole now dotted with tented encampments.
Beyond the fluttering pennants of the great lords who
occupied these pavilions there were boats and barges
plying their way upriver, some to Rouen, others
which would continue on to Paris and perhaps all the
navigable way to fertile Burgundy, for the Seine was
a major artery of trade with the interior, a source of
great wealth to whosoever controlled the river as it
exited to the sea.

To the elderly man who emerged from the deep woods on the high ridgeline, the sight before him spoke of different things: it reminded him of his heritage and the tales he had heard at his grandfather's knee. Once that same river had been the means by which his Viking forbears had terrorised this part of the world, as they had done so many others, sailing their longboats up to and beyond the island on which Paris stood, and besieging the city until paid enough treasure to depart.

The land around this part of the Frankish Kingdom, from the coast to the core, had been rich, fruitful, full of churches, monasteries, castles and walled towns the men from the north had plundered at will; it was rich now, but it was also the land settled by those same raiders for two centuries and thus not for despoliation. There was a part of Tancred de Hauteville that had always hankered after the notion of living in older times, even if the age he lived in now was troubled enough for any man.

The rest of his party, all members of his family, fanned out alongside him. Tancred and his sons were not only on higher ground, but being mounted as well, they were at near eye level with the round, crenellated towers of mighty Moulineaux, which stood at each corner of the curtain walls that connected them. They were close enough to see the separation between the mortar and the stone blocks, as well as the dark slash of the deep ditch before the ramparts, though not enough to see into the great square keep they protected.

Within ballista range the forest had been cleared to deny cover to any approaching enemy intent on battering the walls, but Tancred, who, despite his advanced years still prided himself on his skill, as well as his experience as a fighting man, was adamant the castle was not built in the right place.

'Mind it, some clever clogs will build a contraption that can fire a stone ball further than we now know, and they will gain distance from this high ground. Those walls could be breached and even the keep could be open to a shower of deadly rocks big enough to kill. Duke Robert should have put it up where we are sitting now so it could not be overlooked, and I told the young fool that when he was building the place.'

'Which is no doubt why he sought your advice in all matters since that day.'

'Mind your cheek, boy!'

Robert de Hauteville, named as a child after the very duke just mentioned, showed no reaction to this stricture from his father, nor did he even deign to look as though he noticed the glare which accompanied it. The rest of the family did not react: that was just Robert and his papa, forever in disagreement as they had been on the whole journey and for years prior to that. If anything, they were slightly embarrassed, given that riding to attend a ceremony of great importance – one to which every loyal subject of the Duke of Normandy was ordered to be present – their party was in company with many others travelling on the same errand.

One such group, a dozen knights, rode slightly ahead of them on the narrow highway that ran along the ridge top, with yet more close behind, all summoned to attend upon their liege lord. King Henry of the Franks, was coming downriver from Paris in all his majesty, his purpose to confer knighthood on his vassal, William, the adolescent Duke of Normandy, this on the occasion of his fifteenth birthday.

'Roger,' Tancred barked to his youngest and favourite child. 'Do me the honour of not growing up to be like this one, who, by his manner, is bound to be a changeling.'

Such a statement was nonsense, of course: you only had to see Robert and Tancred together to know that the old fellow, for all his hair was white, his frame somewhat shrunk, with a face lined and craggy, was the sire of this sturdy, tetchy giant. Indeed that was where the constant rubbing up against each other came from: they were too alike.

From a mere ten-year-old, the response was loud and firm. 'I will match his height and valour, Father, if not his conduct.'

'Don't be too keen on the loftiness, lad. There comes a point where it clearly affects the brain.'

'Then I must have more sense than anyone else in the family,' insisted Serlo, who, though a year older than Robert and no dwarf, was nowhere near the size of his half-brother; few men were.

'Are you going to block the path, or move your fat arses on their way?'

The irate voice came from the party immediately behind them, half a dozen mounted men still in amongst the trees, and the reaction was telling. Tancred half-turned to request patience, his face showing no rancour, but in the time he had done that Robert had his sword out from its scabbard, and was hauling on his reins to turn his horse, bellowing as he pushed it through his brothers, as well as the packhorses on which rested the family possessions, back into the woods, demanding to know who dared speak so.

Being family, and with Robert urging his mount to the rear, Serlo did likewise and the remaining two de Hautevilles old enough to bear arms, Aubrey and Humbert, had their weapons out too; even Roger was quick to brandish his knife. The men behind were sharp to the defence, so that in seconds the two groups were ready to do battle. All his sons stopped moving when Tancred bellowed for them to desist.

'What are you, barbarians? Would you have us

branded louts before we even see our duke?'

'By your manner, sir, I mark you as that very thing.'

'Stand, Robert, I command you!'

That was an instruction given just in time: if Tancred had one son who would not stand even a hint of an insult to the family name, it was Robert. Jovial most of the time, with a huge laugh, a mischievous wit and a tendency to backslap painfully, he was also touchy in the extreme, that made more dangerous by a fighting ability formidable even in a family of high martial achievement. Now it was Tancred's turn to bring around the head of his horse and move to confront the complainant, a large fellow in a green and blue surcoat, his head adorned with a plumed bonnet. His voice, when he spoke, was icy cold.

'I was about to beg your indulgence for delaying your passage, to desire you to show a little patience, but that I now regret. You will withdraw the words just used, or what you can see of the castle of Moulineaux will be your last as a man on two legs. You will, I promise, be carried to meet your liege lord and so will the men who accompany you.'

'I request only that you spur your mounts and clear a passage. Should you fail to do so I will be obliged to compel you.'

'We await the attempt,' growled Robert.

Tancred matched that growl, but he was still an old

soldier, who knew that to contest with this fellow and those he led in such a confined space, on the very edge of a forest, would not be wise: much better to be out in the open where he trusted the ability of his sons, as well as his own, to redress any imbalance in numbers.

'We shall ride out onto yonder field, sir, but we will still be in your path. Without an expression of contrition we will stay there.'

'To be swept aside, I do assure you.'

'Roger, stay out of this,' Tancred insisted, which produced, as it would in any proud boy of his age, a glum look. 'Look to the pack animals.'

Chagrined as he was, he obeyed a father he loved and respected, taking from his brothers the required reins and riding out onto the open ground, but away from the direct route that led to the gates of Moulineaux, which lay on the Rouen side of the castle.

The others required no instruction: having grown to manhood at a time of much turmoil in Normandy, such encounters were, if not commonplace, frequent enough to ensure they had no fear or ignorance of what was about to occur. Had this fellow known the nature of whom he was up against, he might have shown more tolerance, for the name of de Hauteville, in the part of the world in which they lived, was one of which men who knew it were cautious. It had been that way for many years now, with each of Tancred's twelve sons showing, as they came to manhood, remarkable prowess in battle.

'Perhaps you should stand aside as well, Father,' sneered Robert. 'Given your years.'

'I'll give you the back of my hand, boy.'

That made Robert smile as, like all of his party, he put on his conical metal helmet; nothing pleased him more than getting under old Tancred's skin.

The other party had not been idle: they emerged from the forest ready to fight, the fellow in the surcoat now similarly helmeted, and concentrating on what was about to happen, neither party paid much attention to the approaching rider, a fellow with a hawk on his right hand, that is till he rode between them, addressing Tancred first and loudly, as he removed his own floppy cap.

'I bid you good day, Uncle, and I observe that years have not dimmed your quick-tempered nature.'

'Montbray!' Tancred exclaimed, what could be seen of that craggy face on either side of his nose guard breaking into a huge grin.

'The same...and how, my cousins, do I find you?'

'Too occupied at the moment for pleasantries,' Serlo replied, 'though happy to see you, Geoffrey.'

The wings of the hawk fluttered and Geoffrey of Montbray turned to face the men lined up to fight his cousins, moving the hawk aside so that they could see he was wearing a surcoat with a clerical device. 'Can I, sir, enquire after your name?'

'Only after you give me your own.'

The response to that came with a slight bow. 'Geoffrey of Montbray, Almoner of Rouen Cathedral.'

'A priest?'

'Yes.'

'You can join with us, Geoffrey,' cried Robert. 'I recall you were good with a weapon.'

Geoffrey replied loudly, but over his shoulder. His gaze was still fixed on the fellow with the green and blue surcoat. 'Can I not now be a man of peace, Robert?'

'I am Count Hugo de Lesseves.'

'Then, Count Hugo, I request that you put up your weapons.'

'You are clearly known to these ruffians behind you. It would be best if you requested they do so first.'

'Uncle, sheath your swords.'

'Geoffrey—'

The voice, no longer friendly, cut off any protest. 'That is a demand, Uncle, and one that will be enforced by Duke William's own knights, who are too numerous even for the de Hautevilles. No weapon is to be drawn on this occasion by anyone, on pain of the most stringent punishments, and that applies to Count Hugo here as much as to you.'

The response was not immediate; it could not be in a land where men were so conscious of their honour, and as they complied, slowly sheathing their swords,

Geoffrey of Montbray hoped perhaps they would see the wisdom of the instruction: with so many fighting men, and touchy creatures at that, gathered in one place, the chances of brawls and worse was too high to leave to fate. Few great magnates gathered their vassals together in one place for that very reason, outside a call to partake in war.

'Now, Uncle, I will lead you to the castle, where you will soon be given opportunity to present yourselves to your suzerain. For accommodation, I am happy to say that I have an apartment of my own which you are invited to share, and stabling space for your horses.'

'My word, Geoffrey,' said Robert, with a grin that was not wholly affable, 'you have risen in the world.'

'I have enjoyed good fortune, Robert, that is true.'

'And no taint associated with our name?'

Montbray rode up to Robert and looked up into his deep blue, penetrating eyes, speaking softly so that his uncle could not hear. 'It would be fair to say, cousin, that the de Hauteville name, these days, does not register within yonder walls.'

Robert bellowed with laughter, causing the rest of his family to look at him with curiosity, but he spoke to his cousin in the same way as he himself had been addressed. 'Never fear, Geoffrey, it will.'

There was a moment of pure pleasure for the de Hauteville clan as Geoffrey led them towards the stone bridge spanning the ditch which surrounded

Moulineaux, and past the line of knights set to prevent unauthorised entry, as Count Hugo, given he seriously outranked Tancred, holder of no more than a petty barony, was politely informed to make his way to the field that ran downhill to the Seine, and find himself a spot on which to camp.

The great keep was packed with humanity: knights, grooms, sutlers and squires; the ground, even if it was dry, churned up by too many hooves and too many feet, as well as deep in dung – if it rained it would soon be a morass – and it was with much shouting and not a little barging that their almoner cousin got them to some temporary stabling which had been erected along the interior of the curtain wall. As he dismounted, a liveried servant ran forward to take from him his hawk, while others at his command led the animals to the narrow stalls already provided with nets of hay and tubs of water.

'Leave your possessions, Uncle, my servants will fetch those.'

Nodding and impressed, the old man, trailed by his sons, fell in behind Geoffrey as he led them to one of the round towers, then through a narrow entrance that brought them to a spiral of steps leading up to the individual floors, each one crammed with people, loud in their hubbub of talk.

'I cannot promise you luxury,' Montbray called, 'but I will see you have a palliasse and enough space to sleep. That and food, of course.'

'For my old bones,' Tancred replied, 'anything that is not a tent on cold ground is opulence.'

The floor Geoffrey occupied was halfway up the tower, just an open space floored in wood with narrow embrasures to let in a little light and air. It was already well occupied, but space there was, as had been promised, and on the long rough-hewn table in the middle, with equally made-up benches on either side, there was food and drink for anyone who wished to consume it, the always hungry young Roger making straight for that.

'He was a mewling child when last I saw him,' said Montbray. 'A babe in arms.'

'Mark him, nephew,' Tancred said, a glint of pride in his eye. 'I rate him the cleverest I have sired.'

'Come eat, Uncle, and tell what news you have of my cousins in Italy.'

The food was plentiful, and soon Roger was joined by his brothers, who used their knives to hack at the joints of meat, that eaten off fresh flats of unleavened bread, accompanied by fruit and washed down with apple wine. But it was obvious that the sons were curious, never having before been inside such an imposing castle as Moulineaux, and as soon as they had fed themselves they were off exploring, the words of their cousin – of the need to keep the peace – following them down the bare stone steps.

Montbray and his uncle were left to talk. Having

grown up with the eldest of the de Hauteville brood, Geoffrey was naturally closer to them, and besides living in the same house as a youngster he had, after his ordination, taken on two duties: priestly ones at the church of Hauteville-la-Guichard, as well as the job of trying to drum a bit of lettering and counting into his uncle's brood. He had also said the rites over the grave of Tancred's first wife, half-sister to the late Duke Robert, worn out by bearing him so many children.

What a history this man had, for he had fought in many places with the same vigour he had brought to procreation: in Spain against the Moors, in England seeking to rethrone King Ethelred, but most importantly at the side of Richard, the then reigning duke, who had held him in such high esteem as a warrior that he had given him his illegitimate daughter's hand in marriage. Tancred had been with Geoffrey's father when he had been killed in battle, taking on the duty of raising his son. Looking at the man before him, whom he loved, it was not possible to ignore how much he had aged since they last met, but the voice was still strong, the memory still good.

Yet as Tancred spoke of his elder sons, all in Italy, it was clear in his now watery eyes that he knew he would never again see them, and there was hurt in that, especially with his eldest, William, who might be his heir to his demesne, but would never return

now to take it up. They talked of how well he and
Drogo had fared, of the money that had flowed back
from their success, which had allowed the others to
follow in their wake, as well as providing the funds for
that which Tancred desired most in the world, if you
excluded their return: a stone donjon from which he
could survey his demesne.

'The foundations are in place, for not even a duke
can gainsay my right to do that.'

'Perhaps, on the occasion of being knighted, our
young duke will see fit to give you leave to build the
rest.'

'There are siren voices against me,' Tancred
growled. 'It is not a thing my neighbours favour.'

Montbray smiled. 'One in particular, I seem to
recall.'

There was no need to say the name Evro de
Montfort: both men knew it and were aware that he,
far richer and better connected than Tancred, still
hankered after the right to call the de Hauteville clan
his vassals. The Contentin, probably the most unruly
province in the ducal domains, was rife with similar
disputes, over land and water rights, or who had the
right to lord it over whom, all going back to the earliest
settlement of the region.

Many times Tancred and his sons had come to blows
with de Montfort's men and just as many times they
had sent them scurrying away nursing their wounds:

the little pouter pigeon, as Tancred called him, did not risk his own skin, for to lose would not just mean an effusion of blood, it would also entail a serious loss of face, and might, if it went far enough, terminate any claim he could make. That he kept up in writing delivered as pleas to the judgement of the ducal court.

For all that Evro de Montfort argued his right, Tancred knew that his nephew was a stalwart voice against him, and perhaps, given he could provide accommodation inside the castle and had so many servants to do his bidding, that rising star was taking him to a level where he would have much more influence.

But Geoffrey knew that what he did was not to make a case for the de Hautevilles: he was confined to denying a right to de Montfort. 'Uncle, I will not fight your suit too hard until I am sure of success. It is best not to press for too much.'

'I trust your judgement,' Tancred replied, though the look in his eyes did nothing to match his tone. 'But I say this, Geoffrey, I have not long for this world, and I would dearly like to see that donjon built before I must confront my sins and my Maker.'

Roger de Hauteville arrived in a flurry of noisy footsteps, his face flushed and eager. 'Papa, I have seen the duke.'

'And did the sight impress you, Roger?' asked Montbray.

Roger de Hauteville looked at his cousin for a while, a man he really did not know, the one-time priest of his local church who had left to find advancement elsewhere. His brothers had praised him as a good friend and a fellow to be seen as like a brother, so he decided to answer with the same truth he would have given his father had he posed the question.

'Not really, he is rather short in the leg, his hair is dark, and he has a shifty look in his eye. Perhaps that comes from his being a bastard.'

'No, it is not that,' Montbray replied. 'You too would have that look, Roger, if you had as many enemies intent on killing you as he.'

# CHAPTER SIX

∞◊∞

All those summoned assembled next morning for the ceremony of knighthood, which took place in an open field bordering the Seine, before a huge pavilion erected to house the King of the Franks, while on the river lay the gilded, blue-painted barge on which he had travelled from Paris and on which he rested at night; no sovereign went lightly into the castle of a powerful vassal on the very good grounds he might never get out again. Everyone there to participate had attended Mass in the grey dawn light and committed their souls to God and their sins to his justice, lords high and low down to the meanest squire.

Duke William entered from one end of the field attended by his most powerful lords, counts, viscounts and clerics, wearing a surcoat bearing the device of his house, two gold and recumbent lions on a background of scarlet, looking right and left as if unsure whether his attendance was wise; the king, in a blue cloak decorated with fleurs de lys, sat on a throne-like chair at the other end, set on a dais designed to show he was above not only the common herd, but his vassal.

Both sides of the field were lined with the cream of Normandy, the men who held the land and the lances who served them, while behind the ducal party came the *familia* knights, all sturdy men and doughty fighters, all dedicated to keeping alive young William the Bastard, the man they served. Should he ever engage in battle, they would ride with him and never leave him exposed, even if it meant the need to forfeit their own lives. They would man his castles, hold safe both his borderlands and battle to keep in check internal rebellion. For that they would be rewarded with many things: regular pay certainly, lands possibly, and for the most favoured or successful, a title of their own.

It was that which Tancred had wanted for his own sons, only to have it denied, to serve as *familia* knights, and it was that which he had raised them to expect. Never had he indicated that as blood relations to the reigning house they had any rights other than knight service, for had he not vowed to William's grandfather, on taking his illegitimate daughter as wife, that should he be blessed with children, no one of his line should aspire to anything above his baronial station.

The whole affair, this confirmation of vassalage, he watched with a jaundiced eye: to Tancred, the ceremony and the fripperies surrounding it spoke of everything he despised about the Franks and their customs – gaudy display and over-elaborate rituals which were seeping inexorably into the court life of Normandy: too many great blasts from trumpets, the top notables overdressed in fine silks, bishops gloriously attired, all attended by fawning servants leading decorated hunting dogs and surrounded – especially King Henry and young Duke William – with what the old man called simpering dolts.

Tancred had grown to manhood when no fighting man feared to tell his liege lord that he was in error: service was a two-way thing, the lord as beholden to his vassals as they were to him. His own grandfather did not fear to restrain his cousin, Count Rollo, the first Viking to trade pillage and sea-raiding for land and a title. Now great lords surrounded themselves with those who agreed with any statement they uttered, however foolish – a point so strongly felt that, inadvertently, he said so out loud.

'No man should surround himself with those who fear to be truthful.'

'I shall recall that, Father,' Robert growled, 'when next you tell me to be quiet.'

The angry rejoinder to that was cut off by the voice of a very excited and eager Roger, pointing at the advancing assembly. 'There's our cousin of Montbray, Papa, in the third rank behind the duke.'

'Look to him, all of you,' Tancred said, 'for if there is to be any advancement for you at this court it will come through Geoffrey.'

'You think he has the ear of the bastard?' asked Robert.

'He has the ear of men who counsel him. You, of all people, must talk with him and seek his good offices.'

Robert de Hauteville nodded slowly; that was why he was here, why Tancred had brought all his sons to Moulineaux. The ducal court was the fount of all advancement and perhaps the rancour of the past could be set aside. For Robert and Serlo, there might be a chance of being taken into ducal service after all; for the rest, like young Roger, if his elder brothers could prosper, then he could do likewise in their wake.

'He doesn't look like much of a fighter, our duke.'

'He's not yet a man, Serlo,' Tancred responded, 'give him time.'

'There are many who will not, Father.'

There was truth in that: for every two men called to this assembly who had obeyed the summons, there was another who had declined, those unprepared to accept the bastard son of Duke Robert as his lawful successor.

For some, not many, their objection was genuine, based on an inability to accept that illegitimacy; for most it was based on opportunity. Not close to the court and the munificence it could disburse, they saw no profit in support, more in rebellion, of which there had been many these last eight years. The King of the Franks had come this day for a ceremony; his previous incursions into Normandy had been to help put down the fractious subjects who opposed William, a boy come into his inheritance aged seven.

Many powerful men had tried to ensnare Tancred into rebellion, holding before him the tempting prospect that his sons, those now fighting in Italy, had a claim on the ducal title at least as valid as the child who held it. To them all he had given his refusal: first there was his own oath, but he also suspected their promises to be false. Ambitious magnates would use the de Hauteville name and connection for their own ends, not something they would adhere to if they managed to unseat William. They sought power for themselves.

Another flurry of trumpets interrupted that train of thought. Reaching the dais, William climbed the steps to kneel before King Henry, who rose from his carved chair to tower over the youth. With a flourish he took out his sword, a weapon of great beauty, decorated with gold and jewels and with a glittering unmarked blade which had never been tested against other metal, the tip of that touching each of young William's shoulders as the king intoned the Latin words of investiture, everyone present aware of the true meaning of what was being said as they heard the responses.

William of Falaise was swearing before all that he held his lands and titles only from his rightful king; that should he fail in his duty to his sovereign those could be forfeit. It was an oath no ruler of Normandy had made since the days of the first Count Rollo over two hundred years before, who had been given Normandy as the price of a lasting peace in place of the constant alarm caused by Viking raids. No Norman ruler since had ever seen the need to publicly bow the knee to Paris, and it was an indication of young William's weakness that it was taking place now.

If Tancred had been disgusted before, he was doubly so now: he had fought the Franks too often, and beaten them every time, to welcome the loss of ascendancy thus implied.

William of Falaise thus anointed, it was the turn of each landholder present to swear allegiance, and given the act of fealty to the Duke of Normandy was made in the presence of the King of the Franks, that too was significant, for each man was also pledging an ultimate allegiance to Paris. First to swear was Count Alain of Brittany, who had acted as William's guardian, keeping him safe from those who desired him dead, and in a strict order of precedence, laid down by the chamberlain of the court, each lord, in turn, shuffled forward to bow the knee, say the words, which were witnessed by the hierarchy of Norman bishops and recorded in a great ledger by a monkish clerk.

Way down the list, it was a long time before Tancred, clad in a brand new surcoat of blue and white, found himself face to face with his suzerain, a boy he had not seen since the day his father first named him as his heir. Close to, the eyes were not shifty, nor were they in any way apprehensive; they were sharp and penetrating, and Tancred wondered if the impression given earlier was the fear of a sudden knife from a youngster unsure if all who had obeyed the summons to Moulineaux were loyal.

When William spoke, it was in a voice well broken and deep, close to being that of a man. 'I have the right to call you "Cousin", do I not?'

Tancred was cautious at such a friendly opening gambit: mighty princes could be devious and there was flattery in those words. 'You have the right if you choose it, my Lord.'

'Then I do so, Cousin, for I have been made aware of your loyalty to my house and the temptations to which you have been exposed since the death of my father.'

Such information could only have come from

Geoffrey of Montbray. Did he have the actual ear of the duke; had he progressed that far?

'Yet you have not rallied to my banner.' That was said in a sharper tone, immediately moderated as the young duke added, 'But it has been pointed out to me that to stand aside can be a wise policy when everything you own is at risk in such a polity as the Contentin.'

Tancred was tempted to rudeness then, and had to bite his tongue: the Contentin was a part of Normandy this young man feared to enter yet to agree it was a place full of rebellion would not be wise.

'I have never once wavered, sire, in my oath to your grandfather.'

'Which was?'

'To always support his sons.'

The eyes of both man and boy were locked, but neither showed signs of anger, and if William was waiting to hear Tancred add the words 'and his son's bastard', he waited in vain.

'I did not know my grandfather.'

'Duke Richard was a great man, and a great soldier.'

'My father?'

'He, too, proved to be a soldier of merit, as I am sure his brother would have been had he lived.'

That produced a thin smile: the elder son of William's grandfather was a man rarely mentioned, but what had been said implied nothing. 'You are better versed in discourse than I have been told, Tancred de Hauteville.'

'I am, sire, what I have always been, a loyal servant of your house.'

'Very well. I would speak with you in private, when time permits, and I have been told it would be to my advantage to make the acquaintance of your sons, who are reputed to be doughty on the field of battle. I have been assured, by the almoner of my Cathedral of Rouen, that I will see them this very day if I so wish.'

'They are present now, my Lord, and await your summons.'

'So be it. When all are sworn, bring them to this pavilion, and they may also bend the knee to the King of the Franks and make his acquaintance.'

'I would wish to bring them all, sire, including my youngest, Roger, who is as yet too lacking in years to bear arms. Yet I have no doubt he will grow to match his brothers.'

'Make it so, Tancred, for as you say, he will grow, and I would have him see his liege lord and remember it.'

Tancred had not been looking forward to kissing the young duke's hand, fearing a cool reception. He did so with enthusiasm now: all the ghosts of the past, thanks to his clerical nephew, were going to be laid to rest.

* * *

'You knew of this, did you not? I sense you did not trust me.'

Montbray acknowledged the truth of that, but with a wry smile. 'I grew up in your house, you must recall. I have seen your temper and I know that bearding dukes is not a thing you fear. I heard of the words you exchanged with Duke Robert, may God bless his soul, the day he declined service to William and Drogo.'

Both men crossed themselves through long habit – liking or loathing meant nothing: a departed soul, noble or not, must be respected. If there was retribution for sins committed in life it was for God to judge, not mere humans.

'And it is not just your temper that makes me cautious. I do not know our young duke so well that I can be sure of how he will act and what he will say. Already he has a reputation for cunning and manipulation.'

'He will not live without it, or transgression – no ruler can.'

'Let his confessor deal with his sins, I must deal with his nature.'

'Will he take my sons into service?'

'I have advised him it would be prudent.' The look on Tancred's face was not one to let Montbray leave matters there, and he was obliged to continue. 'You know the Contentin as well as I, and you know that it would be incautious to lead a ducal host into what could become a nest of vipers.'

'He is not loved there, it is true, many claim for his bastardy.'

Montbray replied, showing a touch of asperity as he began to pace up and down. 'Greed is a more pressing excuse, but Normandy disunited plays into the hands of the Franks. Duke William, even fully grown to manhood, must ever depend on King Henry for support against his own barons; yet Normandy united, he has the power to ignore Paris, like every ruler before him. I have advised the duke, because I was raised there and know the region, that if the Contentin is to be tamed, he must win support there or placate it with fire and sword.'

'That would be wise, whichever course is chosen.'

'And that denying the de Hauteville family advancement, men who are respected there and fight for his cause, does not serve.'

There was a twinkle in Tancred's eye as he responded. 'Not to mention that a peaceful Contentin, wholly loyal to the duke, would finally allow for the appointment of a Bishop of Coutances.'

That stopped the clerical pacing: the Contentin had been the last place settled by the invading Norsemen. Count Rollo, still, in truth, a pagan despite his conversion to Christianity, was never happier than when despoiling monasteries, churches and cathedrals, and he had ravaged the western part of the old province known to the Romans as the Neustrian

March with glee. Not only had he stripped them of their portable wealth, he had stripped them of their landholdings, handing them out to his supporters, like Tancred's grandfather.

But Mother Church had never ceased to reclaim them, as well as the right to parcel it out to its own vassals and had, now, a receptive ear at a court more pious and Christian than that of old Count Rollo, more inclined to side with the church against laymen. The answer to the dispute lay within the boundaries of the Bishopric of Coutances: nothing could be decided without the incumbent overseeing proceedings and judging claims. To ensure none could be settled, suspecting it would not be in their favour, the local barons had ensured for decades that no appointed bishop ever took control of his see. Some elevated clerics had tried, only to be chased out of the Contentin at the point of a sword.

Montbray was shaking his head now, but not in irritation. 'I told our young duke that the de Hautevilles had two valuable assets, their ability in battle and their guile. The see is vacant, and there is no great desire in my fellow clerics to take possession of it. If I can have it, I will.'

'I trust any claims made against my demesne would get a fair hearing, should you do so?'

There was no question what Tancred meant: to him a fair hearing could only mean one that came down on his side. 'I think you would be satisfied with my judgements, Uncle. As for others...'

'What care do I have for others, my boy?' Tancred scoffed. 'Let them look to their own.'

It was under torchlight that the sons of Tancred met their duke, the only one he could truly look in the eye until they were on bended knee being Roger. Close to, the ten-year-old was more impressed than hitherto, as much by the surroundings full of luxury as the majesty of those present, including King Henry. The interview was short, but the words used were important: William of Falaise was sure he had need of men, such as these brothers, to serve him close and much would be gained from a Contentin at peace. So that it was with high step they left the pavilion, to be met by an exuberant father, who knew what those words truly meant. Rebellious barons would be defeated and dispossessed: what lands they owned would go to the duke's loyal servants and his boys would be amongst them.

To celebrate was natural, and that they did, the effect of the apple wine on each very different. Tancred, before he fell asleep, became maudlin and wept for his absent sons; naturally light-headed, young Roger took to staggering about before collapsing in a heap, followed by two of his brothers until only Robert and Serlo were left, though both had wrung a different mood from their imbibing. Robert by nature was a happy drunk, Serlo a morose one, all the resentments of which he was full surfacing the more he drank.

To be taller than most was not enough when you have several gigantic brothers; to be proficient with weapons never satisfied when those same brothers could best you every time. As the youngest of the elder branch, a year older than Robert, he had been a newborn babe when Tancred took a new wife, and had consequently missed the tenderness of his own mother more than his older siblings and he had also grown up seeing the likes of Robert favoured over him.

He could be surly even when sober, and while all the family had mischief built into their being, Serlo had a quality that tended to the devious and slightly cruel. He was also naturally light-fingered, and could be relied upon to lift anything not family-owned if left unattended. The pity was, that night, and in his mood, he took to wandering, with a cheerful half-brother at his heels; a tragedy that they met Count Hugo de Lesseves, he having accepted the hospitality of a noble cousin, and swapped his damp tent for a straw palliasse in the castle; a misfortune that he, too, had partaken of too much wine and had stepped out of his chamber to use the relieving pot.

Bleary-eyed Serlo recognised him, as much by the colours of his surcoat as the contours of his face. Besides that, there was the count's haughty manner, and his words, on being reminded of the previous day's encounter, came out as a near repeat of the insults he had issued then. When called upon by Serlo to withdraw them while still pissing, he turned, laughed, and aimed the jet of yellow fluid at Serlo's feet.

'Leave it be, brother,' Robert slurred, giving Serlo one of his back thumps that were always too hard, making the recipient stagger forward and shoulder the count.

'Get off, you rank-smelling oaf.'

Neither Robert nor the count saw the knife come out, and certainly the victim only knew of it when it entered under his rib cage and upwards, hitting him hard enough to make him double forward until his head was on Serlo's shoulder. The hand that held the blade was moved without a thought, in the way Serlo had been taught since childhood to use it in battle, raking up and across to make sure the stab became fatal.

Robert's vision was blurred enough for him to be unsure what it was gurgling out of the count's open mouth, but it was only moments before he knew it to be blood, and it was only then he realised what Serlo had done. He grabbed him by the top of his surcoat and dragged him backwards, an act which brought out the knife from the count's ruptured guts, sending a fount of blood pumping from the damaged heart. The man was dead before his body crashed onto the stone floor, at which point one of his servants, a young boy, came out and, seeing him bleeding on the floor, let out a high-pitched scream which would not have disgraced a girl.

Still holding Serlo's collar, a rapidly sobering Robert dragged his brother away. Suddenly aware of what he had done, his horrified gaze fixed on the body, Serlo dropped the knife at the same time as his belligerence, and he started to gasp to God for forgiveness, a sound which had turned into a maudlin wail by the time his brother got him far enough away to even begin to think. There was no choice but to wake Tancred, and he, once his head had cleared enough to comprehend the enormity of what had happened, knew he must wake his clerical nephew.

'We must get Serlo away. He will face the gallows if we do not.'

Montbray looked at his cousin, now sat with his head in his hands, clearly regretting what he had done in his moment of madness, while Robert stood at the entrance to the chamber ready to do battle should anyone come for him. For Montbray the dilemma was obvious: if there was not a hue and cry already, there soon would be. De Lesseves' knights, once someone had found their encampment and told them, would either come for Serlo with their swords out or, if they had more sense, make sure their duke knew of this foul murder.

He had a duty to his lord and a duty to God, but overriding that was family. Tancred had raised his sister's orphaned boy as he raised his own sons, never showing them favour over him. He could not stand by to see one of his cousins hang, regardless of the consequences for him. He would have to aid Serlo first and face the wrath of the Duke of Normandy later.

'Serlo,' he barked, 'gather your belongings. Robert, you too.'

'Why me?' Robert protested.

'You might have to fight your way out of here.'

'Horses?' Tancred said.

'Will have to be stolen. I will have enough to do to get you through the gate on foot.'

It took a hard slap around the head from Tancred to get Serlo moving, his words as harsh as the blow. 'Get back to Hauteville-la-Guichard if you can and gather enough to fund a journey.'

'Where am I to go?'

'Not south,' Tancred insisted. 'That will take you through lands controlled by Duke William, and if word gets ahead of you from Count Hugo's relatives you will be taken and roasted over a spit. Go to the coast and seek a boat. If you can get to England you will be safe.'

'Duke William can find me there.'

'You snivelling wretch, do you think yourself important enough to interest a duke? Perhaps, if you had kept your knife sheathed and risen in his service he might have noticed you, but now, you are nothing, not to him, nor to me.'

'And where am I to go, Father?' asked Robert. 'For I shall not flee to England.'

It was Montbray who answered. 'The only place is Italy, Robert.'

'So I must take the risks you will not permit my brother.'

'The case is different. No man can be condemned for aiding his brother. If any of Count Hugo's relations took revenge on you, they would face the gallows themselves.'

'I would rather stay here and face the consequences.'

'If you do,' Montbray replied, 'you will most certainly face the oubliette, and I know that there are men in these castle dungeons who have languished there for years. Come, you must go and go now, there is no time to delay.'

It took all of Montbray's authority to get the two brothers out of the great castle gates, and they had only just crossed the stone bridge when they saw a procession of torches heading their way, an angry crowd of men in green and blue surcoats, which caused them to run to where they could not be seen. For once it was Robert, not Serlo, who came up with the notion of thievery; they could hardly walk to Hauteville-la-Guichard.

'At least we know where there are horses, now unattended.'

# CHAPTER SEVEN

><×><

Arduin of Fassano had a love of making speeches, and no sooner had the entire force made good their entry into Melfi, passing in the process glum-faced peasantry and townsfolk who made no secret of the fact that they knew they had been cheated, than he had them assemble to hear his words. But first Mass had to be said, a prayer made to God to bless this enterprise, and as the priest intoned the ceremony in Greek – Mass being said in the Eastern rite, for there were no Roman clerics in Apulia – it made William think that he would have liked the Mass said in Latin, and by a divine from his homeland.

Norman priests, like his cousin Geoffrey, knew how to fight alongside the men they blessed and confessed. Montbray had wielded his sword and lance alongside his cousins in battle, under the banner of Duke Robert of Normandy, his only concession to his vows the determination to pray for the souls of those slain over their recumbent bodies, while their blood was still warm. Those thoughts were interrupted by the voice of Arduin, who, now that the priest had done with his rite, began his speech.

'It is time to cease to exist like mice in the skirting,' he boomed, to an audience who were not at all taken with the reference. 'How long have you been in this part of the world as nothing but paid swords at the beck and call of others? Yet here before us is a province and wealth under the grip of an empire too distant to rule with wisdom. It is time to reach out with a strong hand and in this I will be your guide. Follow me and I will lead you against men who are as women, who lord it over and exploit this rich and spacious land.'

'Windbag,' said Drogo softly, for he was near the front of the throng.

'Too fond of the sound of his own voice,' opined Humphrey, managing, in his usual fashion, aided by his sour expression, to lard his words with an extra degree of disdain.

'Let him speak away,' William replied, 'as long as he leads us well.'

'It is you we will follow, Gill,' Drogo insisted.

'No!' William insisted. 'There can only be one man in command. Let Arduin be that, and only if he fails—'

'And now,' Arduin cried, loud enough to prevent that sentence from being concluded; he had finished his peroration, a mellifluous one in which every one of those present had been promised the Earth, the moon and the stars, 'let us repair to the great hall, and a feast fit for the men who will humble Byzantium.'

That got him a loud cheer; if there was anything these Norman mercenaries loved it was abundant food and drink.

Prior to sitting down to the feast, William gathered his brothers: he too had something to say, albeit in a quiet way.

'Make it known, all of you, that we are here to stay.'

That produced looks of surprise on every face but that of Drogo; he was nodding as if some long-held thought now made sense.

'I want no act by any man to endanger our position with the inhabitants of Melfi. They are to be treated with respect. Anything taken must be paid for and nothing is to be stolen. Their women are to be honoured, even if they are bought as concubines, for their fathers and brothers will form part of the force Arduin must put in the field. That is to be the same for any place that surrenders to our arms. We are in a territory that is not our own, and who knows what our needs will be? We dare not make enemies in our own backyard.'

'Surely we have the right to plunder?' demanded Mauger.

'We have that right with those who will oppose us, not with the people who will rally to our standard. Now let us eat our Lombard friend's food and drink his wine, and show him all respect, for without him to secure for us a force of *milities* we will have little.'

Both Arduin and William de Hauteville departed the next day, the Lombard to spread the word of revolt, while William rode out, without helmet, hauberk or lance, to examine the whole area around Melfi with an experienced military eye, aware that, for all he had ridden through these parts, he did not know the terrain well enough.

Formidable castles had fallen before, and to his mind, given equal force, the Norman advantage lay outside stout walls, not within them. Already a piquet had been sent to climb the heavily wooded slopes of Monte Vulture, to man the round stone redoubt on its barren peak, thankfully now clear of snow, which had within it a warning beacon that would tell the Melfi garrison of the approach of any substantial force from the Apulian heartlands, giving them the choice of what action to take to thwart it.

He rode first to the east, which dropped away from the high hills that surrounded Melfi to the fertile lands and rolling landscape which led to the lush plains of Apulia, looking for those places where an army could properly and advantageously deploy, examining each valley to see how it could be used by cavalry to outflank an enemy, with the obvious corollary that it could also be used by them to the same purpose. He also needed to seek out those places where an attacking force could rest: open land, well watered, for no army could exist without that precious resource.

William de Hauteville sought to put himself in the mind of an enemy commander, and a competent one, to see the terrain from their point of view. How would he come to Melfi, how would he sustain a siege? It was obvious that one of the strengths of the place was the lack of ability to do the latter in any true proximity to the fortress, to keep enough force outside the walls, to feed and supply them over broken country that was just too far from that endless fertile plain.

Also, in each well-pastured and crop-sown valley he studied, William calculated what it would take to turn it into a desert, which is what would be required to frustrate his opponents should they seek to invest the Normans: to destroy yields in both field and store room and so deny them to the enemy, forcing them to forage far and wide. The peasants who had toiled to reap and sow the land he examined would suffer, but that was their lot: God must care for them, for he could not.

He was sure any threat would come from the

south or east but that did not obviate the need to look elsewhere, and to that purpose he rode slowly north into less bountiful country, looking for anything approaching the same ground conditions. There were few of those in a landscape mostly consisting of rock-strewn hills interspersed with thick woods. Where it was cultivated there was little in the way of flat ground, instead steep and rolling fields, small in size and with the same high hedgerows he knew from home, separated by an occasional clump of trees, which hid the narrow streams and watercourses that fed them.

Any dwellings tended to be of the sod hut type, part sunk into the ground and buttressed with stones, the roofs of some made of thatch, the poorer ones of turf, all placed on hillsides close to rivulets of running water and surrounded by dry stone walls which acted as animal pens; the locals went out to their fields at dawn and retired to the safety of their hut at night, when bears and big cats, not to mention wolves, were out hunting.

They were in those fields now and as he passed by he could see them toiling, at this time of year working to keep at bay the pests that would, if left to prosper, ruin their crops, and it was with some gratitude he thanked his Maker that he had been born and raised to be a warrior. He might respect those who worked the land for their devotion to their drudgery, but he had no notion or desire to join them.

To the north, still within sight of Monte Vulture, the landscape was even more broken, bordering as it did on the mountains, and while some slopes were heavily wooded, at a certain height that gave way to heath where scrub proliferated and no crops could be grown, a place where only goats and sheep could graze, while above that the slopes were barren screed that would be snow-covered in winter. Though he saw no one, he surmised there would be shepherds and the like who could observe him, and if they could they would also see his sword, as well as his blue and white shield of that teardrop shape peculiar to Normans, and mark him as a man to avoid.

The chance of any substantial force coming from this direction was remote. It was too infertile, but William was determined to examine every possible avenue, and that was best done from high ground and, with a wearying mount, on foot. The walk up a narrow track, no doubt cut by herded animals, which led from one valley to a high peak, then down to the next, was steep, even more so on the bare hill to one side.

It was from that direction the thundering, rolling noise came, a large near-round stone, loosing smaller rocks as it raced with increasing pace towards him. His mount, spooked by the noise and with no rider to exert control, reared up and spun to face back down the path with enough force to nearly pull the reins from his hand, and that left William on the horns of a dilemma: if he fought to control his horse they might both perish, so he grabbed his shield, which he had looped round the saddle horn, let the reins go and smacked the animal hard to add to its desire to escape. Then he turned to face the increasing avalanche of rocks.

The boulder which had set off the rush, being the largest, was the most dangerous, for if lesser rocks might maim him, that would kill. Even concentrating on that for no more than a couple of seconds, he saw something behind it, a movement which registered the outline of what looked like a human head at the very top of the slope. Such an observation did not allow for delay: given what was coming his way, there was only one method of survival – shelter – and he began to bound downhill ahead of the inundation, towards the treeline, looking for something large enough behind which to hide.

Only one outcrop, though it looked too small, appeared to give him even half a chance, but there was no time to seek out anything else or make the treeline so he dived behind it, cowering under his shield, trying to claw his way into the unyielding moss which covered the ground to increase his chances. The smaller rocks began to bounce off the shield immediately, each with a resounding thud, and it was only good fortune that those big enough to immolate him either missed his shelter or, on hitting the slab of near-flat rock behind which he lay, bounced enough to clear his shield. In seconds the roar of the avalanche had faded to be replaced by the sound of tearing wood as trees were smashed to splinters. Then there was silence, and with some trepidation William stood upright and, taking out his sword, even if he knew it to be useless, looked up the hill, wondering who it was who had tried to kill him.

He saw not one head, but two, silhouetted against the skyline for no more than another second, which made him turn away quickly to give the impression he had seen nothing. Sword and shield still in his hand, he began to jog down the slope into the trees, then turned to follow downhill, as closely as he could, the line of the path, knowing that somewhere below he would find his horse.

The animal, once clear of the perceived danger, had stopped at the first open patch of decent grass and was now grazing contently, though in the way horses do, it had a wary eye on him as he approached, as if trying to sense his mood. It shied away only once, as if to denote independence, but a sharp word from a man who had owned and ridden the beast for years made it stand still and put back its ears in disquiet, as though it was aware of having let him down.

If it expected to be chastised, no harsh words came:

if William could not have stood still in the face of that rush of stone, why should a more fragile horse? Trained for combat it might be, but it was no destrier, endlessly exposed to noise and threat so that it became fearless. This was a lighter mount bred for movement, fleet of foot but still a prey animal that saw danger everywhere and was blessed – or was it cursed as all equines were? – with near all-round vision. So it was patted and spoken to with gentleness, until those flattened ears were once more up and pricked. Back in the saddle, William made no attempt to retrace his route: instead he headed away from that rising path, along the valley floor in the cover of as many trees as he could find, at an easy trot.

Once he was round the base of the hill he spurred his mount into a faster pace, and emerging from the trees he looked for a way to get to the obverse side of the hill by a longer route, and one that would allow him to do so at speed. Somewhere out there were the people who had set that boulder in motion and there was a very good chance they were on foot. Being on a patch of cultivated land, cleared of obstacles, allowed him to set his mount to a steady canter, and in a short time he could see the entrance to the next valley.

That was when he gave his mount its head, aware that the sound of his hooves on what was soft polder would carry, which might just flush out his quarry on what he could see was an equally wooded lower slope. Even if there was no one to yet chase, there was exhilaration in the mere act of galloping; being a responsible military commander did not allow many opportunities to indulge in such as this: a pleasure he had enjoyed many times as man and boy, bent over the straining neck, the wind whistling in his ears, knowing that each thudding hoof on this forgiving ground would send up a clod of mud to rise in the air behind him, aware also that his horse, like all its fellows, loved to run flat out.

If the pair had stayed in the trees he would have had a hopeless time trying to spot them: it was foolish to break cover and try to outrun a mounted man. The other fact which registered as soon as he espied them was that one was either a dwarf or a boy-child, while the other was shaped like, and ran like, a female. William had his sword out again, and given his mount was tiring he needed to spur to maintain his speed. The child was falling behind and when the other turned to take a hand and help he saw, indeed, that it was a female, a girl not a woman, of no real age.

Time seemed to slow: William saw the dark eyes and tangled long hair, as well as the terror at the sight of his sharp, broadsword blade, now held out from his side in a way that, swept in an arc, would cut in half anyone with whom it made contact. He was sure he could hear rasping breath as well as a gasp of fear as he closed with the pair, who sought to

make a sharp turn to thwart him. Letting his mount
slow, William hauled it round inside its own length
and closed with both his quarry, now so close he could
hear the screams of the child, still lagging behind,
even being near dragged.

Coming alongside now, William's blade swept down,
turned at the last moment, with him reaching low, so
the flat of it took the running boy on the buttocks with
enough force to knock him to the ground. Then he was
ahead of both and turning, hauling on his reins and
pressing with his thighs to take all forward movement
out of his horse so he could block any continued flight,
forcing it to rear and stop.

The falling boy-child had dragged down the female,
and she had fallen to her knees, head down, but that
did not last, and when she looked up at the now
stationary rider the near black eyes had in them no
trace of fear, more of hate. Breathing heavily from his
own exertions, as was his mount, William dismounted
and, sword to the fore, demanded of them who they
were, using Greek. When that brought no response
he tried his limited Italian, another failure which had
him attempting to get an answer in Latin, the most
common language of the world in which he lived, but
one he knew before he spoke was unlikely to elicit a
response.

In doing this he was able to examine the still-
kneeling pair, taking in their rag-like, dun-coloured

clothing which covered their undernourished frames, the filth with which their skin seemed ingrained, that on a dark colouring which denoted an outdoor life, as did their hair, black and matted, their feet bare. The boy could not have been ten years old, but being of stunted growth made it impossible to be sure; the girl was older and beginning to show signs of maturity, and it was to her he barked his enquiry.

Getting no response, William was at a loss what to do: a pair of adult men would now be dead, their heads lopped off while he was still mounted, but he could not bring himself to do the same to this pair, even if they had, it seemed, tried to kill him. Or had they? He had not seen them dislodge that boulder – it could well have been an accident – yet in the eyes of the girl was a look of such deep enmity that implied such a thing was not the case.

Given where all this had happened, in this high country, they were likely to be of shepherd stock, at the very least peasants from a hard-won farm. Their background made no odds: if they had tried to kill him, they should be punished. That they had no idea of his name and position meant nothing: his dress and the fact that he was mounted and armed marked him out as a person from a far superior station in life. The other obvious fact added to his quandary: they very likely spoke a mountain dialect of some language of which he had no knowledge. He had a requirement to find out what had occurred and why, and that could only be achieved by taking them back to Melfi, where there was likely to be someone with whom they could communicate.

The girl finally spoke, in a stream of words that made no sense to the man standing over her, but then, if he knew not precisely what was being said, there was no doubt it was not a fond greeting. The words tumbled out in a stream of what sounded like bile, and whatever she said set the boy-child to tears, which tumbled down his cheeks making furrows in the filth. William swept an arm down and grabbed the boy with enough force to detach him from someone he expected was a sister rather than a mother, which turned what sounded like invective into spitting screams.

Making for his horse, William threw the boy over the front of his saddle and swiftly mounted, aware as he did so of his back being pummelled by the girl: she was certainly a feisty creature and despite what had occurred William could not help but smile, which when aimed at her, sent her into even greater paroxysms of fury. Shouting to silence her he set his mount into a walk, knowing that she would follow: if she had gone to that much trouble to save the boy before, she would not abandon him now.

The sight of the great warrior, William Iron Arm, riding slowly through the steep streets of Melfi, broke the indifference the locals had adopted as a way of reacting to the Normans. The boy, who had fallen silent long before, seeing or sensing the curious people, began to wail loudly once more, again in an incomprehensible tongue, as if by doing so he could persuade them, the townsfolk, to free him. The girl, having walked and cursed for too long, was now too exhausted to utter a word.

That wailing attracted even more of the locals and before long William had a trail of townsfolk at his rear, and he was aware of much angry muttering; what was the boy saying he had done? The crowd stopped walking, if not carping, as men came down the causeway that led up to the castle to observe at close quarters a sight to which they had been alerted by the sentinels, all tall Normans eager to see what it was their puissant leader was doing with these two grimy creatures, and those who had known and served with him long enough to be aware that he was a man who could take a jest began to praise him for the capture of such dangerous foes.

Laughing out loud, William replied, 'Have a care I don't let this boy loose to scratch out your eyes. Now do me a good turn and find someone in the town who has some knowledge of the mountain dialects.'

When the men around him would not cease to laugh, he barked the same request as a command, which was quickly obeyed, a pair of Normans barrelling down to demand help from the still-gathered crowd. That took some time and persuasion: no one in Melfi wanted to enter the castle for fear that, with the devils at present in charge, they would never re-emerge. The gap gave time to enter the keep and dismount; it also gave his brothers, who had no fear of him at all, a chance to take over the ribbing.

'You like them dirty,' hooted Humphrey, quite failing to make humorous what was intended as a jest. 'What is it to be, the boy or the girl?'

'I think you should wash the girl,' said Drogo, who had an eye that could see something to attract him under the dirt and rags. 'Perhaps I should throw her in the trough.'

'You're welcome to try, brother,' William replied, holding the wailing boy-child by the scruff of his smock. 'Me, while I will do battle with any Byzantine who comes near, will leave that to men of more courage.'

'You fear a slip of a girl?' asked Mauger, approaching her, only to recoil, to the accompaniment of much sibling mirth, when she went for his face with her outstretched nails, that before she spat at him.

'Has anyone taken a woman yet?' William asked.

Even Drogo de Hauteville was forced to deny that, and he was the most salacious of the brood, never happy to sleep alone.

'There are some matrons in the castle kitchens,' said Humphrey.

'I've seen them,' hooted Geoffrey, 'arses like a plough horse and arms akin to tree trunks.'

'Just your sort, then,' Drogo retorted, nodding to indicate that behind his brothers, the men who had gone to find someone who understood the local dialect had returned with a very unhappy-looking local, an elderly fellow of greying locks and, judging by his clothing, some prosperity, who had knowledge of both Greek and Latin.

What followed was something of a revelation: there was not a Norman present who thought themselves loved, but in interrogating this girl – the boy, indeed identified as a brother, was too young – the level of hate was enough to induce a degree of increasing anger, given that all present could hear what was being imparted. The girl did nothing to deny trying to kill William, and was only too happy to say why, making very uncomfortable the fellow who had to relay her words, while no doubt trying to hide the fact that he wholly shared the sentiments.

No crime was left unmentioned – if this adolescent had never seen a Norman, she had heard of them – even if it emerged in a stuttered, inchoate way: rapine that included the torching of crops and stored food, the chopping down of vines and olive trees, the slaughter of livestock, theft, the torture of innocents, the hanging and mutilation of men, women and children, with those not so treated left to starve over a foodless winter, and, if any women survived, to bear, the next year, the bastards caused by forced conception.

It was the tale of every invader who ever lived, for those listening knew that a Christian army from east or west would behave no differently and the Saracens were worse: war bore down heavily on those who had no part in the fighting, but it seemed, in this invective, the Normans were seen as more troubling than others, nothing less than a plague. Eventually it ceased: it seemed either the girl ran out of hate and breath, or there were no more crimes to list.

The poor interlocutor, who expected to pay a heavy price for his explanations, now stood with his head bowed, afraid to look a single one of these Normans in the eye. William, throughout, had been recalling some of the thoughts he had mulled over earlier in the day. Personally not overly bloodthirsty, he knew the fellows he led to be guilty of much that had been said: had he not seen them do these very things on more than one occasion? Had he not in Sicily, to deny his Saracen enemy the means of sustenance, laid waste the land and let loose his men to cow the populace?

'Hang her from the walls,' Drogo said, 'and her brother too.'

'How do they live?' William asked, for that had not yet been put to the girl.

Gently the old man enquired, to pass on that the pair came from a family of goatherds, though they had long since lost all but two of their herd.

'The rest of the family?'

The furious shake of the girl's head, and the way she dropped it when that was posed, required no translation: they were very likely orphans, so William looked directly at the old man. 'These things that have been said, you share them, do you not?'

'My Lord...'

'I am not your lord, fellow,' William snapped, taking hold of his sword hilt to drive home the risk the old man was taking: he had no desire to hear either platitudes or untruths. 'But I will have an answer and it must be an honest one.'

The words that tumbled out were not wholly coherent either, being spoken by a worthy trying to avoid condemning himself to the fate Drogo had suggested for the two youngsters. Yet they were similar, albeit mixed, unlike the girl's invective, with many an apologetic caveat. It met what William desired: it told him of the depth of distrust, if not loathing, he and his men faced locally.

He could hang them both: they, certainly she, had tried to kill or at the very least maim him, but would that meet his needs? There were two ways to treat the local population, to further increase their dread or to seek to win them over to his side. Would magnanimity do that? Still holding the boy by the scruff of his smock, William pushed him towards the old man.

'The women in the kitchens, they are local, they will be able to speak with these children?' That got a nodded response. 'Then take them there, have them fed.'

'Gill...' Drogo protested.

William looked hard at his brother, whom he knew to be an avid despoiler of land and crops. Since their relationship was normally friendly, it was a ferocious glare, which stopped Drogo speaking further.

'They are to be washed and found clothing as well as a place to rest. From now on these two are wards of mine. Let that be known throughout the region. We do not make war on children.'

'When you get to the kitchens, old man,' said Mauger, as nonplussed as the rest of his half-siblings, 'keep that spitfire away from the knives.'

# CHAPTER EIGHT

✣

The Normans were not only the best soldiers in this part of the world, they were the most mobile, able to react quickly to any emergency: their weapons were kept sharp, their harness always attended to and each lance had a mount fit to get him to where he needed to be and another trained for battle. Thus they were mounted and ready to ride out within hours, word having come from Arduin that a show of force was required outside Venosa, the nearest large fortified town between Melfi and Bari. Leaving a garrison large enough to overawe the locals, William rode out at the head of his men, on a journey of no more than seven leagues, his hope high that the message from Arduin was correct: Venosa would not open its gates unless it could prove to the catapan, should he too turn up outside their walls at a later date, that they had little choice.

If the people of Apulia had seen Normans before, raiding parties which had come from Campania just to loot and rob, they had never seen them in such numbers, over two hundred and fifty warriors fully armed and ready for battle, the sun glistening on their mail and helmets, as well as the tips of their lances, on each of which fluttered a coloured pennant.

For once, sure no enemy had yet gathered to oppose them, they could ride en masse, without the need to send ahead scouts or to put out strong parties to cover their flanks, which pleased William: he wanted those toiling in the fields to observe their power, in the hope that the more adventurous amongst them, the younger sons who would rail against the life they were obliged to live, would see opportunity and flock to join them as foot soldiers.

Fording the higher reaches of the River Ofanto, the force was soon in a country of rolling fertile hills, the landscape studded with pale stone dwellings, the odd one the size of a proper manor house, most single-storey, stone, round and thatched-roof bothies where humans and animals would shelter together at night. Some of the larger properties were enclosed by a defensible curtain wall, high enough to withstand marauding bands provided they were not too numerous; they usually had also, enclosed behind those walls, barns, cattle pens and pig sties, while outside there lay extensive paddocks, everything irrigated by plentiful streams. No horses were in those paddocks now: at the sight of this host, or hearing the rumour that somehow flew ahead of them, they had been taken into safety.

The open fields, many with standing corn, others meadowland lying fallow, would provide stacks of hay in abundance, which was reassuring: this was a well-watered and valuable country in which the Norman cavalry could operate with some freedom; there would be no shortage of sustenance for man nor beast. It was also, given its obvious wealth and fecundity, a rich source of tax revenue, a land Byzantium would fight hard to hold on to.

Arduin, with his escorts and some Lombards he had already recruited, met them within long sight of the town walls, and he and William rode ahead while the remainder of the force rested the mounts they had used to get here, with the added task of making it seem as if they were also preparing for battle. Approaching those walls, a far from formidable edifice, it was obvious they were in a state of disrepair, so poorly maintained as to make withstanding a siege near impossible.

There was no moat and in several places there were gaps where the masonry had fallen, while all along the walls ramshackle dwellings had been built, now deserted, which also rendered the place insecure. The only thing which looked solid was the great pair of studded wooden gates, firmly shut against these interlopers.

'The populace?'

'Mainly Italians, with a few Lombards, but not sufficient to make them see sense. They surrendered quickly in the recent troubles. I don't think the catapan even bothered to bring an army to menace the place. He just sent them an envoy with a threat, the same as we must do.'

'Then we must encourage the citizenry to repair those walls.'

Arduin looked doubtful. 'They see safety in not doing so. Stout walls would tempt them to defence, to stand out against a proper siege. The catapan, whoever he happens to be, has openly discouraged such activity, knowing it left them dependent on his forces. Such a thing tends to keep people loyal.'

'There are others the same?'

'Many, William, outside the ports, of course.'

'Lavello is in the same state?'

Arduin nodded, causing William to mull over two things: first the aims and ambitions of this Lombard, which would be for a quick campaign to cement his leadership and ensure his place in any future settlement. There was wisdom in that from his point of view: Doukeianos was certainly weak and it might be possible to expel the catapan quickly while that situation pertained, certainly before this Atenulf appeared on the scene. There was also great risk: in his eagerness Arduin might overreach himself, and that took no account of past errors or Byzantine resilience.

As yet, Arduin did not have an army, he had Normans, and while that might suffice here outside Venosa, and would certainly be a factor in any open battle, there was no guarantee the case would be the same in the numerous other fortified towns they must secure if they were to conquer the whole province. Certainly a rapid campaign against a vulnerable opponent might secure them the hinterland, the fertile plains, but would it persuade the citizenry of the Adriatic ports to acquiesce?

That William doubted, despite assurances they could not wait to throw off the Byzantine yoke. It only took one great port to refuse, even if all the others joined the revolt, and that would require it to be invested from both land and sea; success would not be quick, which would give the Eastern Empire ample time to send reinforcements – and with a province of such value at stake, never mind their pride, they would most certainly do so. It would provide, as well, a safe enclave in which they could land.

The Lombards had been in advantageous situations before and had always squandered them, either through their squabbles or outright betrayal by one of their number. The way Guaimar of Salerno had refused to openly support them meant divisions were highly likely to occur in the future. That William de Hauteville did not trust the Lombards was a given: he also felt certain that to subdue and conquer this land so completely that Byzantium would give it up was not something which could be achieved in one swift crusade.

Then there was his overarching aim, which he must keep hidden from Arduin, which was to gain in Apulia land for himself and his family. He needed to prepare for a long, hard campaign, in which those whom he now fought alongside might one day become his enemies, opponents who could come at him from east and west. For that he required to secure an area he and his Normans could control against anyone – not just Melfi and a triangle of mutually supporting fortresses met that need.

Melfi held the passage from the west: from the maps he had studied, good maps originally made over a thousand years before by Roman surveyors, it was obvious that any force seeking to come upon and recapture the great fortress from the east had two obvious routes of approach, the first setting out from the coast at Barletta and hugging the River Ofanto. A wise commander would then base himself on Lavello: the town stood midway between two forks of the river on an open, fertile plain. The other route came here to Venosa, from Bari in the south-east. Whichever was chosen, nothing would serve them better than a fortified base close to Melfi. Even one in a bad state of repair was secure when possessed by an army; these places must be denied them.

'Both towns must be made secure, even if the citizens dislike it. When Michael Doukeianos thinks to come, as come he must, let it be known to him that he will have these places to besiege long before he gets to Melfi, for he dare not bypass them and leave a garrison of Normans to harry his rear.'

'A garrison! That dissipates our strength.'

William nearly shook his head emphatically, but resisted: Arduin had to be persuaded, not pressured in agreement. 'First we garrison them to force the townsfolk to repair their walls, for we have time before the catapan can mount any assault.'

'A quarter, no more.'

'Once those walls are repaired it will require very few men to secure both towns against their own people. They can be fully equipped to withstand a siege if we are forced to withdraw, which will set even a powerful attacker a real problem.'

Arduin could not help but look glum: whatever he wanted to do, he could achieve nothing without William Iron Arm and the men he led. The Norman was wondering if he was having cause to regret his insistence of his presence. Time for a touch of flattery, something to which he knew this man was susceptible.

'And in that quarter you can achieve what no other man can, Arduin. You can raise an army, I cannot, and I promise you, once you have that we will march against the catapan, and under your leadership, with you as our general, we will cast him into the sea.'

'You can repair these walls in time?'

'Three months, Arduin? We Normans can build as well as fight, and we can make others labour. Take the surrender of Venosa, and then set out for Lavello. Once both are in your hands, you can send out word to raise men and arms to every town in northern Apulia, and when they come to your banner and observe how we, the Normans, accept you as our leader, they will also see that they have nothing to fear.'

The notion of taking the town, albeit the act was more appearance than conquest, cheered Arduin somewhat, though deep down he had to be aware that there was no alternative. Once joined by the de Hauteville brothers, who made an imposing sight, he spurred his horse, as did William, who made sure he and his brothers stayed to his rear, made sure that those watching from the walls would see clearly who led and who followed, when Arduin called upon them to open the gates.

In this the Lombard was in his element: not for

him the mere bare bones of a demand, he was gifted a chance to make another speech, one he took heartily. William had never heard the terms of surrender put in so bloodthirsty a fashion. Not for Arduin a simple threat that to refuse would see the inhabitants given no quarter as demanded by the laws of war. He was a general and he was determined they should know it, and know in detail how their houses would be torched, their possessions plundered, their women used as bitches as they watched each man castrated and suffocated on his own genitals.

'If he goes on much longer,' Drogo whispered, 'those walls will come down completely. Jericho would not have needed trumpets if Arduin had commanded instead of Joshua.'

'Give him his moment, brother,' William replied, as the gates opened and a penitent group of the leading citizens emerged, carrying the seals of the town. 'This is his first act as a general.'

It was a flushed Arduin who turned to his Normans and said, in a voice full of arrogance, 'William de Hauteville, I desire to take possession of Venosa in my name.'

Given the message coming out of Salerno had been sent to Bari in a Byzantine vessel, the captain of the ship had little difficulty in getting to see the catapan personally and immediately; the communication he carried was an alarming one, doubly so for Michael Doukeianos, who now knew, if what he was being told was true, that in appointing Arduin of Fassano to hold Melfi, he had made a terrible error. Looking around the faces of those assembled to counsel him, the leading Greek officials of the Catapanate, he wondered which one would be the most eager to pass on the tale of his foolishness in trusting a Lombard to his imperial master. Whoever it was, it would not be well received in Constantinople.

'This information, Excellency, came to me from a reliable source, the servant of a man who has the private ear of the prince.'

'But not from the Prince of Salerno himself?'

'No, and he would feel the need to be cautious, nor would he want it known outside his own very close circle that he is not truly master in his own domains.'

'Who is this man?'

'The clerk to a very important official.'

'That, fellow, is the name I want.'

'I gave my solemn oath to keep that secret.'

'Well,' Doukeianos said, in a quiet way that was even more threatening than any shout, 'it will cost you your lifeblood if you do not answer me.'

The hesitation from the ship's captain, the look at the ground at his feet as well as the despair in his countenance when he raised his head again, was all display: he knew he had to answer with the truth, for he knew that this catapan was not jesting, and, in truth, why should he risk anything for the protection of a Jew?

'The man's name is Kasa Ephraim and he is the collector of the port.'

'A Jew is collector of the port of Salerno?' When that got a nod, Doukeianos added, 'Then this prince is a strange ruler indeed.'

'I was told that the Prince Guaimar would not hold his title without that the Jew had aided him, and that is why he is so trusted, and not just with the port revenues.'

'Explain!'

That demand brought forth the story of how Ephraim had aided Guaimar and his sister to escape the clutches of Pandulf, which in turn had led to that man's downfall and the young man coming into his rightful title.

'His clerk was adamant that without the Jew he would now languish in Pandulf's dungeon and that man would still hold Capua. So he counsels the prince in private, and has his ear in all things. According to the collector's servant the prince is locked in an embrace with the Count of Aversa from which he finds it hard to free himself, since Drengot still has a large force in Campania. He has demanded that the count withdraw his men from the Catapanate, but he lacks the power to insist that he do so.'

'Rainulf Drengot is in his pay, is he not? The Prince of Salerno is also his lawful suzerain.'

'It seems the Normans do as they wish, Excellency,' the captain replied, a remark which set up much nodding and murmuring from the others present. 'But there is more. The Jew has advised his master to seek intercession from the Western Emperor, to threaten to strip Drengot of his title if he does not obey his prince.'

For the first time Michael Doukeianos showed a trace of temper, his voice rising. 'Guaimar does not see fit to send word to me.'

'He fears to betray a fellow Lombard.'

'Arduin?'

There was a deep satisfaction in the messenger's response then; he had thought long and hard how to present this story to the catapan, for if the man was feeling generous the reward could be substantial, and paid in gold, of which he would have an abundance. He had decided very early on, hardly out of sight of the bay of Salerno really, to keep the best till last.

'Not Arduin, Excellency, but the Prince of Benevento.' That finally brought Michael Doukeianos out of his seat, his face so suffused with fury that the captain recoiled, his voice rising in panic. 'The Normans have allied themselves to Benevento, and asked that he lead them in Apulia, since Prince Guaimar refused, even to the point of denying them any supplies on

the way to Melfi. It did him no service. I am told they
stole them anyway.'

The catapan had not resumed his seat and he
walked to look out of an opening in the chamber, away
from the interior so that his face was hidden. Beneath
him lay the port of Bari, full of shipping – but none of
that was his own – and surrounding that a town full of
people, while behind him, standing and waiting while
he ruminated, were the men he had not consulted
about appointing Arduin. The sun shone on the sight
before him, but not in his heart. He realised now the
magnitude of his error: with three hundred Normans
in Melfi he would struggle to retake it, but he knew he
must try.

Yet he also knew he had been lucky: first in the
fact that the Normans were there unsupported by
Guaimar, by far the most powerful of the Lombard
magnates. Had the Prince of Salerno done otherwise
the whole Catapanate would be in jeopardy. He had
also found out what was happening well before the
news would have filtered down to him overland, so he
had gained vital time.

Arduin would not be expecting a response for many
weeks, and his first task would be to raise foot soldiers
from the surrounding land and they would have to be
trained. He still had some proper soldiers, his own
personal troops and bodyguards, as well as some of
the hastily conscripted levies from Bari with which he

had put down the recent rebellion; with luck he might surprise the traitor while he was away from Melfi and get between him and the fortress.

If he could do that and he was weak, he would make Arduin pay for his treachery. As for the Normans, they could be bought off: they always put coin before loyalty to a cause – anyone's cause.

But that brought forth another concern: mounted and already well trained and armed for war they could move swiftly and anywhere, which included the coast, which must be protected at all costs. If Byzantium held the port cities it held a firm grip on Apulia, but they were a rich and tempting prize for men who loved to plunder.

'Captain, to which port are you bound?' Doukeianos demanded, turning round to face a roomful of bland-faced officials, some of whom had served half a dozen previous catapans.

'Ragusa, Excellency, with a cargo of oil.'

'Forget that. You will proceed to Constantinople under my orders…'

The man's hands were suddenly open in protest. 'Your Excellency!'

'Oil commands a good price there too, so you will not lose, and I will reward you for the service. You are to take a despatch which will be written speedily telling the emperor of what has occurred and asking for reinforcements.' Then he looked past the bowing captain, that being enough to send one official off to compose the necessary document. To another he demanded, 'Get me a list of what levies we still have under arms.'

'Excellency.'

The command to a third was just as brusque. 'I want a message sent by sea up the coast, first to alert the ports to the danger, and then a rider sent on to Troia, to the garrison there. They are to send out patrols to scour the border with Benevento. I want to know what kind of support the principality is providing in arms and men.'

A stream of other instructions followed, with the required officials departing to obey. It was an element of the efficiency of the Apulian administration that he had in his hands a paper outlining the message he wished to send to Constantinople with less than half the sand run through the glass, one which he perused quickly before, satisfied, he appended his seal. Quietly, he told the man holding the wax and candle how much to pay the captain for the service required, then ordered him, once the man was on his way, to return on his own.

With everything that could be put in hand complete, Michael Doukeianos sat down to compose a message to be sent to Salerno, one in which he imparted that he understood the constraints under which Prince Guaimar struggled, and also that he was appreciative of the stand he had taken, as well as the steps in informing the Western Emperor. He also wrote that he regretted his own concerns prevented him from offering to bring to Guaimar's aid the kind of force which would put his rebellious vassal, Rainulf Drengot, in his place.

He stopped and smiled then: the last thing Guaimar would want to see was Byzantine war vessels filling his bay. Then he went back to composition.

The fulsome praise which followed was to the prince's sagacity in the actions he had taken, as well as his caution, plus an assurance that once he had dealt with Arduin and recovered Melfi he would be content to leave Campania in peace while he sought to enforce redress on Benevento, albeit he would have no choice but to ask the men Drengot commanded to return to Campania.

Reading it over twice, the young Byzantine general was satisfied that it implied that which he intended: if Guaimar wanted to take part in the dismemberment of Benevento, he, as the representative of Constantinople in Southern Italy, would welcome him, and given that occupied Normans were better than idle ones, such a course might distract them from mischief in his own domains.

He knew the man who had sealed his despatch earlier was waiting and he called him over, sanding and sealing his own message without allowing the fellow to have sight of it. 'This is to go by ship to Salerno, to be placed in the hand of Prince Guaimar and no one else. See to it.'

The message found Guaimar under the walls of Amalfi. Not that he himself was engaged in trying to subdue the place: on land that fell to Rainulf Drengot, who led his Normans as well as the foot soldiers the prince had raised in his fiefs. Likewise at sea, a trusted admiral was responsible for ensuring no ship entered or left the harbour and he had placed stout booms across the entrance to ensure that task was carried out.

To subdue the place would take time, perhaps till they were starving – it had stout protective land walls – but that he had. If he had ever thought he might have an enemy who could trouble him, the response from Michael Doukeianos was everything for which Guaimar could wish. Both Naples and Gaeta, his other trading rivals, were either only too happy to see Amalfi humbled or too afraid of his Normans to intervene. To amuse himself, given he had little to do but inspire the besiegers by his presence, he spent time making lists of those enemy citizens he would hang from the walls, some of whom had troubled his father before him, while also dreaming of one day being acclaimed as a king by his fellow Lombards.

# CHAPTER NINE

∽◇∼

News of that siege naturally travelled east, but it was of no concern to either Arduin or William de Hauteville, except that it kept Guaimar and Rainulf busy. When word came of the approach of a Byzantine army, William was occupied, with the aid of his youngest brother, supervising the reconstruction of the walls of Lavello, which, on inspection, had proved be in a more sorry state than those of Venosa.

Michael Doukeianos knew of the occupation of Melfi by the Normans, knew of Arduin's betrayal: he was heading their way to set matters right, the size of his army unknown. The messenger, a Lombard from Giovinazzo, had set out to warn of the intention, without waiting to assess numbers, but the fellow was certain the catapan could not be far behind: had he not moved like lightning the previous year to crush revolt?

Arduin was travelling throughout Benevento, well to the north, seeking Lombard volunteers, too far away to make any decisions affecting the urgent problem, leaving William to make them instead. He sent word at once to Drogo at Venosa, to Humphrey and Geoffrey still in Melfi, all three to join him while he despatched Mauger with a small party of horsemen to ride down the southern side of the River Ofanto, the route he suspected his enemy would take, to warn of their approach.

Instinctively, he wanted to meet the catapan in the open – the idea of being locked up in a fortress, however strong, was anathema. He also had to take a chance that Michael Doukeianos would not take the direct route from Bari across the high uplands, that he would hog the fertile coastal plain and the port cities, which would provide his troops with both ample sustenance and, if he had time to press into service the younger men, with recruits.

Drogo was with him the next day, bringing in the conroys who had been working with him, supervising the restoration of the Venosa defences; from Melfi came the garrison, excepting a skeleton force to hold it safe as a refuge to which they could fall back if need be. William had at his disposal all the men he could muster.

'He can surely only assemble a small force,' Drogo insisted, 'and cannot field much in the way of trained bands. Moving as quickly as he has, he has not had time to raise fresh levies.'

That word 'time' hung in the air. Doukeianos had been expected to react but he should not have marched so soon. He had come to know of the Norman presence in Apulia long before he should; how had he found out mattered less than his being on the way: that had to be dealt with immediately.

'That lack of trained bands applies to us even more,' William replied. 'We have none at all, and only a few Lombards who have volunteered as foot soldiers.'

None of his brothers, cogitating on that unpleasant fact, seemed willing to offer any ideas. It was William, looking over Drogo's shoulder at the hundreds of labourers he had been supervising, who came up with a solution. They had been forced to the work and, apart from a couple of stonemasons, were the least skilled men in the town. That mattered less than their number; that they would certainly, without training, be near useless as soldiers, was even less important.

He knew there were weapons in the Lavello armoury – swords, shields and pikes. It was a requirement of any sizeable town in the Catapanate to act as an arsenal as well as a storehouse for any passing Byzantine army. The sight of men in such numbers, as long as he had no idea of their quality, might force

Doukeianos to alter his tactics; it might even throw him off balance.

'Drogo, get back to Venosa. I want all the labourers you have employed armed and marched to the east of here.'

'Labourers?'

'Bodies, brother. Let's make our enemy think we have more force than he expects.'

The party from Melfi had brought with them the old Roman maps, and while certain place names had changed in the last five hundred years, the locations of the towns remained the same. Studying them, and working on his earlier assumptions, William surmised that Doukeianos would rest, regroup and recruit at Barletta, but he would not delay there long, given speed and surprise were his most potent weapons.

From Barletta the route to the interior would be through Canosa, large enough to be fortified, his next point to replenish his supplies. From there he would come on to Lavello, then Venosa, and for the same reason: to gather more men and to replenish his stocks of food and fodder before proceeding on to besiege Melfi. He could not yet be aware these towns were already in Norman hands.

If Doukeianos moved at the pace William thought – not slowing his march to forage – to confront him to the east of Canosa would be impossible. To reduce his options it was therefore best to let him advance from there to a point closer to Lavello, where whatever supplies he had garnered would be depleted, which would also hamper his options when faced with an enemy. Inglorious it might be, and when he suggested the thinking his immediate family certainly thought he was showing Byzantium too much respect, but William did not want to fight the catapan, he wanted to scare him into withdrawing: the time to engage him in battle would be when Arduin had created a properly equipped and trained Lombard army large enough to crush him.

Drogo, having fought with his elder brother many times – and having seen the power of Byzantium in Sicily – took it best, sensing after only a moment's thought that this was no time for glory; it was a time for prudence. He at least had discerned they were in Apulia for a campaign, probably an extended one, not some all-consuming battle. That would take time, effort and good fortune. Shouting to his men, he had them mounted and on their way as soon as he and William had agreed to rendezvous on the far bank of the Olivento, the closest north-to-south tributary of the River Ofanto.

'Open the armoury, Geoffrey,' William ordered, as soon as Drogo had departed, 'and let's get these labourers with pikes in their hands. Tell them we will march in the morning and if anyone even looks like refusing they have a choice: they can do as we wish, or hang from the walls they have been working on. Humphrey, take a party of three conroys ahead and ensure we have fodder for the horses and food for all.'

'The peasants and landholders will resist,' Humphrey insisted. 'How do I treat them, brother?'

That was a shrewd question and one William appreciated, harking back as it did to his instructions regarding the inhabitants of Melfi, but this was no time for gentle measures.

'Tell them they have a choice,' William growled, 'they can let us take their produce or the catapan and his army will grab it.'

'No choice at all, then?'

'None. Also send a messenger on to contact Mauger and tell him what we plan.'

There was only one act in the next hours that was not surrounded by chaos: the riding out of those thirty lances under Humphrey. Drumming into the locals what was required of them could not be done gently, it had to be carried out with a degree of brutality, given time was short. William took charge of the few Lombard volunteers, some of whom had seen service before, seeking to teach them a few basic commands and manoeuvres in Norman French – the language he would have to use with his own lances – to turn right or left or to advance; he did not even mention retreat, given it was an option men fighting on foot were prone to take too readily.

Geoffrey had the harder task with the unwilling citizenry: at least the Lombards were enthusiastic. Both brothers worked well into the night to ensure all was made ready, that at least their charges could move forward in relatively disciplined groups, and then when they had done as much as possible, they set guards to make certain none of their forced recruits slipped away in the dark.

Naturally the affair had to be blessed and the priests were summoned to the task before the need for torches had passed, intoning, since this was Byzantine territory, their consecrations in the Orthodox rite. The march began as soon as they had been fed, and William led them away, heading into the rising sun as a straggling line, to the wailing sound of the womenfolk, sure they were seeing the last of their men.

'The catapan is north of the river.' The messenger who, coming from Mauger on a seriously blown mount forced to run hard and long, had found him on the east bank of the Olivento, at the rendezvous he had arranged with Drogo. 'Not south as you expected, and he is pushing his army hard.'

'Horsemen?'

'Few. His men are almost all on foot.'

'Numbers?'

'We were on the far side of the river and they were half a league from the bank. Also there was much dust, but it would take several thousand to kick up what they did.'

William, pacing up and down, tried to work out the ramifications of what he had just been told, and it was troubling: the young Byzantine general had out-thought him. Michael Doukeianos had not acted as William thought he should, given what he suspected he had at his disposal. The numbers suggested he had pressed into service many recruits on the way, while their present location meant he must have moved north from Barletta and crossed the Ofanto where the shallow delta met the sea, and that could only be done by boats brought up the coast from the ports through which he had passed, which in turn pointed to much forethought.

That meant both he and Drogo, yet to join him, would be in very much the wrong place, and if he did not move with speed Doukeianos would have a clear route to Melfi and only a small garrison to face when he got there. The Normans could find themselves fighting just to try to relieve the fortress, and that would mean facing an army in prepared defensive positions – not good for cavalry at all.

There was one chance, but it would have to be taken at speed. From memory he knew there was a mapped river crossing just to the north: a place where the Ofanto, crossing a wide, low plain, was shown as fordable, certainly for mounted men – but not, he suspected, at this time of year and with a river flowing strongly, for those on foot. As of this moment he had no idea how far away Drogo was, and he had with him a sizeable number of the available lances. If he was to have any chance of stopping the catapan he would need every man he commanded.

Decision made, the orders came out in a stream: the messenger to ride back to Mauger on a fresh horse, contacting Humphrey en route and telling them to retire west along the riverbank until they came to the piquet he would leave at the point at which he and his men had forded it, though it should be obvious from the evidence of hundreds of mounts preceding them. Another messenger was sent to tell Drogo to speed up: he must abandon anyone on foot and push his horses hard if he was to be of any use.

'What about our foot soldiers?' asked Geoffrey.

'Find one of the Lombards who looks as if he has a brain. Tell them to march our labourers back to Lavello and close the gates. Then get our men mounted.'

This time the Normans were on the move quickly, watched by their bewildered conscripts, with William trying to calculate distances and how far he could push his mounts, a reckoning made on years of experience. Around seven leagues in any one day, with frequent halts, was held to be a good norm for horses; he needed to do more.

Like every Norman, he had grown up surrounded

by several varieties of horses: those bred for battle, trotting alongside on a short rein, others more fleet, like the one he was now riding, another of the strain he was leading, his broad-backed packhorse. He had foaled them, whatever their type, watched them grow to yearlings, nursed them when sick and come to know each one as an individual: the shy, the biters and kickers, the cunning and the near human in their attitude; but all had common features.

Push any mount too hard with a weighty rider or panniers on its back, eschew the periodic walk, and they would tire very quickly. Put aside any thoughts of a complete break twice a day with water and at least some pasture and even those being led would be less effective if it came to an immediate battle. They required to be fed, as well, and each of his men had only one day's supply of oats on his packhorse, that set against plentiful pasture; but cosset them and Doukeianos might outpace him and get between him and Melfi. What emerged had to be a compromise: he would work them harder than was prudent, but not so hard as to render them blown.

The stops they made were short, and always near some habitation, the numerous hamlets scattered throughout the land next to strips of cultivation, where small amounts of fodder and food for his men could be had; water was plentiful, it being springtime. No one resisted the demand for the last of their produce stored over the winter: no peasant would contest with armed men, especially these giants from the north, for if they had never in their life come across one, the reputation of the Normans was a folk tale well spread. They were sullen, certainly, but offered nothing more than black looks, which matched the increasing density of the clouds overhead.

Getting across the Ofanto at this time of year meant pushing the horses through a river that came up to their thighs, though thankfully the current was slowed by the spread of the flow over the flattish plain. No sooner had they crossed than it began to rain, a steadily increasing drizzle, then a downpour that soaked everyone to the marrow, despite their thick cloaks. William could only hope the same conditions were affecting Michael Doukeianos – nothing slowed foot soldiers more than wet weather: if rain made a horse drop its head, it destroyed much more quickly the spirits of men marching in mud.

They spent an uncomfortable night in the open, hobbling their mounts so that they could graze and sleep as they pleased, necessary with no hay to hand, and rose in the morning to an all-consuming mist that made getting dry impossible. It also prevented William from sending out patrols to scout ahead – not much point in that when they could see little – and it seriously hampered his desire to push on: without sunlight he had little idea of the direction in which to proceed, and it was mid-morning before the sun began to burn it off.

The extra time was good for the horses, and with no actual rain it was possible to groom them, not for beautification, but for their health. Brushing removed burrs, picked up riding through long grass and bushes, which, if left, could break easily into infected skin. The dust of the previous day had already been cleaned from their nostrils and dung residue from their behinds, but in the morning hooves required to be inspected for wear, and oiled to avoid splits that would render them lame, while backs needed to be checked for sores caused by wet saddlecloths.

Not all were in good enough condition to continue: on the march a loss of mounts was inevitable and this was no exception. When they headed out, two of his men were riding their packhorses, their regular mounts unsaddled, limping, and trying to stay with the herd. There was no time to light a fire, to kill and eat them: all William's men had was some stale bread, and dried strips of beef on which to chew.

Those on the best and fittest-looking horses had been sent ahead, their task to look over every high point and ensure their confrères were not riding into a trap, while also looking to the east for any sign of marching men. Those scouts found a grass-covered hill that gave extensive views in all directions, all the way east to the silver ribbon of another river tributary, and stopped, William calling a halt for all as soon as he caught up. The ground on the slopes was dry, the grass at the base thick and green, and if an army had passed nearby he would be able to see evidence and there was none: he had got ahead of his foe. Across a rolling hilly landscape, he should be able to observe their line of march, as well as the early presence of Drogo and his lances coming from the south, allowing him to make whatever dispositions were needed.

All around packhorses had been stripped of their loads, but now, unlike the previous night, the contents they carried were laid out in the sunshine: no fires could be allowed as that would alert the enemy to their presence, although William had a great deal of timber gathered and brought in for later, piling up the wood along the crest of the mount.

Spare leather jerkins and woollen breeches had been donned to allow the ones they had worn previously to dry, and footwear had been removed for the same purpose. Still-wet cloaks covered the grass and they lay alongside chain mail, hauberks and gloves, which if left damp would rust. The men cleaned those when they were dry and their weapons, swords and lance tips, using the same oil as they had previously applied to hooves. William waited till all was done and his men were back to being ready for battle, then, having put out a piquet on the nearest hill to the east, he allowed those who wished to some sleep.

That was not a luxury he could allow himself: looking out over the surrounding landscape, barren and deserted except for the dots of grazing sheep and goats, he searched for a suitable field of battle, the best place to confront Doukeianos, wondering if he would be granted the right to choose it. Given his force was cavalry that should be the case: horsemen could manoeuvre with much more ease than *milities*, however well trained they were. But this catapan had outfoxed him once and he was too wise to think all the choices would remain his, a point he made to his younger brother.

'All I can say for sure is that we got ahead of them.'

'Can we stop them?' asked Geoffrey.

'That I do not know until I see their numbers.'

'And if they are too numerous?'

'We fall back on Melfi and prepare for a siege. At least we know we can outrun them.'

'Not Venosa or Lavello?'

William smiled, aware his brother was asking these things out of ignorance; yet he had experienced battle, having, like William, ridden alongside their father under the banner of Duke Robert. But then so had Drogo, and though he was a mighty fighter he deferred to William when it came to tactics; Humphrey and Mauger would likely do the same. All four were formidable in battle; even if it had only been in mock combat he had contested with them and knew their

prowess. That they could not best him meant less than the fact that they could beat most of the men he led.

Yet they were limited when it came to command; excellent at following instructions – also, certainly in Drogo's case, good at close battlefield control – but none of them could plan what he had in his mind, which was a great deal more than just stopping this approaching catapan and his army. Sometimes William tired of responsibility, and often, at home in the Contentin, he had wearied of his status as elder brother, but that was useless: if it was a burden it was one that could not be put down, and in truth, he would not want to.

'No. If we sought to retire on those, I think this Michael Doukeianos would just bypass us. Melfi is the prize.'

'He will not capture it. The castle is too strong.'

'He does not need to take it, Geoffrey, he needs to deny us the use of it, and the ability to sally forth at will. He also needs to let the Lombards Arduin is busy recruiting know that they do not have Melfi as a safe refuge. Doukeianos has little in the way of strength and a long time to wait before any reinforcements can arrive, and even if he had those he cannot hold Apulia if the entire population rises against him. Doubt of outcome in this is his greatest asset. News that he is besieging Melfi will make many minds cautious, will serve to divide those keen to rebel, and that will do. Byzantium rules by the fear of what its armies might do, not what they can actually accomplish.'

'Better to fight him, then?'

'I will if I can, but that will depend on many things, and not just the size of the force he brings against us.'

'Such as?'

'The quality. You can tell much about an enemy host by the way it deploys. If it is smooth and disciplined then they are likely to be steady under assault; if it is ragged and muddled they will not stand against our lances, and once broken they will not stop but flee the field. The ground too will have a bearing. Following that heavy rain we rode through, it would not be wise for us to fight in a valley until the ground dries out and ceases to be soft.'

Geoffrey acknowledged that: mud would slow the horses, impede any attack and make manoeuvre challenging.

'And since Doukeianos knows this as well as anyone he will seek to draw us into such ground.'

'How do you intend to deal with that?'

'By talking, brother.' Seeing Geoffrey's questioning look, he added, 'For I think the catapan, before he seeks battle, will try to do what Byzantium does best, and buy us off.'

The cry from a sentinel had them both looking south, to a long ragged line of horsemen approaching. Within a glass of sand William was greeting three more of his brothers, but most importantly, for they were weary and damp, he would now be, once they had rested, at maximum strength.

# CHAPTER TEN

❯◆❮

The forward piquet saw them first, just as the sun was setting, and alerted William so he could ride forward and observe, in the gathering gloom, a distant army marching in several columns over a broad front, men to the fore, a sizeable herd of donkeys, mules and probably camp followers to the rear, the only mounted men seeming to be those in positions of command, which cheered him: he would face no cavalry force. It was impossible to tell from this distance the state of their morale, but they could not be less than weary given the ground they had been obliged to cover in the last few days and the fact that they had just had to ford a river, which however narrow a watercourse it was, would make them wet; they were in for an uncomfortable night.

In reality, they should not still be coming on at this
time of day: most armies would have camped on the
far riverbank and crossed in the morning. Looking
up William saw that the sky was clear and the moon,
rising slowly, was three-quarters full, which, given
the mass of stars to aid it, would bathe the landscape
in sufficient light to see. Surely the catapan was not
going to march on in the hours of darkness? If he had
that in mind, it was time to disabuse him.

'Back to the main body,' he said to a man at his
side. 'Tell them to get those fires lit and blazing, all of
them, right along the skyline. Let them see their way
is blocked and in force.'

Signalling to the rest of the forward party, he had
them ride up until they were lined along the crest, in
time for their silhouette to catch the last dying light of
the now invisible sun, but distance and gloom meant
William had no idea if they had been observed. To
their rear the first of the fires began to glow, bright
orange flames and sparks rising into the increasingly
dark sky from a hill higher than that on which they
sat.

There they stayed until all that was left was the
moon and stars, when slowly, William turned his
horse's head and led his men back to the main body.
There, dividing them into three, he set one *battaile*
on foot, out ahead of those fires to protect the camp,
with the flanking sentinels told to keep their eyes

peeled to ensure the Byzantines made no attempt to slip round their flanks. The rest were obliged to sleep in hauberks, with arms and helmets close by, given he had no intention of being surprised. The horses, now rested, were saddled; everything that could be done had been done, so an exhausted Norman commander could himself lie down and close his eyes.

'Rider approaching.'

The dawn had come up with no sign of movement, yet William knew that the catapan had halted on the other side of the opposite hill and made camp, where smoke from the mass of cooking fires drifted lazily into the morning sky, and that could only be because he knew he had failed in his initial aim. The question remained, however, as to what he would do next, and the sight of the lone horseman approaching was, in part, likely to provide some kind of answer.

'No armour,' said Drogo, 'but handsome silks.'

That was plain to all the de Hautevilles, lined up alongside William, helmets on, swords out and stuck in the ground before them, shields on their arm, the purpose to look as warlike as possible. It was certainly in contrast to this gaudily clad messenger, a slim fellow of medium height in splendid blue garments of varying hues, with long black hair, and eyes over a slightly hooked nose, a feature which he looked down with disdain as he reined in his mount and spoke.

'I seek the leader of your band,' he said in Greek.

'Do you speak Latin?' asked William. When the envoy nodded, it was requested he speak in that language: the two older de Hautevilles had some Greek, but the recent arrivals had none. The request was repeated.

'He should dismount,' growled Humphrey, his face plainly angry even if little of it was visible. 'It shows a lack of respect to address us from the back of his horse.'

'I think the quantity of lances you see before you elevates us above a band.'

'It does not exalt you enough to explain your presence in a Byzantine province.'

'Which would matter if we felt the need to explain.'

'Get off that horse, damn you,' Humphrey barked, an outburst which clearly amused the rider, who smiled disdainfully.

'To do so would be to imply that as the representative of the catapan, Michael Doukeianos, I am willing to treat with you as equals.' That was followed by a snort and a snapped addition. 'Which I am not.'

'And neither, I suppose, is the catapan?'

'Most certainly not.'

'Probably too frightened to come himself,' scoffed Drogo.

'You have a message,' William said, 'deliver it.'

'To you?'

'To me, William de Hauteville, the leader of the Normans in Apulia.'

'The catapan has been informed that you have illegally occupied his great castle at Melfi.'

'He has good ears,' said Drogo. 'Or many spies.'

'You are also at large in the domains for which he is responsible, which he takes as an act of war—'

'Then he is blessed with wisdom,' William interrupted. 'For that is what it is.'

The messenger carried on as if William had not spoken. 'You are required to depart these lands forthwith on pain of the most severe punishments.'

'And if we refuse to go?'

The head went back slightly, as though the horseman had something untoward beneath his nose, and it was almost with a sneer he continued. 'The catapan has good reason to believe you have been promised much in the way of reward for your illicit incursion, and he is conscious of the fact that you are mercenary warriors. In the spirit of Byzantium, which is known to be generous, he is prepared to pay to you, in gold, a sum sufficient to make up for what you feel you might lose, as long as you depart.'

'But that would mean Michael Doukeianos knows what it is we want.'

'What else but money?' the envoy sniggered, his dark eyes narrowing. 'What else do you Normans ever want?'

'Respect!' Humphrey yelled, stepping forward till he was right in front of the horse's nose. 'Enough to get off your damned horse and speak to us as equals.'

'That would fly in the face of God's purpose.'

William was about to point out, in a calm way, that insulting the men before him was not the job of an envoy and would hardly aid his task. He never got the chance. Humphrey's mailed fist took the horse right between the eyes in a mighty blow that so stunned the animal it immediately dropped to the ground, poleaxed, taking the sniggering messenger with it. It was only by great good fortune that the fellow avoided one of his legs being trapped beneath it and crushed.

Throwing himself clear he hit the ground with a thud, and as he scrambled away from his unconscious horse, Humphrey grabbed him by the front of his silks and hauled him to his feet, pushing his nose guard right up against the fellow's face.

'Now you are where you belong. Learn, pig, never talk down to a Norman.'

When Humphrey let the fellow go, he nearly collapsed, so shaken was he by what had just occurred. The arrogant look had gone from his face to be replaced with one of complete shock. His mount was out cold, two stiff legs in the air, while it was clear the rider's own pins were visibly trembling.

'Hold him up, someone,' said William. Mauger and Geoffrey stepped forward to stop him tumbling in a heap. 'Now, you will go back to your master on a horse we will provide and tell him this. The way to Melfi is barred, and will stay barred by us. If he wishes to go there he must go through we Normans, which is not something that can be done without much bloodshed, and most of that will fall upon the men he has led here. Tell him to keep his bribe, for we do not want gold we can take at will in the future. He is free to withdraw to the coast and stay there, for this part of Apulia is no longer a fiefdom to Constantinople, it is Lombard. Is the message clear?'

The still-shaken envoy nodded.

'Humphrey, fetch the poor fellow another horse.'

'I'd make him walk, brother.'

William grinned. 'Let us show Byzantium a courtesy they scarcely showed us.'

When the horse was brought forward, the fellow had to be helped to mount. Turning its head, Humphrey slapped it on the rump to get it going; the man on its back was still too much in a state of shock to get it moving himself.

'Why did you punch the horse?' Drogo rasped, clearly unhappy.

'Because I'm not sentimental about them, like you.'

That was an argument the brothers de Hauteville had not heard for an age, but one they had heard too often, for it was a subject on which these two had clashed many times at home. Humphrey had no time for horses; he needed them, yes, and he trained them to do as they were bidden, but affection for them was beyond him. Drogo was the opposite: he had an affinity with equines of all kinds down to the most stubborn donkey. The only thing he loved more than horseflesh was women, the difference being the former never got him into trouble, the latter always did.

'I hope the bugger comes round and kicks you in the head.'

Humphrey spat on the recumbent animal, which had at least opened its eyes. 'If it does I'll fetch you the same clout I gave him.'

Drogo moved forward, shoulder hunched and threatening. 'You and who else...?'

'Enough!' William barked, his hand pointing to the smoke still rising into the sky. 'We have enough fighting on our hands over there.'

'Are we going to fight?' asked Mauger.

'Let us say, brother, we are not going to withdraw. So whether we fight or not is up to the catapan.'

If the message returned by his envoy was not delivered with clarity, there was no doubting the sentiment, and it presented Michael Doukeianos with a real dilemma. What he had with him was not a force any general would choose to take into battle: few, if any of those he led, had served before and they were not suffused with enthusiasm. The rest were new levies, but to withdraw was impossible.

Even if he had known his enemies had possession of Venosa and Lavello, it would not have changed his dispositions: that was an action he would have undertaken had he been in the place of the Normans. Such thinking had been built into his plan to outflank them, to get between them and the fortress. It was Melfi he was after, yet without surprise or a properly trained army, taking it would be near impossible.

As he paced his tent, watched by the captains he had fetched with him – none of them with much experience – he was aware he had to act, yet he suspected outright victory to be beyond his grasp. Up against mounted men, if he prevailed, and he thought he could do that – he outnumbered them by ten men to one – he could not inflict on them the kind of defeat that would force them out of his territory.

It was more likely they would see he was too strong and retire slowly before his advance, taunting him for his inability to pursue at sufficient pace to crush them, drawing him towards Melfi while inflicting the kind of losses on his army that would make it too weak to invest the place. That would leave him at the mercy of a combined Lombard-Norman force, far from safety and short on supplies.

The proper military course of action, now that surprise was gone, was to withdraw to the coast, send out his conscripting parties, set up training for those recruited and those to come in, build an army too formidable for his enemies to withstand, then begin a proper campaign to take back territory piecemeal. Never mind that the Lombards would join the Normans: Byzantium had beaten them too many times in the past to fear them. The Normans would stay in Melfi only as long as they were paid; the trick was to isolate them so that such rewards would be cut off.

Just as he knew that was prudent, he also knew it was impossible: those very Normans were in front of him now and they needed to be overcome, given the reputation for near invincibility which preceded them. The morale of his own host was a major consideration but there were others. To retire before some kind of success had been achieved would lead to a loss of face too great to stomach and it would not go down well at an Imperial Court where he would already be in bad odour.

The solution came to him in time, a tactic that would preserve his reputation, keep up the spirits of his men, without risking any serious loss in their numbers.

'Prepare your levies. We attack immediately.'

'Dawn would be better, Catapan, with the sun behind us to blind the enemy.'

'And let them get away?'

Doukeianos said those words with a jeer, just before he proceeded to outline a plan of attack that would bring about that very thing. Once he had chased the Normans from their positions he could safely say he had achieved all that was possible on this field of battle, that being mounted they were too fleet to pursue. What followed on from that would depend on many factors, but he could rightfully claim to lack the resources to carry on and besiege Melfi.

Watching from the high ground overlooking the Byzantine encampment, with his men mounted, lined up and ready, the shoe of what course to follow was now on the other foot. Prior to assembling they had knelt to pray, with William again deliberating, in between his devotions, on his lack of a priest from home. In Normandy, where clerics bore arms and fought alongside their flock, there would have been someone to bless the men and confess them, then go into battle by their side, ready to deliver the last rites to any who fell: no good son of the Holy Church wanted to go into battle and face death with sins unforgiven.

It looked uncomfortably as if that was about to happen. Even if his men were the best fighters in Christendom, to engage with the odds in numbers so massively against them hinted at folly, and it flew in the face of William's original hopes: he had expected the catapan to do the sensible thing and withdraw, but there was no mistaking what he was observing, a host moving forward to engage in battle.

He could also see what Michael Doukeianos was going to attempt to do: by spreading his forces out to cover a broad front he was planning to envelop the numerically inferior Normans. If they stood to fight in a central position on their high ground they would be bypassed on both flanks, anathema to cavalry; if they sought to engage one flank, the other would wheel to take them in the rear. It was a very simple manoeuvre, which suited the forces the catapan had at his disposal. Sense dictated, in the face of such a tactic, the Normans retire.

Yet William could also see that, even with an uncomplicated design, the men in command were having trouble in arranging their levies in anything approaching reasonable order. As they advanced their line must be solid: if one body of men got out of step with another they would create a gap and that would be dangerous for those who had stepped out too forcibly. Could he bring about such a thing?

It was an axiom drummed into William from his earliest days to do that which your opponent least expected, whether in single combat, a small group action, or now on a proper field of battle. He also had one priceless asset: the men he was facing, from Michael Doukeianos down, even if they had faced cavalry, had never fought men like him before. The very least the catapan could hope for was that the Normans would wait till he came upon them to decide their course of action: engage or retire.

What he would least expect would be a Norman assault which would expose the fact that Michael Doukeianos had committed another blunder: he was bringing forward slow and inexperienced foot soldiers to fight men who had an inherent discipline, the ability to manoeuvre, as well as the speed to do so quickly without losing cohesion. Could William force him to compound such an error?

That speed was quickly evident: no sooner had William appraised his brothers of what he wanted to do than they were moving their conroys to execute the first part of his scheme. Fanning out to confront as much of the enemy host as they could they would appear to be spread too thin. Instead of a tight line there was a large gap between each rider, a perfect opportunity for foot soldiers, once the lines clashed, to surround each individual horseman and bring him down.

As soon as William was satisfied they had deployed as he wished he gave the order to sound the horn, dipped the blue and white de Hauteville banner, which was the standard of command, and set off the advance. It was done at a walk first, coming off their high ground and onto the flat valley below, then, at the sound of another blast, the Normans broke into a trot. William de Hauteville's banner was the only one held aloft; those of his brothers were dipped.

Faced with this unexpected action, and sensing an opportunity, Michael Doukeianos reacted immediately. He could see before him exactly what William wanted him to see: a cavalry force weakened by its deployment, a chance to annihilate these Normans, not by seeking to envelop them, but by closing up his front to present and overcome them with overwhelming superiority. His horns were sounding, messengers were riding to the individual captains telling them what their general wanted, and soon the outer contingents began to trend inwards.

William, in the centre of his line, was watching that manoeuvre carefully, looking for the least sign of confusion. All it took was one eager captain to urge on his men with too much zeal and it would happen, but where in his line would it take place? There was a chance, of course, it would not, in which case the horn would sound and his banner would wave to order his men to retreat.

The Byzantine levies were holding their discipline better than he expected, though with much beating of men with swords to keep them from rushing ahead. William suspected what men he had who had fought in a battle before had been put out front to aid their captains in setting the pace, a shrewd move, and it looked as if the Normans were about to be faced, in extended and vulnerable order, with a wall of pikes, behind them eager men with knives ready to come through the front line to slash at horse and rider.

But they could not hold their discipline, even on a field of battle unbroken by gullies or rocks. Gaps began to appear, the greatest opening up before the men led by Drogo, and William knew that he would see it. He dropped his banner and held his breath until Drogo raised his. That was the signal, and breaking into an immediate canter the Norman line began to close, concentrating around Drogo's *battaile*. Their opponent was no fool: Doukeianos could see what was happening and William suspected it was he who rode forward hard to try to close that gap by halting his troops.

With trained men he might have achieved it, but the actual result was greater confusion, with some men stopping completely while others came on. It was they, partially isolated, who now faced a solid line of Norman lances, and one that would lap round their sides when they met. Compounding what had already gone awry, the captain who led them saw his salvation in an aggressive charge, completely ignoring the horns his general had furiously blown ordering him to halt and retire.

Drogo's banner was now central and the Byzantines were faced with a solid line of Norman lances. There was no escape, though many tried, making matters worse as the Normans got between them stabbing and, when a lance was lost, slashing with their broadswords. Inevitably these untrained *milities* broke and sought to run, in doing so getting in among those to their rear who still held some kind of cohesion, setting off a general panic as each body of men saw themselves in danger from these ferocious horsemen.

Soon the field was full of running men, being pursued by a wall of horseflesh and riders that took a weapon to any flesh that came within their reach. Michael Doukeianos was fleeing too: there was no point in standing still to die a glorious death. Those captains who had not perished had surrounded him and were acting as a shield, and in doing so they had left the men they led to their own fate.

It was foolish to try to surrender, though many made the attempt. A small host facing a massively larger one cannot take prisoners, and in any case these were worthless creatures, not rich men who would command a ransom. Wise heads lay down and pretended to be dead, the imprudent pleaded for mercy and died with their plea on their lips, many of them ridden down and trampled by hooves as well as cut with swords.

Soon the field was clear of fighters, the whole Byzantine host broken and in flight, even those contingents that had not faced battle. William de Hauteville, his arms soaked with victim blood, called a halt to the pursuit when the point of any further havoc had passed. Now he was in among braying donkeys and mules, animals abandoned by the sutlers who had brought them here, they running alongside what women had trailed the host from Barletta.

It was Mauger who found the pack animals that mattered: the beasts which had on their flanks the heavy brass-bound coffers of the catapan, full of the gold with which he had offered to bribe them.

'Find out where we are, someone,' William cried. 'This victory must have a name.'

There were a couple of settlements called Moschella close enough by to provide that.

# CHAPTER ELEVEN

∞◇∞

Arduin was cock-a-hoop when he heard of William's triumph, though that was tempered by his not having been present to lead the fight in person. Ensconced once more in the great hall of the castle at Melfi, his crows of triumph echoed off the walls.

'Never fear,' said William, seeking to bring him back to reality – he was behaving as if the end result of his insurrection was a foregone conclusion: that his enemies would be driven out of Apulia by what had just occurred. 'You will get your opportunity. Byzantium won't give up after one reverse, and I will wager it will be harder to beat them next time. The catapan has learnt about the risks of fighting we Normans.'

Those dark Lombard eyes were alight as he replied. 'They will face a proper army, William, not just you.'

There was some truth in that, for Arduin had been busy: Melfi was already surrounded by encampments full of Lombard volunteers, and more were arriving each day, from Benevento and even parts of Campania, where Prince Guaimar had placed no restrictions on his subjects travelling individually to enlist – not that he would have been attended to if he had. If William had ever doubted the strength of that Lombard dream he had good evidence of it now: they had not seen Byzantium soundly beaten in Southern Italy in decades.

Norman lances came in too, some from Normandy in ones and twos; others were mercenaries who had been in Italy for years, come to swell the ranks of his cavalry, not yet in a flood, but enough to encourage William to believe that more would follow. Non-fighting supporters had come too: farriers to shoe horses and blacksmiths to forge weapons and shape helmets, while men with the right eye for a pikestaff combed the surrounding forests for suitable timber.

There were leather workers and cloth weavers, saddlers and harness makers, cobblers to produce footwear, vivandiers and bakers, along with their women, who would cook and sustain their fighting menfolk on the march. A steady stream of supplies was being brought in by mule and on human backs and, most vital of all, Arduin had found a troop of crossbowmen, not as many as would be needed, but enough to train up more when weapons became available.

A message of congratulations had also come from Salerno, but – and this William held to be strange – it was a verbal one delivered by a messenger employed by Kasa Ephraim. It was also noticeable that whatever Lombard volunteers had come in from Campania few of them, so far, were from that city and its immediate surroundings, where Prince Guaimar's inclination to stand aside would be better known and, besides that, they would have been recently engaged in the taking of Amalfi...

The Jew proved as shrewd as ever: as soon as news of Masseria reached Salerno, he reasoned there might be business to transact with the victorious Normans, who needed someone to keep safe their funds, and also to facilitate any transfer of their plunder home to their relatives in Normandy. The message that was returned to him was that it would profit him to journey personally to Melfi where there was already Byzantine gold, and likely to be more to follow.

Sending money home was an arrangement he had provided for years to the likes of Rainulf Drengot. William and Drogo had used his services before. How he did it over such distances, at the constant threat of banditry, was a mystery, and one he was determined to keep to himself, but the funds to bring south their brothers, as well as the coin needed to finance the construction of their father's stone donjon, still waiting to be built, had been safely commuted back home by Ephraim, who made substantial fees from the transactions.

Those brothers were not present now. Apart from a garrison to man the walls of Melfi the Normans were out doing that at which they were best: raiding Byzantine territory south of Barletta, taking towns and tribute if they would submit, ravaging the countryside around those places that held out – few of those, since the catapan was too busy training his newly raised levies to interfere. With word spread throughout the province, not only of the recent victory, but the fact that the Normans were raiding at will, Lombards were trickling in from the port cities as well, which provided William and Arduin with good intelligence.

It was from that source they heard of the methods of Byzantine conscription – many had fled from the threat of that – an imposition made more harsh by necessity. No one able-bodied was spared: the whole of Apulia down to Otranto, as well as Eastern Calabria, was being scoured for men. Even if they were unwilling to serve they were being dragged in to make up a host big enough to prevail, and the training was as callous as the recruitment. Even forced to serve, they would be better drilled the next time Michael Doukeianos faced the Normans and, to stiffen them, he also had trained reinforcements, a body of Varangians recently arrived from Constantinople.

That news was enough to give William pause: he had fought alongside the Varangians in Sicily and he knew how formidable they were. They were of the same stock as the Normans, men from the Viking heartlands who had gone east into the great wilderness rather than south to the land of the Franks and beyond, using the rivers and lakes instead of the sea to penetrate deep, finally setting up a rich and fruitful kingdom on a great river that flowed all the way to the Euxine Sea and, across that great body of water, to Constantinople.

The men sent to Apulia would be uniformly huge, of a size to match any de Hauteville, and flaxen of hair and moustache. The other quality they had was steadiness in battle: they stood their ground regardless of odds and would rather die than retreat. It was they who had killed off the flame of the last Lombard revolt, and the last thing William de Hauteville wanted to do was to face such men with inexperienced levies, however fired up they were by their visions. Time to dampen his general's enthusiasm.

'The men you have recruited will be a proper army when they are skilled at war, Arduin. I think our encounter with the catapan proves that men who are not tend to be a liability, and they cannot stand against Varangian axes. In truth, right now, only we Normans have any hope of countering them.'

The frown that produced came and went in a flash: now that he had a steady stream of volunteers, now that he felt like a proper general in command of a proper army, Arduin did not like to be reminded of how much he depended on Norman support. William saw it come and go and knew the reason; he suspected if he thought he could beat Byzantium without them Arduin would seek to send them back to Aversa, but he could not, so it did not signify.

'We also move your levies away from Melfi. The countryside around here cannot support them.'

'It can.'

'Not without reducing the locals to starvation.'

'Let them starve; what we have to do matters more than a few famished Italian peasants.'

And they wonder why, William thought, they are not loved, these Lombards. The other thought was the need to give Arduin a pressing reason to fall in with the suggestion he had just made: he would not be coerced into doing the right thing.

'The country around here is not suitable for training large bodies. Besides, more and more recruits are coming in from the land to the east. It would be best, and might increase the numbers, if we were to go towards them rather than have them come all the way to us. Let us gather in one place, Normans and Lombards.'

'You want to stop your brothers?'

There was calculation in that too: the de Hautevilles were sending back to Melfi the contents of the coffers from the towns they were taking, and part of that was going to the man in command – Arduin's little strongbox was filling up as much as was that of the Normans, a reminder that he was not only in this campaign for a dream.

'I want to go to where they are operating and destroying crops and livestock. If we are going to feed our host let's do it with produce from the fields of the Catapanate, not those we possess. Let us make our base at Canosa, not here.'

'We do not have possession of Canosa.'

'Faced with our entire force under its walls and no sign of help, I suspect it will capitulate.'

'And if he attacks us there?'

'Let him break his strength on its fortifications, let him lose men, then let him have the place.'

'Surrender?'

'Draw him on Arduin. If we fully exploit Canosa we will leave him nothing in the way of supplies, and nothing in the way of men either. He will then pursue us to a place of our choosing.'

'I have been mulling over some other plans.'

'And so you should,' William replied, sounding emollient, even if he was unsure he was hearing the truth. 'All I ask is you think on it.'

Pride meant Arduin would not move immediately; indeed he did not do so until the proposed leader of the Lombard revolt, Count Atenulf, arrived. The brother of Landulf, the Prince of Benevento, he was a rather dense young man of no discernible personality and he was certainly no military leader: asked for an opinion on tactics all he produced was a vacuous look and no suggestions. Arduin showed no disappointment, for he was perfect: properly patrician but utterly stupid and malleable.

'I have decided that we must move closer to our enemies, and let them know that we intend to do battle with them. I hope you agree, Count Atenulf?' The pause was long, the eyes opaque, if not actually confused, and it was a while before the youngster nodded. 'Good. We will move two days from now down the Ofanto towards Barletta. We will also examine the possibility of investing Canosa.'

William got no mention for having suggested this course of action, not that he cared. The vanity of other men when it came to making the right decisions was something with which he could easily live.

The wards that William had taken on looked very different from the day he had brought them to the castle, and in the case of the boy the change was more than just the fact that he was clean and had been properly fed for enough time to put flesh on his ribs. When his sister was not looking he had even smiled at their saviour, unlike her: she had a face like a mastiff sucking a wasp and no words of William's interpreter, however soft and kindly they sounded before translation, seemed to dent that. Even if she showed signs of some physical charm, albeit as yet undeveloped, her steady, unremitting and hate-filled glare took away any hint of good looks.

They had names too: she was called Tirena and he answered to Listo, and William was sure they understood more of what he was saying now than they had previously, for instruction in Latin had been part of that which had been provided. Instead of being angered by her intransigence, he admired her spirit, and wondered if it was a common trait in these mountainous regions of Italy, hoping that such a thing might be the case.

The reason was straightforward enough: if his long-term aim was to acquire land and possessions here, he would need to understand the nature of the people. That they, both in the mountains and on the plains, hated Lombards, he knew – every Italian native did – just as he knew why. Wherever they had exercised power, they had done so to serve themselves. But they detested Byzantium too: it was distant and cared only for what it could extract in terms of taxes paid in produce and livestock, this gathered by rapacious collectors who bought the right of assessment, then lined their pockets with excessive demands. His brothers, in their forays, had captured and strung up to the nearest tree a couple of these tax farmers, to the delight of the locals who had witnessed their death throes.

Perhaps the people of Apulia would submit to better rule, laws properly applied and the payment of revenues that did not drive them to starvation, and especially a lordship personal and closely present. The other thing William knew was that, to sustain himself and his house, a reliance on Norman lances, on a steady stream of men coming south, was an unsound policy. Just as now, in league with the Lombards, an army needed foot soldiers. They had to be raised here and perhaps, in time, they could be mounted and taught the same kind of discipline that made the Normans so formidable.

As well as the interpreter, the woman who had been given charge of the pair was present too, a homely creature as broad as she was high, with a face and arms to match, the former red and full, as befitted one who worked in the castle kitchens, the latter more akin to a horseman's thigh than a female jambe. That she had stopped the girl spitting at him was to be lauded, that they were clean too, but her abilities were limited to such cares, while William was wondering how far he could take this.

'You will need to be lettered and numerate,' he said,

quietly pleased that the confusion those two unknown words caused, when translated, at least removed the glare for a second. 'I will employ a monk for the purpose.'

That made the girl Tirena spit again: even folk of shepherd stock knew monks, and knew that too often they were ignorant layabouts who used their supposed piety to leech off those who toiled for sustenance.

'You are nothing but a burden now. I would want you of some use.' He looked at the boy. 'And you will work with my soldiers, Listo, learning to clean and maintain harness and weapons. Perhaps, if the reports of your progress are good, you will be taught to ride.'

The look of delight those words produced lasted only as long as it took the boy's sister to snap at him. Turning to her, William thought it might be better to teach Tirena to be a fighter, given she had all the attributes of an Amazon.

'You, girl, only the good Lord knows what I will do with you. I would give you needles with which you could learn to sew, but I suspect they would end up in human flesh, and mine own if I gave you a chance.'

The departure from Melfi was attended by great ceremony, something of which William heartily approved, being good for morale, even if the man to whom the levies aimed their cheers as they passed left something to be desired. Even sat on his horse behind

Atenulf, at the base of the causeway that led to the castle, he was unimpressed: these levies raising their pikes, swords and axes needed to be inspired; the limp hand Atenulf waved in response made William wonder if he had any red blood in his veins to go with the blue.

Once the last foot soldiers had passed, Count Atenulf set off, in the company of Arduin and William, to make their way to the front of the league-long column, to get out of the cloud of dust these levies kicked up. As he kicked his mount into motion, William took a last look at the ramparts of Melfi, and he was sure, before the head disappeared, that he had caught sight of Tirena peering over and that pleased him.

The sickness came upon William within two days, a sort of lassitude allied to vomiting, which laid him low and confined him to a cot when camped and a litter when they moved. Thankfully Drogo had rejoined, followed by the other de Hautevilles, and they could ensure that the right ideas were being promoted. Training was being undertaken on the move, in the morning before the sun became too hot; the men rested till it cooled in the afternoon, when they would move a couple of leagues to a new campsite, slow progress to their eventual goal, but necessary.

'They're an argumentative lot, these Lombards,' said Drogo, talking while a woman, one of the numerous camp followers, spoon-fed his brother with a potage, the patient reluctant to take more than a couple of mouthfuls. 'No wonder they never win. Anyone gives an order and it's the cause of an immediate quarrel.'

'Will they be ready if we meet the catapan?'

'They will not be a useless mob, but ready is another thing.'

'We've got to keep them away from the Varangians.'

'You can keep me away from them too,' Drogo replied, standing to leave, and pinching the woman's ample arse as he did so. 'I have nightmares about those axes.'

It took over ten days to get within striking distance of Canosa – the host had hogged the Ofanto, living off its supply of water and the fertility of the fields that bordered it – with William still too weak to partake of any duties, and it was with some misgiving he learnt that Arduin had decided to bypass the town and move on towards Barletta: a place, one of the important great ports, the catapan would have to defend.

Much as he disputed the notion he made no attempt to interfere, and it was not from his own ill health: there was no point in having a general then not following his lead, and the whole notion of coming from Melfi was to find the Byzantine army and defeat it for a second time. For that the plains around Barletta were as good a place as any.

* * *

'That, William,' said Arduin, sweeping an all-encompassing arm over the plain spread below, 'is the field of Cannae.'

Weak as he was, William rose from his litter to gaze over one of the most famous battle sites in history, the field where the Carthagian general, Hannibal, annihilated two Roman legions.

'God willing, this is where I want to do battle with them, the place stained with my father's own blood.'

Helped by Mauger, William, worried that Arduin was allowing sentiment to interfere with sound judgement, moved to look around and he could see, from the commanding mound on which they stood, why the field had been fought over more than once. The hill overlooked an extensive flat plain running all the way to the coast, perfect for an army to deploy and also a place giving a good view of the landscape for leagues around. No enemy could approach by stealth, or organise an attack without all their dispositions being obvious. Below, and to the north and west, ran the River Ofanto, providing ample water for an encamped army – vital, since it was now high summer – as well as a supply route for food and fodder.

'I have made sure the catapan knows this is where we are camped and of my intention to advance on Barletta if left to do so.'

'The Normans were chased from the field too, Arduin,' said William, his voice rasping and weak.

'Rainulf's brother Gilbert died here along with a third of the lances he led. It is the only time we have ever been bested in Italy.'

'Then it is a ghost you too have to lay, William.'

They knew Michael Doukeianos was coming as soon as he broke camp. Resting still, though feeling somewhat stronger, William lay in his raised litter at the front of the tent set up to accommodate him. He could watch the battle unfold in the company of those men, some Normans included, who had been left to guard the baggage train, free of mail, warmed by the sun and calling for refreshment while he did so. Truly this was a better way to soldier than to always be at the forefront of the fight.

The Norman-Lombard forces were in place on the gentle lower slopes; it was the catapan who must march to this place and deploy to meet them, which was carried out in what looked like better order than he had managed at Masseria, with the Varangians, very obvious even at a distance, in his centre, the less well-trained levies on each side. Arduin had split and placed the Norman cavalry on the flanks, both to protect the foot soldiers from envelopment and to be there to exploit any weaknesses, and, William suspected, to see first if his Lombards could win without their aid. The crossbowmen stood to the rear, ready to be used wherever they were needed.

These dispositions were not something of which he disapproved; despite Arduin's hopes this would no more be the last battle than Masseria. Byzantium still held the great port cities and most of Apulia and they still commanded the loyalty, albeit by force, of the majority of the Italian and Greek population. If the Lombards could win this fight without Norman help it would raise their spirits; what they could not do, in his estimation, however high their morale might be, was chase their enemies out of Italy.

The surprise, when Arduin ordered the advance, had him standing upright, because that was precisely the wrong thing to do. What the Lombard-Norman host needed was a defensive battle. They held the higher ground, so they should force the Byzantines to attack them, harder uphill than on the flat. The only way to even partially unsettle those Varangians was to force them into the attack, hoping that movement would disorder their ranks: to assault them was to play to their strengths. They would face any attacking force, on foot or mounted, and cut them to pieces with those great axes.

The feeling of hopelessness was allied to William's feelings of physical weakness, and that was compounded by the sight of the front line of the attack growing ragged almost before it had covered a third of the intervening ground. Meanwhile his brothers, Drogo and Geoffrey on the right, and Humphrey and Mauger on the left, had begun to move their lances forward as flank protection, and at the same pace as the marching men, a total negation of their innate abilities. Nothing happened quickly: it was like watching a waking dream unfold, or, if anticipation was added, a potential nightmare.

'Fetch my mail,' he shouted, 'and saddle my horse.'

There was a moment when that order so astounded those who heard it, no one moved, but the subsequent roar from William had people running to obey. Moving with difficulty, he got closer to the small party of Normans guarding the baggage and the temporary paddocks where the mules, donkeys and spare Norman mounts were corralled.

'You, go to Drogo and tell him, whatever his orders are, to attack the Byzantine *milities*.' Turning to another he sent him with the same instruction to Humphrey. 'And tell them to stay away from the Varangians.'

He had to be helped into his mail, all the time watching the Lombards close in on the catapan's centre, thinking that Michael Doukeianos must be relishing what was to come – a half-trained army taking on the very best fighters he had – and he would be right to be so. It would be an assault that, if it was to continue, would have to be over the dead bodies of the very front line. They would then be taken in flank by their opposite numbers.

His horse was beside him, stamping and restless, having a nose for impending battle, perhaps, or just unsettled by the way it had been so hastily prepared, and it was evidence of his continued weakness that helping hands were needed to get him mounted. Spurring hard, he rode forward to where the crossbowmen stood waiting, shouting an order for them to follow him at a run, and as he did that he heard the horns of his own men, and much higher still than the host he saw Drogo lead his lances into a trot.

'That, Catapan, will make you think!'

Which he did: the front line of his levies knelt down and pushed lower their pikes, creating a frieze of points no cavalry could ride into without becoming impaled, the same happening on the left as Humphrey and Mauger advanced. Arduin, moving forward behind his advancing lines, had turned to see William riding down upon him, what could be seen of his face under his helmet suffused with rage. Iron Arm ignored him, his voice like a blasting trumpet as he yelled for the rear ranks to open and let him through. There was no time for a conference, no time to tell Arduin of his error: the Lombards had sacrificed the high ground and they must be halted.

Men fell before his horse as he forced his way into the mass of bodies, using the flat of his sword blade to create a path through which the crossbowmen could follow him, until finally he was at the fore, no more than lance-throwing distance from the blond giants who faced him, the sun flashing on newly polished helmets, their raised axe heads, and the gleaming bosses at the centre of their round bucklers.

'Crossbows, in a line. Aim for their lower legs. When they drop their shields, aim for the eyes. When they lift them to protect their heads, aim for their thighs.'

Once the first bolts were released, and had struck exposed shins, William turned and ordered the front Lombard rank to kneel, another behind them to lace their pikes through that first line, another to stand and present their pikes over their compatriots' heads. There were men carrying spears, and once that solid line was formed they could aim those over the heads of their front with impunity.

That which he had ordered the crossbowmen to do was being executed, which was an appropriate word, as bolts thudded into any part the Varangians exposed. William knew they would not stand and suffer, just as he knew that he and those crossbowmen were between those soon-to-be advancing axes and an impenetrable mass of pikes. But he also guessed that a horn would order the advance, and as soon as that sounded he bellowed for those bowmen to run, hauling round his mount and heading for Drogo's now engaged lances.

The catapan had only seen the Norman tactics at Masseria: here he was faced with a completely different set of problems, as the riders stood off from the pikes and shield wall, and the lances were used at full extent to jab at the men holding them, while swords were employed to cut off the deadly points, thus reducing their deterrent effect. Goaded, they sought to retaliate, opening gaps between shields into which those same lances were cast with deadly effect, that followed by a double horn blast, which had the men who had loosed them ride away from danger in a disciplined group, to be immediately replaced by a fresh line of Norman horsemen, who employed similar tactics.

Cohesion in defence was paramount and the Byzantine levies could not maintain it. Once it failed they were doomed, and now they faced, in their disorder, a solid line of mounted warriors coming at them at a fast canter with lances ready to impale them. And if they did not know of William Iron Arm they saw him, a towering figure bawling instructions and slashing at heads with a huge sword.

When they broke, they did so completely. The same soon happened on the left flank, and that left those mighty and fearsome Varangians trying to attack a solid line of pikes. Even as they lopped the points off the defenders' weapons, taking human heads next, they found Norman lances pressing in on both sides in a way, given they were committed to a frontal battle, that could only have one outcome. Brave as ever, they died where they stood, as those who had come with them to ancient Cannae fled the field.

William was near to dropping off his horse when he approached the titular commander of this victorious host, a man bound to be unhappy, not about the outcome, but by the way it had come about. It did not help that the entire army was yelling *'Bras de Fer!'* in praise of the man to whom they accounted their victory.

Iron Arm gave him an old Roman salute, arm across his chest, and managed to imbue the words he used with significance. 'Arduin of Fassano, you have avenged the blood of your father. It is time to take Barletta.'

# CHAPTER TWELVE

⊃⊂◇⊃⊂

The long ride to the south was a solitary one for Robert de Hauteville, and he had learnt, as had his brothers before him, that those on the route to Italy recognised a Norman when they saw one, and given he was more blessed than most with the physical attributes of his race – the height, girth and that golden Viking hair – and his warrior accoutrements were highly visible, he found that his company was rarely sought, that being especially the case in any settlement which stood on a navigable river. These were populated by folk who chastised their children with threats of the evil Norsemen who had, albeit not in living memory, sailed up those same rivers in their longboats to pillage and burn.

Nor were matters always eased in the countryside:

a giant with lance and sword brought back too many memories to small communities, and in some cases very recent ones, of roving bands, armed and unemployed fighting men, whose only means of existence without war was to rob and defile the weak in any period of peace. To ride into many a hamlet was to find it deserted, the inhabitants taken to the nearest woods until he had passed.

When the occasion demanded he traded to eat, Robert would merely dismount and wait. Peasants and farmers, seeing he was alone, would come out eventually, tightly grouped for mutual protection and carrying various weapons, though they would keep their wives and daughters hidden, to cautiously approach this seeming Goliath. It was a testament to Robert's winning ways that, even bereft of a shared language, he could make friends and gain trust given time. Countless nights were spent round blazing fires in laughter and japes brought on by whatever spirit these yokels concocted to ease the drudge of their lives.

Whenever he could, he sought shelter in monasteries: they, lying as they did on pilgrim routes, had a Christian duty of hospice accommodation, and none would turn him away, but there was rarely joy in their charity. If there was a group of humans who hated and feared the race from which the Normans had sprung, it was the religious one, for their churches and abbeys had always been the first places to be plundered, quite simply because they were the richest in treasure.

Truly pious monks, proper heirs to the monastic founders, were a rarity, and where they existed were much loved by the laity; most were far from devout, inclined to use promises of salvation as an excuse for rapacious exploitation. The hypocrisy of living a life of comfort and ease, of consuming good food and wine, interspersed with endless prayer, not to mention a degree of carnal predation, all provided on the back of serf labour, this while preaching the Saviour's message of poverty and humility, escaped them in the main.

The landscape changed, turning from green to brown, the smell changing from damp grass to burnt earth, the roofs from thatch to red tiles, the bastions and watchtowers from dank, rain-soaked grey to near white. In the high-perched castles, with stout walls, citadels that oversaw every route by which a great fief might be vulnerable to an invading army, he was welcomed by men of his own stamp: knights in service or the lords to whom they were attached, for there was a universal bond between warriors. Men who might themselves travel to fight or serve had an affinity with a lone confrère.

This was where Robert was most at ease, among men of his own stamp, who saw that the blade of his sword had been marked by others while his helmet had dents, and were eager to hear tales of how these marks of conflict had been gained. If he was privileged to dine with the lords of these castles, they were eager to hear of the customs of other courts, and given he had conversed with both the Duke of Normandy and the King of the Franks, it was easy to impress these men, and their chatelaines, with tales of regal magnificence.

Temptation for a vigorous young man was ever present: most monasteries-cum-hospices had a nunnery, if not attached, then close by, places where few of the inmates were truly there as brides of Christ. Most women were in such places against their inclination and in many cases in spite of their expressed will, confined by relatives for perceived or real offences, but more often for mere disobedience: a refusal to marry a designated spouse, a defiance of parents, an unwed pregnancy, a wife put aside, or widowhood which might lead to temptation, that too many times attached to a threatened inheritance.

That chastity was not their paramount concern was hardly surprising; that a hearty young giant was often indulged not at all startling. The monks who saw these nunneries and the females they contained, some of tender years, as their personal preserve, took umbrage. Such a thing was to be expected; that they never challenged a man like Robert de Hauteville showed that if they lacked the tenets of their faith, they were not in want of good sense, for he was not one who feared to box the ears of an ecclesiastic.

For a young man who had only very occasionally left the Contentin, travelling south was an education and Robert drank in everything he saw and heard. Monkish misconduct he had known about since he ceased to be an impressionable youth; peasant exploitation he had seen too often close to home, which contrasted with the care Tancred extended to his tenants and villeins, drumming into his boys that if they had arms, equipment and the right to bear them, it could only be sustained on the back of the willing labour of others.

Yet the depth of some of what he saw shocked him: great monastic and dynastic wealth surrounded by the near starvation of those who toiled to keep their masters in luxury; the barons of those great castles who, in their cups, would curse the dukes and kings they were obliged to serve, and this to a stranger's ears. Some of those chatelaines had made no secret that should this strapping young visitor go a'wandering by candlelight, their doors would not be barred.

By the time he reached the stink of Rome, which was as much created by corruption as human and animal effluent, Robert de Hauteville's education was complete: it only took a short stay in that den of papal iniquity, a city with three different popes, all of them equally corrupt, competing to control the Holy See, each supported by their own warring aristocratic factions, to complete a view of the world in which he lived, one that was utterly jaundiced. It was there he also learnt of the Norman activity in Apulia – news of their victories had reached Rome – which altered his intended destination: no point in going to Aversa if none of his family were there.

'Where are you headed, brother?' asked a sightless beggar at the Appian Gate, a fellow of much experience, who had either been tipped of the approach or knew the sound of a triple set of hooves. Robert's hounds growled at him until commanded to desist.

'To Apulia, friend, to seek my fortune.'

'Is there a fortune there, brother? I sense you are of a kind, one of many who have gone that way. Even if they had gained much, perhaps there is not enough to satisfy.'

The booming laugh that engendered was loud enough to echo off the old and broken walls of the Eternal City. 'I am Robert de Hauteville, and if there is fortune to be had, then I shall have it.'

'Then God bless you, brother, and if you come back this way, do not pass by without gifting me some of that prosperity.'

'Who knows if I ever shall?'

Even sightless eyes can narrow, and the beggar's did so now. 'Take the word of a man who can see with empty sockets, brother, a man who has senses more acute than those of priests. I know from your voice and manner, and that which surrounds you, that you shall come back to Rome, and with more horses and a deeper purse than you possess now.'

'What are you, fellow, a sorcerer?'

The laugh was a cackle. 'No, brother, happen I am a seer.'

That jest got another booming Norman laugh, turning the heads of all around. Robert's purse was near to empty, but he liked the prophecy enough to pass over the smallest of his silver.

'News has just arrived, William, that Prince Guaimar has accepted the surrender of Amalfi. He is busy taking bloody revenge for slights of long duration.'

William, standing by an embrasure, was watching the boy, Listo, practise with a wooden sword. One of the older mercenaries who had come with him from Aversa, a fellow who had been badly wounded at Cannae, had taken to the boy, teaching him not only how to use a toy sword and shield, but how to ride as well. Or perhaps, suspecting he might not see service again, he was looking for a role that would keep him in Melfi.

'I have said before, Arduin, I have no interest in Amalfi.'

'But I suspect you do in the other piece of news just arrived.' Arduin, when William turned, was grinning, in a way that did not please the Norman. He looked too much like a cat who had stolen the cream. 'We have a new catapan, no less than the son and namesake of that devil, Basil Boioannes. Michael Doukeianos has been sent to Sicily for his failures, where I suspect he will rot.'

'Then we should be cautious of him, Arduin, lest he has the same ability as his papa.'

'Who is Basil Boioannes?' asked Count Atenulf, with his usual vacant expression, he having come with Arduin.

It was a question that astounded William: for a Lombard not to know that name was ignorance indeed. It probably shocked Arduin even more: had not the man in question led the army that beat Melus of Bari and killed his father on the very field where they had just been victorious? But if he was surprised, Arduin gave no evidence of it, too accustomed, probably, to Atenulf's density to be stunned.

'No doubt,' Arduin added, 'they think to win a prize with the same blood and name.'

'Has he come with any more men?' asked William, for that, to him, was of paramount concern.

'He has apparently come with nothing but his father's reputation. But the recruiting parties are out again, and they will use the name to gather a host. Also he has the remains of the men who fled the field at Cannae.'

'Then he had better be clever,' William insisted, 'for they could not stand.'

It took several months to discover that the younger Boioannes was just that. Following on from Cannae, William had been cautious in the way he deferred to Arduin, who, though he had praised him for the victory he had achieved, and had taken without a blush the accolades which had come to him, was still rankled by the way he had been so ignominiously superseded at Cannae. Knowing that time favoured the Byzantines, as it always would, Arduin ordered the army out of Melfi and went in search of Boioannes, only to find him as elusive as a buzzing fly.

Every time they got close to him he manoeuvred quickly and efficiently to get clear, sometimes retiring to a fortress – especially when faced with just Norman cavalry – then slipping away from that if Arduin brought up enough men to institute a siege, always with a route open back to the great bastion of Bari. As a campaign it was wearing, especially for the foot soldiers, marching hither and thither with nothing to show for it at the end.

Given that lasted through winter and into the following spring, it became positively dispiriting and the numbers of recruits began to fall as those who had farms slipped away to sow crops while others who had left their trades saw more profit in pursuing them; with plunder they would have stayed, without it they saw only empty bellies, until Arduin was obliged to fall back on Melfi, which only increased the feelings of gloom and the rate of desertion.

'Better to let them go, William,' Arduin suggested. 'If I do they will come back once their crop is in the soil. If I do not...'

That needed no finish: they might not return at all, a thought which made a general become dispirited even more downhearted. He thought a more inspiring leader could have kept them together; a more practical Norman mercenary knew differently: men served themselves, even if they mouthed causes. He also saw the need to ease the man's mind.

'I would do likewise, Arduin, as long as we keep the crossbowmen. And I too will welcome an end to campaigning. I too need to look to my men and horses.'

It was more the latter than the former, but his lances, now numbering near six hundred, were weary too, in need of rest: being in a saddle was better than being on foot, yet it was still hard work. For the horses, the burden of constant campaigning was becoming evident in losses – not deaths but wear: mounts becoming lame, increasing sickness such as laminitis and colic, which rendered them useless. They needed time in pasture, and the stud he had set up would benefit from replenishment.

'We agree, then. Disband the *milities*, leave your men to hold Melfi, and plan a new campaign following the spring planting.'

The next days were marked by streams of foot soldiers heading off to their farms, livings and families; not all, for some so relished the military life that they were loath to part from it, or perhaps home life was miserable. Arduin accompanied Atenulf to Benevento, there to partake of the prince's hospitality and think great thoughts about how he was going to beat Boioannes and then persuade the port cities to join in the revolt.

William was glad to see him go: he did not dislike Arduin and even if his military thinking was footbound he did respect him, but a constant exposure to that Lombard dream was exhausting. In the field they often shared a meal in one another's tent, and while conversation might range over their past exploits in Sicily, which would mull on to a discussion of what Michael Doukeianos might achieve there – generally held to range from little to nothing – it always came back to that which was immediately before them, that inevitably leading to Arduin and his fellow Lombards' aspirations.

Added to that, the opaque Count Atenulf was ever present, asking inane questions or making stupid statements, when not utterly silent and merely looking glaucous. William had acquired the ability to look interested when not, and took refuge in watching Arduin carefully, only listening to those parts of his conversation which bordered on speech-making, seeking to discern from his words the true meanings, which were bound to be hidden. He speculated, too, on Atenulf, on that young man's presence, for it was obvious that their titular commander had personal ambitions and they were not that the Prince of Benevento, through his younger brother, should end up as the ruler of Apulia.

Obviously, having come to this whole enterprise through the Prince of Salerno, there had to be some secret agreement between Guaimar and Arduin, but William doubted it would satisfy this Lombard. It was more likely that Arduin dreamt that somehow, despite his lowly status in the hierarchy of his people, he would come to rule over Apulia himself and, if that were the case, it was also interesting to wonder how he saw himself dealing with the Normans. Would he seek to use them to fulfil his ambitions, or would he try to get rid of them?

Messengers seen from the ramparts to be riding sweating, chest-heaving horses, conveyed danger before they ever spoke and the one who came clattering into the great keep of Melfi was no exception. The shouts that heralded his approach had the entire command of the Norman-Lombard forces awaiting him as he came through the gate.

'Boioannes is outside Venosa with the whole of his host, my Lord, but shows no sign of wishing to instigate a siege.'

'He called on the garrison to surrender, surely?' demanded Arduin, even although the messenger had addressed Count Atenulf.

'He did, then he rode back to his camp, which was in long sight of the walls, and there he stayed, though it is suspected he was making preparations to move on.'

'Then he is coming to Melfi.'

Arduin looked to William, who nodded, knowing that Venosa meant nothing to this new catapan, Melfi everything, and he had no doubt heard that his enemies were weakened. He could also guess at what he planned: if Boioannes could bottle up what forces remained in the fortress, especially the Normans, then he could prevent any of those farmers from coming back to serve after the spring sowing, and behind him, even if it would be difficult to supply an investing army, he had the whole of Apulia to draw on for the supplies necessary to endure a long siege. Thus he would have achieved one major goal, and an immediate tactical advantage.

For the Byzantines such a course of action made perfect strategic sense as well: having lost two battles in open country they had to deny their enemies the luxury of movement. Boioannes might not take Melfi, but he would put an end to that and snuff out the enthusiasm for revolt the previous victories had created. He would also deny his enemies the opportunity to reconstitute their army and, who was to know he would not, in the long months while he was outside the walls, acquire fresh troops from Constantinople and swing the whole campaign in his favour.

'He's more astute than we gave him credit for,' said Drogo.

'And devious,' William added. 'He lulled us into a feeling of security. All that marching to and fro was just to bring about this very thing.'

'He cannot take Melfi,' Arduin insisted, looking at the walls of the castle as though they would somehow bear out his words. 'It is too strong.'

'He knows that, Arduin.' William watched as Arduin took time to get to a conclusion, which with him had been near to instant, one which met his dislike of the notion of being bottled up in a castle, an absolute negation of the advantage of cavalry.

For once the Lombard deduced the same as his mercenary commander. 'And he could not take it even if it is held by only a small garrison.'

'Just as he cannot safely besiege it if he has hundreds of Norman lances waiting to raid his siege lines and kill his foraging parties.'

'Let us consult the maps,' Arduin snapped.

He turned quickly to re-enter the great hall, followed by the Normans. Halfway up the steps he stopped and turned, then spoke, for once, in a terse voice and with a thunderous look, to Atenulf, calling on him to follow. Even that took time for the dense brain to sift, and it was Humphrey, the last to move, who pushed him hard and with little ceremony to get him to obey.

Examining the maps, it was obvious there were many directions in which they could go: towards Campania, which offered a safe line of retirement, should that be required; the least favourable was to the east; the one impossible to think on, to head south into the catapan's line of march. Arduin, with his depleted forces, knowing that on this occasion, while not wholly dependent, he needed the Normans more than ever, asked William to decide.

'North to here,' William replied, placing his finger on an area he had ridden over when first he came to Melfi, close to the spot where Tirena and Listo had rolled that boulder down on him. The high hill that rock had come off, which he now knew to be called Monte Siricolo, gave a good view of the approaches to the fertile valleys over which it towered. There was ample pasture in those, with hayricks left over from the last cutting, and at this time of year the mountain streams were bursting with snowmelt, while the forests would provide wood to both construct shelters and keep them warm in the cold high-altitude nights should they have to winter there.

Added to that, the longer they stayed there the stronger they would become, for if it cut them off from

Campania, that was the main path for the return of the levies who had gone back north to Benevento, and any supplies they needed to sustain themselves could come by that same route. It was easy from there for cavalry to raid south, using the numerous trails through the mountains to achieve surprise. Any siege of Melfi would suffer mightily from constant attacks and the decimation of parties sent out to forage.

'William,' Arduin insisted, 'Boioannes cannot just leave us there.'

'No, my friend, he cannot.'

He did not often use such a term with Arduin, but he did now. There should be nothing in the way of the Lombard seeing what was possible, and that was a place he got to with commendable speed.

'So once more we bring him to battle at a field of our choosing.'

Normans were used to moving at short notice, less so the Lombard levies that had remained, but all were long gone, accompanied by the locals, by the time the catapan's banners were sighted from the battlements. Given the constraints he had laboured under, the losses suffered by his predecessor and the difficulties of recruitment, he had assembled an impressive host, and it was soon obvious he had brought along not just fighting men but artisans skilled in the construction of ballista and the like, who immediately set to work, so that the sound of hammering and sawing floated up to the stout walls.

Left in command at Melfi, with a stiffening of Normans, but mainly a garrison of Lombards, it fell to Humphrey and Mauger, standing on the curtain wall which overlooked the narrow entry bridge, to refuse to accept terms. They listened in silence as the normal threats regarding no quarter were shouted up at them, restraining the men they commanded from any overt displays of either jocularity – showing their bare arses – or expletive-loaded insults, merely acknowledging the message and telling the Byzantines to do their worst.

By the time the party sent to present those terms had returned with the expected refusal, Basil Boioannes knew that his enemy had flown the coop. The men he feared most were outside those walls, not inside, and he was also committed, far from his base at Bari, with a set of shrinking options, the least palatable of which, given the fate of Michael Doukeianos, was withdrawal.

The next morning, he issued instructions that his artisans should keep toiling, with enough men to keep them safe staying behind. Then, once his host had been fed and blessed, he marched them away from Melfi, heading north, knowing that his approach would be observed. So be it: let them stand or flee, but the Normans had to be beaten or driven away.

\* \* \*

That his enemies had come so quickly threw Arduin off balance: he had worked on the assumption that Boioannes would at least make some kind of assault on Melfi before seeking to cancel out the external threat. William was less unnerved: again their young opponent was showing sound judgement, his deduction that the peril would only increase with time, not diminish. Also, when he came face to face with his foes, below the great mound of Monte Siricolo, he did not make the same mistake as Doukeianos: he did not attack, he stood on the defensive and set his men to digging a ditch before the line on which he intended to fight, to slow down, and perhaps kill off, any Norman cavalry assault.

But he did not control the high ground, and could not, therefore, see what his enemies were up to. He tried, sending strong assaulting parties through the low forests and up above the treeline to the barren slopes of Monte Siricolo, but they were beaten back by the same kind of boulders which had so nearly done for William. Because he could not capture those, he did not know that Arduin had sent most of the foot soldiers he had through two high passes on either side of the field of confrontation, to come down on the Byzantine rear.

William's task was simple, and this once it was the Normans who aided the Lombards, not the other way round. They attacked Boioannes, but only to fix him in front, using the crossbowmen to inflict casualties, serious enough, but not sufficient to break the line, while the enemy crossbows were brought forward to counter them, thus removing them from where they would be needed. The Norman cavalry, in lines, under Drogo and Geoffrey, rode forward as far as that freshly dug ditch several times, cast lances, then retired to jeers from their enemies, with William's eye firmly fixed on the piquet sitting atop Monte Siricolo.

The signal that Arduin was advancing came as a column of smoke, made black by throwing pitch on it, and William took command of his men, with his brothers alongside him. They were in one tight line now and they began to walk forward, as the first yells echoed off the hillsides, the shouts from the rear of the Byzantine host that there was an attack coming from that quarter.

If these Apulian levies that Boioannes led were not the same men who had been at Cannae and Masseria, they were well aware of the defeats that had occurred there. Added to that, it takes little to break the spirit of a force bent on defence when they discover that there is an enemy behind their lines, while before them, coming on like a tide of death, are the mailed knights of Normandy.

Arduin lacked force, but he had the option of retiring to the fortress of Melfi, because he had strength in abundance to brush aside anyone who tried to stop him. Thus his men had nothing to fear as they charged through the Byzantine baggage to attack confused troops who were not yet fully prepared for battle, and the cries they sent up, first of alarm and then of betrayal, totally destroyed the unity of the men facing the Normans. They were more concerned with what was happening behind them than in front and numbers began to move backwards in confused groups.

Where that happened the ditch no longer protected them; odd that those who stood their ground had a better chance of survival, because for once, the approaching horsemen were not intent on maintaining a solid line, they were intent on exploitation. Before the opening gaps the lances spurred their mounts. Where Boioannes's men stood, the threat before them trended left or right to bypass them. It took no time at all for those stalwarts to realise that staying still would see them eventually surrounded and slaughtered, and just as the first lances struck home, practically the whole Byzantine line broke and fled, compacting back on a rear already in chaos, which had men spilling up the surrounding hills to seek safety.

Boioannes, with those men who attended him personally and nowhere to go, stood firm, prepared to sell their lives dearly, and it was an indication of how comprehensive the collapse of his army had been that they were so quickly surrounded. William halted his men and stood off till Arduin arrived and called upon his opposite number to surrender. There really was not much choice, except death, and the catapan called upon his companions to put up their weapons, then came forward holding out his sword.

To the disgust of William and his brothers, Arduin stepped aside and let that idiot Atenulf accept it in the name of the Lombard revolt.

# CHAPTER THIRTEEN

∽◇⌐

Within a week the whole of Apulia learnt young
Basil Boioannes was a prisoner and Byzantium had
suffered total defeat, so that leading Lombard and
Italian citizens of the great port cities, in conclave and
with their Greek inhabitants overawed or frightened,
decided that backing the revolt was a more promising
policy than standing aside. Messages of support
flooded into Melfi, but were seen for what they were:
precautionary olive branches to the now dominant
power in the land.

The news of what had happened at Monte Siricolo,
and the consequences, also travelled like a brush
fire to Campania, there to reach the ears of Prince
Guaimar, now back in the Castello di Arechi, and he
hastily sent for Rainulf Drengot. Was it time for the

Count of Aversa to call upon those mercenaries of whom he was the titular leader, to assert his rights? If it was, his suzerain intended to accompany him. Was there about to be a division of the spoils? Not to be there might be foolish.

Guaimar's regular meeting with Kasa Ephraim allowed him, before Drengot arrived, to test out how he should act towards William de Hauteville and an ambitious Arduin of Fassano; there would also be the puffed-up brother of his fellow ruler of Benevento to be taken into consideration. The Jew had been dealing with the Normans throughout their campaign using a travelling agent, but like everyone Ephraim employed, the fellow had an acute eye, so his master knew more of what was happening in and around Melfi than the ruler of Salerno.

'I have to be open and say that the news, such a total overpowering of Byzantium, surprises me.'

Kasa Ephraim hid a smile as he watched Guaimar weigh in his hand the heavy leather purse he had just gifted him: there was a time he would have waited until his collector of the port had gone. The young man had become less discreet in his avarice, as well as more competent at calculation. Now he could hand-evaluate the contents and guess the amount of his secret revenues.

'I thought it would take years, quite possibly a decade, and even then...' Guaimar did not finish that sentence; it was not necessary. 'So now we must, earlier than we suspected, see how this affects the Principality of Salerno.'

Watching him still, as he began to pace, the Jew could guess at some of what was on his mind: he would be concerned that his warning to Michael Doukeianos might be exposed by this sudden Byzantine reversal. Having arranged it, Ephraim was less so: it had been delivered with a discretion which was under his control, and by a ship's captain who regularly bribed him to be allowed to smuggle, so he would say nothing. Any accusation from another source could be easily denied and put down to mischief-making by the Eastern Empire.

The other problem was more serious: having gifted oversight of the revolt to another, how could Guaimar, in light of the speed of this success, bolster his own claims to what might very soon be a nascent Lombard kingdom?

'We are secure in the matter of sending word to Bari?'

'*You* are very secure,' Ephraim replied, with an emphasis on the first word that Guaimar did not miss.

'I have let it be rumoured that Amalfi is responsible, by a claim to have been told to me by a fellow we racked, before putting him to burn at the stake.'

'Then you have even less to fear, honourable one.'

'The Prince of Benevento must be wondering what to do with Apulia.'

'I would advise that it is not yet there for him to dispose of.'

'Byzantium has been beaten.'

'Defeated in battle, not yet beaten. They will not, I think, give up such a rich and fertile province without yet more effort. The revenues of the Adriatic ports alone are too substantial.'

'You know this?' Guaimar demanded. This Jew had sources of information which made his look pale; for Kasa Ephraim trade, risk and the contacts that went with it were personal. For the Prince of Salerno such activity, performed as it was by others, was merely political, which meant he relied, for information, on his courtiers. 'I am, as you know, surrounded by people who do not always tell me the truth, they tell me what they think I want to hear.'

'It is the fate of princes. Your council fear more for their place and their privileges. They also know rulers can be capricious.'

Guaimar smiled, which made human a face that had increasingly become solemn as he grew into his responsibilities. Few people spoke to him so directly as this Jew: only his sister, in truth.

'You do not fear my caprice?'

'I fear only my God.'

'So, speaking the truth, advise me.'

'Do not be hasty, honourable one.'

'Are you saying I should not travel to Melfi?'

'You have that right, but I think it too soon to make enemies. Better to make friends.'

'Go on.'

'Count Atenulf is a foil for his brother, is he not?'

'Of course, no one would follow that fellow. I have heard he is a fool.'

'A prince who is a vassal of the Pope.'

'So?'

'Apulia, in its religion, is mostly Greek. The people who live there, even those who are Lombards, after hundreds of years of Byzantine rule, look to the Patriarch in Constantinople for spiritual guidance. A Prince of Benevento, a vassal of Rome and a worshipper in the Latin rite, may not be to their taste.'

Guaimar nodded: what Ephraim was saying made good sense; even if it appeared the revolt was succeeding, nothing was yet settled.

'I would also suggest that city states like Bari and Brindisi, even if the Lombard sections of the population are now in the ascendancy of opinion, have enjoyed so much privilege under Constantinople that they will be reluctant to bow the knee to anyone. In pledging to the revolt they may have acted out of prudence, not conviction. Their actions henceforth will be regulated by fear, and I doubt any Lombard prince can command enough force to compel deference.'

'They would not see Amalfi as an example?'

'They are much more formidable than Amalfi.'

'So whoever wanted to rule in Apulia, unless they have an emperor to sustain them, would still need the Normans.'

Ephraim nodded, pleased that Guaimar obviously accepted the same constraint applied to him, without it having to be openly stated.

'They are warriors you control through Rainulf Drengot.'

Guaimar smiled again, but it was more wolfish than his previous good humour. He would not admit to Ephraim he had been worried, unnecessarily so.

'Let me travel to Melfi. After such a victory there will be much business to be transacted with those people, more than I can entrust to another. You should not venture out of Campania, but stop before the border.'

Guaimar's eyes narrowed suddenly: those Normans would tell this Jew who handled their money things they would not impart to anyone else. Would he pass it on? 'As long as you act for me.'

'Honourable one, who else would I act for?' The Jew then nodded to the bulging leather pouch on the table. 'Quite apart from personal affection, there is the question of my own interest.'

* * *

'Arise, Count Rainulf.'

Guaimar said those words in a soft and friendly voice, hinting that for his vassal to kneel to him was unnecessary. The man in question knew better: if he had not wanted a public display of fealty Guaimar would have received him in private instead of his audience chamber, and not subjected his old bones to the dipping. Seeing him struggle to rise again, one of his attendant knights stepped forward to aid him, only to be brushed away. He was not so aged he needed lifting!

Watching this, Guaimar could see that the years were continuing to take their toll of this one-time puissant Norman – or perhaps he had not yet recovered from his effort at the recent siege. Odd that his ears seemed so much bigger, and those on either side of a face now losing the ability to hold firm the flesh. The cheekbones were very pronounced now, in a countenance that had once been so puffy as to nearly conceal the eyes. Yet there was no denying his success: not only did he have Aversa and his rewards from Amalfi, but he had long ago replaced the Wolf of the Abruzzi as a bane to the great monastery of Montecassino.

Where the late unlamented Pandulf had ravaged monastery lands and beggared the monks, Rainulf was more measured in his actions, forcing the abbot to cede land, so that Rainulf's most loyal followers gained much of their income not from his purse, but at the expense of the monastery coffers. Even that failed to ease the threat of Norman brigandage – only distant warfare did that – just as it did nothing for the transferred tenants.

Rainulf's Normans had fought at Amalfi, but as soon as that was over, those not part of the garrison had gone back to raiding their neighbours. This Rainulf saw as none of his concern; he had to keep content men bred to war and in search of wealth, and with no war still to fight, and in consequence no plunder, this was his way of providing for them and stopping the discontented from sliding off to join William de Hauteville.

The Abbot of Montecassino had appealed to Guaimar to intervene, as he had to both Rome and the Prince of Benevento, but those were pleas made to deaf ears: if Rainulf's unruly Normans were not occupied ravaging the abbot's lands, they might well find temptation elsewhere. Let them stay out of Lombard territory. Letters had been despatched to the emperor in Bamberg, but he, newly elected and of tender years, was a man with much more pressing concerns in Germany; Italy could wait.

Guaimar was remembering how much he had once feared this man. But no more: he was sound in his inheritance now and he had command of Rainulf Drengot in his own domains, which gave him deep satisfaction. The Count of Aversa needed his prince as much as Guaimar needed him, perhaps more, given his continuing difficulties with Rome, a matter not helped by the continuing dispute about who, in fact, out of the competing contenders, was truly Pope.

'I am obliged to ask after your family.'

Not my woman, or my son by name; my family, thought Drengot. I'm damned if I will mention to you the woman who shares my bed.

'The boy is hale, sire, and growing.'

'And how do matters progress in your annulment?'

If the courtiers attending in the chamber did not laugh outright, there was certainly more than a hint of suppressed mirth: Rainulf knew of the jokes that they told each other about him and the woman he wanted to marry, so much younger than he. Why could not that bitch of a wife of his expire? He was a man who had torched nunneries in his life and he longed to do that now, with one of the inmates still trapped inside. But it would not serve: he was no longer a mere knight with a lance, a sword and nothing in his purse – he was too elevated, too prominent a figure. Excommunication, which would surely follow, would not aid his cause.

'I have asked Pope Benedict to tell me what would be needed to facilitate matters, but he seems very reluctant to name me a price.'

'Benedict is having trouble holding on to his office, Rainulf. There are those in Rome who challenge his right to his title. Perhaps you should consult with them too.'

Suddenly Drengot's voice became weedy and pleading, he knew he was being guyed. 'There can only be one true pontiff, surely, but is it not a shameful thing, sire, that such a man holding such a holy office seeks a bribe to do that which is right?'

One of those attending, so ancient now he had earned the right to be seated, was the bent-backed Archbishop of Salerno, who frowned mightily to hear the Pontiff he and Salerno supported, the man who actually held both St Peter's and the papal castle of St Angelo, so traduced. Taking advantage of his years and his mitre, he barked out a response.

'The case must be examined, Count Rainulf. You say the marriage was not consummated and can thus be annulled, the woman you married denies it. Are you suggesting the Holy See pay to investigate the true facts?'

'I say the Holy See should take the word of an imperial count before that of—'

Guaimar interrupted sharply, it being a chance to beard his vassal on safe ground. 'The sister of an imperial prince, for if Pandulf has been deposed, he once held that estate?'

'Prince no longer, sire,' Rainulf spat. 'His fief is a

Byzantine dungeon and he is lucky not to have had his eyes put out.'

Said with such obvious bitterness, Guaimar was tempted to remind Rainulf Drengot of how he had once loyally served the man they called the Wolf of the Abruzzi. But it would not do, his responsibility to his rank and office demanded that he put such a notion aside, for that would be a jibe too far. Truly, being a prince took some of the joy out of life.

'Come, Rainulf, and let us retire to my private chamber, to discuss matters in Apulia.'

Unbeknown to Robert de Hauteville, his arrival in the hill city of Benevento coincided with the day Count Atenulf had set aside to show off his prisoner, a matter delayed and arranged so that the population could demonstrate their feelings for this hated Byzantine catapan. He had found a place to lay his head, and to stable his horses, in a religious house half a league away and, alerted to the proposed celebrations, he made for the walled city on foot. The gates were guarded, but such was the crowd coming in from the surrounding habitations that spread out from the citadel, he was not challenged as he would have been on a normal day: a man of his appearance always was.

Once through those he entered narrow streets thronged with people, all in the kind of mood prevalent in the more robust religious festivals, with drinking and dancing, some even running to costumes of the kind worn by fools, and he had to push his way through the crush, curious as to what the fuss was about; to him the term 'catapan' was, if not unknown, then certainly not a familiar title.

In quizzing the locals – not without difficulty, their Latin was strangely accented to his ears – he heard of the great victory achieved by the brother of their prince, a mighty warrior who had, they stated proudly, almost single-handed, humbled Byzantium. Having been kept outside the walls for a week, the prisoner was to be brought into the city, hauled through the old Roman triumphal arch, much carved with symbols of ancient military victories, then led through the streets to his ultimate humiliation in the amphitheatre.

With his height, Robert had no difficulty in finding himself a point from which to observe, nor in seeing the captive, a distressed-looking fellow in a wheeled cage, of swarthy complexion and lank black hair, wearing a white smock. It did not stay that for long: as soon as he emerged from the city side of the arch the pelting began, all the filth of the streets and more beside hurled with screaming abuse at a victim who took it with commendable stoicism, looking straight ahead and not reacting unless hit by an object large enough to make him jerk.

Behind the cage, in plumed helmet and glistening

armour of a kind worn by the ancients, rode his captor, Count Atenulf, who had won, according to his brother's subjects, not one battle against the mighty Eastern Empire, but three. Robert's enquiries, to find out if any Normans had been involved, were greeted with scathing dismissal: Beneventian generals needed no help from northern barbarians. Those who said such things, once they raised their eyes and realised they were talking to one of the breed, and an angry one at that, soon took to grovelling, but all that led to was an admission of ignorance.

Moving with the crowd was a jostling experience but at least he had the power to ensure he had the space to stay upright. So great was the crush in the confined streets that people were falling and being trampled on, and more than once Robert reached down to heave some unfortunate to their feet, lest energetic stamping turned into bloody mutilation. The outer walls of the amphitheatre, when he finally reached them, reminded him of the Coliseum he had seen in Rome, a once mighty edifice suffering for its years and looted by local builders for its stones, so looking like a ruin.

Inside it was different: a theatre for drama not games, with the rows of stone seats already nearly full. In the middle of the performing area stood a magnificently clad reception party waiting for the mighty Count Atenulf, and further enquires established that the main figure was the Prince Landulf himself, while it was made plain to this boorish, nosy visitor that the fellow in the mitre and robes was an archbishop. This was said with pride, Benevento having the blessing of the Pope, their ultimate overlord, to keep it safe. The rest of the people present, male and female, were members of the prince's court.

Entrance delayed until the amphitheatre was full to bursting, while soldiers with flat-held pikes joined them on the rim to keep the crowd in check, and with people now hanging off the outer walls, the cage was finally dragged in. The occupant was now covered from head to foot in ordure, his hair soaked and hanging down where it had been covered in piss and spittle, standing in a pile of rotting vegetation trapped by the bars. Yet still he stared proudly ahead, and Robert could not help but admire him.

Atenulf dismounted, took off his plumed helmet, and knelt before the prince, to be then raised by his brother and embraced. The high cleric got a kiss on his episcopal ring and bestowed a blessing on the bowed head, before showing some Christian charity: he made the sign of the cross at the caged catapan. Taking a crown of laurel leaves from an attendant, the Prince of Benevento crowned his brother as the Caesars had once crowned their triumphant generals, then Atenulf spun round to face the people, and to accept the roaring accolades of those assembled.

# CHAPTER FOURTEEN

✖

The recipient of those laurel leaves would have been less pleased, or in his case utterly confused, had he been further south at a meeting convened by Guaimar at the near-ruined castle of Montecchio, just inside his own territories. Nor was the Prince of Salerno entirely happy. He had to listen to the envoys from the great port cities treat him as if he was of no account, not that they favoured anyone above him. They repudiated the leadership of a fool like Atenulf and they were not prepared to take orders from an upstart like Arduin of Fassano. As for the Normans, they were nothing but brigands.

Arduin, in the face of such contempt, was furious, while Rainulf Drengot looked as though he had been slapped, which given his past exploits, was absurd. A party of Normans from the fortress of Troia, as massive and as hard to capture as Melfi, had finally come south too, and they had reacted noisily to accusations of brigandage. They had also made it plain they had no interest in furthering the ambitions of anyone but themselves. Long in the service of Byzantium, if that power was removed, they cared only about who would take up the burden of paying them; William de Hauteville did not allow himself any expression at all.

'If you put aside cohesion,' Guaimar insisted, still trying to work through his proxies, 'you will find yourself back under the thumb of Constantinople.'

'We have walls to resist Byzantium,' the envoy from Brindisi insisted. In the case of his own city he was right, and his next words underlined the disparity of interest amongst these mainly Lombard envoys. 'Let Arduin and his Normans control the countryside. As long as they hold that, no siege of our port can succeed.'

That set up a clamour, as each representative bellowed about the needs of his own community, proving that the one thing that did not exist was unity of purpose.

'What do you think, Gill?' said Drogo, using, as he habitually did, the French diminutive of William's name. The de Hauteville brothers were standing far enough away to talk quietly, observing proceedings. 'Guaimar looks as though he has bitten one of those lemon fruits we found so abundant in Sicily.'

'They are greedy, Drogo. They want to run their own affairs and pay taxes to no master, with us, or the Lombards led by Arduin, fighting a Byzantium army in the open to keep them free to trade.'

'Surely they would pay for that service.'

'They might,' cut in Humphrey, his brow as usual looking furrowed, 'but it would be a fee collected after service not before, I'll wager.'

'You mean they would not pay for our lances?' asked Mauger.

William replied, 'They would only pay if they felt secure. They would feel secure only if Byzantium was booted out of Apulia for good. Who then would they have to fear?'

'Me!' young Mauger replied, vehemently.

Humphrey had a laugh that always sounded derisory, never humorous, and that came out now, his upper teeth jabbing into the skin below his mouth. 'That is a thought which will scare them rigid.'

William called upon both brothers to hush: that exchange had been too loud and earned a sideways glance from Guaimar, now speaking again.

'You are glad to be free of Constantinople, are you not?'

The envoys exchanged glances, none of them friendly to him or to each other. They had come from Brindisi, Monopoli, Giovinazzo and Barletta, and while most were Lombards, there were Greeks and Italians too, while back in the cities from which they came were more of all three races to whom they were answerable. It was telling that no representative had come from Trani, a majority Greek port still loyal to Constantinople. The entire party who had travelled all the way from Taranto was actually Greek, but they shared with the others a desire to cast off the same oppressive yoke and the impositions that went with it.

The looks nailed another one of those problems for that tiresome Lombard dream: not one of these mixed-race city states really looked with favour on the idea of a South Italian kingdom, and that applied to the many Lombard citizens, even run by one of their own kind. To such worthies, all wealthy traders in their bailiwicks, that was only replacing one tax-raising power with another.

It was a Lombard from Bari who answered. 'That we are, and to a man we share the dream of the late Melus and we look with favour on his son Argyrus.'

'Liar,' hissed Geoffrey de Hauteville, which got him a nudge from William.

Not that his older brother disagreed: he had come to see the name of Melus as a talisman that could be trotted out without much attachment to sincerity, and the idea that the late leader's son could oversee a revolt was just as disingenuous. Argyrus, as had already been proved, did not have the stature to compete with the likes of Guaimar or the Prince of Benevento, and if such powerful Lombards as they would not bow the knee to him, then these city states had a ready-made excuse to do likewise.

William's eye was drawn to Kasa Ephraim, who stood well back, taking no part in the discussions, but with a half smile on his face. He, too, understood perfectly the nuances of the negotiations and the fact they were going nowhere. He had not had a chance to speak with the Jew since he arrived, but he knew he would. Ephraim had not come with Guaimar, but separately, two days after the prince, and he had yet to sit down with the Normans, William included, and contract his business.

But he was a wise old owl, a man who could see which way the wind would blow and plant his crops to avoid damage, to protect, in his case, his wealth. William was looking forward to talking with him, and seeking his views on what he was now witnessing, as the wrangling continued without any solution in sight.

'I urge you to talk more amongst yourselves,' Guaimar concluded, 'and will gather again on the morrow.'

As the port envoys filed out of the great hall, Guaimar signalled to Rainulf, Arduin and William to join him in an antechamber. He was already on his way to that smaller room, his face dark with anger, before the others moved.

'They must be made to bend the knee,' he spat, as the door was closed behind William.

'To whom?' William asked.

Guaimar nearly spoke the truth and said 'To me', but he stopped himself, still wishing to uphold the fiction that he had no ambitions to be the man who ruled, falling back on the usual mantra. 'To the revolt.'

'Only force will persuade them,' William said, then added, 'the ability to breach their defences, and those, with stout walls in good repair, we lack.'

Being true did not make it palatable: the ports were rich enough to keep their defences in proper repair. It would require a fleet to block the harbour, need siege engines or trained men to sap under the walls and undermine them, as well as enough force to take advantage of any breach created by their efforts. Guaimar's sour reaction gave Rainulf Drengot a chance to favour William with a look that implied he was fearful, which got the older man that de Hauteville smile which so infuriated those on the receiving end.

'Arduin,' Guaimar demanded, as though he would have the answer.

He had one, but it was not to the taste of the Prince of Salerno. 'If you were to take the field, sire, and—'

'What would Landulf of Benevento have to say to that?' Guaimar interrupted.

He really meant Byzantium, who still had troops in Sicily, only a few days sailing from Salerno, and a massive fleet, should it be sent from Constantinople, to transport them to the bay on which his city stood. Benevento was, in terms of places to plunder on the coast, safe: the wealth of the principality was all in the interior. It was still too soon to openly declare himself.

'Besides,' Guaimar added, 'I have still not fully subdued Amalfi.'

That was received with polite disbelief, but if others were troubled, William was quietly content. Dissension amongst the Lombards suited him and when the meeting broke up he emerged in good humour. Days went by in fruitless discussion, time in which William and his brothers could leave them to their quarrels and escort Kasa Ephraim the short distance to Melfi, there to discuss both how to send funds back to Hauteville-la-Guichard and secure a safe place for that which they intended to keep.

'You do not trust the fortress of Melfi?' Ephraim asked, amused, looking around the formidable walls.

'We don't trust the people we share it with,' spluttered Humphrey, braying with laughter.

'These two tried to kill me,' William said, quite taken by the reddening of Listo's cheeks, the reminder embarrassing him. Both now spoke good Latin: the boy's sister Tirena understood as well, but was, as usual, less contrite, though she no longer looked at William with studied loathing.

'And you spared them?' asked Ephraim.

'We had only just taken over the castle and the locals were fearful. It seemed a good way to show we were not here to plunder them.'

The Jew nodded. 'You show more wisdom, William, than some of your fellows, who only know how to burn and lay waste. What do you have in mind for them?'

'Listo here wants to be a soldier.' That had the boy stretching, and though still small he had put on quite a few inches. 'For Tirena, perhaps she will become wife to one of my lances.'

William hid a smile to see that look return. He had caught her more than once watching him from some place she thought hidden, that first day from atop the ramparts. She had also taken to carefully dressing her hair and seeking out fetching clothes, which given she too had grown and filled out, had revealed a comeliness that had not been apparent under her previous filth and demeanour. Drogo had to be warned off with the threat of a lance up his arse if he laid a hand on her.

'It is interesting, my friend, is it not, that when the people of Melfi look to the castle, they see one of their number not only fed but cosseted?'

'These two are hill people, goatherds, but you are right. It makes for a peaceful life.'

'I am told your men are instructed to respect them too, on pain of dire punishment.'

'We live amongst them, they grow our food; to despoil them is stupid, and one peasant with a sharp knife, loose in the paddocks or stud on a dark night, could do more damage than a regiment of Varangians.'

'It would be especially foolish to plunder them if you have ambitions to rule over them.'

'Like Prince Guaimar, you mean?'

The silence that followed that question, from a man who was not normally short of words, was telling. William could see Tirena was intrigued too, reminding him of what he had noted more than once: she had a sharp native intelligence, on this occasion able to discern an atmosphere which was not quite as it should be.

'Listo, see to my friend's goblet.'

'I wonder,' Kasa Ephraim said, without looking at William, instead examining his fingernails, 'if you and I should talk about things until now left unspoken.'

'The choice is yours.'

William was looking at the Jew with a curious expression: Ephraim was not one to break a confidence for him, nor did he think he would do it for Guaimar of Salerno, but he was clearly ruminating on something profound, fingering his refilled goblet in a way that implied calculation.

'What, William, do you think are the chances of a Lombard kingdom in South Italy?'

'I have the same thoughts on that as you.'

Ephraim smiled as though William had uncovered some secret, and he did not pretend surprise or ask a stupid question like how this Norman could know what was in his mind.

'And even if it could be achieved, it could not sustain itself,' William added. 'The Lombards are not good at rule and they are especially not good at acting together. Petty jealousy would tear it apart.'

'Not even if Guaimar was to declare himself?'

'Your prince wants the spoils without the blood, which may serve in Amalfi, but is no way to command loyalty in this part of the world. Besides, he was appointed, or should I say restored, to his fief by the Western Emperor, Conrad. How do you think Constantinople would see his attempt to elevate himself from prince to king?'

'They would see it as imperial encroachment.'

'More to the point, my friend, the present Emperor of the West would see it as committing him to the defence of Apulia, and I think an imperial edict would come from Germany telling Guaimar to withdraw his candidacy lest he provoke a greater conflict.'

Ephraim nodded: the two remnants of the old Roman patrimony lived in a mutual regard based on never driving the other to feel threatened. Thus, for years, Byzantium had stayed out of Campania, while Bamberg had avoided encroaching on Apulia.

'Did you know, William, I have a wife and children?'

'No, but it does not surprise me.'

'I often think what I will leave them, apart from what I own.'

'What do you wish to leave them?'

'That which any son of Abraham wishes to bequeath to his offspring, a secure place in which to live. That is my sole concern, and one I pursue relentlessly. I am minded to go wherever that can be promised.'

William felt the slow smile of understanding crease his face, and oddly, because he was looking at Tirena, she, mistaking it, gave a hint of a smile in return. But he was not really looking at her, he was thinking that Kasa Ephraim had just offered him his support. A bargain had been struck, and it had been done so by a very clever man, because it had been made without a word being said, or a promise made, by either party.

That frame of mind was ruptured by Mauger rushing in, his voice breathless. 'Count Atenulf has sold Boioannes back to Byzantium.'

'What?'

'And he has kept the gold to himself.'

'He is truly a Lombard,' said Kasa Ephraim.

'But that is not the most surprising thing, brother. Wait till you see who is the messenger.'

The figure that filled the doorway made William wonder if he was looking into a piece of polished silver with magical qualities, for it was like looking at a younger version of himself. His hair had some grey now; that of his brother was still pure gold.

'Do you not know me, William? I was once your squire and watched you fight the brother of the King of the Franks.'

'Robert?'

The nod was slow, then the deep-blue eyes turned to look at, first Kasa Ephraim, then at Listo and finally at Tirena, who was wide-eyed at this apparition, so like the man who now held her as ward. The voice was as deep and the air of being in command of all around him prevalent too, a self-confidence that was devoid of the taint of arrogance.

'I have come to make my way, William.'

Unbeknown to Robert, William's thinking was still taken with the chicanery of Atenulf. Also, selling Boioannes was an act that could not have been carried out without the connivance of his elder brother. Thus he was frowning, and Robert, who had seen that expression too often on the face of his father, reacted to it.

'Do I warrant a proper welcome,' he growled, 'or am I to be treated like an intruder by a man too grand to acknowledge his own flesh and blood?'

William was not accustomed to being addressed so and the frown turned to a glare, the voice taking on an equally angry tone. 'You say you have come to make your way. Well, when I have seen you fight I might consent to let you stay, but, mark this, you will sit well behind the rest of your brothers and they will prosper before you do, for they have done service.'

'I should have stopped in Troia, as I was asked to do.'

'If you wish to return there, do so with my blessing.'

'William...' Mauger protested.

Robert did not let that intercession interfere with his anger at a greeting so at variance with his expectations. He had travelled too many leagues to get here and sacrificed too much. 'What makes you think I require your blessing?'

'You will starve without it.'

'I think,' said Kasa Ephraim, 'that I had best depart.'

'If you wish, friend,' William replied, with a glare that now included Mauger. 'And you can take these two with you, for I have people whose interest I care about to attend to.'

Turning away from the doorway, William nearly burst out laughing. Tirena was favouring his half-brother Robert with the kind of fierce glare she once reserved for him.

'Murder?' said Mauger, shaking his head in disbelief.

'He was drunk and so was the man he killed. The duke was about to take us into service, but that went by the board as soon as Serlo stuck in the knife.'

'What about Father?' demanded Geoffrey.

'I assume he came home, but I was gone by then.'

'You left him at Moulineaux?'

'I did what he commanded me to do,' growled Robert. 'I saw Serlo onto a boat in the bay at Granville and came south. I wonder now if it was wise.'

'You caught William at a bad time,' Drogo insisted. 'Perhaps an apology...'

'If he wishes to give me one I will take it!'

Drogo shook his head: that was not what he meant but there seemed little point in saying so, though he did think this younger sibling of his had an arrogant manner.

'Do we know if Serlo got to England?' asked Mauger.

'How would I? His fate is in the hands of God, and if he has drowned, what of it? He would certainly have seen the end of a rope if he had been taken.'

'He's your brother.'

'He's my half-brother, just like William, so before you chastise me for a lack of concern, take him to task, or are you all too afraid?'

If there had been any sympathy for Robert de Hauteville then, it evaporated. If he had not been blood, there might have been murder in Melfi.

# CHAPTER FIFTEEN

❧❦❧

In a world where news travelled slowly, normally at the pace of a walking man or a sailing merchant vessel, the death of the Eastern Emperor, Michael IV, spread like wildfire, because it directly affected the life of everyone in half of Christendom, as well as having a bearing on relations with the rest. Given the unrest in Apulia, it acted to create as much confusion as it did to engender raised hopes. Michael IV had, from humble beginnings, proved to be a successful ruler, in that he had held together an empire many of his neighbours, all of them ravenous for a share of the spoils, saw as ripe to fall apart. He had also managed to survive in the cauldron of imperial politics to die a peaceful death.

Once a handsome courtier and junior officer,

brother to a hugely powerful court official, Michael had become the lover of the fifty-year-old Empress Zoë, and had succeeded to the purple on the death of her first, ageing husband. That was an end replete with all the attendant accusations of assassination: first, it was rumoured, he had been left debilitated by frequent doses of a slow poison and, when that failed to send him to his grave, with a drowning in his bath.

Michael, it transpired, had not only kept Zoë content, but several other concubines as well, though increasingly epilepsy, the affliction from which he suffered, had seriously impeded his abilities as both a lover and an emperor. It was a measure of the authority of self-interested courtiers, not least a brother who acted as the power behind the throne, that a man so distressed by increasing illness could reign for so long.

The succession was always a fraught affair, so to those observing and calculating their own position, the tangled skein of Byzantine politics would now become even more unpredictable as those who hoped to inherit the power of the deceased fought for influence. The news that the heir to Imperial Purple was another Michael, related by marriage to the deceased emperor's father, Stephen – a one-time ship's caulker risen to the rank of admiral – arrived hard on the heels of the first, and a steady stream of rumour mixed with fact followed as the drama of imperial succession was played out.

Zoë must have approved of the new Michael, yet he demonstrated scant gratitude for her support. Once installed as emperor, she had been banished from the city to a nearby island in the Sea of Marmara, her head shaved and her wealth purloined, but being much loved by the citizens of Constantinople, as well as heir to the ruling Macedonian house, that had caused riots in the Byzantine capital.

Michael V, appearing for the games at the Hippodrome, had been pelted with stones and shot at with arrows by the mob, causing him to send hurriedly for Zoë to appease their wrath, but, even if he showed her to the crowd to prove she was free, he had acted too late. In yet another twist, Zoë's hated sister, Theadora, who had been shut away years before, was dragged out and acclaimed as joint-empress. Michael, called the Caulker because of the profession of his father, who had taken refuge in a monastery, was hauled into a public square and had his eyes put out.

Zoë was left to co-rule with her sister, but that did not last: she would rather have shared power with a horse. Within months, and now in her sixties, Zoë had taken a third husband, while Theadora was sent back to the nunnery. The new emperor, to whom Zoë was happy to surrender her power as well as her charms, was a one-time courtier, now styled Constantine IX, leaving everyone who passed on the story of these events to wonder at how such an entity as the Eastern Roman Empire could last.

That last tranche of news, the name and identity of the new emperor, came to Apulia with a nasty sting in the tail, for Constantine, as was usual, had reversed many of the acts of his predecessors, which meant that the favourites of both Michaels had been sent to the dungeons, while many of those they had imprisoned were freed and reinstated to their previous rank. One such was the general called George Maniakes, and he was on his way to Apulia to restore the power of Byzantium. Having escorted Kasa Ephraim back to Montecchio, prior to his onward journey to Salerno, William and Drogo were once more face to face with Prince Guaimar.

'Height,' William replied, when asked to describe the man he had served under in Sicily, his palm going above his head by three hands. 'Arduin will confirm that.'

'Did he not nearly strangle the old emperor's brother?' asked Guaimar, as Arduin nodded.

'It took three of us to stop him,' said Drogo, 'and even then I'm not sure we did by force.'

As an admiral, Stephen, the caulker, had been useless, only in place because of his connection to the ruling house, and George Maniakes had made no secret

of the fact that he despised him. An arrogant man of
incredible strength, as well as size, that strangulation
had been a one-handed attempt at murder, which
would have succeeded had he not been stopped; but to
lay hands on a man with such powerful connections
had not been wise and had led, once news got back to
Constantinople, to his downfall. It was a fitting irony
that this happened just after he had achieved his
greatest campaign successes, the defeat of the main
Saracen enemy followed by the capture of the most
important city in Sicily, the great port of Syracuse.

Due to that same arrogance, as well as the
increasing conceit which came with victory, he had
fallen out with William, denying the Normans, as well
as a body of Varangians led by Harald Hardrada, the
right to plunder a city they had helped to capture, and
one which had refused terms when besieged. All knew
the laws of war and the citizens of Syracuse were no
exception: a walled city offered terms of surrender,
that then forced an army to invest and subdue it,
forfeited the right to mercy.

Maniakes had claimed Syracuse, once the Byzantine
capital of Sicily, as a recaptured city, not one taken
from the Saracens, nor was he prepared to compensate
Normans or Varangians from the Syracuse treasury
for their loss – anathema to men who fought for both
pay and the spoils of war. Furious, both William and
Hardrada had withdrawn their men from the campaign

and left the island, the Normans returning to Aversa, while Harald Hardrada travelled back to Norway, where his brother was king, his now leaderless troops returning to Constantinople.

'His Achilles heel is that temper,' added Arduin: he had also suffered from the egotism of Maniakes, treated like a servant rather than a captain, glad to see him replaced, only to find himself so underwhelmed by the capabilities of his useless replacement that he too had come home.

'He thinks himself the greatest general since Alexander,' added William.

'Yet his reputation...?' hinted Guaimar.

'He is a good general,' William replied, 'and I don't doubt he will be a formidable opponent.'

Guaimar glanced at Rainulf Drengot, as if looking for inspiration, but none came from that source, and it was obvious to those watching him closely, the two senior de Hautevilles and Arduin of Fassano, that the prince was on the horns of a dilemma. Here was the very situation that had made him originally cautious in his aid for the revolt. He had come to the very borders of his domains, to this ruined castle of Montecchio, in the belief that matters were proceeding to a point of settlement; but Byzantium was not prepared to give up on Apulia so easily.

'What about the forces he has?'

It was Arduin who replied. 'Maniakes will have

no more men to choose from than either of those who preceded him, but he is a more ruthless recruiter and, I would suggest, he will use them more wisely.'

'But will he prevail?' Guaimar demanded, in a voice that showed the exasperation he felt at not being provided with concrete help to make a decision.

'Nothing is certain in war, Prince Guaimar,' said William, with a gravity he certainly did not feel. Indeed, without showing it he was amused by the way Guaimar was wriggling, like a worm on a fish hook.

'I cannot see that we can now achieve anything here,' Guaimar concluded.

Again he glanced at Rainulf, again in vain: the old Norman warrior was either not willing to help him with a way to extricate himself, or he did not see the problem. As soon as news of the Maniakes appointment had reached Montecchio, those representatives of the Adriatic ports had hurried back to their homes, knowing full well that they would be the primary targets of the new catapan the minute he landed. They had departed with nothing decided regarding the future.

'I think it best that we return to Salerno.'

Those words finally stirred Rainulf Drengot from his torpor. 'You mean run away!'

As a choice of words it was not only too obvious, too undiplomatic, it was very embarrassing, and even if he had become practised at dissimulation, Guaimar's cheeks flushed and his response was brutal.

'I do not mean run away,' he barked. 'But nothing can be done regarding the future until the threat of Maniakes has been dealt with, and since neither you or I are likely to engage him in combat we would best serve being out of the path of those who must.'

It was now Rainulf Drengot's turn to flush, but his cheeks reddened with anger at being so publicly rebuked. 'Then I ask to be allowed to fight.'

'In what capacity, Count Rainulf, and who will look after matters in Aversa?' The use of his title, something Guaimar rarely employed, was as shrewd as the mention of his fief, a sharp reminder of the Norman's vassalage as well as his dependence on the prince for other matters. 'This was a question I thought settled.'

'You are, at present, in no danger,' said William mischievously. 'I doubt the new catapan knows of your presence on the border.'

The reply was given with all the creativity required of an imperial prince, and in a voice once more under control. Any irritation was in the eyes alone: Guaimar knew he was being bearded.

'I do not fear danger, William, but I fear that matters might go to rack in Salerno if I am away too long, and that may be even more true of Amalfi.'

Unbeknown to both Guaimar and Rainulf, that was exactly what was happening in Campania, not in newly conquered Amalfi: a full-blown uprising of the peasantry in the lands around Montecassino – not on those worked by the monks, but those forcibly granted to Rainulf's lances as demesnes. Uncontrolled by their nominal leader, the Normans had grown more and more greedy, not only bearing down on their own people, but increasingly raiding their neighbours, stealing harvested crops and the produce of the vineyards, creating a dangerous head of fury.

Worse, they were inclined to treat their womenfolk as chattels to be used as and when they wished, and that was doubly the case when they went pillaging. Even if he knew little of what went on around Montecassino, it was an attitude William had observed and disliked since his arrival in Aversa: the way his confrères treated the locals, as if they were raiding the land instead of living in it. His notion that they should remember how their forbears had settled Normandy, and how they had come to live in harmony with those over whom they exercised lordship, when mentioned to others, seemed to have no impact and had fallen on deaf ears.

To be seen as worse than the Lombards was stupid, but it was brought on by the mercenary status of the Normans. When gathered, and especially when in their cups with too much wine, they would wax nostalgic about the land they left and the one to which they were determined to return, which flew in the face of experience. Some did travel back to Normandy, but most left their bones in Italian graves, and had the prayers paid for by their compatriots said by priests or monks who knew nothing of their antecedents, but were well aware of the way they had lived their lives, one in which their redeemer had much to forgive.

Retribution came at the monastery itself, where a captain called Rodolf had stopped at the monastery church to pray, in the company of some fifteen of his men. No Italian, indeed few Lombards, would seek to challenge a Norman when he was wearing his weapons, but there was one occasion when even these warriors were obliged to divest themselves of their swords, for it was sacrilegious to take those into a church; bloodthirsty they might be, but they were also deeply pious, many never letting a day go by without Mass being said so they stood in good stead with God, and this day was no exception.

The monastery servants had seen those gathered weapons and seized them, ringing the church bell as well, a signal that the monastery was in danger, to summon all within earshot to its defence. When Rodolf sought to lead his men out, curious as to the cause of this commotion, he found the church doors barred, that was until the peasants who had come to the aid of their church entered, using those same swords left behind to slay men who, for all their prowess, only had their knives with which to defend themselves. By the time the monks arrived to seek to mediate, all the Normans had been slain.

From that, the revolt spread, so that no Norman, by the very nature of their existence, living in small isolated bands, was safe; nor, given the number of people committed to this revolt, was Rainulf Drengot when he rode out with a larger number of his men. A hurried plea came to Melfi for support, a request that some of his lances be returned to help him regain control; that was an appeal William was ready to turn down, and for two good reasons: Rainulf had brought this upon himself and, quite apart from that, he had, in George Maniakes, an enemy much closer, who to his way of thinking was a more potent threat, especially given the tactics he had chosen to employ.

With few experienced men to do his bidding – he had brought no more than five hundred soldiers with him – George Maniakes resorted to terror in order to make his enemies fearful. Wisely, he began his campaign well to the south, as far as possible from Melfi and an army that could beat him if engaged. Instead of landing at Trani, staunchly loyal to Byzantium and reasonably close to his enemies, he made his landfall in the far south, below Brindisi.

Raising what conscripts he could, he bypassed that great port city, it being too strong, and force-marched his men on to Ostuni. Normally this hill town, perched on a rocky outcrop half a league from the Adriatic, was a place no serious general would have troubled to capture, and it was one that had shown no stomach for either intrigue or revolt in previous decades. That, against the likes of George Maniakes, was not enough to save it.

Poorly defended, with no garrison, a broken-down watchtower and cathedral atop the mount on which it stood, and with walls much-pilfered for house building, fortifications that had not been maintained for decades, it had no chance of resistance and the citizenry knew it. Envoys bearing gifts of food and wine were sent out as soon as the Byzantine force was spotted moving up the coast accompanied by a small fleet of supply ships.

Pitching his tents in the narrow strip of land between the outcrop and the sea, George Maniakes received those envoys and took their gifts just before he personally, with a sword big enough to match his great stature, took their lives by lopping off their heads in a quartet of single blows. Then he sent his men into Ostuni with instructions to show no quarter, and for once, that was an order strictly applied. Every man found was killed, the women of all ages raped before joining them in death, so that the narrow steep-stepped streets of the town ran with great effusions of blood.

Those children who had not fallen to blows from

swords, knives and clubs were brought out onto the plain, the older ones set to digging a pit deep enough to hold their bodies, one they were thrown into as soon as it was completed, joined by the younger children down to toddlers, the earth they had toiled to remove thrown over them to suffocate them while they still breathed, their tears and wailing wasted on the ears of the tyrannical general who had ordered this massacre.

Houses and the cathedral were torched after being despoiled, everything of value going to Maniakes's men, for they were wise enough to torture the people who might have something to hide before despatching them to meet their Maker, and for those who resisted, the mutilation of one of their children or the brutal deflowering of a pubescent daughter was usually enough to loosen parental tongues. Livestock was driven out to be slaughtered on the beach, those not roasted and eaten were salted and barrelled to provide supplies.

As always – and it was a mystery to those who had pillaged Ostuni – there were some who survived their efforts at total eradication. Forced to flee the inferno of their burning dwellings, and with fires too good to waste, many were roasted alive over the flames so recently used to cook food. Maniakes ordered that half a dozen be spared, young men who could travel with speed. These he ordered out of his camp, with food and water, to travel in all directions and tell the surrounding towns and villages what they could expect.

It is probable such places thought it a warning not to resist. It was not that: for most it was a notification of the coming storm. Town after town, and every hamlet in between, saw the same treatment, and as George Maniakes marched up the coast, sending raiding parties inland where there was something to pillage, assaulting towns with his whole force if they warranted the effort, he turned the province into a desert in his wake.

The roads of Apulia were lined with rotting bodies swinging from the trees, with the cadavers of women and children putrefying by the roadside. The message was not for those little towns and rural settlements, it was for the port cities that had the ability to defend themselves: do so, and this is what you will face – utter and complete destruction and death.

It took time for the news to reach Melfi, and that came with the first of the port cities to submit. Monopoli, originally, in antiquity, a Greek settlement and still mainly that in sentiment and religion, was too close to the mayhem in its hinterland, too aware of the fate it faced, to hold out, lacking the military mind and judgement that would have advised it do so, for in truth, even if it was not large, it was rich enough to keep its walls in good repair and George Maniakes did not yet have the forces or equipment to take a place of that size.

But the terror, allied to the Greek inheritance that went back to pre-Roman times, worked its devilish magic, and the bloodthirsty catapan was shrewd enough to offer to spare them chaos, thus underlining his message to those further up the coast. Yet every able-bodied man of the right age in Monopoli now found himself a soldier in the service of Byzantium, and the treasury of the port was plundered as a means to pay them.

For Arduin, when he heard what was happening, the problem was acute: previously, marching his men to fight had involved no extended distances. To stop this new threat required him to take his volunteer *milities* far from their homes, families, and more importantly for the majority, their fields. Yet to do nothing was to watch Apulia burn and Maniakes get stronger, for it was obvious that each port up the coast would follow Monopoli and submit as soon as they saw the Byzantine host outside their walls. Something was needed to inspire them to resist, and also encourage his army to fight far from its home. In the new titular leader, Arduin thought he had the answer.

'William, this is Argyrus, son of the great Melus. Landulf of Benevento has finally relented and sent us the leader we require.'

William nodded and looked the young man up and down, noting that he seemed, just by the look in his eye and the way he held himself, to be a better prospect than that idiot, Atenulf. About the same age as the newly arrived Robert, he was not martial in his bearing, being slim of build, but William had to remind himself that it was an error to judge Lombards, Greeks or Italians by the same yardstick he applied to Normans.

'I bid you welcome, Argyrus. I hope you are aware that it was you we looked to before the Prince of Benevento sent us his brother.'

'Arduin spoke with me then, and I will not hide from you that I was made angry by the prince's decision. Not that I could make that too obvious: I was, after all, a guest in Benevento.'

A strong voice and not lacking in wisdom, thought William, certainly clever enough to keep his head on his shoulders: for guest, read near-captive.

'With Argyrus as our leader, William,' Arduin crowed, enthusiastically, 'the men who have volunteered will march anywhere, to the ends of the Earth if need be.'

That piece of hyperbole was taken for what it was, a way to flatter this new talismanic arrival.

'You have heard of the depredations of George Maniakes?' Argyrus nodded. 'Arduin and I have thought on how to counter him; I wonder if you have any notions of your own.'

Unlike Atenulf, who would have been floored if
required to answer to his own name, the young man
replied with speed and precision, yet so quickly that
William guessed he must have been primed by Arduin
regarding what to say. That mattered not, it was only
important that he grasped the essentials and agreed
with them.

'Maniakes is marching up the coast, gathering
strength with every place he subdues but does not
destroy, yet we have to hope that Brindisi and Bari
will hold out as they have done so often in the past.
Not even George Maniakes is going to devastate the
two greatest sources of revenue in Apulia, even if he
had the force to breach their walls, which I doubt he
could yet muster. Our aim is a revolt which will rid
South Italy of Byzantium for ever, is it not?'

William nodded: he and Arduin had discussed this
often, and though they had their differences, they
agreed on that.

'Maniakes, while he has burnt and despoiled
everything around it, has spared Monopoli, therefore it
is probable to assume he will do the same to Molfetta
and Giovinazzo and, if he could come far enough
without a battle, to Barletta.'

Given another nod, Argyrus continued confidently.
'But before he can get to Barletta there is Trani, and it
is my view that in order to show that we, the Lombard
revolt, can not only win battles but take cities, I

suggest we invest that port and do to those loyal to Byzantium what Maniakes has done to others.'

'Brilliant,' said Arduin, 'do you not agree, William?'

Tempted to sarcasm, William expressed himself with more care. 'A wise course of action, but it will not be easy. Trani has stout walls.'

Argyrus stretched a tad, to show fortitude. 'Then we must build siege engines capable of breaching them.'

'At some point we will have to meet and defeat Maniakes.'

'Of course.'

'And given his penchant for destruction, the further south that happens the better.'

'If we take Trani, it will so lift the spirits of our troops, who will have gold in their purse and the blood of Greeks on their weapons, taking them further will be easy.'

Robert de Hauteville, complaining loudly to his bored brothers about the inactivity of the Normans, did not see William enter the chamber behind him. If he had not been so obsessed with his argument, that they should be out harrying this Maniakes instead of leaving him to do his worst, he might have noticed the looks on the faces of those he was addressing: not any warning, but more interest than they had shown hitherto. Not even the one closest to him, Mauger, was going to miss the upshot and fun to be had from this.

'He can't supply all his needs from the sea. He must forage, and when he does we should be there to kill his parties. And he sends detachments to attack the smaller towns, not his whole force, people we could easily beat.'

'You are welcome, brother, to ride out of here with your weapons and do what you wish.'

Robert spun round, then back again to scowl at his now grinning brothers. 'It may not sound like sense to you, William, but it does to me, and not to take on an enemy when the chance presents itself smacks of caution.'

'I cannot help but think our father should have administered to you a few more smacks as you grew up. It might have beaten some sense into your head.'

'He would have needed a club,' wheezed Humphrey, quite taken with his own joke.

'We have mobility while Maniakes has none,' Robert protested.

'Leave us,' William insisted, waving a peremptory arm at the others, a gesture that was not well taken: William was normally more careful of their pride. But they complied, knowing it was Robert at fault, given, in the short time he had been present, he had shown an ability to rile William that was unusual.

'Sit down,' William commanded. Set to protest, just for the sake of it, Robert finally shrugged and complied. 'You are new here, so I will forgive your ignorance.'

'I—'

Robert got no further, and William shouted at him to be silent.

'Do not question my tactics any more than you would question an order in a battle. I presume Father has taught you to do that! There are things here you do not understand, and if you wish to, silence and listening would be a better method than prattling to your brothers and trying to undermine me.'

'I do not seek to undermine you.'

'Then what have I just heard you do?'

'I am suggesting a course of action, a more honourable one—'

William cut across Robert again. 'One you suppose me too stupid to see?'

Robert, for once, replied in a somewhat chastened tone. 'I am sure you have considered it.'

'And discounted it, for which I think you will grant I must have a reason.'

Not accustomed to conceding much to anyone, it was a reluctant reply that emerged. 'Perhaps.'

'We are about to march out of here...'

'To where?'

William shouted again. 'To where I command our conroys should go. You are a lance amongst others and sharing blood with me grants you no rights above another. We are going to fight, and when I have seen what you can do, I will decide if you are an asset or a liability. If it is the second of those, you may as well load up your packhorse and go back to Normandy for I will have no use for you here. Until then, do as you are ordered.'

Robert was seething, but his voice was not raised as he answered, it was icy. 'I will make you eat those words, man to man if need be.'

'You are here to try to kill our enemies, not your relations.'

'My brother and I wish to accompany you,' said Tirena. 'It is not nice to be here when everyone else is gone.'

'To do what?' asked William.

'Listo will be your squire and look after your weapons and horses.'

'And you?'

The eyes, which had been looking at him eagerly, dropped then. 'There are things I can do.'

'You are still a child, Tirena.'

That got him one of those glares he remembered so well. 'I am not. Ask the other women and they will tell you.'

William was tempted to laugh, but he knew that would not be taken as he intended. This girl was too serious to see that it would be brought on as much by warmth as surprise at that which she was clearly suggesting. Slowly he nodded.

'Very well, Tirena, but remember you must do as I command.'

Meant to deflect what she was obviously proposing, it had exactly the opposite effect, as she dashed forward and flung herself at him so furiously he had no choice but to catch her, and she showed remarkable tenacity in the way she hung onto his neck. Finally he got her free and gave her a look that matched any she had ever given him.

'Behave, or stay in Melfi! Now, get your brother, and both of you see to my panniers.'

# CHAPTER SIXTEEN

><><

Trani had defensive walls that were indeed formidable, running right to and beyond the seashore, high and crenellated, with stout gates. The location of the town that supported the twin wooden jetties of the port, laying on a flat plain, meant that to invest the place was practicable as long as the besieger was prepared to be patient and had vessels able to enforce a blockade and stop supplies of food and reinforcements. Arduin had no ships, but he had absolute confidence that no more troops would arrive to aid the defence: the only ones close by were otherwise engaged.

Maniakes had finally decided he had enough strength for a siege, and had chosen to subdue Bari: thus he was too occupied, though there was no news that he had been reinforced. So if Constantinople would not support him there, they would not do so to protect a less important Byzantine outpost. The defence of Trani would be left to the citizenry, and they could be overcome if the right tactics were employed, which meant avoiding the gates, with their overhanging brattices designed to drop boiling oil and heavy rocks upon anyone attacking. Instead he would seek to mount an assault by siege tower at a point along the curtain wall.

The land to the north was low-lying marsh, too full of bog to support anything weighty. It was yielding even now, in early spring, useless for large numbers of soldiers on foot and thus even more so for cavalry. While those marshes acted as a protection for that portion of the defence, they also presented a barrier to the occupiers. They would struggle to sally out to a poorly manned frontage with any hope of achieving sudden surprise – soft marsh would slow them as well, giving a chance to react: by the time they reached firm ground, the mounted Normans, able to swiftly deploy and now close to a thousand in number, would be waiting for them.

And it was soon obvious that those marshlands were best avoided: troops bivouacked near there showed early signs of sickness, and that was not something the besiegers could afford. Every military leader knew that more sieges were beaten off by illness than stout defence, so while that part of the lines had to be covered, the troops, Lombard infantry, were rotated away from the place, to less miasmic climes, on a regular basis.

Inland the terrain was earth-covered rock and, being near level, perfect ground on which to construct the siege tower that would, if properly employed, soar above the walls of the port city. Those who would man the parapet might have a leavening of professional soldiers – an experienced captain from Byzantium was in the town, as well as a personal envoy from the new Emperor Constantine, there to stiffen the attitude of the defence – but even with such aid, the besiegers could count on a lack of discipline as well as a want of cohesion. Their only hope of relief lay in the abandonment of the siege of Bari: if George Maniakes came barrelling north with all the men he could command, he would have to be met in the field.

Their new titular leader, Argyrus, being untrained in military matters, was wise enough not to interfere in any discussion of tactics, though he always attended and listened carefully to what was being discussed. He took to riding around the lines with an escort of men he had gathered, so he could be seen, using his prestige to encourage and cajole. He also rode out to bolster the efforts of the timber-cutting parties; the kind of wood necessary to build a massive siege tower was not readily available close to Trani and had to be cut and dragged from the forested hills inland, an arduous task given there was no flowing watercourse on which to float the logs; movement was accomplished by a combination of men and mules.

Cavalry they might be, but there was no ease for the Normans in this: when not on their mounts foraging for supplies, they were stripped to the waist, helping to drag timber, or sawing and trimming tree trunks with the Lombard *milities*, using their strength where that was required – once the bigger logs were at the construction site – to haul on rough, hastily rigged cranes in order to get aloft the weighty main-frame timbers, these resting on the wheeled flatbed base and greased axles which would be used to move it forward to the walls once a path was cleared of rocks and any depression filled in.

As the carpenters sawed and trimmed, supplies of rope and canvas were brought down from Barletta, as well as grappling hooks fashioned by blacksmiths, the ropes entwined into ships' cables of a thickness that would allow the tower to be pulled, the canvas used to produce long fire screens which, wetted prior to the assault, would hang around the tower so that flaming arrows could not set the whole thing alight. Once the frame was complete, the carpenters could cut wood and smooth it for the higher platforms and barricades, and trim rough dowels to hold them in place.

Flat timber was used to fashion ramps with arrow slots for the crossbowmen. These would be dropped onto the top of the walls once the tower was hard against them, the first task being to grapple the whole structure so it could not be dislodged. The small number of fighters first to attack, the most formidable Normans, would then make sure it stayed there, holding off the inevitable counter-attacks, while others rushed up the interconnecting ladders in support, before moving over those same ramps in such numbers as to overwhelm the defenders.

'We will be able to offer terms within the week,' said Arduin, looking at the tower taking shape, an object that could easily be seen from the walls. 'They must know that once this is employed, unless it is destroyed, they cannot hold out.'

When construction reached a point where the physical attributes of his men were no longer required, William instituted training in the kind of combat they would face. On foot, it was based on the basic unit of Norman warfare, the ten-man conroy – if their leader knew anything, it was that men did not fight for a cause or even for plunder: they fought for each other. The Norman system meant that not only did these warriors ride thigh to thigh in battle, they camped together round their own fire, ate together and slept in near-touching distance. A warrior would not sacrifice his life even for a glimpse of heavenly paradise, but he would give it freely if one of his confrères was seen to be in mortal danger.

Robert had been placed under the command of a captain called Hugo de Boeuf, an old fighter and experienced leader who had seen and survived much combat in both Campania and Sicily, as well as being a man William trusted to keep in check his brother's bumptious nature. It was evident that Robert fitted in quickly because, when it came to mirth, he and his companions were the ones who seemed to laugh most, however hard and unpleasant was the task allotted to them.

Given that included tree-felling, woodcutting and hauling on crane ropes, Robert was to be seen, like his fellows, stripped to the waist. William had to admit himself impressed by the girth of his shoulders and the obvious strength of his muscular arms. He lifted and carried things other men dragged, singing ribald songs that his fellows took up, thus easing their labours.

Now he wanted Robert training to be first onto those walls, and that, too, would no doubt be impressive if you discounted his oft-mentioned assertion that he knew more about fighting than any of his brothers. William had the carpenters construct, out of sight of the walls, a mock-up of a tower platform, raised off the ground, complete with a ramp, as well as a wooden palisade set along the ground to represent the parapet, the idea to stage as near as possible what would actually happen once the tower was pressed and held against those walls, using as defenders better, more experienced fighters than those the attackers should actually face.

While that was being constructed, normal training was resumed, and it was in such activity that William found himself up against Robert, employing the kind of wooden swords they used in the manège at Aversa in everyday training. Rarely ever beaten on horse or on foot – and only then by a piece of startling guile – William Iron Arm found he had a real battle on his hands, and he could see from the flinty look in the eyes on either side of Robert's nose guard, as well as the weight of the thuds on his shield, the determination to beat him into submission.

When it came to using the mocked-up platform, one thing was quick to emerge: the very simple fact that if the calculation for the tower height were correct, they would, on the first point of engagement, be attacking from a higher level than the defence. William, leading those defenders, had the great pleasure, during the first attempt, of sweeping his mock sword under the point of Robert's shield, so taking away his feet, causing him to collapse in a heap, to be finished off with a stout and painful stab at the chest, a fate suffered by most of the men led by Hugo de Boeuf.

The chastened attackers, who would probably have had their feet sliced through in a real battle, gathered to discuss how to overcome this, with Robert first to speak, posing a question to his conroy leader. 'This is false. As we approach, the crossbowmen will keep down the heads of the defence, will they not?'

A bent-over Hugo nodded, as he rubbed a sore shin where it had been clobbered hard by a defender, before agreeing. 'And so those on the walls will be thinned and the ones who take station right before the ramp will be forced to duck, and thus be under it as it drops and out of the fight—'

'So we fight to right and left,' Robert continued, interrupting Hugo and ignoring the look that implied such behaviour was not right, that Hugo was the leader and these were conclusions he should state: with this de Hauteville he was wasting his time. 'We should come down crouched behind our shields and use weight to just push back the defence. We can't really do battle with them until we are on the parapet.'

'The crossbows—'

Robert cut across him again. 'Must keep the defenders away from the grappling hooks.'

'Will you hold your tongue,' Hugo yelled, in a voice loud enough to carry to William. 'I command here.'

While Robert, who could see William glaring at him, mumbled something about only trying to help, it was obvious from his bodily reaction that he was less than pleased to be so publicly admonished. Yet no one could doubt he had the right of it, and that he had nailed both the problem and the solution in less time than Hugo, this proved by the partial success of their next effort, one marred only by the time it took to execute the manoeuvre, which added to the time it would take to achieve their ultimate aim: to get to and open a gate.

It was no good to insist that in fellow Normans they were up against men of greater height, strength and fighting ability than those they would be likely to face, the whole idea being to identify problems in advance, and that led to another platform being built at the top of the tower and balustraded, accessed by yet another ladder, which the bowmen could use to overlook and aid the assault while still keeping the defenders away from the grappling hooks.

Time and again they went at it, William changing the men engaged on both sides so that everyone knew what to do and what they would face. He even had his heavily mailed and armed lances, himself included, running up and down the ladders to time how long it would be before they got to the top and became effective, an activity that, like most of what had gone before, required copious amounts of watered wine for dry throats, this while Arduin drilled his volunteer *milities* for the task they had to perform, to attack in force any gate the Normans managed to get open.

As darkness fell, William retired to his tent, there to be looked after by his two wards, who had insisted on taking on the duties. Listo saw to his equipment, cleaning it of the dust and sweat with which it had become stained, while Tirena provided warmed water with which he could remove those same commodities from his body, and fresh, more comfortable clothing. She also supervised the preparation of his food, with an air, much resented, that indicated she did not trust those who did the cooking not to poison him.

Once fed, and attired in loose garments, William made his nightly tour of the outposts, checking that his men, on the part of the lines for which they were responsible, were in place and awake, stopping occasionally to talk, and also to look at the walls of Trani, lit by flaming torches that cast a low glow of light onto the ground below so that no sudden night-time assault would be possible.

Traversing the southern edge of the lines, alongside those marshes, he stopped to watch the dancing fireflies, wondering at how God had made such creatures, but that only led him on to wonder at how that same deity had made humanity in his own image, yet he had set men like him on a path that led to death, mostly for others. Crossing himself, just before he slapped a biting insect, he was also thinking Arduin was right: with the tower probably no more than a day away from completion it was time to offer the citizens terms.

The proposition would be simple: open your gates and give yourselves over to the Lombard army, in which case the city and the people within it will be spared. Refuse and you will face fire and sword, for if you force us to bleed to capture, then you will lose more blood as a consequence, and if required to continue once the gates had been breached no citizen of the town, of any age or sex, would be guaranteed to survive.

That thought made him gloomy, and, sick of the buzzing of flying creatures in his ears, he made his way back to the quarter housing the tented encampment of the leaders of the host, where he came across Arduin and Argyrus. They were in conversation outside the latter's tent and, being called to join them, William did so.

'All is ready, William. Tomorrow at first light I will call for the gates to be opened.'

'Arduin thinks they will refuse, William, how do you see it?' asked Argyrus.

'I think if they were going to surrender they would have sent out envoys by now. They can see what we are building and they know that once it is employed, unless they can destroy it immediately, they are doomed. My mind is set on the assault.'

There was a short silence then: regardless of how good the men who would attack, some would die, and since William was going to lead the supporting fighters personally, and would thus face the defenders near to their most potent, he might be one of them.

'How I wish I was going to be there alongside you,'

said Argyrus, his eyes alight with enthusiasm.

William took that for what it was, wishful thinking: this young man could not fight like a Norman and would probably struggle to match the men of his own race. Utterly untrained, he would just get in the way, in fact he would probably get someone killed trying to keep him alive. But it was a worthy sentiment to express at such a time and it would have been churlish to react with the truth.

'You lead our men through the gates, Argyrus,' then he looked at Arduin, to reassure him he saw him as their commander. 'Alongside our general.'

Argyrus sighed. 'I doubt I shall sleep. My blood is racing.'

'I shall,' William replied, 'and so will you when you become accustomed to nights like this.'

'Of which we have had many, have we not, William? And we will have more before our cause triumphs.'

Looking at Arduin, William could see, once more and reflected by the flickering torches, the light of that Lombard dream in his eyes, and he wondered how the man could sustain it after the rebuffs he had suffered at Montecchio. Putting aside his own ambitions and imaging the result after which Arduin hankered, what was there for him if they were ultimately successful? The envoys from the other port cities had openly repudiated him, as well as mouthing meaningless platitudes when it came to Argyrus, while Guaimar was playing such a double game he could hardly look for support there.

Was it that he would be satisfied to see Apulia free of Byzantium? Did he hope that Argyrus would somehow overturn any objections from the other Lombard powers and succeed in uniting the factions, thus gaining his reward as the man who had aided him to power? These were too many thoughts to be harbouring at such a time of day. William had had a hard day's training, with more to come in the morning and quite possibly real fighting instead of mock combat. He was tired.

'Time to sleep.'

The oil lamps were low in his tent and there was silence from the other two cots. Having said prayers, then disrobing, William lay down and closed his eyes, but sleep was slow to come as he ran over in his mind what might happen on the morrow, envisaging the attack, almost hearing the clash of swords and the shouting of men engaged in deadly combat, himself included. In doing so he had the thoughts which had plagued him often, of how close he had come in the past to death, seeing the blows that he had deflected which might, had he not been both good and lucky, have got through.

He was just drifting off when his cot dipped to one side and he half-raised himself sharply: a secret knife in such places as Italy was always a possibility and assassinating leaders was a particularly good way to thwart a siege, but that turned to first surprise and then to slight annoyance as the girl Tirena wrapped her arms round his naked upper body.

'Back to your own cot,' he whispered, insistently, but that only increased the force of her embrace: she was now clinging to him and he was aware that she too was naked, her pert young breasts pressing into his flesh.

'You fight tomorrow,' she hissed, 'and I fear for you.'

William wanted to scoff but that seemed ridiculous in the face of the thoughts he had just been harbouring, so he sought to deflect her obvious concern by addressing worries she might have. 'Never fear, Tirena, you and Listo will be cared for.'

Even whispered, her reply was vehement. 'You can be very stupid!'

That said, her hand shot down to his crotch and took hold of his penis, and even if he had wanted not to react, he was a man and could not help it as she tugged at it with the same urgency she had no doubt once used on a goat's teat. Drogo might accuse him of behaving like a eunuch, but William de Hauteville was far from that: he had the same desires as his rampant brother but he attributed to himself more self-control.

That was not the case on this night and under the pressure of this girl's enticement. It seemed only seconds before he was astride her, hearing her gasp with a combination of satisfaction and pain as he entered her, grateful that all thoughts of what might happen at sunrise had been driven from his mind.

The alarm, much shouting and cries of agitation, were slow to penetrate William's brain, and as he awoke, the surprise of finding someone else in his cot, huddled close to his body and asleep, took a moment to register. But those shouts coming through the canvas allowed no time for delay and he was up and at the tent flap in a flash, in the process waking the girl. Standing naked and looking out, William saw without difficulty what the noise was about: the flames from the burning tower rose high in the sky, illuminating the ground all around, as well as the silhouetted figures running around it.

Some were trying to throw water to douse the conflagration, but given it was blazing from base to top, with cinders rising into the glowing orange and yellow fingers of flame, it would be useless. But he did register that fresh-cut timber, even if it had had several days to lose its sap, should not burn with such ferocity. It could only have gone up in the way it had because of sabotage.

'Fetch my cloak,' he commanded, watching as Tirena ran to obey, wondering at the sudden tumescence the sight of her young moving and naked body produced.

Once she handed it over, her black eyes wild with fear, he responded softly. 'Go back to your cot and wait for me.'

The last three words assuaged her fears and made her smile, and as she was only half his height, the kiss she planted on him was closer to his chest than his face. He was gone before he realised what she had done, only aware of that mark of affection when the slight night breeze touched on the moisture her act had left behind.

The whole camp was awake now, all gathered around this unwanted bonfire, looking up with a mixture of anger and wonder as the labours of weeks was consumed.

'Stand back,' he yelled, 'all of you.'

That was a command slow to be obeyed, even if it was much repeated, but the crowd had retired before the weight of the structure, acting on the destroyed lower parts, began to buckle and slowly fall. There was a strange grace to that, so slowly did it happen, that shattered by the crash of contact as parts broke off sending sparks flying in all directions. By the time it was down, Arduin was standing next to William.

'It was set alight after being drenched,' he said,' I can smell the pitch.'

William was looking at the faces all around, lit by the orange glow, including his brothers. 'Who was guarding it?'

'A party of my men were set to watch it,' Arduin replied, shaking his head. 'Ten in number. Those not speared I saw with their throats slashed.'

'Where's Argyrus?'

Arduin looked around, as had William, scanning the faces, easily able to identify those he knew. 'I pray to God it is not he.'

'Then why can we not see him, or any of his escort?'

'Perhaps he still sleeps.'

That got the Lombard a look, one he had to acknowledge despite how bitter it made him feel: no one could sleep through the noise of a whole camp rudely brought awake and the light from such a blaze.

William and Arduin saw Argyrus at first light. They were standing by the still-smouldering embers of the tower with the acrid taste of smoke in their throats. He was looking over the walls of Trani, while all around him the jeers of the defenders rose and fell in mockery. There was no need to wonder at what had caused his betrayal: it would be Byzantine gold, as it had been in the case of Atenulf selling his prisoner. Angry as he was, William could at least see what had prompted the young man's treachery.

Since his father's death he had been a prisoner of Byzantium, and who knew what his feelings were truly like towards them? Released, he had become the pawn of others more powerful than he, sustained by the hope that things would at sometime turn to his advantage. He had been used by Landulf of Benevento and surely he had been told of the council called by Guaimar, where he had been extolled by his fellow Lombards as a potential leader with obvious insincerity: whatever they saw him as, it was not as a future ruler. If Argyrus had any sense, he must have seen, too, in the Prince of Salerno's manoeuvring, a future source of disappointment, so he had decided no doubt to take what was on offer now, in place of the uncertain rewards of the future.

Arduin was near to tears: for him this was no mere setback, it was like a physical blow. Who now would lead the revolt and provide a banner around which the ordinary Lombards, those who sought only freedom, could rally? He had been looking into their faces since the first grey light tinged the morning sky, and had seen in their expressions, as the word spread of this treachery, coming hard on the heels of what Count Atenulf had done, how badly it had affected them. The question was unavoidable: would they still fight?

'Do we rebuild?' William asked. He, at least, had no doubt what his men would do: they were professionals when it came to fighting. 'It is for you to decide.'

'I need to gauge the spirit of those who have volunteered.'

'Their spirits will be lifted by your determination, Arduin.'

'I will gather, then, after they have prayed and eaten, but I have to tell you, William, at this moment I cannot think what words I will use to inspire them.'

As the day wore on, with a listless besieging host clearing up the charred mess of that burnt tower, Arduin kept putting off that which he knew he needed to do. For all he had a silver tongue, he felt it would need to be diamond encrusted to overcome the disillusionment which was apparent in every face with whom he exchanged a glance. Equally troubling, and a problem that had him sulking like Achilles in his tent, was what to do next if the siege was not to be pressed, for if these men he led, Normans not included, would have been reluctant to go so far south as to fight George Maniakes before, they would be even more so now.

He looked up angrily as the tent flap was hauled back, prepared to snap that he wanted to be left in peace. But they were not words he could use to William de Hauteville.

'You had best come, Arduin. Trani has opened a gate and is sending out envoys carrying olive branches.'

He saw them as soon as he emerged and moved to the edge of the camp, with William on his heels, the olive branches of peace being waved above their heads, and when they spoke, to tell him why they were now ready to hand over their port city, he had to stop himself from laughing out loud. George Maniakes had rebelled against Constantinople, lifted the siege of Bari, had his troops declare him emperor, and had set off in a fleet of ships for the lands of Romania, intent on toppling Constantine.

'Argyrus?' he demanded.

He had fled by sea, and once they had entered the city, and were on the jetty that made up half the harbour of Trani, they could still see the sails of his ship beating up into an unfavourable wind as he sought to escape their vengeance.

Over the following week, Arduin began to sense that the betrayal of Argyrus was impacting on him, and that was compounded by what had occurred with the idiotic Count Atenulf: it was in looks and conversations hurriedly abandoned whenever he appeared, and it was from his fellow Lombards that he felt the most distaste – the ordinary Norman lances, as they always had, paid him little attention. He had had his men in the palm of his hand until that siege tower was destroyed, able to rouse them to great deeds with his rhetoric. They had been fired to take Trani and spill their blood in doing so.

Yet now, only days later, if he issued a command, he had to wait for it to be obeyed, and when the men he led were collected in numbers such an order led to a ripple of unpleasant muttering, not silenced by their captains, a sure indication of a serious loss of authority, and he knew in his heart that what he was witnessing was impossible to repair.

There was little point in seeing it as unfair: yes, it was he who had started the revolt, but it was also he who had sought that titular leader around whom the Lombards could unite, never doubting in his own mind that it could not be himself. Both had betrayed the cause he espoused, and it took no great imagination to discern that he was being held responsible, being examined, in covert looks, in a way that saw him in the same light, even now that victory was at hand.

Alone in the villa he had taken, overlooking the harbour of Trani, idly throwing dice onto a table, which held a meal unconsumed since the night before, he was forced to examine, as the first hint of grey tinged the eastern sky, his options. News had come that Prince Guaimar had departed Salerno and was on his way to Melfi, where he had called a great council of all who mattered in Apulia. Sure he was entitled to much reward, Arduin had serious doubts as to whether he would get his just deserts, and he would certainly never receive that of which he had entertained in many dreamlike fantasies: real power in the province he had helped to conquer.

The realisation, which he had always known but now saw with great clarity, did nothing to reassure him. Without the Normans he was nothing, especially if he would struggle to command his own volunteer levies, many of whom, in any case, were drifting away. The atmosphere in his military lines, in the rows of Lombard tents which surrounded Trani, as he had walked through them that day, had been rank with dissent and suspicion.

For the tenth time he unfolded the note which had been pressed into his hand as he made his way through the bustling town on his return, an act carried out with such speed and in such a crowd that all he had seen of the deliverer was the disappearing back of the cowl on his head. The words he read only underlined the thoughts on which he had been ruminating, as he wondered if the people who had sent this to him had also fomented that suspicion he had felt in the looks aimed at his back, from the same eyes that would not engage with his own.

It was impossible to put out of his mind the meeting Guaimar had held at Montecchio, to forget how the delegates who had come from the port cities and inland towns had made it plain that they had no real regard for him; that they saw him as no more than an instrument of Norman ambition and would certainly not now wish to see him elevated to a position of any authority. Was he that, a dupe? Was such a role all he could claim? Had he been a tool not only of Norman aspirations but also those of Guaimar, who had done nothing to raise him in the eyes of the Apulian Lombards?

And what would happen if that were true? If he could not command his own levies – and he certainly would never command the likes of William de Hauteville or the Normans he led, if he was not trusted by Guaimar or his fellow Lombards – for what was he working, what ambition of his own was going to be fulfilled? The other objects on the table were his personal possessions: a bundle of clothing, including a heavy purse of gold, the contents of his now empty strongbox, the rewards he had garnered from his campaigning. Clothes he did not need, his new masters would see to that.

With a heavy heart, Arduin of Fassano stood up, picked up the leather purse and exited the villa through the terrace and gardens that led down to the harbour. The note lay still on the table, and that would tell all who wanted to know where he had gone, though he did wonder if they would reason out why. The boat he had been told to expect was waiting for him, and as soon as he climbed aboard the sail was lifted aloft on the mast and he headed out to sea, ready to accept from Byzantium the same kind of offer which had suborned Argyrus.

The news was not slow in coming to William, for the villa he occupied was only a stone's throw from that of Arduin, and while his brothers were loud in their condemnation he was less so. Firstly, he felt unwell and lacked the energy to fulminate. But there was another reason: he alone had some inkling of what had prompted the Lombard's flight. The question which occupied him was not that it had happened but what to do about it.

'Find the trumpeter,' he commanded, 'and call an assembly. The men must be told.'

Hurriedly obeyed, the whole host, Norman and Lombard, was gathered by the time he exited the city gate, and he knew by the buzz of talk that news of Arduin's betrayal had spread. There was no platform from which to address them so he clambered with some difficulty onto the embers of that siege tower, from where he could be seen by all, wondering, as he began to speak, if his voice would carry.

'I do not have the silver tongue of Arduin—' He had to stop then, the name made them react with boos, cries of shame and whistles and he had to wait some time till it died down. 'But I do have one virtue: there is no chance that I will ever take Byzantine gold.'

'That would depend on how much they were offering,' he heard Humphrey, who was just below him, say.

'I come here not to address the men I lead but to talk to you all. You have been thrice betrayed.' More braying greeted that, and another pause was necessary, besides which he needed to take a firm grip on a protruding bit of burnt timber to steady himself. 'So the time has come to find a leader who will never desert you.'

Drogo, as usual, was quicker to pick up what was needed than the others, and he stepped out and pulled out his sword, raising it in the air as he cried, 'I follow William de Hauteville, my brother. Who will join with me?'

That the Normans reacted positively to that was only to be expected, and their yells, as well as their swords or lances, rent the air. What was less expected was the reaction of the men Arduin had recruited, and it was an indication of how far their leaders had fallen in their eyes that they, too, loudly acclaimed William as their leader, and in amongst the shouting he could hear there were voices vowing to follow no other.

'There you are, Gill,' Drogo shouted into his ear. 'You have an army. All you need now is an enemy.'

'Never fear, Drogo,' William replied, his fist raised to accept the continuing acclamation. 'There are many out there, and not just from the east.'

# CHAPTER SEVENTEEN

∝◇∝

The meeting Guaimar called at the castle of Melfi had nothing in common with that which he had held before at Montecchio in the previous year: that had been a muted affair. Now he was in Apulia in all his pomp, bringing along with him not only his court, but his wife and children, as well as his sister, an imposing caravanserai, and the summons for all the powerful people of the province to attend on him was just that: not couched as a request, but as an instruction they would disobey at their peril.

Rainulf, still troubled by the rebellion around Montecassino, had been summoned too, but the one person not asked to attend was the Prince of Benevento, who was brusquely informed that should he or his brother show themselves they risked both life

and limb from their fellow Lombards, still incensed by
the way the captured catapan, Basil Boioannes, had
been sold back to Byzantium. Cunningly, Guaimar
went out of his way to plant in men's minds that he
was responsible, too, for the defection of Arduin and
Argyrus.

So they came again, the leading citizens of the
towns and cities of Apulia, some travelling through
lands still suffering the devastation visited upon
it by George Maniakes, which stood as a reminder
that caution was a policy best kept in reserve, and if
they travelled knowing that Guaimar was intent on
asserting some kind of authority, they also did so with
the certainty of the need for their own independence.

The Normans of Troia had agreed to actively
participate in the revolt, greeted, as they joined, by a
less-than-fit William – his journey from Trani had been
made in a litter. He had spent much time welcoming
like-minded bands from all over South Italy, lances
who had become aware that prosperity, if it were to be
had, was to be found in Apulia. Given there had, over
the course of the campaign, been a steady increase in
the numbers of men William commanded, the Normans
had grown to constitute a far more formidable and
numerous force than that which had originally arrived
in Melfi. More importantly, these warriors owed no
allegiance to Rainulf Drengot and now outnumbered
the men he had brought from Aversa.

After much feasting and talking over several days, which William pushed himself through on willpower, with the various delegates seeking allies or common positions, everyone who mattered was gathered in the great hall of the castle, the babble of noise deafening as it echoed off the bare stone walls. Guaimar had overseen the making of a high dais on which he could disport himself, dressed in silken garments with more than a hint of purple, a signal to all that he now saw himself as the overlord of all who had obeyed his ordinance. He wanted to look majestic, and he did, but when he finally imposed silence and sought to issue various edicts, he found he lacked the power to command: not one of the constituent bodies in the hall were prepared to just stand and allow themselves to be dictated to.

One by one they stated their objection to that which Guaimar was obviously seeking to impose: his own regal ambitions. Again the first to baulk were the port cities, with their mixed populations, who had no intention, individually or collectively, of dipping the knee to the Prince of Salerno, however he chose to style himself, nor did they wish to pay for Norman support.

They would look to their own walled defences to maintain themselves, and hire their own mercenaries, if need be, to protect their newly gained freedoms. Had one of their number not just seen off George

Maniakes? It seemed pointless to seek to get them to agree that it had been the man's ambition, not their efforts, which had sent him east.

Next came hostility from the Lombards of the inland towns and cities, where if they were not in a majority they formed the leading citizenry. Though the word 'king' was never mentioned, it was made plain by allusion that they had no desire to accept as sovereign a man who had stood aside from the fighting and all the losses of wealth and people that had entailed – an impostor, who had now come to claim the rewards.

William de Hauteville, the single most powerful person present, said nothing, and merely kept his own counsel, partly through a feeling of lassitude, but also from policy. Eventually, after much rancorous debate, Guaimar called for the meeting to be adjourned until the following day, and, plainly unhappy, stormed off to the part of the castle set aside for his use.

'They must have an overlord,' Guaimar shouted, vehemently yet safely, given he was in the company of his sister and the man he trusted most to advise him.

'I suggest,' said Kasa Ephraim, in his habitually calm manner, 'they will not have anyone who styles themselves king.'

'Is that not what we fought for?' the prince replied, which led the Jew to wonder if he knew the meaning of the word 'hypocrisy'. Not that he was troubled by the notion – it was the habit of princes – but if Guaimar thought in those terms, and worse still, spoke like that, he would only alienate those he was trying to persuade. 'Do they not realise what we all have to gain by being united?'

'Men see things from their own standpoint, honourable one.'

'The Normans are behind this,' Berengara claimed. 'None of these cockroaches would dare gainsay you if they knew the Normans would back your claim, but did we hear any of them speak?'

'Do you see a Norman hand in this, Ephraim?' demanded Guaimar.

'No. I doubt they care what title you adopt. They care more about what rewards are bestowed on them.'

'Reward is all they care about,' Berengara spat.

'It is they who have fought, Lady Berengara, and it is their skill at arms which has brought such victories...'

'Don't forget the Lombards who fought as well.'

Kasa Ephraim merely nodded at her, and addressed his next words to her brother. 'Only one question matters, honourable one: can Lombards, by themselves, hold Apulia if Byzantium sends a new catapan with an army at his heels to retake it? There is no certainty the Italians will fight to preserve a Lombard state. Who then will ensure security?'

The question that hung in the air was just as potent. Could the Prince of Salerno stand against such a force without the aid of Norman mercenaries? Only they could prevent a reverse, and it had not escaped notice that even the Lombard levies now accepted William de Hauteville as their leader. Guaimar could style himself by whatever appellation he desired; without men to sustain it, a title was worthless.

'I would also suggest, my Prince, that given the numbers to which they have now risen, to have them back in Campania would be troublesome. Best they are kept away from your domains.'

The Jew did not add what he knew and had discerned in his conversation with William de Hauteville the previous year: the Normans were not going anywhere, they were in Apulia to stay.

'I must speak with Rainulf. He must bring his men to heel.'

At that moment, it was William who was speaking with Rainulf, and the words he was using were not being well received by the elderly Count of Aversa, who had sought to berate him for his refusal to answer his previous appeals.

'You stood by while your fellow Normans were massacred by peasants.'

A weary William replied, 'I was otherwise occupied.'

'You should be occupied as I direct.'

'No, Rainulf, you no longer command me or the

men I brought to Melfi – *I* do, for they have been with me too long, both here and in Sicily. As for those who have come of their own free choice...'

'Many of those men you brought to Melfi are mine and I need them with me north of Capua.'

'Perhaps some will agree, Rainulf, not many, and I grant you permission to seek them out.'

The explosion was immediate. 'You grant me—'

'Yes,' William replied, in a soft tone. 'Perhaps the notion of slaughtering poor peasants will appeal to them more than plundering Byzantine treasure.'

That calm interjection was like throwing turpentine on flames: Rainulf was so incensed he could barely breathe and his words were far from easily comprehensible. 'You swine...you nobody... I raised you up and I can cast you down... I—'

William's shout stopped him dead. 'Enough!'

'You owe me allegiance.'

'I owe you nothing,' William replied, with equal force, an act which required much effort. 'I have seen you in private to do to you that which you would not have afforded me. If you want to be humiliated I will have the horns sounded and every Norman in Melfi gathered for you to address, and they can do so in full sight of everyone else present, Guaimar included. Then you can tell them they are yours to command, Rainulf, which if you are lucky will only gain you a sight of their bared arses. If not, you might pay with blood.'

Rainulf's hand went deliberately to the hilt of his sword, which got him an icy response.

'Draw it if you must, Rainulf, and though it will give me no pleasure to kill you, kill you I will.' There was a moment then when pride fought with good sense, until William, too powerful even in the grip of a fever for the older man to challenge, gave him a reason to concentrate on the latter. 'If you care nothing for your own life, think of your woman and her child.'

'You owe me everything.'

'I did owe you, Rainulf, for you trusted me once, you raised me and named me as your heir. But you took something away from me and I have now taken it back. You have your county of Aversa, you have many lances, if not as many as I, rest content with that, and whatever crumb Prince Guaimar is prepared to throw you in Apulia. I'm sure he will give you something.'

'You will fly too close to the sun, William de Hauteville.'

'Better that, Rainulf, than to grovel in the mud for what you would grant me. I will put out word that anyone who wishes to return with you to Aversa is free to depart. I will do no more than that.'

Once Rainulf had departed, William had to sit down: he was weak and he could feel himself shaking, cold even as he could feel the sweat on his brow and in the crook of his back. It was Tirena who led him to his cot, laid him to rest and fetched cold water to mop him down, listening as, in a fever, he went forwards and backwards in his life, cursing sometimes, at others weeping for the sins he had committed. It was near dawn before he fell into a troubled slumber.

Still weak in the late morning, William nevertheless dragged himself to where he needed to be, fully dressed and armed, so that those he led could see their general parade along the battlements of Melfi. Every time a group spotted him he was cheered. If they saw behind him the boy Listo, they knew him now to be a squire. If they also observed Tirena, who was much concerned for her lord and master, that had them nudging each other in the ribs, for it was no secret what she had become.

Beneath and below, Guaimar was struggling with a dilemma. In trying to make the best of bad circumstances, Rainulf could not avoid letting slip how much he had lost control of the mercenary force he had once led, one now massively more powerful, and, in doing so, he forced upon Guaimar a complete change of approach.

The prince had hoped Rainulf, for all the problems he had left behind, still had some authority: he now knew without doubt that he had to deal with William de Hauteville, and that whatever he was to achieve here in Apulia could only be attained by his good grace. Allied to William, he could overawe the others; without his aid, all he had was bluster.

'I cannot think you could delude yourself into expecting more. The Normans have never done anything else but betray our house.'

'Berengara, please,' Guaimar pleaded.

He pointed to the others in the room, not just his courtiers, his wife and children, but Rainulf Drengot as well. She was, as usual, saying things in public best aired in private, yet his sister was seen by those who advised him as more than her station implied. They had been through much together: he had said many times, and in public, that without her by his side in his youth he would not hold his title. She had suffered with him and travelled with him, and used her wiles to charm the emperor who had restored him to Salerno. In short, she was seen to stand so high in his esteem that to command her silence in such a gathering was difficult.

'Why should I hold my tongue, brother?'

Guaimar nodded towards Rainulf. 'For propriety if for no other reason.'

'We are talking of Normans. Surely I do not need to remind you of what they are capable.'

'Am I to be publicly insulted for my loyalty—?'

There was a sudden wail to break Rainulf's response, as Sichelgaita, Guaimar's baby daughter, let everyone know she was unhappy. Looking at her, and not for the first time, her father was given to wonder at her: from where had the girl sprung? Younger than her brother, she already outdid Gisulf in height; her hair was, unlike his own dark locks, the flaxen colour of her mother, her eyes a startling blue, and she was growing at a rate. Her throat was not left behind in this, and her cries, as she struggled with his wife, filled the room.

'I think my niece wails for our impotence, brother,' said Berengara maliciously, looking at Rainulf. 'When a treacherous slug can prate about loyalty...'

'If you were a man you would be dead by now,' Rainulf responded, his eyes now so narrowed that they disappeared into the purple folds of his face.

Berengara tilted her head and sneered. 'If I were a man you would have been dead years ago, Rainulf, and the rest of your Norman pigs as well. I'd rather trust a Saracen than you—'

'Stop,' Guaimar shouted, though whether at his still-wailing daughter or his sister no one could initially tell. 'Sister, you go too far.'

'Brother,' she replied, as Sichelgaita took to whimpering: the shout had alarmed her. 'You have never gone far enough.'

'A ruler cannot always do that which he wishes, however tempted he might be.' There would have been silence, if it had not been for the sound of Rainulf Drengot storming out of the chamber. 'There goes the only hope I had, Berengara, of enforcing my will on those gathered here, and not for the first time your tongue has run ahead of your brain.'

'I will not be chastised for speaking the truth.'

'I think the problem is, sister, you have never been chastised for anything, but I tell you, this day you have forfeited something, and I think you may come to regret it. Now, leave me, all of you, and someone go to William de Hauteville and ask him if he would attend upon me.'

'William,' Guaimar said, in a friendly tone, 'are you unwell? You look pale.'

'A fever, no more. It will pass.'

'It has come to the point where you and I must talk.'

Not willing to let him forget, William responded. 'Have we not talked in the past?'

The prince nodded, even if he looked less than pleased to be reminded of the divide-and-conquer game he had played between William and Rainulf. But he was still the most powerful lord in Campania, so he was not about to let pass such an obvious admonishment. His voice was sleek with insincerity as he responded, saying to this Norman very much the same as he had earlier said to his sister.

'The needs of state come before private inclinations.'

'And that is more true now than when I sought your help.'

Guaimar had to look away then: this damned Norman had found a sharp way to tell him the boot was now on the other foot. 'You did not speak at the great gathering, as others did.'

'I had nothing to say.'

'You must have…' Guaimar waved his arms, as if the word would not come.

'You have changed since first we met.'

Both would have little trouble in recalling that encounter, with William forcing the young man, an innocent in negotiation, to be open about that which he wished to conceal. How different Guaimar was now: as devious and conniving as every other Lombard magnate in the south of Italy.

'I was a disinherited youth then. I am not that now.'

'No, you are a man and a prince, but if you can recall that first meeting you will also remember that I am not one to waste my breath, nor am I inclined to weave spells before making my case. I prefer to talk plain and to the point.'

'Are you daring to rebuke me for the way I go about my affairs?'

'I am daring to say to you that you have in mind words to use. Offer me what you have so that I may judge its worth. I am too weary for your sport.'

'You are so sure I have something to offer?'

'I am sure you have no choice but to make me one.'

'You get above yourself,' Guaimar replied, with a hiss, for the first time letting his frustration show.

'Is it really necessary for me to spell out that which you already know, that you have no power in Apulia unless I agree to it? I asked you to remind Rainulf of his obligation to me in the matter of the succession to Aversa, but you chose to play the prince and deny my claim. Now I can claim what I want.'

'No, William, you can make a claim but it will have no legitimacy unless I agree. Swords and lances count for much, but they do not count for everything. You may choose to give yourself a title, you may accept the acclamation of those you lead, but it will be a bastard one unless you have a suzerain.'

'I will settle for a title that matches that of Rainulf.' Guaimar was nodding, but that stopped as William added, 'So will my brothers.'

'What!'

'Land and titles.' He nearly said 'except Robert', but decided not to bother. 'And then, whatever elevation you visit upon yourself, we will kneel before you and swear fealty.'

'What about the port cities?'

'Give them free status. You might as well since they will not agree to anything else, and, Prince Guaimar, there is enough land and wealth in Apulia. You do not need them too.'

The next words from the prince were bitter. 'Anything

else about which you would wish to advise me?'

'Just one, sire,' for the first time granting the prince the kind of respect to which he was accustomed. 'It would cement the arrangements if you were to grant me your sister's hand in marriage. I might add, I will agree to nothing else if you do not assent to that.'

If William had slapped Guaimar, Prince of Salerno, he would not have produced a more shocked reaction.

Guaimar, left alone after that talk, had much on which to ruminate: he had tried to marry Berengara off more than once, to various Lombard dukes of places like Teano and Gaeta, and even a nephew of Naples, but such attempts had foundered on her insistence on marrying a man of her own choosing. Really, he should have put his foot down long ago: he was a ruler, she no more than a woman, to be used as a diplomatic pawn to keep safe their patrimony. That was how alliances had been gained and cemented since time immemorial.

Yet he knew why he had acquiesced: it was her bravery and that shared past of daring escape and difficulties. He recalled now how, aged no more than fourteen years, she had offered him her jewels, this to facilitate his escape from Salerno and the clutches of the cruel and rapacious Pandulf of Capua. He had already tried to rape her and would no doubt make a second and more successful attempt. Guaimar would get away; she was willing to stay and face what she must.

Likewise in Bamberg she had played cat and mouse with the Emperor Conrad, a man like any other, who had seen before him a beautiful young lady not averse to his advances. Berengara would have surrendered her virtue if it had been called for; she had made that clear to him. That it had not been required did not lessen the proposed sacrifice.

Yet there was no doubt that since then he had overindulged her, a fact made obvious by the way she had insulted Rainulf to his face. Her tongue had ceased to be a weapon and become for him a liability, and that had been plain to see in the distressed faces of those courtiers who had been present earlier, it being a look he had observed before. Salerno needed her to act as a princess should, not, as she thought, a woman acting as his equal.

Odd, thought Guaimar as he prepared to confront her, in all my decisions as a prince, this might prove the hardest.

'Never. I would rather take the veil.'

'I must tell you, sister, that is your choice, for I will not be gainsaid in this. Policy requires it and you must succumb.'

Guaimar could see she was hurt, her eyes left him in no doubt, and he knew why: he had never spoken to her like this before – he had always been a brother not a ruler. 'We are no longer children, to play games as we wish.'

'So I must play what game you choose?'

'If I could have it otherwise, I would, but everything I have set out to achieve here in Apulia will come to nought unless you agree.'

She shouted then. 'You are asking me to marry a Norman, to be brought to the bed of a man from a tribe I despise, to have me lie beneath him as he uses me as his chattel and to bear his children, who I will despise also!'

'You must do as I say.'

'No, brother, if it is that or a nunnery, I will take the veil. I will not be whore to a Norman.'

'Very well,' Guaimar replied, which should have made Berengara suspicious: he had long since ceased to be the kind of person who gave up easily, and he was a prince who knew that men such as he had had trouble always with unwilling female relatives. He would get his way, with the help of an apothecary if he could not have consent.

Berengara went through the ceremony of marriage to William de Hauteville in a daze, induced by the infusion she had unknowingly consumed, before the whole assembly gathered at Melfi, a signal to them all that these Norman de Hautevilles were no longer mere mercenaries: they had become lords in their own right and elevated enough to be attached by matrimony to a princely house. Drogo orchestrated the acclamation of Guaimar as Duke of Apulia and Calabria, and he in turn granted William the appellation of count, with the land and title of Ascoli, then acknowledged him as what his confrères now hailed him, the Norman leader in Apulia.

Drogo got Venosa, lesser demesnes being granted to the rest of the de Hauteville clan, except Robert, who was, as his nature dictated, furious. Rainulf was given a small barren county near the coast as a sop, not enough to satisfy his pride, while Melfi was to be held in common, the place where the one-time rebels could combine to hold on to that which they had gained. Yet no sharp eye was required to note that the garrison now was entirely Norman and that the captain of the castle was none other than William de Hauteville.

The nocturnal part of the nuptials, after much feasting, passed for Berengara in the same haze as had her wedding and the effects of the drug only wore off as she slept. When she awoke, the first thing she registered was the fire in her lower belly, which told her, along with the bloodstained bedding, that she had been violated. Next she realised that the chamber she was in and the bed she occupied was not her own, a mystery soon solved by the great banner hanging on one wall, the blue and white standard of the de Hautevilles, spilt across at an angle with a chequer in the same two colours.

Of the man to whom she had been given there was no sign: he was in another chamber, with the arms of the shepherd girl Tirena wrapped around his naked, sweat-soaked, but slumbering body.

# CHAPTER EIGHTEEN

>∘◇∘<

News of the triumphs in Apulia had been slow to reach Normandy, but when it arrived and was digested, it stirred ambition in many a thwarted breast, not least in the still-unruly Contentin, though the knights in that county were not alone in seeing that opportunity, much frustrated in their homeland, was truly on offer in the fiefs of South Italy. What had been a trickle of lances heading there did not turn into a torrent, but instead of men travelling in twos and threes, bands of warriors now formed, sometimes as many as fifty in number, especially of those who had no love for, or saw no future in, serving the present duke.

William of Falaise made no effort to stop such men departing: he saw much advantage in the removal from his domains of those who might unite to oppose his rule. It was like cutting off an affected limb. Tancred, still under a cloud, was unsure what to do about the rest of his sons. Roger was, of course, too young, but there was no doubting his desire, once he had reached his majority, to join his mercenary brothers. Serlo was safe from ducal justice in England, serving in the far north, protecting the coasts of Mercia against the Danes, but that left four sons still to decide on their future. The only solution was to seek advice from his nephew.

If the uncle had suffered banishment from court, Geoffrey of Montbray had endured just as much, even if he was still, in the physical sense, close. Prior to the murder of Hugo de Lesseves he had been climbing to prominence in the councils of the dukedom. Given his role in extricating the culprits, he had then been frozen out as untrustworthy, though there had been no attempt to remove him from his ecclesiastical office.

Yet Duke William was not so rich in clear-sighted minds that he could forgo one so sound, one so attached to his cause, and nor had the victim of Serlo's knife been a man he had much favoured, so slowly but surely Montbray found the atmosphere thawing in his favour. Thus his advice to his uncle was that it would be best to wait: perhaps if he could be absolved of blame so could Serlo's brothers; perhaps there was a chance of ducal service after all.

One knight fired with the desire to go to Italy was

Richard Drengot, a nephew of Rainulf, and such was his attraction as both a person and a leader, and so well found was he in monies commuted back from Aversa, that when he rode off from the family lands around Alençon, he did so at the head of forty knights, all well mounted and equipped. In his progress south he suffered none of the travails of those who had gone ahead individually. Richard Drengot travelled in the style that suited his attachment to his uncle's wealth, the only experience he shared with the likes of Robert de Hauteville that of passing through a Rome of still-warring popes.

He and his band were not far south of there when an even more potent force arrived from the north, a whirlwind that would shake the Eternal City to its foundations: the new arrival was no other than the Emperor of the West, Henry III, heir to Conrad Augustus and a man committed to putting an end to the stench of papal politics. Trained since childhood to exercise power – he had been King of Germany since the age of eleven – Henry, a conscientious and overtly pious ruler, knew he would never have integrity in his domains without an end to the machinations of the Roman aristocracy and their endless warring over who held the office of pope.

Although a cause of endless dispute, every Emperor of the West held that the papacy was an office in their gift: no man could rise to be pontiff who did not have their approval. Opposed to that were not just those Roman aristocrats but also a majority of cardinals, bishops and abbots of the great Christian monasteries. Even in his own German domains siren voices were raised against what was seen as imperial presumption, but it had been a right exercised by Charlemagne and no successor of his was inclined to surrender it.

Riding in Henry's entourage was one of the holiest men in Western Christendom, Suidger, Bishop of Bamberg, and the aim of this imperial mission was made plain at once: a synod was convened in St Peter's at which all of the three competing popes whose rivalry had so rocked Rome were dethroned, and Suidger was proclaimed as Pope Clement II, his task, to bring back to order the Church of Christ, to put an end to simony and the selling of indulgences, and to perform the ceremony of marriage for Henry and his imperial bride.

So honest was this Suidger that, even with imperial approval, he insisted his elevation be confirmed by a convocation of the leading churchmen, so, for the first time in decades, one upright and properly holy man held the office of pontiff without dispute, yet it was an office with temporal as well as spiritual responsibilities: the Papal States were extensive in both land and wealth and they bordered on Campania and Apulia, so naturally lay matters were also raised at the imperial synod, not least the turmoil in the south.

The removal of Byzantium from Italy was to be welcomed: it had been a desire for centuries, though one every emperor had struggled to achieve. The Eastern Empire was formidable, and even if it was rocked by constant succession strife, even if in the last four hundred years it had lost all of Arabia, most of Persia and the entire North African coast to Islam, it always seemed able to regenerate itself closer to its spiritual homelands. Now it seemed, at last, it was on the rack of near expulsion.

Yet no imperial ruler could be content with vassals appointing themselves to lands and titles, so the great cavalcade, with the Pope in attendance, made preparations to proceed to Capua where another synod would be convened to deal with these temporal problems. Guaimar would be summoned, along with Rainulf Drengot, the de Hautevilles and the Prince of Benevento, now in a state of open conflict with Salerno, to attend upon their ultimate liege lord, Henry III, Emperor of the West.

'Argyrus got more than gold, William,' reported a dust-covered Drogo, freshly returned from an expedition to the south and now drinking successive goblets of wine to get that grime out of his throat. 'The Emperor Constantine has appointed him Catapan of Apulia and he has taken possession of Bari.'

William sighed. 'A city that assured us of their

support not two months past. Lombards are bad enough, brother, but a combination of them and Greeks is worse. I pity the Italians, though I have no reason to think them more scrupulous.'

'You would be wise to think so. Look what they did at Montecassino.'

'The men they slew got their just deserts at Montecassino, brother. You will get no less if you steal the sustenance out of people's mouths. But let us concentrate on the enemies before us.'

'Argyrus is safe as long as he stays within the walls of Bari.'

'Which he will not,' William replied, with a weary expression. 'He must come out and seek to retake the Catapanate.'

'He cannot do that, Gill, unless Constantinople gives him a powerful army and no other city has declared for him. Nothing has altered.'

'Sadly, no.'

'You did not think it to be over so soon?' Drogo asked.

'No, but I confess to being fatigued with war.'

Drogo grinned. 'I admit you look peaked. Is that not too much activity in the bedchamber, Gill, keeping two women content?'

'Such exertions never harmed you.'

'I think you have told me often, brother, we are very different.'

Said with humour, Drogo could not fail to notice that William was indeed looking drained, and if it was not by endless warfare and intrigue, it could just as easily be brought on by his assumption of too much responsibility. The fever he had suffered from previously had abated, but the marks of it were upon him. Nor did he allow himself respite: he took everything on his shoulders and he had a set of brothers and subordinates happy to let him carry the burden. The jest about the bedchamber could not hide the fact that he had other concerns.

Like his brothers, the title of count, by which William was known, had been granted to him by the acclamation, to be reluctantly confirmed by Guaimar in his capacity as the self-styled duke of the province, in itself a suspect creation. It was one that was open to challenge as to its legitimacy, for only the power of his sword and the ability of the men he led made it real. Not wishing to be beholden to any other power, the only way to make it more than that was by the continuous application of force of arms, so in time it came to be accepted by all.

Added to that, William needed to produce an heir, a child who would cement his position in the same way little Hermann had done for Rainulf, in fact he could go one better, for a child of his present union might have a future claim on Salerno and Capua. He never mentioned it, but he had, like any man who had risen as high as he, dynastic ambitions for his bloodline.

Never spoken of, William de Hauteville still felt the slur of being refused recognition as a blood relative of the House of Normandy. He longed one day that an heir of his would treat with a Norman duke as an equal. The way to wipe out that old affront was not only to gain his own title but to pass that and more on to a legitimate heir who would, in turn, have sons of his own.

Despite his efforts, and they were resolute because they needed to be, Berengara showed no sign of becoming with child. It was no secret that nothing had happened to abate her hatred for Normans, and if that had at one time been concentrated on Rainulf, it had moved from him to William. Her strength of feeling was as strong as ever, and that applied to her determination. Every conjugal act was a battle bordering on force and she had to be kept away from any public gathering so that her insults would not be aired in a way that diminished her husband.

The brothers would have discussed it with him if William had been open to such, but he was not. Drogo, for one, would never have married her, but had he made that error he would now be looking for a way to put her aside and find another, not, in his case and given his reputation, necessarily in that order. William would not do either: to his brother he was too upright for his own good.

'So, Drogo, how do we deal with Argyrus?'

Normally, William would not have posed such a question. While he was happy to listen to advice, it was he who decided what course of action to follow.

'We could invest Bari.'

'Not yet.'

'It is the right thing to do.' That got him a shake of the head, and that smile which implied secret knowledge. 'I have often wished, Gill, that you would be more open with me. It is as though you lack trust.'

William's response was quick, but good-humoured. 'Only with women, Drogo.'

'Then why not invest Bari?' William made to respond but Drogo cut him off. 'Before you say it is too formidable to capture easily, I know that. It could take a year or more, but at least if we were outside his walls Argyrus would be kept from mischief.'

'You must see that if we institute a siege it must be carried through to success. We could not afford to fail, regardless of how long it took.'

Drogo nodded. 'We have the means to win.'

'One day, Drogo, Bari, and all the other port cities, will either acknowledge we Normans as their overlords or they will burn, but if we were to do that now, to whom would the ultimate gain accrue? Bari defeated would trouble the others, which might bring that which neither they nor we want.'

'Guaimar as king.'

338 Jack Ludlow

'Do not think he has given up his dream. He got his Apulian title by chicanery, if he wants to take the diadem let him get it himself. I will not fight and spill Norman blood to have a crown put on his head.'

'And your own.'

That made William laugh. 'Not mine either, Drogo, but perhaps my son or grandson will aspire to it one day.'

'Then, Gill,' Drogo hooted, though he did register that William had been more open with him than hitherto, 'much as it pains me to say so, you must get into your bedchamber this very minute and get busy.'

The summons to attend upon the Emperor Henry at Capua came at an awkward time: Argyrus was doing that which William predicted, raiding out from Bari, but always with a line back to his base should he be threatened, which had Norman cavalry engaging in fruitless and dispiriting pursuit, for he never let himself be faced by a combination which included soldiers on foot. He was also showing a skill William never thought he possessed, which made him wonder if there was a secret direction behind his actions, a proper soldier.

Whatever the Lombard traitor did, it had to be ignored, for Henry could not be: to do so would risk such an affront that it would turn the emperor against the whole de Hauteville family, and the consequences of that could be enormous. Yet it was also an opportunity: provided the price of vassalage was not too high he might be able to acquire imperial confirmation of his title, and his brothers likewise. The dukedom of Apulia might be recognised as well, which would not be to his liking and could create future difficulties with Guaimar, but the solution to that would have to be left to time. Also paramount was the need that his wife should accompany him, not a notion that was well taken: Berengara refused point-blank.

'You will accompany me even if I have to lash you to a litter,' said William. 'I will not be embarrassed before the emperor by your absence.'

'And I suppose your little shepherd girl will be taken along to provide you comfort?' Berengara responded, her voice, as it always was, dripping with bile. 'There will be no embarrassment there, I think.'

'If you refuse me comfort—'

'Do not pretend you would not use us both in a like manner if I allowed it.'

'I will use you as I have the right to as your husband.'

'Then make sure we do not pass a monastery, for if I have the chance I will escape and slam the doors behind me.'

'Which I will burn down.'

'Not because you value me.'

'Bear me sons and I will leave you in peace.'

'Any son I bear you I would strangle at birth.'

'This is futile,' William yelled. 'Make yourself ready for the journey, and when we get into the company of the emperor hold your tongue or, believe me, you will make the return journey in a penitent shroud and bare feet, lashed to a rope that will be tied to my horse's tail.'

William would have been surprised if, having stormed out of the chamber, he had returned moments later: Berengara was in floods of tears, for this was not the life she had imagined for herself.

'I cannot take you with me, little one.'

William felt the head lying in the crook of his shoulder jerk, but Tirena did not sob, as he feared she might, even when they were upright and facing each other, but she made no secret of her unhappiness, which made him feel wretched. Nor did he really want to explain to her that he must, in the imperial presence, behave properly, for there was much at stake. This Henry was reputed to be a principled fellow much taken with prayer and confession, not long wed, who might take a dim view of someone attending upon him in the company of an obvious concubine.

How different it was when he was with this girl. She made him laugh, she made him happy and she brought out in him a love of the bawdy, a side of his character he kept hidden from even his own brothers, who saw him as somewhat dour. Had she been of the right blood he would have wed her in an instant, not least because she so wanted to please him, a feeling he had to be guarded about reciprocating.

William actually fretted about raising her hopes: the girl knew his marriage was far from blissful, just as she knew it was not based on affection. He realised that one day, even if it would render him miserable, he might have to send her away: should fortune favour him with an heir, he would not raise the boy in close proximity to such an evident mistress. She would never starve: he would help her to find a husband and provide for any children she had, and he reassured himself the course he had in mind was the right one; but would he not be as miserable as she?

The ride into Capua, from his tented encampment, on the day appointed for the synod, brought back many memories, not least that in this locality Normans were not loved: the looks they received from the population as they made their way from city gates to the castle left them in no doubt that time had not abated the fear Capuans had of these blond, blue-eyed warriors. Then it had been just him and Drogo, now it was all six of the brothers de Hauteville: even Robert was in his entourage, riding alongside the litter in which sat Berengara, the drapes firmly closed.

But there were other memories, more pleasant: it

was here he had ceased to merely be a mercenary lance without patrimony and had become, or so he thought, heir to the County of Aversa. He had ridden up to the gates of the twin barbicans of the castle he was now approaching as an imperial messenger, to demand its surrender. Now he was coming to it as a warlord in his own right, older and, he hoped, wiser.

The walls and gate were manned by imperial troops, Swabians by the look of their accoutrements and speech, who demanded to know his name and title before allowing him admission to the inner keep, this accompanied by suspicious looks at the powerful escort of fifty lances William had fetched along. From there, once dismounted, the senior members of the party made their way to the great hall he had visited so often in the past, in more disordered times.

Guaimar was already present in all his pomp, as was the Abbot of Montecassino, who looked daggers at them, as he would at any Norman, while on a dais sat two men. One, young and fresh of face he took to be Henry, the other, given his pontifical garb and his great age, undoubtedly the Pope. Rainulf was standing by the aisle, with a stalwart-looking young fellow by his side who William suspected might be his nephew, Richard, news of whose arrival from Normandy had filtered through to Melfi. Clearly, if it was, and given his presence at such a gathering, he already had the ear and trust of his uncle.

The Dukes of Naples and Gaeta were identified by the gonfalons retainers held over their heads, proud men and Lombards, owners of their own fiefs, who nevertheless knew they held their titles by imperial favour, and it was telling the distance that existed between them and Guaimar, whom they knew to be ambitious that Salerno, having subsumed Amalfi, should surpass them as the greatest trading port of their shared coast. To these lords he was a constant threat, having, as he did, Rainulf's still-numerous Normans at his beck and call.

The surprise of the gathering, in fact no less than a shock, only revealed itself after they had made their bows to the dais and been welcomed by the emperor. Standing to one side, partially hidden, stood Pandulf, the one time Prince of Capua, the man known as the Wolf of the Abruzzi, in what had been his own great hall, this before he had been deposed. Hasty questioning of the others, gathered as they retired, revealed the truth: if the release of George Maniakes from his dungeon had been one of the Emperor Constantine's little surprises on his accession to the purple, this was another, potentially equally troubling. Pandulf had been freed and sent home, in the certain knowledge that he was bound to cause trouble among his fellow Lombards, which could only benefit the Byzantine cause.

'So, William de Hauteville,' Pandulf said, having

made his way through the throng to sidle up to a man
he had once tried to recruit, the very fellow who had
seen to it he lost his title. 'I find myself addressing a
very different fellow. You have risen in the world.'

The Wolf had aged, hardly surprising for a man
who had spent years in a Byzantine oubliette; at one
time darkly handsome, he was now drawn-looking
and his black hair was streaked with grey, but the
dark, dancing eyes were the same as was the voice,
one which William knew to be silky and insincere, but
also one which wove a spell on the uninitiated, which
seemed to be able to embrace and render congenial
whichever person he was addressing. And there was
the smile as well, slightly crooked.

'And you, Pandulf, have risen from the dead.'

'If it were not blasphemous, I would compare myself
to Christ.'

'I do not recall that you feared blasphemy or
damnation,' said Drogo.

Pandulf ignored that remark, looking past Drogo
and his brothers to Berengara, the eyebrows lifting
and the smile broadening in mock wonder. 'And you
have taken as wife the beautiful Berengara, William.
How I envy you such a prize.'

There was mockery in those words: Pandulf was the
kind to ferret out gossip and he was telling him that
he knew very well how troubled was that particular
relationship, just as William knew they were meant

to rile him. All his life he had reacted to people who attempted that with a slight smile, one which hinted at an interior superiority. Generally it infuriated the recipient; there was great pleasure in seeing it work on Pandulf now, but the question still remained: how had he got to this place at this time? Being set free by Constantine was one thing, being invited to a synod set up by the Emperor of the West quite another.

That he had charmed this new emperor was later obvious and not wholly surprising: he had done the same to this young man's predecessor until his depredations had forced Conrad to act. When called forward to speak, admitting his previous errors and seeking forgiveness, Henry listened intently. William just had to look at the face of Guaimar of Salerno to know how badly he took the re-emergence of the man he held to be his greatest enemy.

The Abbot of Montecassino looked as if he would happily forgo his vows and commit murder to be rid of a man who made the Normans appear like saints. It was hard for Rainulf too, for he was in the presence, not only of an abbot who gladly would list his sins for an imperial ear, but also of two magnates he had at one time, and in turn, betrayed, while he was about to kneel before the only man who could legitimately strip him of his title for the activities of the men he led.

But whatever Guaimar and Rainulf felt paled beside that of Berengara, who for once spoke to William in a voice not dripping with hate for him, her gaze fixed intently on Pandulf.

'Kill that man, cut out his living heart, and I will give myself to you willingly, and perhaps bear you the child you desire.'

Robert de Hauteville replied, not William, in a voice too loud, as usual. 'You have asked the wrong person, Lady Berengara. If you want someone killed you should have asked me.'

Before either she or William could respond to that, Henry stood, and looking out over the assembly at the many armorial devices which identified each grouping, his face creased with curiosity. 'Where is the Prince of Benevento?'

Someone, a court official no doubt, responded in the negative, which produced a look of anger and a voice to match. 'Not yet here on the appointed day! Send messengers to seek him out. He is my vassal and he should be in attendance.'

The voice that responded was so soft it was difficult to hear, but the words were much repeated afterwards, as the newly elected Pope Clement leant across and reminded the emperor, and not entirely to his liking, that in strict truth Benevento was a papal fief, not an imperial one.

# CHAPTER NINETEEN

∞◇∞

Emperor Henry III, looking out over the assembled gathering, was not happy and he had good reason: there was not one person present who did not give him concern, and one still absent that made him furious. Added to that, every voice he heard, be it in private or public, was committed to condemnation of the actions of another.

A nobleman from Amalfi, dispossessed by Guaimar and lucky to still be breathing following the sack of that place, denied the piracy of which that city state was accused, in turn condemning the other trading ports for secretly undermining imperial edicts regarding fair trade and tariffs. But these people never did anything other than curse each other, making it difficult for a distant and German-based overlord to sort claim from counterclaim.

But there was no doubt they all shared one thought: Salerno was the real problem. They were sure the ruler of that city, with Amalfi already in his grasp, had continuing plans of conquest, which meant no one was safe. Henry had the power to reverse that, to force Guaimar to give up Amalfi, but would that be wise? Guaimar was undoubtedly ambitious and there was no knowing where that would lead. He needed to be checked but it would not be good policy to humiliate him.

The idea of an independent king ruling in South Italy, wherever he sprang from, was not one to appeal and the outlines of such a polity seemed to be taking shape. Not content with Amalfi, Guaimar had self-appointed himself to Byzantine Apulia and then gone on to grant land and titles to the Normans who were once in his pay: the emperor had no idea of how much those mercenaries led by William de Hauteville owed to him in return, and that he needed to establish.

Rainulf he was sure of: Guaimar's vassal in Campania was seemingly under his thumb, but he was out of control on the edge of those domains, nothing more than the leader of a marauding gang of robbers sucking the wealth out of church lands, and despite his recent troubles he still mustered an impressive force; combine those two bands of mercenary warriors under Guaimar's leadership and they would be a power that even the whole might of the empire would struggle to contain.

Prince Landulf of Benevento would be at risk as well as the rival ports, but when it came to what they had done in Apulia they did not garner much imperial sympathy. Landulf had been just as ambitious and duplicitous as Guaimar in support of revolt, with the appointment of his brother and the subsequent encouragement of Argyrus, and where had that led? Worse, despite a clear summons, he had yet to appear, and that bordered on an affront to his imperial majesty, one which would definitely have to be dealt with.

Henry knew two things: that Lombard rivalry, while troublesome, was less of a concern than that one of these magnates should rule over the rest, because they were not the kind to ever be content with what they held. Given power over the whole south they would next be at the Papal States and the imperial fiefs to the north. He also knew that whatever dispensations he made in this part of Italy must somehow hold once he had departed, which had to be soon. He could not afford to be away from Bamberg too long.

What he required was not continued turmoil but a balance of power that left everyone dependent upon imperial endorsement and one which would not drag him into conflict with his fellow emperor in Byzantium. The idea of forcing the inhabitants of Apulia to resubmit to Constantinople was an attractive one in terms of keeping the peace, but it was also impractical: his writ ran even less in that part of Italy.

Given the day had been taken up with ceremony, his decisions had been postponed till the morrow, which allowed for much intrigue as those who sought imperial favour attempted to bribe Henry's officials. It also gave time for those who felt themselves in some way threatened to seek allies with which to fend off the emperor's wrath. Guaimar definitely felt at risk: the good relationship he had enjoyed with the previous emperor had not been carried over; if anything, he suspected he was perceived as a disturber of the peace, so he sought the support of William de Hauteville, needing to speak quietly in a doorless antechamber.

'We must stand strong in the face of the emperor.'

'He is not yet my emperor, Prince Guaimar.'

'I am his vassal, you are mine.'

'Only when Henry confirms us both in our Apulian titles. If you are not Duke...'

The rest of that sentence had no need to be completed, and judging by the look on Guaimar's face he thought what had just been said to be a real possibility. William was more sanguine about his own future, because he held the ground: not only Melfi and the country around, but Troia too, now that his fellow Normans had joined him. In numbers, his lances had risen to some fifteen hundred: he was powerful enough to fear no one. Certainly he desired his title to be confirmed but he was not prepared to give up any part of his recent gains to get it.

'How much do you trust Rainulf, William?'

'I think that question is more important to you than to me.'

'Pandulf free is unsettling, and what is he doing here at this imperial gathering? He has fooled Henry and he could have Rainulf's ear, as he has had in the past, and whatever he says will not be to the benefit of either you or I.'

Guaimar had not been the first one to visit him: Pandulf had that honour, seeking in near whispers to enlist William's support against both Rainulf and Salerno, with much gold on offer if he agreed. Never one to needlessly deny a possibility, William had merely demurred, but he did wonder if Pandulf knew him at all. Much as he had come to dislike Rainulf, he would do anything in his power to avoid fighting his own kind, for the very simple reason that it would be a bloodbath in which the only people to gain would be the Lombards.

Now Guaimar was at the same game! They were both as bad as the other, weaving what they saw as their spells as if those they were addressing lacked any insight. Guaimar did not seem to be able to discern that William was no longer acting as his proxy: he was acting for himself and his family. Pandulf, likewise, saw him still as a mercenary to be bought.

So wrapped up in their own dreams were they, neither could see how the power to decide had passed from their hands, so he listened to Guaimar as he had listened to Pandulf, without commitment.

That they should call upon him was to be expected: both were jockeying for imperial favour and afraid of censure from the same source. Rainulf had the same dilemma, but his calling was a surprise, and it was immediately clear to William that his presence in his chamber was due to the young man he brought with him, who did indeed turn out to be his nephew. In fact, it was young Richard who did the talking.

'My uncle fears that one of these Lombards will seek to use us against the other.'

William had to wonder who had visited them before they came to him, just as he had cause to conclude that if they had been called upon by Pandulf or Guaimar then this Richard had immediately seen the risks and so the need to consult with him. It must have taken a strong argument to get his uncle to come anywhere near a de Hauteville.

Looking straight at Rainulf, William replied. 'I do not know if I have the words to reassure him.'

Richard responded, while Rainulf's purple face closed up in disdain. 'I think it best to ask you to consider what purpose would be served by such an action.'

'I think you will find, should anyone suggest such a

thing, I would come to the same conclusion as you.'

'It has not, then, been proposed?'

William just smiled: this fellow seemed shrewd enough to guess the truth, so there was no need for it to be said out loud. 'We have little to fear. Your uncle has his County of Aversa and numerous lances, I have my men and my aims in Apulia.'

'The emperor could strip me of that,' Rainulf growled.

'To what purpose, Rainulf, and if he did, who is going to take it from you?'

'We both know,' Richard replied, 'that you are the only one who can certainly do so. Henry's escort of Swabians is not enough and Guaimar would need allies to try.'

'You have my word, I have no interest in Aversa.'

Rainulf made no effort to moderate his tone. 'Can we believe you?'

'We have no choice, Uncle,' said Richard, looking William right in the eye.

The sudden appearance of a servant at the chamber entrance had William flicking his eyes to look past this youth. 'His Imperial Highness requests that you attend upon him.'

'Tell him I would be honoured to do so, just as soon as I have finished with my guests.'

'There's nothing more to say,' barked Rainulf.

'No,' William replied, 'there is not.'

'You have not asked us for any pledge,' said Richard.

'It would be meaningless.' Seeing the youngster's face change, for the first time showing anger, William added, 'But I see you as a person of sense and I hope you see me in the same light. As long as your uncle has you to advise him, as I once did, I doubt either of us has anything to fear.'

William left them standing there and went out of the arched doorway, immediately aware of his brother Robert leaning against the wall. 'Have you been listening?'

'I have,' Robert replied. 'You said I have much to learn, so I am doing that.'

'And?'

'What you said in there, as regards Aversa, might not hold for ever.'

'Not much does hold for ever in this part of the world, Robert. If you wish to learn, learn that!'

'I have no idea how to style you,' said Henry, as William gave him half a bow. 'I am not yet minded to greet you with the title Prince Guaimar granted to you.'

There were many courteous ways this emperor could have greeted him. In choosing those words he had deliberately sought to diminish William, and not being prepared to accept that, his response was brusque.

'Then we share a dilemma, sire. Given what you

have said, my suzerain is not you, it is the Duke of Normandy.'

That had the emperor looking at those around him, his own courtiers, all military men by their bearing, as well as the armed Swabian guards present, with raised eyebrows, as if he was shocked. 'Conrad told me, when he returned to Germany many years ago, you de Hautevilles were a proud lot. Too proud perhaps.'

'No more so, I suspect, than was he. I think it necessary in a warrior to be that.'

There was a definite prod in that: Conrad Augustus had proved himself in battle; this Henry was yet to do so and William knew by the emperor's piqued expression he had struck home.

'The question is, William de Hauteville, is what am I to do about you?'

'Are you asking me to advise you?'

'No!'

'Then I am at a loss to know how to respond.'

Henry waved an arm towards his Swabian guards. 'You get above yourself. I am the elected head of the Holy Roman Empire and I am unaccustomed to being so addressed by a mere mercenary.'

'Something more than that now, I think.'

'You are nothing, William de Hauteville, so much so that one word from me and these men who guard my honour will cut you down.'

That really got under William's skin, and his reply

was a hiss. 'If they do you will never see Germany again.'

The emperor's response was a bark. 'You threaten me?' When William gave him that knowing, superior smile it was just as effective on him. 'Do not smirk in my presence. Do you not know to whom you speak?'

'As of this moment, you are a young man who is not even beginning to achieve that which you set out to do, which is to get me to beg on my own behalf, and that of my family, that the titles we have been given should be confirmed. You wish me to plead. If any of these men who advise you have the courage to voice the truth, they will tell you I have no need to do so.'

'And if I declare you an enemy?'

'That is your right, yet I have taken nothing from you. Everything I have was once the property of Byzantium. I can, however, give you Apulia, by acknowledging you as my imperial suzerain.'

'And Guaimar of Salerno, what of him?'

'He is already your vassal, do with him what you will.'

'Am I to take it you will not support him?'

'You could have asked me that at the start of this conversation, so now I will answer the questions you should have posed, the ones which concern you, to which I would have responded with the truth.'

'I think I must judge whether someone is being truthful.'

'Then take it as you will. I owe Guaimar nothing, even if I am wed to his sister, and I will not pledge the men I lead to any enterprise you fear he may have in mind. I will not, either, combine with Rainulf Drengot and the lances he leads on any imperial fief.'

'Easily said, and just as easily denied.'

'Then listen to this. Neither will I stand aside, and nor will my family, if he is threatened. It is not for the love of Rainulf but because I will not see my fellow Normans put to the sword, and I have good grounds to feel they would treat me likewise. Understand that if you threaten one of us you threaten us all. Now that you know my mind, you may make up your own, and I will await whatever your pleasure is.'

William spun round and walked out, without bowing, leaving behind him a buzz of angry talk, not least from an emperor screaming that he would 'not be treated in such a manner'.

'That's no way to address an emperor,' said Drogo, quietly, once William had apprised his brothers of the results of his discussion. By the expressions on most faces, they agreed with him.

'I think those he looks to for advice told him one thing, and I enlightened him.'

Mauger responded to that. 'Which is all very well if he believed you.'

'It makes no difference if he did or not,' boomed

Robert, in a carrying voice that had his siblings gesturing to him for hush, given that, gathered in the open-arched and stone-walled antechamber, they could be overheard if they spoke too loud. Robert's response was a dismissive glare. 'Unless he is prepared to fight for his pride, he must swallow what you give him.'

'You know nothing,' Drogo growled.

'I know power when I see it,' Robert replied, 'just as I can smell spoken shit.'

'Your nose is too close to your arse,' barked Drogo, who had come to actively dislike this bumptious younger brother.

'The emperor is far from weak,' Geoffrey insisted.

Robert scoffed at the same time as he glared at Drogo. 'He is also far from Apulia and unless he is prepared to come to that place with an army—'

William interrupted. 'Which he could do if we gave him cause.'

'Bearding him might do that.'

Looking at Humphrey, who had voiced that concern, William was wondering if his gloomy brother might have a point. He had not intended to rile Henry, but he had found his imperious manner hard to stomach. Yet he was the elected emperor, and entitled to respect. Was that a sign of hubris? Was he becoming too used to authority to be guarded in his tone?

That thought evaporated as he realised the company he was in: his brothers would defer to him when they thought he was right, they did not fear, and never had feared, to tell each other they were wrong. As for Henry, if he wanted respect he should show some instead of talking to him like a lackey.

'Are we in any danger here?' asked Robert. 'The emperor's Swabians hold the castle gates.'

That was possible, though unlikely. If Henry wanted to, he could stage a sudden arrest and throw them into the dungeons of this very place, which William knew, having visited them when it belonged to Pandulf, to be deep. It was the kind of ruse the Wolf would have employed and he did seem to have, as Guaimar had implied, the emperor's ear.

'I thought I was the suspicious one,' Humphrey scoffed.

William was less certain and he knew the imperial escort outnumbered his own, large as it was: they also had more in numbers than Rainulf and he combined.

'Best be safe. Robert, go to the apartments of Rainulf and speak to his nephew, not him. Raise the possibility and tell them to be on their guard, and that we will stand with them if they are threatened. Mauger, go to the quarters where our men are billeted and tell them to sleep in their mail, with their swords at the ready.'

It was a restless night for them all, and at first light it was necessary for William to test his reactions when he first heard Berengara retching; having been raised in a home where the birth of a child was an annual event, he needed no telling what the sound portended. He also knew, much as the sound pleased him, there were many ways of getting rid of an unwanted pregnancy and he recalled her threats; she would have to be closely guarded from now on.

Around him the castle of Capua was stirring, the smell of fresh baking from the kitchens permeating the chambers, and since nothing had happened in the hours of darkness he stripped off his mail and upper clothing, then dipped his hands in the chilly waters of the bowl of water to wash his face. The scuffling sound of feet had him turning quickly, but not speedily enough, and although he managed to deflect the assassin's knife away from the centre of his body, it entered the flesh of his side.

He knew he had shouted, knew he had hold of the hooded man trying to kill him, but he could see the eyes and make out the intention: that knife had been pulled out to inflict another stab and he, being stripped, was near defenceless. The sword flying through the air was no more than a flash of steel, but the bellow that accompanied it was more than that. The blade hit the man before him, and even if it did not penetrate, it was enough to distract him from the blow he was trying to deliver, enough to allow William to gain some space between them.

It was Robert who followed that sword blade, grabbing William's assailant in his great big hands and twisting and lifting him at the same time, so the sound of the snapping neck was as clearly audible as the snapping of a dry twig. William by that time had doubled over his wound, his hand over it, but his eyes seeing the blood seeping through his fingers. Suddenly the chamber was full of people, all his brothers and more beside, and as he lifted his head to one side he saw his wife standing holding the curtain that concealed her bed, and the concerned look on her face mystified him, not least because of all the people in this castle who might want to kill him, she could be one.

'It would take too long to list those who might be responsible,' said Drogo, and he was right: the Emperor Henry, Pandulf, Guaimar, Rainulf were all suspect, and that left out the notion that Argyrus had sent someone from far off Bari to carry out the deed. William did not mention Berengara, and in truth the look of concern she had carried when she saw him wounded might actually have been for the father of her coming child.

'Is the council going ahead?' William asked, feeling the bandages in which his belly was now swathed.

'It is.'

'Then get me on my feet.'

'Not wise, Gill, that was a bad wound and the monk who treated you said you should remain still to let it heal.'

'If there is someone at that gathering who is responsible for this I want them to see my face. Now do as I ask.'

It was a painful struggle for William, and there was no way he could dress himself, a task carried out by Drogo and Listo, with his other brothers, Robert excluded, looking concerned. Finally he stood – or was it swayed? – in his family surcoat, striped in blue and white, as his sword was strapped to his waist. An imperial order dictated he should not wear arms, but that was one William de Hauteville was determined to ignore.

On the walk to the great hall of the castle he had to stop several times, to lean against a wall and gather himself, but when he entered that huge chamber he stood alone and upright, his family several steps behind him, before a crowd of nobles and churchmen who parted so that his view, from doorway to dais, was uninterrupted. Many present were surprised, but that did not indicate guilt. It took much determination to walk as if unwounded up that aisle, but walk he did, until he stood before the Emperor Henry, fixing him with a look that was as questioning as it was discourteous.

'We are glad to see you are well, William. We have

cut off the head of your assailant, even though he was dead, and it now sits on a spike by the outer walls.'

His brothers were beside him now, Drogo and Geoffrey so close that he could, if he needed to, lean on them, and when he spoke he managed a voice of full strength. 'Let it be known, sire, that to kill me will avail whoever tried to carry it through of nothing. You see beside and behind me my brothers. If you wish to contain the name of de Hauteville you must kill us all.'

'You have my permission, William, to be seated in my presence.'

'I thank you, sire, but that is unnecessary.'

'Gill,' Drogo hissed.

'Then let it be known,' Henry said, standing, and his voice ringing out, 'that in my office as elected emperor, and with the blessing of the most holy Pope Clement, I hereby repudiate the title taken unto himself by Guaimar, Prince of Salerno, in the territories recently wrested from Byzantium. He was granted the title of Prince of Capua by my predecessor and that grant I now repudiate in its entirety, and with the title thus being vacant I appoint to it, with all its lands and revenues, the previous holder, my most loyal servant, Prince Pandulf.'

'Sire,' Guaimar protested, but he got no further.

'You have Salerno and Amalfi, Guaimar, be content.'

Naples and Gaeta were grinning: anyone standing close to Pandulf would have heard the Wolf say, under his breath, 'You have them for now, Guaimar.'

'And for you, William de Hauteville, I invest you with the title of Count and Master of all the Normans of Apulia and Calabria, and charge you to hold those provinces in my name.'

The escort William had brought to Capua were all in the keep when he emerged, looking pale but still on his own two feet. They cheered him to the echo, and two of his brothers took his arms to aid him to stay upright.

'I can look Normandy in the eye now,' William said. 'How I wish our father, Tancred, was here to see this.'

'He will hear of it, Gill,' Drogo replied. 'Now you must rest.'

'I must have a seal made. I need to send greeting to my cousin and namesake, Duke William, and I also need to request that he give my father permission to build that stone donjon he has dreamt of all these years. He cannot deny it now I have my title!'

# CHAPTER TWENTY

∞◆∞

The emperor, feeling his work was done in Capua, moved on to Benevento to censure the prince of that fief, only to find that Landulf would not open his gates to admit him or the Pope. Verbal thunderbolts thrown at the walls had little effect: there was not a person inside who did not suspect the purpose for which Henry had come, even if they disputed his right, namely to depose the ruler and replace him with some unknown quantity. If Landulf was not universally loved – he was too fond of display and a spendthrift – they were not prepared to trade him for someone imposed on them: that someone might be Pandulf the Wolf.

They might make jests about there only being one letter between them, but there was a lot more than that: Landulf was foppish and a little foolish, but he was not overtly cruel. His near namesake was the kind to hang his own citizens from his walls if they displeased him, and his dungeons, in his previous incarnation as Prince of Capua, had never been less than full to bursting. Rumour had it that he was filling them again: those he felt had betrayed him, if they had not been wise enough to flee, were paying a heavy price, some with their very lives.

Having only a small escort and thus lacking the military means to impose his will, the emperor was obliged to ask his newly appointed Count of Apulia for help, something an ailing William declined to provide, replying that in his new capacity as an imperial vassal he was too busy in his own province to even think of Benevento, and besides, it would involve a siege for which he lacked both the equipment and the time. In order to avoid a more pressing request he took his army off to the south to find and fight Argyrus, despite his brothers' insistence that he was too ill to lead men into battle.

Thus a seething Holy Roman Emperor persuaded Pope Clement to excommunicate the whole population of the city, before he was obliged to retire north, blustering as he departed – for that was all it was, and a serious loss of face for a man not long elected. But before he left he let it be known that Benevento, both city and principality, was subject to his deep displeasure and that anyone who could bring the miscreants to book, and bring Landulf in chains to his imperial capital of Bamberg, would earn his gratitude. Given the only force with the power to carry out this task was Norman, it was nothing less than an invitation to William to put aside his southern adventures and take the province to the north.

Had the message come to him when healthy he might have been tempted, but he was fevered and in a sick bed, rarely able to speak, surrounded by anxious relatives and priests praying earnestly for his recovery: he had taken to his horse too soon, long before he had fully recovered from the wound to his innards. Sometimes he spoke, at other times he shouted out, a jumble of memories and aspirations, at one time even speaking calmly to ask if a message had been sent to his namesake in Normandy regarding his request.

It was Humphrey who led a force north to take Benevento, and with enough men outside their walls to eventually overcome the defences the people of the town saw safety in deposing Landulf and sending him on his way into exile, then, after a decent interval to allow him to get safely clear, to open their gates to the Norman host. An extensive and fertile province soon found itself at the mercy of bands of Normans, riding in raiding parties, who now acted like the overlords of the principality.

* * *

*Bras de Fer* was dead long before permission to build a stone donjon reached the tiny hamlet of Hauteville-la-Guichard. The time it had taken to come as a request to Duke William and to be acted upon took several months. It came to a manor house in which old Tancred was also fading from long years, sheer fatigue and all the wounds his body had borne in a life of combat, not aided by too hearty an appetite for the pressed products of his orchards. He would be buried beside both of his wives, whose graves lay in the churchyard where Geoffrey de Montbray had christened all his sons.

Roger, now with spots and a broken, rasping voice, was the one, along with his sisters, to greet the messenger, none other than their one-time family confessor. Geoffrey of Montbray was on his way to Coutances to adjudicate the disputes of that vacant and troubled bishopric. The rest of the de Hauteville brothers were fighting in the service of Duke William, helping him to subdue the last province of Normandy to hold out in its entirety against his cause, their own Contentin.

Tancred raised himself enough to see the first stones laid, but did not live to see his dream completed. He passed to the other side with the last rites of his nephew in his ears and the images of his distant sons before his eyes, seeing them as they were, as their younger selves, with full-flowing fair hair and deep-blue eyes, laughing, fighting, riding in the fields below the manor, training with weapons to be the warriors he wanted them to become. Roger apart, they were that now and he would be soon.

But most of all he saw the face of his eldest, his true heir, and the image of William was of him standing at the top of the old wooden tower overlooking the demesne, now being replaced by that stone donjon, as he handed him a cloak on a cold autumn day many years before, the one in which he had ridden away from his birthplace for ever. He would have thanked God, had he known, that he died in ignorance of his firstborn preceding him to the grave.

The deep knife wound was not the sole cause of his eldest son's demise, though it had so weakened William that when his fever recurred, a reprise of that from which he had suffered at Trani, he lacked the vigour to hang on to life, and hardly had the strength to hold hard to his brother's hand as the end approached. His body was wasted, no longer that of the warrior he had so proudly been, and the voice as he spoke was so weak Drogo had to lean close to hear him.

'If I have a son, Drogo, raise him to make me proud.' Drogo did not look round to where Berengara stood, with her swollen belly that might contain a boy-child: he feared to look into her eyes lest he see in them a degree of pleasure for what she was seeing. 'He will, at least, have my title.'

'He will, brother,' Drogo replied, though he had doubts if that would be the case.

The Normans would not follow an infant, regardless of how much they esteemed his father: they were now too numerous and eager for further conquests and they had enemies to hand who they would ride out to fight; they needed at their head a man of similar stature to the dying man on the cot. William's title was too new a creation to have built within it the kind of loyalty that had sustained Normandy, and it would take a strong hand and a good leader to merely hold on to what had been gained. There was no king of the Franks nearby, either, with an army to protect any child inheritor, just the bind that held together the males of de Hauteville.

One by one they came: his brothers, to kneel at his side and kiss his fevered brow; the last to do so Berengara, who allowed his hand to feel the kick of the child she was carrying. But she shed no tears, for she would not, even in the face of a coming death, be a hypocrite and pretend a love she did not possess. Tirena had to wait till he was cold to weep over his cadaver, and she had to be dragged clear, sobbing, as the monks came to prepare the body for burial. Drogo had her sent to a nunnery as soon as she had said her farewells, while her brother Listo was sent to become a monk.

The requiem mass for William de Hauteville's soul

was said in the Latin rite, as befitted a son of the Church of Rome, and his remains were interred in a vault in the local church, a building surrounded by row upon row of the silent men – Normans, Lombards and Italians – that William had led into battle. If they had come to mourn his passing, they also had a deep and abiding interest in what would happen next: they were an army now, ready to live off conquest and that alone.

As the brothers emerged into the strong sunlight, with Drogo at their head, the warriors with bowed heads ceased their prayers and one senior Norman captain, Hugo de Boeuf, who had a clear notion of what was required now, raised his head to yell out, in a clear and carrying voice.

'All hail to Count Drogo!'

The silence that followed lasted a very short time, until the cry was taken up by every throat, growing to an endless roar until it echoed off the high hills surrounding the town and castle of Melfi. The man being acclaimed stood stock-still and confused, still mourning for a brother he loved.

'I do not want this,' he whispered, even if he knew it to be the only solution to the thoughts he had as William was dying.

'You must take it, Drogo,' said the next oldest, Humphrey, 'for if you do not we may as well saddle our mounts and head back to Normandy.'

Geoffrey and Mauger concurred, pushing him to the fore, but it was the brother he liked least who decided Drogo, for Robert de Hauteville said in a hard tone, 'If you don't accept it, Drogo, I will.'

Slowly, and not entirely willingly, Drogo raised his arms to accept the acclamation, which had the serried ranks of warriors break, as they rushed forward to lift him on their shoulders. The man they were carrying was praying that he had the strength not to disappoint them.

Before a month went by, Rainulf of Aversa followed William to the grave, leaving his young son Hermann as heir to his title, and his nephew Richard Drengot to lead his lances and guard the boy, given one was needed. The emperor's dispensations achieved very quickly a result he had surely not intended: certainly he had split the sources of power in Southern Italy so that no one magnate could overawe the others, but that had quickly turned into a low-level conflict which sat on the brink of breaking out into all-out war, as Pandulf sought to regain all of that which he had lost and Guaimar manoeuvred to block him.

Naples and Gaeta were busy seeking defensive alliances and the Abbot of Montecassino was firing off endless missives to Bamberg, insisting on imperial protection for his lands and revenues. Pandulf, in the past, had reduced the place to such penury by his depredations that the monks had been obliged to leave the monastery just to find the means to eat and drink, and that was after he had stripped the place of not only its accumulated treasure but its priceless library of illuminated manuscripts.

The Prince of Salerno's first act on hearing of Rainulf's demise was to hurry to Aversa, to the stone donjon which lay hard by the base camp the old Norman had created so many years before, near to a town now in its own right, not to pay his respects to the dead but to converse with the living; Richard Drengot made sure that once the ceremonies of welcome were over he received Guaimar on his own.

The prince sat silently for some time, looking at a room where the bare stone walls had been broken up by tapestries and the furniture was more suited to a villa than a defensive donjon. 'The first time I came here I was a callow youth with a message to your uncle from the late Emperor Conrad. William de Hauteville was present also, in fact he did all the talking. It was from those discussions that Rainulf got his title.'

'My uncle told me of that meeting.'

'You are aware of what has occurred at Melfi?'

It was an abrupt gambit, but Richard was not fazed. He nodded and tried to give the appearance of a man who had not thought something of the same would be best here, his voice, as he replied, sonorous with responsibility.

'Hermann's father, my uncle, bequeathed me a sacred trust, Prince Guaimar.'

The man he was talking to understood how overweight that statement was: too laden by far. Sacred indeed, and why refer to Rainulf in such an abstract manner? 'Or he left you a heavy burden, Richard.'

'It is not one honour would allow me to put aside.'

'Honour and prudence are not always compatible.'

The pause which followed seemed longer than it was in actual time, as each man waited for the other to voice the conclusion. Finally it was Guaimar who broke the silence, but he knew, given Richard's response to his first mention of Melfi, it would be unwise to be too direct.

'When I heard that Drogo de Hauteville had assumed Bras de Fer's title, my initial response was anger, for his presumption and also for the sake of my sister's then unborn child.'

'Truly it is a pity she bore a girl. A male nephew in place might have gone a long way to restoring that which the emperor removed.'

Richard said that with a wry expression: Guaimar was in no position to challenge the imperial dispensations and they both knew it.

'I admit that was a consideration, but then I thought on this. How could a child, even if Berengara had borne a lusty and healthy son, not only lead the

Normans in Apulia but control them?' Richard did not respond so Guaimar continued. 'I think we both know that the two go hand in hand.'

'I cannot do the same as Drogo.'

'He was acclaimed. I am told he was fearful to accept and I am bound to enquire, though you seem to share that reluctance, why your case is different.'

Richard hesitated to speak, as though the answer required some thought, but Guaimar knew that to be prevarication: he must have considered this deeply. 'Drogo now leads a force very different from the men of Aversa, more mixed, lances from many different parts of Italy who came to join only after the successes achieved by his brother. They care only for what profit will come to them from conquest.'

'And the men here do not?'

'Captains like Turmod have served my uncle for decades, have lived here for all that time, and there are others of the same mould.'

For all this fencing, both men knew what Guaimar wanted: a guaranteed commitment from Rainulf's nephew to take his side against Pandulf. Richard knew, regardless of his wishes, the Normans of Aversa would be caught in the middle of any Lombard dispute, and right at this moment he was unwilling to pledge to anyone, not prepared to place any faith in the promises he would receive from both Salerno and Capua. If Rainulf had gone, he had not done so without making sure his nephew understood his task was to protect that which the Normans had gained.

Yet he had died still not married to Hermann's mother, still waiting for a papal dispensation, although the new Pope Clement had promised it would be forthcoming at Capua, which left Richard in the same position as Drogo de Hauteville: for all that a goodly number of the men he now led were loyal to Rainulf's memory, just as many would not bow the knee to a child, and a bastard one at that.

Good sense dictated he put the boy aside and assume the title of count in his own name, yet Guaimar, who wanted him to take that route, also had to consider what he was being told: such an open declaration might split the men of Aversa asunder, which would leave the whole of Campania, and Salerno in particular, with the worst of both worlds, having to treat with multiple Norman leaders instead of one.

'I was Rainulf's suzerain, so it falls to me to confirm the title of whosoever succeeds him.'

Ultimately it was up to the emperor, but he was far away in Germany; Guaimar was sitting opposite. 'True, as long as it is accepted.'

Ever wily, Guaimar saw the solution clearly. 'It is also my right, should an acceptable heir to a title be in his minority, as Hermann is, to appoint his legal guardian. I take it if you were granted that office it would be accepted by all?'

'I think it would.'

'Then we require that the men Rainulf led be gathered, along with Hermann and his mother, so that I can promulgate such a dispensation.'

Guaimar was smiling at Richard Drengot, not just because matters had been satisfactorily concluded. He was wondering if, having had power and having to exercise it for at least a decade, his honour to his uncle's memory would stay so strong he would be able to give it up.

No man, unless his election was mired in corruption, came to the papacy in the first flush of youth, and Clement was no exception: the one-time Bishop of Bamberg had been in his sixties when Henry brought him south, and travelling for nearly a year had taken its toll on a man more accustomed to a cloistered life. Few popes reigned for long periods, and that did nothing for the stability by which the Holy See was governed. Nor was any deposed pope, still living, free from a desire to resume a position which brought with it great wealth and the ability to dispense much munificence in both money and lucrative offices.

When Clement passed on there was much talk of his being poisoned, an accusation which attended the death of any man who had been pontiff. That was added to by the way the once deposed Benedict resumed his occupation of St Peter's until a newly elected pope arrived from the north. Clement's successor, again sent by the Emperor Henry from Bamberg, lasted no more than twenty-three days before he too went to meet his Maker, both events stirring the endemic and centuries-old dispute between the convocation of cardinals and the emperor about who had the right to choose the next incumbent.

Yet both wanted a strong pope, albeit Henry did not desire one who would challenge his authority, and for once, when they were called together to elect a successor, they were in utter agreement about the next candidate. Bruno, the Bishop of Toul, was not only a divine, he was also a soldier who had led part of an imperial army under Conrad. Tall, strong of limb and with russet hair, the Alsatian-born Bruno was imposing in person as well as piety, but he was also a man known for his steely determination.

While he was happy to accept the nomination from the bishops and abbots of Germany and Italy, as well as the emperor, Bruno, like Clement before him, insisted he would not take up the office unless the people of Rome accepted him also. Thus, dressed in simple pilgrim garb, he made his way to the Eternal City and by this straightforward approach won the hearts and affections of the most cynical populace in Europe, and was thus consecrated to universal acclaim as Pope Leo IX.

The office he came to still had all the problems

faced by his predecessors: endemic simony, where rich benefices were traded for money payments to candidates who cared not for their flocks but for the profit of the place. Indulgences sold to forgive the most heinous sins and tithes that should have been commuted to Rome for the upkeep of the church spent, instead, by those who collected them, on personal luxury.

Leo had forced from the Emperor Henry a reaffirmation of his temporal rights in the Papal States, as well as an imperial admission that Benevento was a fief of St Peter's and his responsibility. Hearing this, the people of Benevento, having found the Normans to be unpleasant masters, sent envoys to plead for mercy, and they also wished for protection from increasing pressure on their entire principality from the Normans. Leo lifted the excommunication and promised to visit their city to ascertain for himself the extent of Norman depredations.

Added to that problem were the ongoing conflicts to the south of his territories: as Guaimar fought with Pandulf, Naples played both off against each other, the people of Amalfi rose in revolt, to be severely crushed, this while the Normans of Aversa increasingly encroached on the lands of Montecassino, while their counterparts in Apulia seemed to have lost all cohesion and turned from war to outright banditry.

An active fellow, Leo set off south himself, to find

out what could be done to both protect his own states and bring some order to those between them and the toe of Italy. Once in the Principality of Benevento, and seeing for himself how it was being ravaged, he set out for Salerno, summoning Drogo de Hauteville to meet him there. To both he and Guaimar, he would bring to bear the entire authority of this new and muscular papacy.

# CHAPTER TWENTY-ONE

✄◊✄

William de Hauteville had been right to consider Argyrus, on first acquaintance, to be somewhat callow, if far from stupid. What he had failed to discern in the young man was an ability to learn and to do so quickly. In deserting the Lombard cause his sole prompt had been the certain conviction that their whole stated dream was based on either hypocrisy or personal ambition of such a high order, from the likes of Guaimar of Salerno, as to render that dream unattainable. He was also aware that for all the mouthed platitudes about his father Melus, he, as his son, was a tool to be used, not a person to be elevated.

To get himself appointed by Constantinople as catapan was remarkable: no Lombard had ever held such an office, yet he had managed to convince the

Emperor Constantine that only one of his race stood any chance of regaining for Byzantium control of its South Italian provinces. It was not only in Apulia they had lost ground: Normans had moved into Calabria as well over the previous decade, building castles like the great edifice of Squillace, which was as potent a defensive bastion as Melfi.

What he could not persuade them to do was to provide him with the kind of force denied to his predecessors, so on arrival in Bari, Argyrus knew he was in for a long campaign in which his best weapon would be guile, not strength. Handsome, personable and not by nature cruel, he had won over much of the population of Bari and he had intimidated the rest. So he had, with the port city's formidable defences, a place of refuge. The burning question was how to expand out from that in the face of the military superiority of the Normans. Lombards worried him less, they could be bought or overawed, but as long as the likes of William de Hauteville had ambitions in Apulia he would never gain victory.

The near assassination of William had not brought with it the hoped-for break-up of cohesion. A new strategy was required and his original attempt to construct an alliance which would overcome the Normans fell at the first hurdle: he sought to engage Prince Pandulf of Capua in a joint conspiracy against them, and the early results were promising from a man who lived for intrigue. But Pandulf let him down, as he had done most people in his life, though Argyrus found it difficult to curse him for the mere fact of dying.

It was odd, following on from that disappointment, that in re-examining his options a clearer strategy emerged, one which seemed to have with it a greater chance of success. First, he must use what weapons he had, but his greatest asset in forming a body of opposition large enough to triumph was being brought about by the very people he wished to remove. The Normans were their own worst enemies, creating adversaries amongst the very people they needed to win over.

'How can I prosecute a war, when I cannot even be sure that the men I command to assemble will come?'

If it was worded differently, it was in essence a complaint that Drogo de Hauteville had been making for two years now. The men his brother had led might have acclaimed him, but he lacked the authority which William had exercised with such ease, given the composition of the men he led had changed and he lacked, due to the cunning of Argyrus, an enemy in the field to fight and defeat. Staying close to Bari, Argyrus was like an itch Drogo could not scratch, but he had made life more difficult merely by being, then doubled that by inactivity.

Certainly the number of lances Drogo commanded had increased substantially from the day when he and William had first arrived in Melfi, but so had the problem of keeping them content: they had come for land and plunder and Apulia was not a place where ground was freely available to give away. Drogo could not just dispossess the local Italians and Lombards to facilitate the elevation of his confrères without creating an uprising. But lacking that and the plunder that came from successful war, they were inclined to outright banditry, giving that precedence over service to him as their titular leader, and ignoring any strictures he tried to impose.

'Salerno,' said Humphrey, as they crested a rise to see the whole bay and city laid out before them. 'You can smell the wealth from here.'

'And I can smell trouble,' Drogo replied.

'This Pope Leo has been a soldier, Drogo. He will know that fighting men are hard to control.'

'Our own are worse.'

'You would be the same if you had no other choice.'

'Are you going to argue with me again?'

The mutual glares which followed that snapped response underlined that these two brothers had never been bosom companions, indeed Drogo often found the company of the one he liked most, Mauger, just as hard to take, given all of them were inclined to dispute any decision he made. Now, instead of being together continuously, as they had under William, they saw each other rarely, tending to remain in their own fiefs when not called upon to combine for some military venture.

That applied especially to brother number four, Robert, who Drogo had come to actively loathe, but he had got rid of him by some distance, having sent him to a particularly unrewarding part of Calabria, where, when he was not fighting malaria, he did battle with the intransigent locals.

Spurring his horse, still scowling, Drogo led his men down into the natural amphitheatre that was Salerno.

The summons from Pope Leo was one he could have ignored: this was not a man he feared outside his ability to deny him the sacrament by excommunication, but it was politic to obey. Guaimar would be present too and, like Drogo, would mouth platitudes to the Pope about future behaviour, because with Pandulf gone to meet Satan – Heaven for such a man was out of the question regardless of how many indulgences he had bought – the Prince of Salerno, now related to Drogo by marriage, was once more eyeing the vacant fief of Capua.

Meeting Berengara again was as unpleasant as it had always been: having a half-Norman daughter had done nothing for her hatred of the race, but Guaimar was fulsome in his greetings, eager to engage Drogo in schemes of infiltration and conquest of Byzantine territory, but he made no mention to Drogo of Capua: for that he would rely on the man who now styled himself Richard of Aversa.

'And how is Rainulf's boy, Hermann?' Drogo enquired, when that name cropped up.

Guaimar knew he was being mischievous, but he could not let that show. 'I have no idea. He is, I suppose, as well as can be expected.'

Drogo doubted Richard would actually kill the boy, but he was sure that he had been put aside. Guaimar knew that for certain: as he had suspected, Richard had come to be at ease with his command. The prospect of relinquishing it had no doubt preyed on him before he had been officially appointed as guardian, and that would not have eased with power. There was some admiration for the way Richard had gone about things: he had quietly removed the child from view while he was too young to do anything about it, an act which would have become increasingly difficult as the boy grew to manhood.

'All I know is that Richard has proved to be a most loyal vassal.'

'And we both know how difficult it is to be that,' Drogo growled.

'Time to meet our spiritual overlord,' Guaimar said, as he led the way into the chamber where Pope Leo awaited them.

\* \* \*

'This letter is from one of your fellow Normans, Count Drogo,' said Leo, waving a piece of heavy parchment. 'No less a person than the Abbot of Fécamp.'

'I fought alongside a bishop of that diocese once. He was a doughty warrior, as, I am told, Your Holiness, are you.'

Leo knew when he was being flattered, and his freckle-covered face showed it, not that he much liked it. 'Let me read to you what he says.'

'If you wish, I can read it myself.' That surprised the Pope: few men of Drogo's stamp were lettered. 'I was taught by the priest of our family church, my cousin, who has recently been appointed, as you will know, to the See of Coutances.'

'Geoffrey of Montbray is your cousin?'

'He is, and no doubt the Duke of Normandy had some say in his elevation, since he looks to him often for counsel.'

'The Duke did request he be given Coutances, it is true, and I was happy to oblige him. But this is wandering away from that which we are here to discuss, which is the sheer outlaw nature of the behaviour of the men you are supposed to lead. Listen!'

Leo started to read, looking at Drogo as each point was made. The abbot had been on a pilgrimage to Jerusalem, and like many travellers to the Holy Land he had taken in many a shrine en route. One such was the cave of St Michael on Monte Gargano, which was in the province of Benevento. The land around the shrine was overrun with Normans, and though they had respected the abbot as coming from their homeland, what had happened to him and what he had been told by the local Italian and Lombard population had made him seethe with anger and disgust.

'"No Norman traveller is safe in that part of Italy, so much did the locals hate them, and passing through was no protection from reprisals. He had been threatened personally, had nearly lost his possessions, only saved by his clerical office, but had since met many who had indeed been robbed even of the clothes in which they stood, this after their horses had been stolen. Some had even been whipped by angry locals as retribution for the losses they had suffered in destroyed crops and torn-out vines..."

'Need I go on, Count Drogo?' There was not much to do but answer with a shake of the head. 'But I shall, and I will enumerate the complaints I have had from Benevento, which might I remind you is my own fief. Homes and fields of corn burnt to a cinder, women raped and tiny children hoisted on the points of Norman lances...'

'Your Holiness, you know that people exaggerate.'

'Exaggerate!' Leo shouted, in a voice more suitable to a soldier than a cleric. 'I have seen these things for myself. It must cease and I will hold you, and you alone, responsible for seeing that it does.'

Drogo, who had been submissive, felt his gorge rise. Who did this ginger-haired sod think he was? He might be Pope but he was talking to a de Hauteville, one who was not, and never had allowed himself to be, browbeaten by anyone, especially in the company of not only Guaimar but also the whole papal entourage. He was about to shout back, he even had a notion of clouting the Pope round the ear, when a vision of his elder brother swam before him. William would have known how to deal with this, would have had the words to turn away the papal wrath while giving nothing in return. The Pope was asking for the impossible: the men he was talking about were warriors. What did he want them to do, take up the plough?

It took great effort to control his voice, but he did manage it. 'I will do as you ask, Your Holiness.'

'You swear on the Blood of Christ?'

'I do,' Drogo replied, crossing himself, as much from fear as from piety: that was not an oath to be taken lightly.

'So be it, Count Drogo, but be assured I will hold you to that. Now, Prince Guaimar...'

Drogo listened and determined to learn. Guaimar deflected every complaint directed at him with consummate ease and silken replies, showing such ability that Drogo was jealous, something he related to Kasa Ephraim when he called upon him later that day.

'Our prince has now had much practice at dissimulation, Count Drogo.'

'I think he might have learnt from you.'

The Jew smiled, and even if he had aged, it was a pleasing thing. 'You flatter me, Count Drogo, but you have come here to transact business, I think.'

It was Drogo's turn to smile. 'I think your ventures are safer than my coffers.'

Ephraim now transacted commercial undertakings for the de Hautevilles, trading in commodities on their behalf and increasing a wealth that was fed by land income and the tribute from the Lombard and Italian nobles of Apulia who looked to Melfi for protection: odd that some of that security had to be provided against men to whom he was titular overlord.

'All business has its risks, Count Drogo.'

Thinking of his soul, Drogo replied, 'None, my Jewish friend, compared to the risks of being in my position.'

Argyrus had worked hard to ensure that, when he struck, it had the desired effect. Money was his weapon, the means to pay for betrayal, but that was not the only tool in his armoury. Unaware that the newly elected Pope had left Rome for Campania, he had sent an embassy to the Holy City, to the Duke of Spoleto, whose lands lay to the north of Benevento, as well as selected people in that province, his aim to build a coalition against their common enemy. But first he had to decapitate the monster.

Drogo, not long returned from Salerno, was to be taken when he was at his most vulnerable, on a Sunday when he attended church on a saint's feast day, the means of his assassination a disgruntled monk, found by Argyrus's agents, who knew how to handle a sword. He assured those who recruited him that not only could he get close to Drogo de Hauteville, there were many men locally who would aid him, but the spider at the centre of the web made an impatient man wait until all else was in place.

Having served with the Norman-Lombard army outside the walls of Trani he knew the names of the most important leaders, not just the de Hautevilles. Humphrey, Geoffrey and Mauger had their own castles ands fiefs, and attended their own churches to hear Mass, but there were others capable of taking over from them, so men had to be put in place, reliable men who were not only willing to strike but able to recruit fellow assassins, for Argyrus was insistent that no one killer, acting alone, would succeed: look what had happened with William.

'The one called Robert I know least well.'

'He is stuck in deepest Calabria, my Lord, and though he is hated we have not yet managed to get anyone to accept the task of killing him.'

'Yet all the others are ready?'

'They are. They await only a day on which to strike.'

Argyrus had before him a list of Roman saints' days and he calculated how long it would take to send messages to those recruited and awaiting the sign to act. He could not risk a lost opportunity: conspiracies were fragile things, and they became even more so the longer they went without execution. Looking a month in advance he put a finger on the Feast Day of St Laurence and deciding said, firmly, 'That is the day I have chosen. See to it.'

Drogo, accompanied by his wife and a newly born son, saw Listo, dressed in his black Benedictine habit, and scowled, as it was not a sight that pleased him. In truth he felt slightly guilty at having sent him and his sister away, given it was not an action of which William would have approved, but then his elder brother had been a bit soft in that way. Drogo would not harm a peasant for no reason, but he had no love for the breed, seeing them as impenetrable and stupid in the main, and when occasion demanded that they suffer he had never been one to hold back. Their crops and vines he would destroy and the Good Lord help any of them who tried to resist.

To him St Laurence was a martyr especially to be venerated, not least because his saint's day was always the occasion of a great banquet, and Drogo loved feasting and drinking, which always led to carousing. Also, since the same saint was the patron of prostitutes, there was no disgrace in having a few along to entertain him and his companions afterward, once he had sent his wife off to her nursing and her bed.

Gaitelgrima had gone ahead into the church, and he was waiting until all his companions were present, some ten in number, those Normans he counted as close friends, slightly put out that two of his brothers, Geoffrey and Mauger, whom he had summoned, had yet to arrive. Humphrey had got the backwash of the papal strictures on the way back from Salerno; the other two were going to get a lecture too, and be told to keep their men in check. When he had dealt with them he intended to call in all the Norman captains for the same purpose.

Unbeknown to Drogo, at that very moment seven of the captains he was going to berate were dead, all of them caught overnight, in their beds, by assassins, all Lombards or Italians who had infiltrated their castles and donjons in the disguise of servants. Where there were women or wives present they died too, and any children young enough to be slumbering in close proximity to parents. Those given the task of killing Geoffrey and Mauger failed – they had been unable to penetrate their too well-established households – and had decided to follow them as they set off in the predawn to attend upon the summons from Drogo.

The Norman captains who died, including Hugo de Boeuf, were unarmed, or their weapons were too far away from them to be of any use. The de Hauteville brothers had theirs and were mounted, so when a dozen assailants tried to ambush them on the road they found out to their cost just how much these sons of Tancred had learnt from their warrior father. Not one of the assassins survived as the two brothers swung their swords and manoeuvred their mounts, the horses taking most of the knife wounds, necessary to fix the men wielding them so they could be cleaved in half by a single mighty blow.

Drogo was unarmed and no one saw Listo draw a weapon from under his habit, the sign for the men he had recruited to aid him, all dressed as Benedictines, to do likewise. Ready to enter the church, Drogo and his companions had laid aside their swords, and crowded into the narrow church doorway they had little room for movement as the two dozen men struck with knives, clubs and swords from both within and without the building. Drogo was a hard man to kill: even with several wounds he fought on with fist and boot trying to break through to where his weapon lay.

It was Listo who struck the fatal blow, taking a sword and slicing through Drogo's shoulder, covered with a blue and white surcoat but with no protective mail, the blow cutting down and smashing bone as well. Drogo fell to his knees but yet struggled to arise again as several men dressed as monks went for him with knives, stabbing him repeatedly, shredding his now blood-covered garment; the last sight he had as he spun from them was of his companions lying dead in a heap, crowded in the doorway of the church.

Listo's mission was to kill the boy-child as well, and his mother, if she resisted, but the pile of bodies, some still twitching, blocked the entrance and he knew that if he stayed too long retribution would be swift. As soon as he had struck the first blow women had screamed and men had rushed for help, and this in a place full of warriors who would tear him limb from limb for what he had done.

'The horses,' he shouted, throwing off his habit, no more a monk now but instead, as he saw it, a soldier in the service of the enemies of the Normans. The mounts belonged to the men the party of assassins had killed, not enough, for they were too numerous. But they were not hulking Normans, they were, even doubled up, a load the animals could bear and they rode out and south, heading for distant Bari and safety.

Geoffrey and Mauger, bearing wounds of their own, and with only one horse between them, arrived to find Drogo laid out on a slab of church marble, the wounds on his body now dark gashes edged with black congealing blood, with his young wife kneeling by, keening in sorrow while a nurse sought to calm her baby.

'Take them home,' said Geoffrey, 'and call upon the monks to come and prepare the body.'

'My Lord,' said one fellow, 'it was monks who did this.'

'No,' Mauger replied, 'no man of God committed an act like this.'

Over the next days they found the extent of this plot, as news came in of deaths all over the lands the Normans held. Humphrey had survived by a stroke of luck, having decided to spend a night away from his own castle, but when he heard of what had happened he dismissed every servant he had, not knowing which ones might be traitors. His next act was to call to Melfi all those who had acclaimed Drogo and he successfully called upon them to elevate him: he had no trouble at all in seeing the need for the succession to the title to devolve upon a grown man.

# CHAPTER TWENTY-TWO

>o◇o<

After a whole year, Robert de Hauteville was sick to death of Calabria and he put the blame fairly and squarely on his brother Drogo, who had sent him to this godforsaken part of the world where more men died of disease than combat, to his younger sibling's mind, just to get rid of him: he had hoped with William gone that Drogo would give him a chance to distinguish himself. What he had given him instead was a thankless task.

Nominally part of the Byzantine Empire, it was a province for which they cared little. If Campania and Apulia were fantastically fertile, capable of producing two harvests a year, this was the opposite, with mostly poor soil, and hilly and rocky where it was not covered in tangled woodland. There were fertile pockets, but the inhabitants suffered from exploitation, as well as constant incursions, from an enemy the people of this part of the world had lived with all their lives, and their grandfathers before them: ship-borne Saracen raiders.

Sailing from North Africa and Sicily, they could land anywhere on a hundred leagues of coast to rob and despoil at will, usually long gone with whatever treasure and slaves they had acquired by the time any distant Byzantine forces even heard of their incursion, and such forces were rare: mostly the Calabrians were left to defend themselves. Likewise they were left alone to rebuild their shattered communities, but as soon as they were perceived to be of worth the raiders would descend once more to wipe out any progress in both population and prosperity.

Having done their worst they would retire to their safe harbours. As a result of these raids, every place of value, mostly scattered along the coast, was well fortified and stocked for a siege, so Robert, with his limited numbers, found it difficult to gain entry to any of the towns that might benefit from the presence of a Norman overlord, which the Italian inhabitants were determined to repulse anyway.

Yet they needed protection, for they lacked the one thing that would guarantee that any Saracen raid could be repulsed, for their walls were not sufficient to repel such a determined enemy if they pressed the seige. They needed the help of proper fighting men, not only as a garrison but also as a mobile force that, alerted in time, could descend on the raiders and annihilate them. The only way to make safe the whole region was to inflict such reverses on the Saracens that they sought their gains elsewhere.

Constantly rebuffed, the Normans found themselves raiding isolated farmhouses and villages just to survive, and that provided a diet insufficient for the needs of big-boned men who were accustomed to eating well and often, as well as the numerous horses they needed to maintain their fitness to do battle. Such raiding created resentment and made matters worse, till the locals would have been hard put to distinguish between a Norman and a Saracen.

The only people in Calabria who seemed to have full bellies were the Basilian monks, who, like their Church of Rome brethren, had expropriated the best land for the cultivation of both vines and crops, all worked by put-upon peasants. One monastery in particular attracted the attention of Robert de Hauteville: Fagnano was walled enough to repel all but the most determined assault and covered a large area on a high and easily defended hill. This overlooked a fertile, well-watered valley and constituted a perfect site for a castle that could dominate not only the immediate neighbourhood but the entire country for leagues in all directions.

From such a bastion, impregnable if properly constructed, and with small garrisons dotted around the coastal towns, he could create the security the region required, and with that would come control. Fagnano had been raided more than once by Saracens, and reduced to a ruin many times for lack of external support. Robert had offered the monks protection, only to be rudely informed, as they barred their gates in his face, that they looked to God for that, not ruffians from a land of barbarians. Little did they know with whom they were dealing!

'They are monks, Robert, it would be a sacrilege to force entry.'

Robert looked down at the speaker – he looked down on most people – and scowled. For all his natural good humour, he had been sorely challenged by the task in these parts. Also, he did not like to be argued with any more than he enjoyed being rebuffed by well-fed monks when he was hungry: stripped, he could see too clearly his own ribs.

The man who had said those words, Gartmod, his second in command, was a pious warrior indeed. He came from the Norman town of Eu: at one time, in the first days of Norse occupation, the capital of the whole Normandy province. He had been brought up in the cloisters of the monastery there as an orphan, which had deeply affected him. Robert knew him to be a man who prayed to God more times a day than any

Saracen, but he also esteemed him when it came to combat: he was a doughty fellow with both lance and sword, and a dependable subordinate.

'Do you see anyone around these parts whose spines are not visible on their bellies? Do you see a dwelling that does not let in rain when it pours?'

There was truth in that: the abodes that dotted the landscape, homes to those who worked the land which surrounded the monastery, were modest indeed: there was not a single stone dwelling of any size.

'If God has chosen to grant prosperity to those who do his work, who are we to see fault?'

'I love our God as much as you do, Gartmod, but he did not grant them the land they live off, they took it by telling the peasants hereabouts that they would show them the way to eternal salvation. What they have done is condemn them to starvation instead. Every one of them looked well fed, but did you see how fat was that abbot, the one who refused me entry? He had a belly like a pregnant sow and that face tells me he takes wine so copiously you could get drunk on his piss.'

'I still say—'

'Shall we put it to the vote?' Robert demanded.

'I know which way that would go.'

'Because your confrères have more sense than you.'

'They are less godly.'

'Tell me, Gartmod, anyone who isn't.'

'The peasants you talk about will not thank you for destroying their monastery.'

'Who said anything about destroying it?'

'If not that, then what?'

Robert put aside his slightly belligerent tone, to adopt one more companionable, though even then his voice was gruff. 'We've been here in Calabria a year, my friend, and what have we accomplished? Nothing is the answer. Am I to go back to Melfi and say that we had to abandon all hope of adding this to the territories we Normans control? Every town has denied us entry and we have wandered around looking for a place to settle.'

'And you want that to be here?'

'Look at it, Gartmod, it's perfect. The monastery itself is already formidable, but imagine a castle at the top of that hill with storerooms full of food. We can build quarters to support the kind of force that will make the Calabrians see sense. Look around you at the hills in the distance and imagine beacons atop them. We are no more than ten leagues from the sea in four directions, so we would know of a Saracen raid before they beached their ships.'

'Then let me speak with them.'

'You think to succeed where I have failed?'

'I shall seek to convince them it is the will of God that we have come here.'

'Very well, try.'

While their mounts grazed contentedly on the rich grass of the valley floor, Gartmod made his way up the hill to attempt at friendly persuasion. When he returned covered in the content of the monks' privy, which had been dumped on him from atop the walls, even his Christian forbearance was overstrained. He was just as keen as Robert de Hauteville to teach the monks a lesson, but at a loss to know how to do it without an assault and the inevitable violence.

'If we spill blood the whole countryside will rebel against us.'

'Fear not, my friend, I have a plan.'

And Robert did, the first part of which involved he and his men riding away as if they accepted they could not have their wish, but that was only to get out of sight and to find a place to camp overnight. Then, choosing the least tall and the darkest of hair, he had them use the juice of tree bark to darken their skins, this while those who were good with wood fashioned a makeshift coffin. That done, they were told to don the hooded cloaks that every man had in his pannier.

What the monks saw from their elevated position at dawn the next day was a body of mourners bearing and trailing that coffin. Mourners in such numbers denoted someone of means had expired and needed to be buried in consecrated ground, a service for which the monks could charge a decent fee either in produce or, if it was truly a wealthy individual, in coin. Slowly

the party, heads covered and bowed, wended their way
up the road that led to the heavily barred gates, with
much wailing rising and falling from their throats.
One of the Normans who had originally come from
Aversa, and had been in Italy for many years, went
ahead to seek entry in Greek.

The gates swung open and the mourners bore
the coffin into the large open and paved courtyard,
with a well-stocked fishpond in the centre, the whole
surrounded by solid-stone double-doored buildings.
Further on there were some stables and a mill,
well tiled and weatherproof, the whole assembly of
buildings buttressing the outer wall, with what looked
like dormitories flanking the church at the furthest
point from the gate. The place reeked of prosperity
and it was full of monks seemingly in prayer for the
departed soul, but they were cautious folk, for those
same gates were being quickly closed behind them.

As soon as they heard the wooden bar drop to
secure them, the mourners let go of the coffin, which
falling to the ground and far from well built, fell apart,
spewing out the swords and shields with which it had
been weighted. At the same moment the heads of
the faux mourners were uncovered, the hooded cloaks
were thrown back and the monks of Fagnano found
themselves facing fully armed Norman warriors who
looked intent on killing each and every one of them.

Men who give their lives to God in poverty and true

righteousness are brave, and would probably have stood their ground, willing to meet their Maker if that was his will. Those who use piety as an excuse for avarice and a life of comfort lived off the backs of a put-upon peasantry are not. The wailing now was coming from the monks as, to a man, they dropped to their knees, hands clasped in front of them in supplication.

One fellow was not cowed, for the bells at the top of a tower were ringing furiously, summoning the people of the valleys, who looked to the monastery for eternal deliverance, to defend their place of worship, which set off the animals penned and cooped; so as well as the ringing and wailing the air was full of bleating, mooing, screeching geese, braying from the donkeys and alarmed clucking from the ducks and chickens.

Robert sent men to check the storerooms and brusquely ordered that the fat abbot be fetched. In his less-than-perfect Greek, once the man was kneeling before him, he gave the bloated divine a choice: the monks could stay and help the Normans build a castle, or they could be cast out to sustain themselves in the same manner as the peasants they exploited, while he and his men destroyed every building in sight.

'I would roast you over a spit, myself,' he barked, jabbing his blade gently into the unresisting fat of the abbot's huge belly. 'Though God knows how much wood I'd need to cook you right through.'

'Robert, there is a mob of peasants coming up from the valley.'

'The storerooms?'

'Near to full,' replied one of the men he had sent to check, who was now slicing and distributing bits of a smoked leg of ham. 'Sacks of corn, hams and cheeses, enough to feed us for a year, and wine – flagons full of it.'

'Open them up and somebody get up the bell tower and stop that ringing.'

That done he ordered the gate unbarred and partially opened, then went to stand in the gap, sword in hand, as the mob approached, carrying with them the implements they used to reap, sow and harvest, which could be just as deadly as any weapon wielded by a warrior. It would have taken more than a man of his height and presence to stop them, and Robert knew that what slowed their approach was not the threat he presented but the curious fact that he was facing them alone.

He searched for a leader, there was always one or more in a situation like this, a person the others would look to for guidance, and the fellows were not hard to spot, they being the ones who were shouting and gesticulating the most. So intent were they on their purpose they did not look behind them, for if they had they would have dispersed. Having a voice that went with his stature, Robert yelled that they should do so now.

At first they ignored him and he had to repeat the call twice, preparing himself to step back behind the line of the gate, which would be slammed shut; he was as brave as they come but not fool enough, with only his sword as defence, to die under a hail of blows from hoes and scythes if the people he confronted were too stupid to listen.

The change in the shouting was enough to tell him that someone had cast a backwards glance, and that was enough to alter the tone from belligerence to apprehension. From the bottom of the hill came a line of fully armed and mailed Normans, a hundred in number, lances at the ready, more than enough to massacre, at will, the mob Robert faced. This time, when he shouted that they should stop, they obeyed. His next shout brought his lances to a halt as well.

There was a risk in him stepping forward, right up to the front line, for all their fury had not abated, but Robert sheathed his sword and dropped his voice to disperse any sense of threat, asking in a level voice for whoever led this rabble to show themselves. That led to much shuffling: vocal and brave before, those who had been the most vociferous now did not want to be identified, but their even more fearful compatriots pushed them to the fore. Speaking even more softly, and having to repeat himself so they could comprehend his accent, Robert invited them in Greek to follow him, so that they could see for themselves the monks were unharmed.

Still reluctant to follow, he had to take one by the arm, a quite sturdy and stocky fellow of half his own height, to lead him through the gate. Trying not to tremble, for he thought he might be about to die, the peasant followed reluctantly and Robert took him across the paved compound of the monastery, past the kneeling but unharmed monks, to the first of the storerooms, standing back to let him enter.

He was guessing that whatever produce the peasants of the valleys delivered to their monkish masters they never saw it in its full measure, and judging by the look of wonder on the fellow's face he was right. Calling forward the man who spoke better Greek, he had him explain that the peasants outside could come in twos and threes to be given some of this largesse.

'Tell him we are here to stay, but we will not harm their monks, but protect them. We will also protect the valleys that lead to Fagnano as well as all the land around, so that no Saracen dare ever again trouble the province.'

Robert doubted the word province would make much sense, but the word Saracen did, for without a force to deter them they had come here enough times to make their name a potent and fearful one. But it was what he said next that really hit home.

'The abbot and monks of this monastery will, in future, work alongside you to seed, plough and grow, and in doing so they will render better service to God than they do now. That will be needed, for the able-bodied men hereabouts must help us quarry stone to build a fortress into which you may flee and be secure should anyone come to despoil your lands. Now go back through the gate and tell that to the others.'

Just about to do as he was bid, Robert spoke again, and these words were chilling. 'But know this, we can make war on you as easily as we can make war on those who would ravage your lands. You will show us the kind of respect you show these monks, or those lances and swords you see will be used against you.'

In twos and threes the peasants came through the gate, many looking fearful still, and most reluctant to take from the monks they revered or feared that which they had grown to keep them portly. There was no mystery to their caution: simple folk with simple needs, their dreams tended to be fixed on the next life, not this one, and the men from whom they were taking this food had convinced them they had the path to salvation, a message much repeated in the services held in the nearby church which they were obliged to enter through a separate outer door.

Though God-fearing, Robert was of a mind to think otherwise: that if God needed slugs like these to carry his message – and he had met too many well-fed monks in his life not to think of them as such – then he was not the Saviour of Holy Scripture.

'I think it would be good to have a Mass said for our souls,' said Gartmod.

Robert burst out laughing, his booming mirth bouncing off the surrounding walls. 'I think the roasting of some of that beef and pork which is yet on the hoof would do more for our souls than prayer. We have fasted long enough, brother.'

The soubriquet given to Robert, who was busy laying out plans for his castle walls, following on from taking over the monastery, became common amongst the Normans, and was repeated often enough to make those monks who accepted the new dispensation curious. They tended to be young as well as inquisitive, less resentful and, in truth, still retained some of the devoutness that had brought them to Fagnano in the first place. Eventually one of them plucked up the courage to ask Gartmod, who had shown himself to be a pious fellow and less likely to take offence.

'Guiscard?'

'It is a word I do not know,' the monk said.

'Neither would you, for it is Norman French.'

'But what does it mean?'

'It means cunning, which our leader most certainly is.'

When Robert heard it he wondered if he might not be known by a more suitable soubriquet, like that of his eldest half-brother, William. *Bras de Fer* sounded better than Guiscard, which could also mean weasel-like. Yet he knew no man would dare to use it in that sense and let him know they were doing so. In time he became comfortable with it, even to the point where some of his lances dropped his given name completely.

# CHAPTER TWENTY-THREE

∋∘◊∘∈

The multiple assassinations ordered by Argyrus had checked the Normans, but it had not stopped or removed them, underlined by the fact that Pope Leo was in constant receipt of complaints that his territory of Benevento was still being ravaged by roving bands of mailed warriors. Added to that, the grip of the Normans on the principality, despite assurances that they were not encroaching, was increasing. Appeals to the Emperor Henry to come south once more, this time with the whole might of the empire behind him, had produced nothing, leaving the Pontiff at a loss to know what to do – doubly frustrating given his background.

When the envoy arrived from Argyrus asking for permission to come to him, it took no great leap of imagination to conjure up a very good idea, in

advance, of what he wanted to talk about. Argyrus
had to travel incognito, secretly by ship from Bari to a
point further up the Adriatic coast, before journeying
inland, with Leo coming east to meet him at a secluded
monastery high in the Apennines. They met alone,
without attendants and devoid of the trappings of
their responsibilities, Leo ostensibly on pilgrimage,
Argyrus just an unknown traveller, the latter opening
the discussions with a blunt statement of the truth.

'The Normans are as much a plague to the Church
of Rome as they are to Byzantium.'

Considering those words, with fingers arched before
his mouth, Pope Leo was also sizing up this Lombard.
He saw before him a solid-looking young man of fine
countenance, with a direct gaze and a lack of the
kind of excessive gestures or eager explanation which
denoted insincerity.

'Does the Emperor Constantine know of this
meeting?'

'No, Your Holiness, the court of the man I represent
is not a place for confidences any more than Rome.'

'Are the Normans not Christians?'

Argyrus knew the Pope was avoiding the point and,
he surmised, seeking to find out, before he committed
himself, the nature of the person with whom he was
dealing.

'Of a kind, though I sometimes wonder if there is
a God, given that what they often do deserves that

they be struck down by a bolt from Heaven.'

Leo replied, wearing a thin smile on his pale lips. 'There is most certainly a God, my son, and should they seek his intercession he will forgive them.'

'Do you?'

'For their sins?'

'For their actions in your fief of Benevento.'

Those arched hands parted to show open palms, and the freckled face took on a querying look. 'Christ bore a cross to his Calvary, is it not fitting that the heir to St Peter should have the same kind of burden?'

'So you are saying that you will turn the other cheek.'

'When I first came to Italy it was as a soldier in the service of the Emperor Conrad – a bishop, yes, but a warrior who would not have recoiled at taking the life of anyone who opposed the imperial host. If I saw before me now a single head that I could remove, and by doing so eradicate a problem, I would be a soldier once more.'

'That has been attempted.'

If he had hoped to shock Leo by a near open admission of secret murder, Argyrus failed: he was greeted by no reaction at all, so he was left to pose another question. 'And if you had an army?'

'Would you be offering me one?'

It was now the Lombard's turn to smile. 'Part of one, yes, for if I had the force necessary to defeat the

Normans I would not have come to you here, would I?'

'No. But you must know I do not have an army of my own to bolster yours.'

'The day may come when you need one.'

'And you think that day is near?'

'What, Your Holiness, do you think the Normans will do once they have swallowed all of Benevento?' That being greeted with more silence, Argyrus continued. 'I think you must see that is what is going to happen, which will bring them to the borders of your own Papal States.'

Leo leant forward, nodding. 'This I know.'

'I cannot see what will satisfy them, can you?'

'And you are suggesting?'

'Force is the only thing they understand, and their removal from Italy is the only thing that will bring peace. Get the Western Emperor to join with the forces of his imperial cousin and together we will have an army too strong for the Normans to oppose.'

'I am not sure Henry would wish to see Byzantium fully in control of Apulia once more.'

'He would rather have a de Hauteville?'

'No man relishes the choice of the lesser of two evils when he does not know which is the worse.'

'We had peace before, we can have peace again,' Argyrus insisted. 'And I do not think it should be just the combination we have mentioned. You have massive authority through your office. Let us gather together all those who have suffered from Norman brutality, including Salerno.'

'Guaimar?'

'He has suffered more than most and he can hardly be said to be master in his own domains when he has Norman vassals like Richard of Aversa who do as they please. If he joins with us, others will follow, but no request from me to him would get so much as a hearing, but from you...'

'You wish to remove the Normans from Italy?' Leo asked.

'Yes, but we must defeat them in battle first, then offer them that as a way out.'

'And if they refuse?'

'Then they must die, every one of them, down to the last boy-child. It is the only way.'

'Would God forgive us for that?'

'Would God forgive us for doing nothing, Your Holiness?'

'I must go to Bamberg,' Leo said, after a lengthy pause. 'I must seek help from the emperor in person, but I will write to Salerno.'

When Guaimar received Pope Leo's request to join in a grand coalition against the Normans he knew it was not a matter he could discuss with his council: the mere mention of it in public and it would be known in Aversa before a day had passed. In any other matter requiring discretion he might have sent for Kasa Ephraim, but he knew the Jew had extensive dealings with the Normans, so he could not be sure that any advice given would not be tainted by that connection. It was an indication, and an uncomfortable one, of how isolated he could become in such matters that the only person he had whom he could trust as a sounding board was his sister Berengara, and he was most discomfited, on broaching the matter, to be greeted by derisive laughter.

'How long have I sought this,' she said, 'and how many times have you ignored me?'

'I hesitated to even ask you. You have a half-Norman child.'

'I have a girl-child who has tainted blood, but I will raise her to hate the Normans as much as I do. Did not her own relatives disown her?'

'I have often wondered if it was you who had Drogo murdered.'

'How I wish I had, and I would give my all to the man who did.'

'So you had no hand in that?'

Berengara produced an enigmatic smile, one her brother had seen before and he knew was designed to bait him: he would never know if Berengara was guilty or not, for he would never hear either an admission or an outright denial from her lips.

'Why did you laugh when I asked you if I should accede to Pope Leo's request?'

'How many times have you told me, brother, that a prince can not always do that which he wishes?'

'Many times, for it is no less than the truth.'

'So how do you think it makes me feel to tell you that if you agree to join Leo in his struggle against the Normans you would be a fool.'

'Why?'

'You know why, Guaimar. Look at a map. Richard of Aversa is between us and Rome and the de Hautevilles are on our border with Apulia.'

'Argyrus could keep them occupied.'

'If I hate the Normans, brother, I distrust Byzantium more. He would be happy to see Salerno humbled and then come to our aid when the city was in ruins.'

'The depth of your thinking on this surprises me, Berengara.'

'Why? Because I am a woman?'

Guaimar denied that, but they both knew it to be a lie.

'So you think I should stand aside?'

'I think you should return a polite response to the Pope saying that your honour does not permit you to attack one of your own vassals.'

Now it was Guaimar's turn to laugh. 'You expect the Pope to believe that?'

'Who cares what he believes, brother? Much as you seek to blind yourself to it, I am my father's daughter. He had Salerno taken from him by Rainulf and Pandulf and I often wonder if you recall how close we came to joining him in that simple tomb in which we buried him. Let Leo and Argyrus beat the Normans, and when they do we will rejoice, but I will not see Salerno destroyed first, which she will surely be, and long before either of those two can do anything to save us.'

Argyrus had entertained mixed hopes for Guaimar: he knew for the Prince of Salerno to join with him and Pope Leo would require a degree of daring. No one depended on Norman lances more than he and, while he was capable of raising armed levies of his own, as he had done in order to take Amalfi, the backbone of any force he had ever put in the field came from Aversa. What did surprise him was the way Guaimar decided to let his refusal be known: what should have been a secret, both the request and his negative response, were now known throughout Italy, severely denting any hopes of engaging the help of the other Lombard magnates.

Somehow that had to be reversed; all problems, to a mind like that of Argyrus, had a solution, while added to that was his ability to think ahead, so in order to hedge against a Salernian snub, and with other possibilities in mind, he had sent a trusted envoy to Amalfi, which might prove to be an Achilles heel, to assess matters.

That the adherents of the deposed duke hated Guaimar went without saying – they had seen power stripped from them – just as most of the citizenry disliked being ruled by another. But, from distant Bari, it was impossible to know if such hatred could be put to good purpose. The reports that came back, of seething discontent, were welcome.

Naturally, when it came to seaborne trade, Guaimar had favoured his own merchants over the needs of Amalfi, so that the once prosperous port saw the commerce off which it had lived leaching inexorably to Salerno. Being a Lombard allowed Argyrus to understand his tribe in a way that the Byzantine Greeks had never quite managed; was it not that very quality which had persuaded the Emperor Constantine to appoint him as catapan?

The leading citizens of Amalfi, be they dispossessed aristocrats or impoverished traders, were Lombards, and though they might mouth other sentiments, and pray mightily for Christian salvation, money, and the power that went with it, was their true divinity. Their other weakness was a lack of tribal loyalty, again something they would mouth, but a feeling which came a poor second to personal advantage.

Nestled in a precipitous coastal valley, connected to the interior by a pass through the surrounding mountains, and, within it, buildings piled on precarious slopes one on top of the other, it was a place built for intrigue. But the garrison and governor Guaimar had installed, supported by Normans, held the round tower that dominated the port – the easiest point of ingress and egress – feeling safe in the knowledge that control of trade from that near impregnable citadel gave them the key to an untroubled occupation.

They also held the two land gates to the city that fed a narrow coastal road: let the Amalfians grumble, and no doubt conspire, in their cliff-hugging dwellings. They lacked the means to strike out at those who lorded it over them. No adult male was allowed to bear arms, on pain of incarceration; any numerous gathering would be brutally dispersed so that conspiracy was confined to small numbers who dared not coalesce. Fear and an iron fist ruled Amalfi but the contact between oppressor and oppressed was non-existent: the former stayed in their bastions, the latter avoided them completely.

That was the message sent back to Argyrus: discontent was one thing, the ability to act quite another. The envoy had, of course, misunderstood his master's purpose. The catapan, who would, if he had been required to, have held Bari in much the same fashion as Guaimar held Amalfi, had never thought that a revolt inside the port was feasible. What he wanted to know was the willingness of the leading citizens to act against Salerno, if he could give them a method of doing so.

Perusing the list his envoy had brought back, he chose for his purpose the well-born over the trader, for the latter would always weigh the righting of a grievance against the cost. Dispossessed nobles were more given to emotion: raised in luxury from birth, they were men who would have grown up seeing power as a birthright, and the removal of it as a personal slight. It came as no surprise to discover that many of such had landed estates outside the actual port, well inland over the mountains, with numerous tenants and peasants to work their soil.

Calling his envoy, he instructed him in what he had to do: to take a ship back to Amalfi, one which would sit in the harbour, its load of weaponry hidden in the holds, and prepare the city to rise up against their oppressors. He was then to find those well-born malcontents and get them out of the place. Once on their estates, they would be met by numerous and armed fellow Lombards who would aid them, as long as they equipped their own people to fight as well, the promise held out of the casting-off of the Salernian yoke. That they would be unaware of the hand of Byzantium in their task was all to the good.

Guaimar was an accessible prince, a man who did not fear to walk with a minimal escort through the streets of his city, nor was he excessive in the way he lived his life: he would not have Normans guarding

the Castello di Arechi, a fact which went some way
to mollify his sister, angry that he associated with
them at all. Salerno was a teeming active port, a place
hemmed in by hills but with a wide sweeping bay that
left it open to cooling breezes, as well as the occasional
hot African wind, and it was as wealthy now as it had
ever been, with much building going on, some of it
financed by its ruler.

Ships came in from all over the known world
with silks, spices and valuable commodities, while
from the Campanian hinterland the produce of the
fertile province, capable of double harvests, flowed
out: grain to feed the people of Rome, olive oil with
which to cook and keep going the lights that allowed
for life to continue when the sun set, fruit that grew
in abundance in the orchards, and wood from the
forested foothills of the mountains.

Every ship entering or leaving paid customs dues,
these taken in by the collector of the port to add
to the secret stipend he gave to his master from
smuggling. Kasa Ephraim was a busy man, with
much to concern him in the way of trade, for he had
multifarious interests, and the need to push his way
through crowded thoroughfares in the company of his
coffer-bearing servants meant he had no eyes to spot
anything unusual, not that the sight of half a dozen
well-set young men in such a prosperous city was
that.

If Argyrus had spies in Amalfi, he also had people who were his eyes and ears in Salerno and they told him, after months of observation, that the one time it would be certain that the Prince of Salerno would be in his Castello was the day the Jew delivered the port revenues. They had also found out from gossip in the wine shops that Guaimar was wont to meet his Jew in private after the transaction of official business, with no one else present.

The group that had trailed Kasa Ephraim was not alone: there were others in the city, all now armed and each one with a task to perform, some to take important buildings, others to take care of anyone who might raise resistance, but most important was the group who gathered outside the gates to the Castello di Arechi, becoming in time so much part of the landscape that if the guards at the entrance had noticed them at all, they did not stand out now.

There was no way of seeing through the stout stone walls, the time to act was a guess, based on the exit of some of Guaimar's council, who would leave the Castello once the public business had been transacted. As soon as they were out of sight, the Amalfians struck. The guards – in truth, in such a peaceful city, long past being alert – were the first to be killed. While half the raiding party entered the Castello, others, the younger ones fleet of foot, were sent as messengers to tell the rest to act. Inside the building, for all that any shouts echoed off the walls, the doors to each chamber were built of stout well-seasoned and heavily studded timber, and so muffled such cries.

Kasa Ephraim would have died had he not just left the prince, having said farewell to Guaimar just as his sister and niece came into his presence. As it was he found himself knocked to the ground as those intent on killing Guaimar, six in number, swept past him towards the unbarred door to the chamber he had just left. The Jew was not a fighting man, but he was a clever one. Seeing the flashing knives, already dripping with blood, it took no great imagination to understand what was happening, just as he knew that alone he could do nothing to prevent it.

The cries of alarm and one scream, he heard as he pulled himself upright and hurried for the exit. Behind him, unseen, those six assassins had stopped before the Prince of Salerno, who seeing their blades and being himself unarmed knew what he was about to face. He pushed his sister and her child behind him, and with a voice carrying as much command as he had ever been able to muster, demanded to know who came upon him in such a fashion.

'Amalfi has come for you, Prince Guaimar, to seek redress for the blood of its people.'

'Strike and your city will burn, I swear,' Guaimar spat back. 'Not a stone will remain standing, not a life will be spared.'

'Then, Prince Guaimar,' the leader replied with a grim smile, 'we have nothing to lose.'

The assassins rushed towards him and hit out with their blades, surrounding the prince and stabbing with fury. The last words he said before he fell to the ground, with blood spurting from dozens of wounds and his garments already bright red, were 'Spare my sister and her child.'

That was not to be: the task was to kill off the House of Salerno; Berengara and her daughter, widow and child of William de Hauteville, died within moments of Guaimar and from those same knives.

Kasa Ephraim knew the Castello well, having served both the prince and his father. He made his way to the family apartments, where he spoke, in a voice he could not believe was as even as it sounded, of the danger they faced. Like every castle of the age in which they lived it had a private as well as a public entrance, and not just for fear of murder: all princes liked to be able to come and go unseen. If the Jew did not know where it was he suspected it existed, and he told Guaimar's wife and children, most particularly his fourteen-year-old son, Gisulf, to get out of the Castello at once.

'Take nothing, for you have no time.'

'The prince?'

Though he hoped he was wrong, the Jew guessed he was right. 'Will be dead by now. Go.'

No one demurred when he followed; he, too, felt that only by leaving could he survive. In the harbour, one fast sailing ship was hoisting sail, not from panic or fear, but to carry the news of the death of Guaimar round the toe and boot of Italy to tell Argyrus of the success of his plan.

The news of the murders came to the Norman host, gathered between Melfi and Benevento, through Guaimar's cousin, Guy, Duke of Sorrento, who had escaped the city and ridden hard to deliver it.

'The road to Aversa was blocked and there were Amalfians at every post house to stop any messenger changing mounts.'

'But not on the road to Melfi?' demanded Humphrey, his beetle brow creased.

'No.'

'That does not make sense,' said Mauger.

'Perhaps it does,' Humphrey replied, his suspicious nature working overtime, as were his prominent teeth, chewing his lower lip. 'I smell another hand in this.'

'Argyrus!' growled Geoffrey.

There was a silent exchange of looks then: one thing did not need to be stated, given they all knew of Pope Leo's scheming. With the Pontiff trying to contrive an alliance to defeat them, and an army gathering north of the city of Benevento, an important fief like Salerno, who had proved to be their only dependable ally, could not be allowed to fall into the hands of someone who was an enemy. If Argyrus was involved that meant Byzantium, the worst possible opponent, given he might control the city and a hinterland that, in league with Rome, would see them surrounded.

'William's child was murdered as well?' asked Mauger, sadly, more sentimental than his brothers. Guy of Sorrento nodded. 'Then we have a blood reason to intervene.'

'If we move on Salerno,' Humphrey nodded, though he looked less grieving than Mauger, 'he will move on our Apulian possessions while we are gone.'

'The Pope?'

'He is still assembling. Leo cannot threaten us yet.'

'So we stay,' Mauger asked, 'or move south to block Argyrus?'

Since the loss of both William and Drogo, Humphrey had grown in both confidence and authority: he was very much in command now.

'Leo is at present no threat. Geoffrey will lead half our forces to confront Argyrus. If we are wrong and he does not move from Bari then no harm will be done. If he does, and you cannot beat him, you can delay him Geoffrey, giving the rest of us a chance to rejoin.'

'And Salerno?' asked Duke Guy.

'As long as we can block the catapan and Leo does not move, the men who killed Guaimar will see their own guts before they die.'

'I thank you,' he replied, relieved.

'We will, however,' Humphrey said, 'need to be recompensed for our assistance. Guaimar was a wealthy man and Salerno is one of the richest ports in Italy.'

The bargaining that followed, for high sums of gold, might have embarrassed a man of tender feelings. Humphrey de Hauteville was not that man.

# CHAPTER TWENTY-FOUR

Robert, still castle-building in Calabria, heard of what had happened at Salerno long after matters were resolved, and he heard of how the hand of Argyrus had been exposed. The catapan had indeed moved out from Bari as soon as the ship from Salerno brought news of Guaimar's assassination, and it was suspected he had sent word to Pope Leo asking him to act as well, but as soon as he met Geoffrey he knew that, even if he could beat and pursue him, he could be putting his head into a Norman noose, so he withdrew.

Humphrey, having joined with Richard of Aversa, had descended on Salerno within four days, a speed which had thrown the Amalfians off balance, causing most of them to flee. The assassins thought they had time to consolidate their position in Salerno when they had none. They thought, also, they had time to overcome the garrison of their own home city, now besieged in their bastions in a port in full revolt; that too was in doubt.

The Normans had gathered on the way the news that Gisulf had been taken into the Castello di Arechi, now barred and held by the most stalwart Amalfians, though it was said he was still alive, so Guy of Sorrento was sent in to offer them terms. Spare Gisulf, free him, and they would live, kill him and they would die – as they must for foul murder – and as an added incentive Amalfi would be spared sack and utter ruin.

The offer was refused. If the Amalfians thought that in holding Gisulf they had an unbeatable hand, they again underestimated the Norman mind. Richard of Aversa descended on Amalfi like a whirlwind and relieved the garrisons. The men in the Castello di Arechi were brusquely informed their own families – wives and children – had been taken as hostages, which allowed Guy to negotiate for Gisulf's release, and as soon as he was freed his uncle bent the knee and did homage to him as the new ruler of Salerno.

'He should have taken the title himself,' Humphrey complained, as he saw Guy kneeling. 'Gisulf is but a boy, and not an impressive one at that.'

'It was a selfless act,' Mauger replied.

'Stupid,' his elder brother spat. 'Salerno needs a strong hand, not that of a weakling.'

'So what do we do?'

They were in front of the Castello di Arechi, still occupied by the Amalfians, with crowds of Salernians not far off, at least out of the range of a crossbow bolt, seemingly cheering their new prince but probably more relieved that they would be allowed to return to making money. Between the crowd and the Castello stood a line of mailed and armed Normans.

Humphrey, biting hard on his lower lip, finally said, 'What can we do, but the same?'

He led Mauger forward and knelt before the young Gisulf, which was followed by the entire contingent of Normans. The youngster looked confused about how to respond, until his uncle told him to gently raise Humphrey up and thank him, which the boy did.

'The assassins?' he asked Guy.

'Will come out now. I have told them they will be spared.'

'Did you?'

'Yes, we need peace and reconciliation more than we need more bloodshed.'

'Then let us see them.'

Guy of Sorrento went to the gates of the Castello di Arechi and called for the men to come out, reiterating that they were safe. Slowly they complied, two dozen of them, blinking at the jeering which came from the citizens gathered at a distance.

'Your weapons?' Guy said.

Unsheathing their swords they threw them to the ground and moved forward to stand before Guy and the de Hautevilles, at which point Humphrey growled, 'You spared them.'

'I told you,' Guy replied.

'Mauger,' Humphrey called, unsheathing his broadsword, his voice rising as he shouted. 'We did not!'

Mauger had followed his brother; his sword was out and employed in moments, swinging left and right, smashing bone as well as slashing flesh, and the men who had killed Guaimar were cut to ribbons with a staggering degree of Norman ferocity.

Guy of Sorrento was shouting in protest, Gisulf was wailing in fright, until Humphrey stood before him, the decimated bodies at his back, a bloodstained figure towering over the boy.

'Don't weep, lad,' he said. 'My brother and I have just saved your life.'

The news of Guaimar's murder was at first a cause for some rejoicing in Benevento, though Pope Leo felt the need to be muted in his gratitude that the greatest obstacle to the alliance he was creating was gone. Then came the Norman retribution, shocking both in the swift manner it was carried out and worrying to those who had joined the papal forces, not least in the way that Salerno and the Normans had combined.

Men began to desert the papal cause, especially when news came from southern Apulia that Argyrus had been obliged to retire on Bari.

Pope Leo was not one to be idle: off he went once more to Germany, to try again to persuade Henry to help him. Not being entirely successful, he had trouble, in the imperial presence, in hiding his anger: there was, to his mind, a dereliction of duty in Henry not accepting that problems in Southern Italy demanded his full attention. However, thanks to a noble relative, he returned with something: a body of seven hundred Swabian infantry, soldiers every bit as professional as the Normans, though he was required to find from papal funds the money to pay and maintain them.

These would form the nucleus of his army, which was made up of levies from all over the north, and with that Swabian core, those who had seen prudence in returning to their homes began to flood back in until Leo had under his command a swelling and formidable force. Humphrey, realising this, sent an offer of parley. It was an indication of Leo's growing strength and confidence that he dismissed it out of hand.

'Rider coming,' called the sentinel atop the first finished tower of Robert's castle. 'And he's Norman.'

Robert, now using what had once been the fat abbot's private chamber, heard the cry and put aside his quill, where he had been examining the income of his new estates which had come in from his edicts: payment from the use of the corn mill as well as the use of the large monastery ovens for baking; there were others for water and grazing rights, permission for two young lovers to set up house together and myriad other impositions by which a lord maintained himself and his knights.

There were outgoings as well, some in hard-won money, unlike most of his income, for Masses to be said, implements to be purchased from the coast so that those working the land could increase their yields, as well as the purchase of seed and better strains of livestock, but that had been offset by the abundant medicinal herbs which the monks had grown and never exploited: he had been able to trade them profitably. He would only prosper if those below him did so too: he might have argued with old Tancred endlessly, but he had learnt from him as well.

By the time he exited the chamber the rider, on foam-flecked mount and in the de Hauteville colours, was clattering into the courtyard that would, one day, be the keep of his castle, and the message he bore was a command from Humphrey to leave Calabria and come at once to join his brothers: the whole Norman presence, not only in Apulia, but in Italy, was in jeopardy.

'He's not talking sense,' Robert insisted, having got

the messenger into his quarters and put something to drink in his hand.

'He is, Robert. The whole of Italy has combined to put an army in the field – Argyrus, Pope Leo, the Duke of Spoleto – and there are even contingents from the valley of the Po.'

'With not a decent soldier amongst them.'

That's when he was told about the Swabians.

Mounted and fully ready to travel, leading three horses, Robert leant down to give his parting instructions to Gartmod. Humphrey might have said *every* lance, but he was not going to completely abandon what he had so far built, on the very good grounds that he might never get it back again: he would leave here three conroys to make sure the monks did not seek to steal back their possessions.

'I know I can trust you to treat the peasants well, Gartmod, but do not get too soft with the monks.'

'I will not whip them.'

'I never have either.'

'You threatened to, Guiscard.'

'And they believed me, which was all that was required. But keep safe what we have built until I can return and finish it.'

'God speed, Robert,' Gartmod said, slapping the flank of his mount, 'and may God preserve you.'

'He does not want to see me yet, my friend,' Robert

called, adding a booming laugh as he rode out of the gates with his men behind him. 'He fears to lose possession of Heaven.'

'Raising foot soldiers has been difficult,' Mauger said. 'The Italians and Lombards are backing the Pope, but we managed to get some Slavs from across the Adriatic.'

'How many?' asked Robert.

'Four hundred.'

'That should scare them,' Robert replied with deep irony. 'According to Humphrey, Pope Leo has over five thousand.'

'If he combines with Argyrus...'

There was no need for Mauger to finish that: the two armies would crush them and it was the primary task of Humphrey, who as Count of Apulia was the leader, to ensure that could not happen. Right now, aided by Richard of Aversa and his lances, he was manoeuvring to drive Argyrus away from a junction with the papal force.

'And Leo?'

'Two to three days' march, we think.'

'It would be best to be sure, Mauger, we cannot afford to be wrong.'

Knowing he was older, Mauger was tempted to tell Robert not to teach his grandmother to suck eggs. But he also had to acknowledge that this younger brother of his had grown in stature: not in height, he had too much of that already, but there was a steadiness about him which he had lacked before going to Calabria.

From being bumptious, and while not losing his love of a good belly laugh, he had become more serious-minded, and Mauger had watched him as he intermingled his lances with those holding the fortress of Troia, so that they could operate efficiently as one, and he was forced to admit that when it came to commanding men this brother had the measure of him. Mauger was not feeble, but neither was he vain, and he told Humphrey when he rejoined that if he had any sense he would give Robert a serious role in the coming battle.

'Over you?'

'If need be. It is important we win, not who gets the glory.'

Geoffrey had been left with a force to mask Argyrus, to convince him he still faced a Norman army that he must take a detour to manoeuvre around.

'Then you fight with me. We march tomorrow to block the road to Siponto, the route by which Leo can join with Argyrus.'

'Do we have a plan, Humphrey?'

'We do...to talk.'

The papal army was a slow-moving beast and Humphrey had all of his forces in place before them

in two days. They were encamped before the town
of Civitate, their backs to the River Fortore, in
number certainly double the Normans, if not more.
Some indication of the coalition Pope Leo had put
together could be seen from the rank of their leading
enemies: Rudolf, son of Landulf and the titular Prince
of Benevento, the Duke of Gaeta and the Counts of
Aquino and Teano, even the Archbishop and many of
the citizens of Amalfi, together with men from Apulia,
Molise, Campania, Abruzzo and Latium.

The brothers de Hauteville, with Richard Drengot
in company, rode forward to parley, hoping to meet
with Pope Leo, a man to whom they could appeal as
good sons of the church. He was not foolish enough to
put himself in a position of denying them succour and
had stayed in the Episcopal Palace in Civitate, but
it was noticeable, as they closed with their opposite
numbers, the commanders of the papal forces, that
Leo's standard as pontiff, the *vexillum sancti petri*,
was there with them. Such a meeting demanded
courtesy: there was much hatred present, but it had
to be hidden.

It soon became obvious that the men to whom they
were talking, polite as they were, had no interest in
anything other than battle or surrender; Humphrey
tried, Richard of Aversa tried, and they both sought
together a way out of the impasse, using ever more
convoluted arguments which fell on stony ground.

Finally Robert spoke up, suggesting that as the day was getting on they should both retire to consider matters, to perhaps continue on the morrow, a notion which annoyed his oldest brother, but one which he made plain made sense as soon as they parted company.

'We can't blather on, Robert, or we will have a Byzantine army at our back and this lot in front of us.'

'I know that, Humphrey. Why do you think our enemies agreed to keep talking?'

'So I fail to see the point...'

'The point is, brother, we should attack them at dawn.'

'Break the parley?'

'Brother, we did not actually agree to talk on the morrow. Did you not hear me say, perhaps? They will be getting ready to talk, to delay again, we will be ready to fight.'

'I have heard of your new name, Robert,' said Richard Drengot.

'What?' Humphrey demanded.

'In Calabria, it seems, they call him the Guiscard.'

'They can call me any name they like,' Robert insisted. 'If we let our opponents set the terms of the battle they will do so to suit their purpose, which is to wait for Argyrus. If we want a chance to win we must suit ours.'

'Is it honourable?'

'Honour, Humphrey, goes to the victor.'

They were lined up and ready to do battle before the sun tipped the eastern sky, but their enemies were not in disorder: they, too, had disposed their forces for a fight. Humphrey had split his army into three divisions: he held the centre, before a small hill that part-masked the enemy centre, and left, which judging by their visible standards comprised of Italians, with the Swabians on the papal left. Richard of Aversa was on the Norman right, all cavalry, while Robert commanded the mixed horse and infantry on the left wing.

The formation the papal army had adopted, strung out in a thin line, was that required to attack, sensible given their numerical superiority. Robert had insisted the Norman host could not wait for such an eventuality – their power lay in assault – they must initiate the contest, and after much discussion, given that had been agreed, Richard of Aversa moved forward on the right to hit the Italian line.

It was true they had probably never faced Norman lances advancing on them steadily and in an unbroken line; it was also true that their military skills would not have been of the highest, but they should have held until at least the assault made contact. They did not: the Italian levies broke before the Norman horsemen could even cast a lance at their running backs, and with a great yell Richard ordered the pursuit, which took his men, slashing and killing as they went, all the way to the Fortore River, into which they drove what Italians remained to drown or swim.

Behind them, matters had developed against Humphrey, assaulted by the Swabians who had attacked him before his lances could get moving, and they were formidable enough to remind those who had fought Varangians of the quality of those Norsemen – they were big men, on foot, who would not fall back before repeated mounted assaults. They began to push Humphrey's division back. With Richard of Aversa fully engaged, that threatened to turn the battle into a Norman defeat.

It was Robert who saved the day: ignoring what opposition remained before him he wheeled his division to the left and attacked the Swabian flank, driving it in. They did not break, but they were forced to retire, falling back in solid formation to the crown of the small hill at the middle of the battlefield. With the return of most of the men led by Richard of Aversa, and the fact that everyone else had fled, they were surrounded and doomed, but a call for them to surrender with mercy was thrown back in Humphrey's face.

The Swabians died, as Normans and Varangians would have died, fighting to the very end; the men who slew them, on foot too, slipping and sliding on a grassy bank so soaked with blood it had turned to mud.

That section of Richard Drengot's men who had forded the Fortore and rode into Civitate found Pope Leo in a state of shock. All around him were men fleeing past, including those who had led the papal army, heading out of the town to the west to get away from the Norman sword blades. Faced with a pope, and being Christian soldiers, the men who came upon him were in awe, the leader actually kneeling before Leo to give a kiss to his proffered pontifical ring.

'I must ask you, Your Holiness, to accompany me back to the camp of Count Humphrey.'

'No, my son. Tell your count I will remain here. Tell him I will not flee, for God has made a judgement this day, and as his Vicar on Earth, I must bear the consequences.'

'I will leave men to guard you.'

'Against whom?' Leo said, angrily. 'Even my bishops have fled.'

'We have the Pope in our grasp,' crowed Humphrey, having taken over the tent of the leaders of the now defunct papal army; he had also taken over the papal treasury. 'How I long to laugh in his face, the red-haired Alsatian swine.'

'It must be blasphemous to call a pope that,' said Mauger.

'I will make him eat dirt, brother.'

'You have not said anything, Robert,' enquired Richard of Aversa. 'I cannot believe you have no thoughts on this.'

'None that anyone will listen to.'

'What do you mean?' Humphrey demanded.

Robert half threw up his hands in a gesture of frustration. 'Take your revenge, Humphrey, and enjoy it.'

'Why should I not?'

'Because it will not serve, brother.'

'Serve what?'

'Our interests. If we humiliate the Pope, do you think the Emperor Henry will let that pass? No! He will not and we will find ourselves facing an even bigger and better army within a year.'

Richard Drengot spoke up again. 'What would you do?'

'I would go to the Pope in all humility,' Robert replied, 'and ask his forgiveness.'

'What!' Humphrey yelled.

# EPILOGUE

><><

It was in Humphrey's nature to explode: he could not help himself, being a passionate man, but he was not stupid, and once Robert had explained his thinking he began to see the sense of the argument, as did the others, Geoffrey included, who had come to join them now that Argyrus was fleeing back to Bari.

No military force, Robert insisted, however powerful, could stand against the authority of the Pope, and as they talked, these Norman warlords, it became obvious, at least to Richard of Aversa, that there was a shift in where the power lay. The more Robert de Hauteville talked, the more it became apparent how far-seeing he was in his thinking. Apart from that, the quality of command oozed from his every pore, as it had once oozed from William *Bras de Fer*.

'The men Leo assembled had one aim, to kick us out of a land in which we are determined to stay. How do we avoid another coalition being formed next year, or in the years after that, with the same aim? We cannot, unless we make an ally of the one man who can bring such a force together.'

'What about the Emperor Henry?' asked Humphrey.

'I was not in Rome long,' Robert replied, 'but I heard and saw enough to know that not only do the people of that city resent imperial interference in papal elections, every high cleric does, too. The day must come when Rome stands up to Bamberg and tells whoever is Holy Roman Emperor that it is the task of the Church to anoint its leader, not of a lay emperor to appoint one.'

'That is an argument a hundred years old,' Geoffrey pointed out.

'Which means it's an argument unresolved, but there is more.'

'My head is sore already,' Humphrey moaned: he was a fighter, not a thinker.

'Byzantium in Italy?' Robert asked, his mind back in Calabria and the services he had attended, all conducted in the Eastern Greek rite.

'What has that got to do with it?'

'I suggest we go to Pope Leo, and offer to him Apulia and Calabria as provinces owing allegiance to the Holy See.'

'Give up what we have fought for?' asked Geoffrey.

'No, gain title to what we have fought for. No pope can hold them without military force. Let us become the arm of the Vicar of Christ.'

Leo, expecting to be humiliated, was utterly thrown when the de Hauteville brothers and Richard of Aversa entered his chamber and immediately fell to their knees before him. Humphrey, as the commander of the army that had defeated his, was the one to speak, but all present knew the ideas were Robert's.

'Your Holiness, we beg you to step outside this palace and give your blessing to our host assembled.'

'Bless them?' He had been thinking of excommunicating the lot.

'There is not a man amongst them who does not fear eternal damnation for taking up arms to oppose Your Holiness.'

'And that,' Robert added, since Humphrey had seemingly forgotten, 'includes us here before you.'

'Amen to that,' added Richard.

'I...'

Knowing that Leo did not know what to say, Robert rose, which brought to their feet the others, and indicated he should follow. The square before the Episcopal Palace of Civitate was crowded with Normans, and as soon as Pope Leo appeared all fell to their knees, and the sound of their request for forgiveness rippled through the multitude.

'You see before you,' Robert said, 'soldiers willing to die in the service of their faith. They are children of a Christian God and they are yours to command.'

'To what purpose?' Leo asked.

'To wrest from Byzantium, and bring into the fold of Rome, the misguided peoples of Apulia and Calabria.'

Leo was no fool. 'You are offering to serve me?'

'We are offering to acknowledge you as our suzerain, and to hold in your name – and those who succeed to the mitre – as your vassals, the lands so described.'

Robert could almost see Pope Leo's mind working: here was a man who thought he would have to forfeit Benevento, being offered not only the retention of that but also two huge provinces instead.

'We see our task as building churches to the glory of our God, but we cannot do that with you against our enterprise.'

'I must think on this,' Leo said.

'It is yours to take or deny.'

Suddenly, Leo raised his hand and gave a papal blessing to the still-kneeling Norman army, muttering in Latin the words that went with that, which had the men, once they had crossed themselves, rising to their feet to cheer.

Robert whispered to his brothers and Richard, 'Try kicking us out of Italy now!'